Lost
Indecision's Flame

Book Two

by JS Ririe

Jan Hill Books

Praise for: Lost - Indecision's Flame by JS Ririe

"JS Ririe is a very popular writer around here with the Indecision's Flame series. Her books are spiritually uplifting and interesting. My girls fight over who's reading them first." - Eddie S.

"Loved it!" - Lisa M.

"I just finished *Indecision's Flame* and loved it. Can't wait for the next one to come out." - Julie G.

AUTHOR'S NOTE: Since the setting for this novel takes place in the Australian Outback, certain colloquial words like "bloody" instead of "very" have been used to set a more authentic flavor. Please join my mailing list and stay updated with my latest releases and more. The link to join is: http://eepurl.com/dCPYVf.

Dedication:

For my grandmother, Viola Ririe, who gave me a love for the printed word and the desire to become a writer like her. She was my hero - never too tired or busy to tell me a story or just listen when I needed to talk.

~JS Ririe

Chapter 1

I don't remember falling asleep, but I must have because Trevor's knock on my door the next morning brought me upright bed. I knew I'd been thinking about birthdays when I'd crawled underneath my covers, but for the life of me, I couldn't remember a single one of my own, except for the last one I'd spent with Becky and Ben. There had been cake with candles and presents, lots of them.

Becky had given me a new sweater, a muted yellow, my favorite color. She said it wasn't cashmere but it sure felt like it. Ben's parents had given me several church books and his grandmother a set of dishtowels she had embroidered. In fact, all of his siblings had given me a little something to remember the day by, but his gift had been the one to move me to tears. It was my own set of scriptures with my name engraved on the soft, blue leather, and a forever message written inside the front cover. I read it every night before going to bed.

It still bothered me that I couldn't remember much about my childhood. The therapist I had seen once or twice after being a victim of sexual assault had told me it was perfectly natural for someone who had been through traumatic experiences like I had to have lapses in memory, and that when my body and mind had recovered sufficiently I would be able to recall most of what I thought I'd lost.

But I wasn't sure that was true. It had been over three years and nothing had happened yet. I was still having trouble processing most of my past and learning how to express what was really on my mind. Still, I had noticed one area of rather surprising growth the past few weeks. I was learning how to accept other people, forgive their sins and weaknesses, and I wasn't running away from anything. I was confronting my father's upcoming death, trying to be there for everyone who needed me, and I was even learning how to bite my tongue when it came to my dealings with Jake.

"Hey, Brylee," Trevor called out, interrupting my musings. "Can I come in? I have been up for ages, but didn't want to wake mum and father."

I blinked a few times allowing the world to come into focus. Exhaustion was my new state of being after days spent in turmoil and fear. In ways, falling asleep as I had last night without feeling compelled to dwell on unanswered questions had been a huge relief. I much preferred thinking happy thoughts about the life I wanted with Ben, but most of those had fled since coming home. It had been nearly two months since we had seen each other. That was longer than we had been engaged before I left.

There was no denial in my thoughts as I sat there in the growing light. I knew I was risking the life and eternity I so desperately wanted by staying here in the land of my birth just waiting for my father to die, but how could I have chosen otherwise? I kept recalling what he said the night before about the importance of including both sides of the family when a couple decides to get married.

Ben would never meet anyone from my past unless I invited him to come. My family might not be anything like his, but they had given me undeniable characteristics and traits, and I needed to get to know as much about them as I possibly could. That was the only way the disillusionment and loneliness my father had described in my mother could be averted. But as much as I wanted Ben to meet my father, LeAnn and Trevor, I never wanted him to meet Jake.

He was the most offensive man I had ever met, but I understood why my father had kept him around. Besides being part of the family, he was doing work Jack Hawkins was no longer able to do. For that reason, I was trying not to hate him, even though he was not at all like the man I was going to marry. I had been more than blessed to meet a man as handsome, kind and loving as Ben.

"Of course you can," I said, realizing that I had to stop my destructive thoughts before they ruined Trevor's birthday.

The next instant, the door flew open, and he raced across the room.

"I can't wait to open my gifts," he said, as his feet left the bed and came down with a thud that lifted my own legs in the air.

"Slow down," I told him as I pressed the fleshy part of my hand into my forehead. I could feel the beginnings of a headache. If I didn't take something soon it could turn into a migraine, and I would have to spend the rest of the day in bed with the blinds drawn.

"You aren't sick, are you?" he asked as his feet hit the bed once again, and he sank to his knees.

"Just a little headache," I assured him with a smile. "What time is it anyway?"

He looked at the travel alarm clock on the nightstand by the bed. "It's almost seven."

No wonder he was so anxious for the day to begin. People got up before dawn in the outback. It was the only time of day that was even remotely pleasant in the summer. Once the sun came up, the temperature climbed to over 105 degrees by mid-morning. My body was still having trouble adjusting to the change in climate, and breaking a sweat before I even made it out of bed was far from pleasant.

But the coming of this new day, which should bring so much happy anticipation since it was my little brother's birthday, would just bring more uncertainty and increased worries about how much time our father really had left.

"Have you been downstairs to make sure your mother isn't up?" I asked.

"Five times!" he admitted. "Uncle Jake was drinking coffee in the kitchen when I went down last. He told me not to bother them and then took me to help with his chores. I had already taken care of my animals, so when I came back to the house and they still weren't up, I decided to check on you."

I opened my arms to him. "Come here, little brother."

He slid across the light comforter until he was in my arms.

"Happy eighth birthday." I kissed the top of his head. "We have some wonderful surprises for you today."

"What are they?" he asked, pulling himself out of my embrace so he could see my face. It took so little to please him, and I wished I didn't feel like such a grouch.

"I can't tell you," I said as his face turned from expectancy into a frown. "But if you will play in your room for a few minutes while I get dressed, we can go downstairs together and get this day started right."

Trevor jumped down from the bed, but before turning to go, he reached up on his toes and kissed me on the cheek. "I'm so glad you are here. I don't ever want you to leave."

"Me either," I said as tears tickled my nose and the door closed behind him. I would stay here for as long as I could, but I couldn't forget about my own life forever. I wanted to be Ben's wife. It was the only thing that kept me going.

I took a quick shower, put on a pair of Capri's and a light cotton shirt and pulled my hair into a ponytail for the day. It was pointless to apply makeup or curl my hair. Once outside, I would sweat off any sign of femininity in a matter of minutes, but I did apply a light coat of waterproof mascara just so I would feel a little more alive.

A few minutes later, I was standing in front of the kitchen sink looking at the small hill behind the house. It was covered with dry brush that was the home to countless varieties of insects, but I still loved climbing it as a child looking for unusual rocks until my mother told me it wasn't ladylike to get all sticky and dirty. So I had learned to play quietly in my room with a meager assortment of dolls, books and color crayons until she was ready to teach me my lessons, tell me a story or play me a song on the piano.

No wonder I couldn't remember much about my childhood. The days had drug endlessly on with little to do and no one to share anything with. I was glad Trevor had parents who wanted to spend time with him. I just wished it had been the same way for me.

Trevor must have tired of waiting for me upstairs. I had knocked on his door on my way down the hall, and there had been no answer. I had even listened at the bottom the stairs to see if I could hear his voice coming from the master bedroom, but it was still silent in that direction too. Since he wasn't in the kitchen either, I figured he was most likely back in the barn with his animals. They seemed to provide him with the companionship he needed when the adults in his life were occupied with ore pressing matters. I might have liked having something like that of my own when I was his age, but the possibility of me raising orphaned animals had never even been entertained.

I looked up when the swinging door between the formal dining room and the kitchen swung open. LeAnn was still in her bathrobe and looked even more tired and discouraged than I did.

"How's father?" I asked as she got a cup of coffee and sat down at the kitchen table.

"He had another rough night. I don't know how much longer he can go on. Every breath is a struggle, and he is so weak."

"Do you think today will be too much for him? Jake and I could take Trevor on the carriage ride."

The beginnings of a headache must be affecting my sanity to suggest such a thing. How could I even think of Jake and me in the same sentence? He hated me, and I'd had more than a belly full of trying to be nice to him.

"I don't think there is anything you could do to keep him here—short of tying him to his bedpost. He is so excited to get out of the house and into the outback again. It's like this land with all its beauty and ugliness is part of his very soul. Sometimes I think he loves it as much, if not more, than he loves his family."

I sat down beside her in the chair at the head of the table where my father usually sat.

"That's because they are the same thing to him. Everywhere he looks he sees family and what they sacrificed so we could be here. Sometimes I think there is a little bit of aborigine in him. He sees how everything is connected, all the plants and animals and us. We can't survive without them, but they seem to do well enough on their own."

LeAnn smiled. "I guess I have always known that. After your mother died and you left, I tried to get him sell everything to Ned so it would remain in the family, and we could move away where he wouldn't have so many sad memories. But he said he would rather die than be separated from Hawkins' ranch. I can't begin to imagine how he is feeling now that he knows he doesn't have much time left to enjoy the things he loves."

"We can't think that way," I told her, placing my hand over hers. It was cold. "We need to cherish every moment we have together, and we cannot let him see how scared we are."

"Are you really scared, Brylee? I know you love your father, but you have Ben waiting for you back in the states. How long will feel you can stay here with us once your father is gone?"

"Brylee's not going anywhere," Trevor announced as he came into the kitchen through the back door, allowing it to slam shut behind him. "She told me so just a few minutes ago. Didn't you?"

I choked back the confusion that was ripping away at my heart. It was impossible to be two places at the same time. "I will be here for as long as I'm needed or wanted," I told him.

"Then you will always be here," he said as he threw his arms around my neck and clung to me with all the strength his little arms possessed.

The look on LeAnn's face was impossible to read. There was too much pain and lost hope written there.

"Let's not worry about anything today except your birthday," she addressed her son. "Now, come over here and give me a hug like you did your big sister. Your father is getting dressed. Then we will open prezzies."

Trevor did more than give her a hug. He kissed her upturned cheek before pulling away. "Can I go see him now?" he asked.

"Sure! You can help pull on his boots."

When he had gone, she fixed me with a glance that asked the question she had not dared vocalize while Trevor was there.

"Did you mean what you said to him, Brylee? I don't think he could take losing you after his father is gone."

"I meant it," I replied. "I will be here for as long as anyone needs me."

"What about Ben?"

"Ben knows this is something I need to do."

"But what if he gets tired of waiting? What if he gives you an ultimatum? Blokes don't like being separated from the women they love. It is far too easy for them to seek solace with someone else."

"Ben's not like that," I told her. "He knows how important family is."

"Then why hasn't he come to join you? He certainly knows how much you need him right now."

My chest heaved with emotions I wasn't ready to face any more than she was willing to accept what would soon be happening to her husband. Ben should be here. I certainly needed him, but he had just started a new job, and I didn't feel right about asking him to come when there was no way of knowing how much time my father had left.

"I haven't asked him to come," I slowly admitted.

"Why not? Don't you want him to meet your father? I know Jack wants to meet him. He's told me that several times already."

I looked down at the worn tablecloth and tried to order my thoughts. I didn't know if I was being selfish, protective or just plain worried about potential difficulties, but something had kept me from extending the invitation. "I do want him to come, but Ben just started a new job. Besides, father could have months left."

She shook her head and looked sadly at me. "You know that isn't true, love. Your father is barely hanging on to life. I pray every night that I won't lose him before morning, and I pray every morning that I won't lose him before night. We are not talking about months, Brylee. We may not even be talking about days. Your father is down to his final hours. Don't ask me how I know that. I just do."

Her words left a huge, cold and empty spot in my heart. My father really was dying, and if I wanted him to meet the man I was going to marry, Ben would have to come now, new job or not.

"I don't know what is wrong with me, LeAnn," I told her. "Maybe I haven't asked him to come because it makes everything so final. As long as Ben's not here, I can go on deceiving myself that there is plenty of time for them to meet, along with resolving everything that went wrong between father and me over the years."

I wiped away tears as I looked at one of the pictures that hung on the wall. It was a watercolor of the ranch house and surrounding homestead that my mother had painted when I was a little girl. I could remember watching her as she sat at her easel in the only shade she could find mixing paints and applying colors with soft, delicate strokes. I had wanted to join her but had been afraid to ask. Maybe, in her own way, she had learned to love at least part of the outback. Why had I not remembered that until now?

LeAnn rested her chin in her hands. "I am sorry for bringing up things that are none of my business. It is just so hard trying to be pleasant when all I want to do is to scream and throw things. I simply do not understand how can God take away a husband and father who is needed so much?"

I wished I had an answer for her that would lessen her pain, but there was nothing easy about death, even when one knew it was just the beginning of the next part of living. And if I was being truthful with myself, I wanted to throw things and scream every bit as much as she did.

"Listen," she said. "Why don't you go out to the bunkhouse and help Jake bring in the prezzies so Trevor can open them."

"You aren't going to wait until later when we have cake and ice cream?"

She looked at me with surprise, and I realized the mistake I had made. That was the way birthday parties were celebrated with Ben's family in America, not here.

"I'm sorry," I told her. "I momentarily forgot."

"No apologies," she replied. "You have been gone for a very long time."

Yes, I had been gone for longer than I had ever anticipated, but how could I have forgotten something as simple as opening birthday presents at the breakfast table? Even if we hadn't been a loving, demonstrative family, we still followed certain traditions.

"Do you need some help with breakfast or lunch?" I asked her, trying to postpone the inevitability of having to face Jake for as long as possible. I didn't like being around him. His icy ogling made me uncomfortable. We were always just one heartbeat away from another fight or a showdown of words, and we had promised LeAnn to be civil when addressing each other so she would have one less thing to worry about.

"Everything for lunch is ready. All we have to do is pack it in a basket. I made sandwiches last night while you were talking to your father. As for breakfast, Trevor always eats a bowl of cold cereal when he gets up, if I'm not here to fix something else. He's had to learn how to do a lot of things for himself. I could make an omelet if you like. I know your father will only eat a bite or two of whatever is placed in front of him. It nearly breaks my heart every time we sit down at the table together."

I felt her pain, but before I could comment on what she had said, she broke into tears and literally ran from the room. I contemplated following her, but what could I say that would help? Empty promises meant nothing now. We all knew what was going to happen far sooner than we wanted it to. Still, the open display of emotion I had just witnessed made me wonder how much of what I had seen from her over the past few weeks was simply an act.

Forcing myself from the chair I was sitting in, I crossed the kitchen floor to the back door and pulled it open. The air outside was already oppressively warm, and I wished I didn't have to leave the air-conditioned house to face a man who would only say something snarky and ruin what was left of a day that had barely begun. As my feet carried me across earth that was too compacted to support any life, I wondered why so many conversations were left unfinished and why so many ended in tears when what we really needed was to be supportive with each other.

Perhaps it was because no one had any answers. I certainly didn't know why I had not asked Ben to come so he could meet my father, and I definitely didn't know how I was going to decide between him and my family in Australia once that time came. Losing the man who had helped give me life was just the beginning of the tough decisions I would be forced to make. Denial and avoidance would not longer be possible.

I knocked on the bunkhouse door several times and called out Jake's name, but he didn't respond. Either he wasn't there, or he was ignoring me. That was fine by me. He was a strong, independent, resourceful man, and he would made it abundantly clear that he did not need my help for anything.

Turning my face towards the barn, I decided to check on Trevor's animals before returning to the house and make sure he was actually with them. Watching Newton's difficult and tragic birth made me appreciate the survivors of the outback, and the elements that seemed to control it. I wasn't sure that Newton's safe delivery was an actual miracle since Jake had been there, but it was certainly a tender mercy for my little brother. The distraction of caring for his orphaned animals kept him from thinking so much about our father.

When I slid the heavy barn door open, I heard Jake whistling as he put the harness and reins over the head of the old, black horse that would be pulling the buggy. He sounded almost happy. It was a most unusual sound.

"Excuse me for interrupting," I said.

He stopped what he was doing and glanced in my direction, his brow furrowing as he did so.

"Is there something you need?" he asked in a most agitated voice. Apparently, he was saving his civility until it was necessary to be polite.

"LeAnn sent me to help you carry the presents into the house. She wants Trevor to open them before we leave."

"Is that so," he said, draping the reins around the top board of one of the stalls.

I wondered how Trevor had missed the buggy and horse, but then his animals were in a different part of the barn, and he had certainly had other thoughts on his mind.

"Then I suppose we had better do as she asked," Jake continued. "We wouldn't want to ruin the day, even if it means we will have to spend a great portion of it together. Are you sure you can be pleasant that long?"

He walked past me and out the barn with not so much as a backward glance. His long strides took him to the bunkhouse much faster than my shorter steps did, but when I got there, I saw that he had left the door to his dwelling open for me.

"Don't just stand there like a whacker waiting for an invitation," he called out as I stood riveted to the plank floor underneath a simple, metal awning. "You can't help me carry anything if you refuse to come in and get it. I'm not going to bite you, not yet anyway, but you will have to excuse the mess. I have never been much into housekeeping."

He was right about that. His bed was unmade and there were clothes hanging over the back of the chair that stood in front of the old roll-top desk that had been in my father's den when I was a child. I wondered who had decided to move it. Heirlooms should not be given to someone who would not appreciate their value.

"Why don't you get some of those small packages on the table. I have the dog in the bathroom. I didn't want Trevor to see her. He has a habit of entering without knocking."

"Is that a problem for you," I asked.

"Why should it be? I practically raised the little nipper when your father was out of commission."

I hated the way he sometimes talked, even to and about people other than me. "I was only interested in Trevor's coming here this morning, Jake."

His reply was curt and to the point. "No! I saw him in the kitchen first and tried to keep him occupied since you were not around to do it."

I scowled and then took a quick look around as I walked over to the table. Besides the bed and the desk that was strewn with papers, a sofa and wooden coffee table was sitting in front of the window. Dirty coffee cups had been stacked on one end, with a pile of books and a picture of a girl with light brown hair on the other. I wanted to inspect it more closely but didn't dare. There was also a kitchen table with two metal-backed chairs.

"Are you ready?" Jake asked as he stepped back into the room with a dog carrier in his right hand.

"How's Baby doing?" I asked, picking up as many presents as I could carry.

"Will you quit with that ridiculous name?" he almost snarled.

"But I thought that was the puppy's name. Janet called her that at the airport"

"The dog is Trevor's, and he will be the one to name her," he replied, not allowing himself to be goaded into saying anything about one of the women who was so obviously interested in him.

"You're right," I said, gritting my teeth and picking up the skateboard in my free hand.

I hated feeling on the defensive every time I was around Jake, but he made me feel useless and incompetent. How could I possibly work with him when father was no longer around to run interference, or to keep me from saying exactly what was on my head? It wouldn't take all that much to push us past what had only been verbal confrontations until now.

"Here, let me help you with that?"

He reached out to take the skateboard, but I instinctively stepped backwards.

"I've got it." I replied.

"Suit yourself! I was just trying to be a gentleman. There is plenty more for me to carry."

I could have relented and acted more agreeable myself, but pride would not allow it. My reaction was childish and silly, but I simply didn't care. Being beholding to Jake Johnson for anything would only give him something more to hold over me.

Father and Trevor were sitting at the kitchen table waiting for us. LeAnn was packing food into a wicker basket. The puppy, who had been quiet until now, let out a little whelp when Jake set the kennel down on the floor.

That one little whimper was all it took for Trevor to jump down from his chair and race across the floor.

"Is this for me?" he asked, as the latch on the kennel door moved upwards and the small, energetic bundle jumped into his arms and began licking his face. He giggled excitedly as he turned his head back and forth trying to escape the puppy's greedy tongue.

"Well," LeAnn said, crossing the room to his side and kneeling down on the floor beside him. She stroked the puppy's soft, rust-colored hair as she looked lovingly at her son. "I guess that means you want to keep her."

"I've been wanting a puppy forever," he exclaimed holding the squirming mass out so his mother could see her better. "What's her name?"

I opened my mouth to answer and then remembered what Jake had said about the name one of his girlfriends had given her.

"She's your puppy," LeAnn told him as she took the little dog from him and held her close, almost like a baby. "I think it's only fitting you name her."

"Then I am going to call her Copper because she looks just like the shinny new pennies Brylee and I dove for in the pool."

His remembrance of our brief trip to town touched my heart. I walked over to our father who was sitting in his chair at the head of the table and put my hands on his shoulders. There were tears in his eyes, and I knew he wished he could be on the floor playing with Trevor and Copper, but he had to conserve his strength if he was going with us today.

He put one unsteady hand over mine. "LeAnn told me all the trouble you have gone to so this day can be extra special. You never cease to amaze me with your thoughtfulness, love. Trevor is going to need you so much when I'm gone."

"Not as much as I am going to need him," I whispered into his hair. I didn't know what any of us would do when Jack Hawkins was no longer around to guide and protect us. He was the glue that held our mixed-up family together.

"Thank you, ever so much, father," Trevor said, scrambling up from the floor after his mother returned the puppy to him. "I love Copper all ready."

Our father took the wriggling puppy Trevor handed him and set her down on his lap. He seemed to lack the strength necessary to even hold her upright.

"She is a real beauty, son, and she is your responsibility from now on. You will have to make sure she gets food and water and lots of attention. You will even have to groom her and see that she is house-trained."

"I'll take real good care of her, father. She can sleep in my room, can't she?"

"I don't see why not. She will want to be close to you since she hasn't been away from her mother very long."

It was a tender scene—a little boy, a dying man, and a small, new puppy. It tore at my heart with such force I had to back away so I would not destroy the moment.

"It's going to be okay," Jake whispered, brushing my shoulder with his hand. "Jack's children are tough. They can make it through anything."

"I hope you're right," I replied, surprised by his unexpected show of compassion after my earlier outburst. "No little boy should have to lose his father."

"We don't always get what we want. Sometimes we just have to get back up and go on fighting, even when we don't have the stomach for it."

When I glanced up at him, I noticed that the hard lines on his face had softened.

"I don't want to fight about anything more today, Jake," I said, wondering if he was thinking about the girl in the picture on his coffee table. "I just want my father to get well."

"I wish I could give you that gift," he responded. "You are a good woman, Brylee. Trevor is lucky to have you for a sister."

He had just given me two compliments. Who was this man standing so near me I could feel his warm breath on my neck? And what had he done with the Jake I had come to know and almost detest because of his arrogance and distain? Perhaps he was caught up in the tender scene between father and son just as I was, and that had precipitated his unusual display of compassion. Maybe it had even caused him to think about his own father—someone I knew nothing about.

"Trevor needs all of us," I said, my brow knitting in a quizzical frown. "I know he loves spending time with you. Though I don't know why since the two of us seem to be nothing more than thorns in each other's sides."

I recognized how rude and unladylike my comment was the moment the words slipped out, but I couldn't retract them. Jake had taken off the boxing gloves, and I should have been more willing to follow his lead. But the truth was, I didn't trust his motives for being nice, even to make Trevor's birthday more enjoyable. And I was so used to sparring with him that any change in our method of communication was jarring.

"He's a great kid," Jake said, choosing to ignore my lack of manners. "If I knew one of my own would turn out like him, I might just consider finding a good woman of my own and settling down."

"There are a lot of them out there," I replied, not wanting to make too much of what he had said, or the cold chill I had experienced that made the hair on my arms   stand erected. "I'm sure you would not have to look very far if you set your mind to it."

"I don't know about that," he said, glancing down at my left hand where the diamond on my engagement ring was sparking in the sunlight that came in through the kitchen windows. "From where I stand, all the interesting ones have already been taken."

I looked away from him too shaken to respond. He liked rattling me, especially when I least expected it. That was the only reason he said what he had. It was payback for my comment about thorns. But in the time it took for me to internalize what had really happened, he had moved away from me.

"Hey sport," he said to my little brother who had not left our father's side. "How about opening the rest of your gifts so we can get on to the next big surprise."

"I can't believe there are more," Trevor said, excitedly taking one of the wrapped packages from the stack on the kitchen table.

He left Copper to settle down in our father's lap. I watched as the man who would not be with us much longer stroked her soft hair. His eyes were glassy-looking, and I couldn't begin to imagine the pain he was in knowing this was the last birthday he would spend with his son, the last birthday he would spend with any of us.

Trevor tore at wrapping paper until he uncovered new khaki-colored shorts, some t-shirts and underwear, a waterproof watch, and the skateboard with knee and elbow pads that I was giving him. There was also a game of monopoly and a box of dominos—activities our father could share with him if he felt strong enough.

"I love everything," he said, moving around the room and giving each adult a hug and kiss. "This is the best birthday ever."

"And it's not over yet," father said. "I think Brylee and Jake have another big surprise. Why don't you run along with them and find out what it is. I will stay here and help your mum with our lunch."

I wanted to ask him if everything was okay. He was in a great deal of pain—anyone could see that—but he was determined to give Trevor a birthday he could always remember with joy. And it appeared to be working because my little brother seemed to forget the man whose hand lay so heavily on the little birthday dog's back as he quickly followed his uncle.

"I can't believe there's more! This is even better than Christmas."

But at the sound of his excited voice, Copper jumped to the floor, nearly crashing into her new owner as her nails hit the polished linoleum and she slid forward.

Trevor laughed and gathered her into his arms.

"Go out to the big part of the barn and see for yourself what is there, but hang on to that puppy," Jake told him. "We don't want her to get hurt."

"Do you think we have made a big mistake?" I asked as soon as Trevor was out of hearing distance, and we were on our way to the barn too. The hot sun beating down unmercifully on my shoulders was causing the sweat to form on my brow.

Perhaps the outing would be too much for my father. He was already bushed, and he had not even left the house.

"A mistake about what? Things seem to be going pretty damned good, when you consider the circumstances."

"But I don't know if father will be able to handle the buggy ride. He is in so much pain, and I'm not sure he will be able to stand on his own."

"You can't change what is happening, Brylee. Cancer's a bitch, but I know LeAnn will up his morphine so he can go with us today. You can't take away his dignity by treating him like an invalid. It's all he has left."

"But I'm worried."

"Who isn't? But I don't think what your father does or does not do right now is going to matter much. We both know the end of his story."

I felt the bile in my stomach rise to my throat. I didn't like being reminded of the inevitable. Father wasn't going to get well, and all the praying in the world wouldn't change that.

"Hey, sport," Jake said, entering the barn before I did. "I see you have figured out the rest of our surprise. How do you like the old buggy?"

"It's splendid, but I can't get in it with Copper," Trevor replied as a frown formed between his eyes. "She's too wiggly."

"I'll take her," I told him, opening my arms to the active, little puppy I had held during the flight from town to the ranch. She pressed her soft hair into my face as I watched Jake push Trevor upwards and into the driver's seat.

"Can I drive it, Uncle Jake?" he asked. "I know I can do it. I am a whole year older now."

Jake laughed and swung himself up beside Trevor. "I do believe you could manage this old plow horse just fine. But would you mind if I get us out of the barn. We'll have Brylee open both doors so we can get out."

"I can do that," I said as I retraced my steps towards the outside of the building. The heavy wood doors creaked on their rusty hinges as I slowly pushed them open with my free shoulder and arm. Copper responded to the agitating noise by struggling to get free.

"You're not going to get hurt," I said, trying to calm her. "Just lie still in my arms like a good little girl."

The puppy immediately quit squirming, and I momentarily wondered if she understood what I was saying. Dogs were very intelligent animals, or so I had heard.

Together, we stood out of the way and watched as the grizzled, black horse pulled the old, blacktopped buggy into the hot, summer sunshine. I was surprised at how good it looked after having spent the better part of fifty years stored away in some shed. The springs underneath the driver's seat barely creaked as Trevor bounced excitedly up and down. This was turning into an amazing day. If father weren't ill, it would be close to perfect.

Jake went into the house to help LeAnn with the food while I stayed outside to keep Trevor company and make sure that the horse—old as it was—didn't get away from him.

"You look pretty good sitting up there with the reins in your hands, little brother. Are you having a good time?"

He looked down at me with sad, knowing eyes. "Everything's bonzer! I just wish father didn't feel so bad. Is he coming with us for a ride?"

"That's the plan," I told him, trying not to choke on my words. "This is your day, and he wants to make sure it is s a happy one."

"Can we take Copper with us? She won't want to stay here by herself."

"Why don't you run into the house and ask? We wouldd have to bring food and water for her."

Trevor handed me the horse's reins and then climbed down the side of the buggy. There was a step to help him, but his legs were too short to make it to the ground without jumping.

"Come on, Copper," he said, taking the small puppy from me. "We have to talk to mum, but I know she will say yes cuz it's my birthday."

I climbed up into the driver's seat, knowing that it wasn't in LeAnn's nature to deny such a simple request, especially when her son was losing so much. The old horse seemed unaware that he had been handed off to someone else. Maybe he was used to it, and maybe he was just too old and tired to care. I knew exactly how he felt.

Chapter 2

The ride to the glen where we were going to have lunch was pleasant. Trevor, with Jake sitting next to him to take over if the trail proved rough, guided the horse whose steady hoof beats were somehow reassuring. I sat on one side of my father, and LeAnn sat on the other. He winced when a wheel hit a rock or a rut, but he just gritted his teeth and pretended he was doing fine. Still, I couldn't help but noticed that LeAnn gripped his hand even tighter whenever she suspected he was in more than the usual amount of pain.

As we rode along, I tried to see the land as my father was most surely doing—through eyes of love for something that had been the foundation of his life. To an outsider, the scenery was anything but spectacular, just a few Gum and Eucalyptus trees and lots of tall, dry grasses and shrubs that provided homes for far more insects and small animals than I could imagine. I just hoped we would not run into any more snakes, poisonous or otherwise. I'd had my fill of them the day before.

"I love this land more than any place on earth," my father suddenly said. "It's so good to be outdoors again."

LeAnn looked at him with great tenderness. "I have to admit that the first time you brought me out here I wasn't exactly excited. All I could see was brown everything, but you have shown me the unsung beauty of the outback. It is my home now, and nothing will ever change that."

"I am going to miss everything so much," he said, inhaling more deeply the oxygen that was making his labored breathing easier.

LeAnn's eyes began to mist over. "It just isn't fair, Jack. I am trying to be strong for Trevor, but I don't want to be here without you. We have been together for so long, but there are times when it seems like we just met. You are the reason I get up in the morning—my reason for living and breathing."

I didn't want to intrude on their private conversation, but we were pushed so tightly together underneath the carriage's awning that I wouldn't miss a word they were saying, even if I plugged my ears or began humming something loudly in my head.

He patted her hand. "You can do anything you make up your mind to do, love. It took an incredibly strong woman to bring me back to life after I lost both my wife and daughter."

"I want to be strong, Jack. I try so hard for Trevor, but to tell you the truth, I wish I were going with you. There just won't be anything left when you're gone."

"Nonsense," he chided. "You are a young, beautiful woman, and I do not want you to spend the rest of your life alone."

She tried to protest, but he silenced her with a look I couldn't see.

"I'm not saying that I want you to find another husband and make a new life right away, but I don't want you sitting around and mourning forever either. I want you to be as happy as you can possibly be, and if that means letting another man love you, I don't want my memory to stand in the way."

"But that will never happen! You are my soul mate, Jack Hawkins, and there isn't another man on God's green or brown earth who can ever take your place. That's the way it has always been, and that's the way it will always be."

Once again, I silently prayed that the love Ben and I now shared would remain as strong as the love between LeAnn and my father. It was something very rare and surprisingly beautiful. But our journey through life had just begun, while they had been together for nearly fifteen years working through problems that would drive most couples apart.

I turned my head to look at the small pink and yellow wildflowers that had managed to survive several years of drought. They were nearly hidden amongst the withered, brown grass that was home to so much that could not be seen. I wanted to see life and the world the way God did, and that included the fact that death was not meant as a punishment. All of his children were given a certain amount of earth life to do as they pleased, but when that time was up, nothing could stop the inescapable. I just wished my faith was stronger. I couldn't begin to imagine what my future might bring.

"We're here!" Trevor shouted a few minutes later as he pulled back on the horse's reins. He sat there beaming with pride over his accomplishment while Jake jumped down and secured the line around a tree. I knew how much my father hated being on the receiving end of help, but he didn't say anything, even when Jake offered him a hand so he could make it from the buggy to the ground without falling.

"You handled that horse mighty well, son," he said, trying to adjust the oxygen tank that hung loosely over one shoulder. LeAnn moved in quietly to lend her support.

"I knew I could do it! Thanks for letting me, Uncle Jake."

Copper had fallen asleep in my lap, but the moment she heard Trevor's voice, she was wide-awake and shaking with anticipation. It was uncanny how rapidly she and Trevor had bonded.

LeAnn and I spread out the blanket we had brought from home underneath the branches of a large Gum tree and set the white, wicker basket of food on its edge. As always, LeAnn seemed to know everything that would make my father more comfortable and had brought a camping chair for him to sit on.

She had packed ham sandwiches, potato chips, pickles, beans, olives, cookies and carrot and celery sticks, with iced tea to drink. She had even been thoughtful enough to bring lemonade for me.

Father sat in his chair in the shade of the old tree that did little to lessen the intensity of the heat, greedily taking in the ambience of both the family and the country he loved. He looked peaceful and happy, even though he consumed little. He knew his time on earth was almost over and had accepted it. I wished I could do the same.

It was a hard to eat even a well-planned and tasty meal, and I had trouble forcing each mouthful down. I tried not to think about what life would be like with both of my parents gone. When I had run away from home after my mother's accidental death—I had to use that term now because entire truth had been verified—I had known that my father would still be here waiting for me if I ever decided to come back. But when I left Australia again, there would be no returning home. Everything I had always considered my legacy would belong to someone else.

After lunch, father closed his eyes, and LeAnn sat down on the blanket in front of his chair and put her head in his lap. He put his hand on her hair and began stroking it gently. I tried not to stare, but was consumed with the strangest feeling. It was as though I was looking at a scene that had been played out possibly millions of times since the earth began—a moment suspended in time when two people had thoughts for no one but each other. How I wished it had been like for my parents, but more importantly, would Ben and I have moments like that to remember?

That nostalgic thought changed quickly to another as I began to realize that I wanted to be the one sitting on the ground in front of my father with my head in his lap and his hand gently stroking my hair. But I had lost that right by abandoning him, making his life so intolerable he had nearly drunk himself to death. LeAnn and Trevor had saved him and become the family he could truly cherished. How could I ask for any concessions now? My life had become like the old adage about a person making his or her own bed and then having to lie in it. But for me, it was a mighty hard and lumpy mattress.

The rest of the outing was more or less uneventful. Trevor played with Copper, LeAnn closed her eyes when father did, and Jake disappeared—destination unknown.

I found a log underneath a nearby tree and sat down to think. So many things in my life had changed recently. Had it only been a little over two months since I had come home? I could barely remember being in L.A. with Ben, even when I looked at the ring on my finger. It seemed like another lifetime, and I speculated as to how I would feel about Australia once I returned to American soil. Would I forget what had transpired since my arrival, or would a part of me always feel like it was missing because I had left so much behind?

My elbows were on my knees, and I leaned forward until my face was resting in my palms. I felt so numb and empty inside even now. This land was incredibly silent and lonely when there was no one to share it with. No wonder Jake was so angry all the time. He had to miss civilization, even if he claimed to be a loner. No wonder he sought refuge with the women in town whenever he could. They must help him feel alive.

That wasn't so hard to understand. Everyone needed human contact, and not just from family members. My own longings for Ben were intensifying. I needed him to hold me in his arms and kiss away all my doubts and uncertainty. His gentle, undemanding love had broken through my fear of being hurt so unmercifully again after being sexually attacked while studying at the university. It had helped me find peace of mind and self-acceptance. The security I felt in his presence was sorely missing right now.

"What do I do, Heavenly Father," I soundlessly prayed. "How I am supposed to keep my promise to my earthly father? He expects me to stay here and help run the ranch with people I barely know, and all I want to do is go home to Ben where I won't have to worry about a man who hates me, a woman who basically stole my mother's life, and a little brother who doesn't even know how soon everything in his world is going to change."

I sat quietly waiting for the Holy Spirit to fill my soul with a burning like it had when I was searching to know if the gospel was true, but nothing happened. Maybe I wasn't asking the right questions, and maybe God expected me to use what I had already learned to make a few decisions on my own. Either way, I felt more abandoned than I had after losing my mother.

"You had best wake up, or you will find yourself face-first in the dirt," a deep voice broke into my worrisome thoughts. I didn't have to open my eyes to know that Jake had come back from wherever he had gone.

"I wasn't sleeping," I defended myself as I looked up at him. "Just thinking."

There was no need telling him that I had been praying and hoping for an answer that hadn't materialized. Jake was the last person in the world who could appreciate what I was going through.

He sat down on the log beside me. "You could have fooled me, but then I don't expect to comprehend how the female mind works—awake or asleep. Besides, there can't be two other people on the planet less inclined to understanding each other than the two of us."

"I would like to understand you, Jake," I said. "It would make working together so much easier, but you don't think I belong here and maybe you are right. Perhaps I am fooling myself in thinking I can stay here and be of any real value after my father is gone. It's not like I have the tie to this land that you do."

"That sounds like a copout, mingled with self-pity, to me. We don't always get to decide where we end up. Sometimes, we simply have to make up our mind that we are going to do something simply because other people need our help."

"It's not always that simple," I retorted.

"Hell, if life were bloody simple, few of us would be where we're at. Still, I'm staying right where I am regardless of what you decide to do."

"I want to keep my promise to father. You have to know that by now."

His caustic laugh only made our conversation more difficult. Trying to explain myself was futile since he rarely believed a word I said anyway.

"Good on ya!" he smirked. "You've got guts for giving it a burl and staying this long. I will give you that, but your return still seems a little convenient to me. I don't believe in coincidences."

His attempt at camaraderie was gone.

"I came home when I did because Ben wanted me to make things right with my father before we were married. I had no idea he was sick. How could I have known? I had been gone for a very long time. Why can't you understand that?"

"Because I'm a cynic with a bad attitude towards most everything in life that doesn't sit right with me. My sister has worked hard on this ranch. It's her home, and I won't let anyone take it away from her."

"I know you love your sister, and I would never do anything to hurt either her or Trevor. They're part of my family too."

"But they were forced on you by a wedding you weren't expecting, and you haven't known them long enough to form any kind of serious attachment."

"You're wrong about that!" His constant accusations were becoming arduous, and I was tired of trying to justify my actions. "How could I not love my little brother and the woman who has made my father so happy?"

"But what if your father has left everything to them? I know he had a will drawn up long before you came back. You were out of his life. He had no reason to believe he would ever see you again."

I looked down at the hard-packed earth under my feet and tried to identify the reason behind Jake's continual false allegations. The ranch was barely providing a livelihood for the people who lived there. How could he possibly think I would lay claim to any of it? My life was already planned. I was going to live like a fairytale princess with Ben in L.A. where the weather was temperate, and I could raise my children in the peace and security having the gospel in my life had brought.

So I took a deep breath of dry summer air and set my chin, hoping I looked strong and not merely obstinate, when our eyes met.

"My father has the right to leave his possessions to anyone he wants."

A smug smile touched his lips. "And you are trying to tell me that you won't be upset if your inheritance goes to someone else? I would be mad as hell if it were me."

"But I'm not you. I went to college so I could take care of myself."

He snorted, a most annoying sound. "That's a noble endeavor, but a little naïve, don't you think? You may not need this ranch for a living since you already have some stupid bloke who is willing to take care of you, but what about all those personal items that belonged to your parents and all the greats? And what if at some point you could use a little extra cash in your pocket? Selling the ranch could be very profitable."

I looked out over the barren, but somehow beautiful landscape that my father loved so much. I didn't have the personal investment in the ranch that LeAnn, Trevor or even Jake did, but I liked to think I was a better person than someone who would fight over materialistic things. Ben and I would be okay. He had a great job, and I would find one as soon as I returned to the states.

Still, Jake had a point. There were objects in the house I would like to have. Things to remind me of home and family when I was half a world away, and things I could pass on to my own children some day.

I could feel Jake's eyes still resting on me, and knew he was waiting for an answer to his allegation. I would have to choose my words carefully so there would be no further misunderstandings. I had come home unexpectedly, upsetting their lives, and had no idea what my father's will included. I only knew he had changed something because I signed a paper Buck Henry brought the day of the wedding without even reading it. Maybe Jake had learned of that transaction and suspected something he couldn't prove.

"I love this ranch," I told him. "And I always want to feel welcome here because it is where my parents and ancestors lived and where I grew up. But Trevor shares those same genes, and I would never deny him or anyone else a livelihood. Ben and I don't need any money, but yes, there are a few small things I would like to have one day."

"Small things?" he queried. "What about your mother's baby grand piano and china? LeAnn uses those things. She might not want to part with them."

"If she doesn't, I will get over it. But I think you underestimate both your sister and me. Notwithstanding the strange circumstances of our meeting, we have become friends."

"I have seen plenty of friends squabble over things far less valuable or important than an inheritance."

His eyes were hidden behind his ever-present sunglasses, but I still looked directly into them praying I wouldn't flinch.

"So have I, but relationships are more important than material things you can't take with you when you die. That should be clearly evident right now."

"Still, they can make living a hell of a lot easier."

I shook my head. "There's no winning with you, is there?"

He leaned his head back and laughed. "I may be a bit of a hard head, but I owe a lot to my sister. She raised me after our parents died and is losing the only man she will ever love. I don't want her to lose her home too."

"She's not going to lose her home or anything else," I assured him, even though I knew it was another empty promise. Nothing in life was guaranteed. We might not be here tomorrow, any of us. But I knew for a fact that I would never take anything from LeAnn or my little brother, if they truly wanted it, no matter how much it might mean to me. I had the Aussie blood of past generations running through my veins—blood that believed in honesty, family and commitment to beliefs and causes. I didn't expect to be handed an inheritance. All I wanted was my father's love and forgiveness.

Suddenly it occurred to me that everything Jake accused me of could be pointed directly back at him. Maybe he was the one who wanted to get his hands on the ranch so he could sell it or keep it for himself. LeAnn trusted him, and with both my father and me out of the way, he would have little trouble getting whatever it was he wanted.

Perhaps he was already skimming a little off the top and feared being caught. My father had not been well for a long time. Why else would a well-built, hard-hitting and virile man like Jake Johnson be hanging out on a ranch that seemed doomed to fail? He liked women and excitement too much, and family loyalty only went so far. Had my father suspected that something was amiss? That might be the very reason he had practically insisted that I learn where the finances stood and would be around long enough to make sure his legacy would be passed on to Trevor before abandoning the proverbial ship.

"What's your real stake in all of this?" I demanded before my courage drained. "You're still young enough to get married and have a family. Would you bring them out here to live like you have been doing the past few years? And what if you just got tired of living in the outback? You have your plane. You could go anywhere in the world if you wanted to."

He flashed me a searing glance and ran his tongue around his lips before answering.

"It sounds like I am not the only one with trust issues. You think I'm only here for potential landfall, and not just figuratively speaking. Is that right?"

Warning signals zigzagged across my brain, and I looked down at the dirt that covered my boots. Had I made a huge mistake pointing my finger at him? Under the circumstances, I could ill afford making him a bona fide enemy. We might not trust each other, but more unfounded accusations would only create a deeper rift, and I had the distinct feeling that he could be an incredibly dangerous man.

When I didn't say anything, he gripped my arm until it began to hurt.

"You find me contemptible, don't you, Miss Hawkins? But I assure you my feelings for my family are as genuine as yours. I would not hesitate stomping into the ground anyone who tried to hurt them. And for what it's worth, I did consider getting married once. It didn't work out. Maybe I have just decided that no woman is worth all the trouble she causes."

His admittance frightened me as much as it tugged at my heart. I would die if I didn't have Ben.

"But what about companionship, warmth and growing old together? Don't you want those things?"

I never wanted him to know that LeAnn had already told me about the girl he had lost—the girl who had run away right before their wedding and died. It would give anyone cause for self-preservation.

"I can get all the companionship I need from the girls in town, and who says we are all going to grow old?" he responded, practically tossing my arm aside.

"It's our only option, unless we . . . ."

"Die first," he finished for me. "My folks were killed when I was five. Guess I don't remember much about them so I can't be overly sentimental. LeAnn's the only family I ever remember having."

"I'm sorry," I told him.

It was another justifiable reason for distancing himself from others, but unless he was willing to open his heart to someone he would be dead in all the ways that really mattered long before his earthly life was over.

"Look," he said. "I'm not complaining. Life is what it is. Not everyone is as lucky in love as you claim to be."

I glanced over my shoulder. Father and LeAnn were both awake and talking quietly. Trevor was trying to teach Copper how to fetch a stick. It was the perfect picture of family serenity. I was glad they would have this day to remember. Too bad Jake and I were so determined to find fault with each other. We needed a happy day to recall when what awaited us was over too.

"Life sucks," Jake suddenly interjected. "People who find their soul mates should be able to spend more time with them."

"Does that mean you believe everyone has a soul mate?"

"Hardly," he responded, diverting his eyes to a line of black ants that was meandering over the brittle earth in front of us. "I believe that some people, like Jack and LeAnn, are just plain lucky. Most of us are doomed to wander through this life of misery alone."

"That is a depressing way of looking at it."

"It's how I see it! Do you really believe this bloke of yours is the only man you could ever be happy with?"

"I haven't really thought about it. I only know I am a better person when we are together."

"That's not much of a reason to marry someone. Shouldn't you want to be a better person on your own?"

"I suppose, but I'm certainly not sorry we met. He is the most incredible man in the world and has given me something I never imagined possible."

"You are such a child," he mocked. "He gave you a cause to believe in, that's all. Religion is just an opioid of the masses used to dull the senses so people will stay in line. I would venture to say you haven't had enough experience with life to know the difference between what is good and bad for you yet. Or you might just be an optimistic, but rather deluded, soul."

"And you have no optimism at all," I retorted. "I happen to believe that everything happens for a reason."

"What possible reason could there be for your father dying? It seems like an awfully cruel God that would tear a husband and father away from his family."

We were moving into uncharted—and even dangerous— territory. All civility would crumble into name calling and accusations if I said anything more he might take opposition to, but I couldn't let him belittle the kind, eternal Father I had come to love over the past few months.

"Religious beliefs can't be argued," I told him as I straightened my back. "I love my father and wish he could live forever, but that is both selfish and unrealistic because it's not going to happen."

"All I hear is a useless bunch of rhetoric," he said, as his dark eyes seemed to pierce into mine. "I thought you religious types had all the answers."

I met his latest challenge head-on.

"I haven't even figured out the questions. All I know is that we will not be asked to endure more than we can handle, as long as we are willing to turn to God for help."

He threw his hands in the air and then brought them down to rest on the top of his head. "I hope you still feel that way when your father is gone. All the religion in the world won't take away that pain. Death is the end. There is no getting around that. You will soon be alone, just like me."

"I will never be alone," I shot back. "I have a new family here, and I have Ben waiting for me. And you are wrong about God. He cares about every single one of his children."

"There you go again," he said, drawing his well-built frame off the log we had been sharing. "You can believe anything you want to! Just don't come running to me when your whole world falls apart, and your God isn't there to pick up the pieces. That truly is a living hell."

He turned and walked away. Had I been much older and wiser, I might have called him back to discuss a way of fighting some of his demons. I had never known a man who was so disillusioned about both life and love. If anyone had need of the Saviour's redeeming grace Jake did, but he was too proud to ask for help. He would consider it a sign of weakness.

"Hey, Brylee," Trevor said as he and Copper came running over to me. "Father said to tell you it's getting late and there is work to be done before we have cake tonight."

I smiled up at him. Copper was bouncing around on the ground at his feet.

"I'm coming, little brother, but Jake just took off towards the dry creek. Do you want to go after him, or do you want me to do it?"

"I'll go, but I better carry Copper. I don't want one of those big, mean snakes to get her."

"Smart boy," I told him as he gathered the squirming puppy into his arms. "It is always best to be on the safe side. I will help your mother load things into the buggy while you are gone."

It had been a good day, I decided on the short ride home, despite Jake's dismissive and contemptuous attitude. In many ways, I felt sorry for him. He had allowed a relationship with the woman he loved to destroy his sensitivity and caring, and seemed determined to keep all emotions locked deep inside—other than the anger and hostility he lavished on me. Maybe it was easier for him that way, but I certainly didn't want to return to the hopeless, raw feelings I'd had after my mother's death, or the dark and dismal years that came after.

I would be eternally grateful Ben had come into my life, but what if he got tired of waiting for me or found someone else? That was one tragedy I would never survive. There had to be a way to keep our long distance relationship flourishing until I made it home. I hadn't even asked Uncle Ned if he had telephone service outside the country. He was miles closer to town and a little more connected to the twenty-first century since NJ and Molly had just left their teens. My cousins knew about technology and would want to stay connected to the rest of the world when they came home from the university in Sydney for a visit.

Uncle Ned and Aunt Nora were waiting for us on the veranda when we got back to the house. Trevor was the first one to jump down from the buggy. He had decided to let Jake drive so he could hold Copper. It was almost as if the little dog had become his lifeline to a reality he felt but did not understand.

"Look what I got for my birthday," I heard him shout as I helped LeAnn get my father out of the buggy and back on solid ground. He looked exhausted and as if he were in a great deal of pain, but I knew he would somehow find the strength to make it through the rest of Trevor's birthday. It was just one of those tender mercies God granted to his children, even if they claimed not to believe in him.

"Are you sure you don't want to go in and lay down," LeAnn was asking him as they walked slowly towards the house. She was carrying his oxygen tank, and he was leaning heavily on her arm. I had wanted to support him from the other side, but he'd told me he would rather I carry the blanket and picnic basket so it would not have to be done later. My heart stopped me from arguing with him. His self-respect was all he had left, and I would help him retain it for as long as humanly possible.

"Thanks for making this day happen," I told Uncle Ned when I joined the rest of my family on the veranda where they were still talking about the day's adventure.

How funny it seemed to be including so many people in my declaration. I had always considered my mother as my only real family until recently. We had done everything together, and it was disheartening to realize that it shouldn't have been that way. In addition to never getting to know my father, I had never really gotten to know my uncle, my aunt or my cousins. It wasn't going to be easy leaving any of them behind when I returned to the life Ben and I had planned.

"It's the least I could do, love," he said, putting his arm around my shoulders. He smelled of stale tobacco and musky sweat. But then, who didn't? It wouldn't be life in the outback if neighbors couldn't smell each other coming. The heat was always intense, and habitual smoking and drinking were just part of living.

"I hope it didn't take too much out of father," I said. "I worry about him so much."

"I know you do, but his life is in God's hands now. Hawkins' men may not be church-going, but they do have a healthy respect for a higher power."

"Father claims he doesn't believe in God."

"Your father is a self-made man who never had the need for anything more than what he could see or feel as long as he could take care of himself."

"And now that he can't, he is reconsidering? Is that what you're trying to tell me, Uncle Ned?"

"Death has a way of equalizing everything. One might not believe there is something more than this life, but it's hard not to entertain that possibility when the end is near."

"Is that how you feel?" I asked.

"Sure is! I don't like the idea of losing my brother any more than you like the idea of losing your father, but there isn't a damned thing we can do about it."

Tears that had been tickling my nose all day broke lose and slid down my cheeks. Uncle Ned pulled me closer.

"None of us are super-human in that regards, love. I can't imagine my life without Jack, but I can assure you of one thing. It isn't any easier for him to leave us than it is for us to watch him go. He's only hanging on because there are still a few things that have been left undone."

I looked around to see if anyone might be overhearing our conversation, not that it really mattered, but everyone else had gone into the house.

"How can people know when they have done everything they could or should?" I asked as a cold sickness rose within me.

I believed with all my heart that a different, more glorious life existed after death, but Uncle Ned and my father were right. Without proof, I could only walk by faith, and right now, I was having a great deal of trouble doing that. I needed Ben's strength, comfort and assurance to get me through what was yet to come, but I still hadn't asked him to join me.

"You're consulting the wrong man with deep questions like that," Uncle Ned said. "I told you Hawkins' men were God-fearing, but that doesn't mean they know what is going to happen once the old ticker stops working. I like to think we will all be saved like Father Frederick proclaims, though I have no idea what that means for reprobates like your father and me. We have lived life pretty much on our own terms, never really paying much attention to what the good book actually says."

"I think God understands human nature since he created us, but I also believe he wants each one of us back with him someday."

"That is mighty astute thinking for one so young, Brylee."

"Not really," I responded, suddenly feeling not quite so brave discussing religion with my uncle. My knowledge was incredibly limited, but I could offer him a glimmer of hope. "This life can't possibly be all there is, or we would not have been given families to love . . . ."

"I miss him so damned much right now, Brylee, and I haven't even lost him yet," Uncle Ned interrupted, his voice cracking with emotion. But he didn't seem to mind that he had let me see his softer side. "He's my big brother and I have relied on him my entire life. I am going to feel like some wallowing whale out of water without him here to lean on. We have been best friends since the day I was born."

My hand went reassuringly to his arm. I hadn't given much thought as to how my uncle must be feeling. I had been much too wrapped up in my own grief and impending loss.

"I am sorry for not being there for you, Uncle Ned. I never even considered what you were going through."

"You can't be faulted for that!" he replied. "Maybe we can be there for each other from now on. I really am glad you decided to stay—for the time being anyway. Hell, we might even be able to convince you to stay here permanently."

"I would do it in a heartbeat, if I didn't have Ben and our life together to consider," I told him with a painful smile.

"And there is no way you could talk that young bloke into moving here?"

"What would he do, Uncle Ned? He's a city boy who has never even seen a ranch. He would go crazy out here. It can be very lonely, and he is incredibly close to his family."

"If you get married, you will become the most important part of his family, and there is nothing saying you would have to live way out here. Edna's growing. I'm sure there would be plenty of opportunities for an enterprising young lad."

"I guess nothing is impossible."

"Not if you really want it. I have been thinking a lot about Nora since your father's wedding. I always thought that loving each other was enough, but I want my kids to belong to us in a legitimate way like Trevor does now. How is that for coming to God under a great deal of pressure?"

"I think it's a wonderful idea, and know Aunt Nora would love it," I said, purposely ignoring his reference to what amounted to not much more than deathbed repentance. My family believed in that, just as they believed that going to confession absolved them of any past sin. Because of Ben, I knew differently now. Christ's Atonement did not come without a great deal of humility and work on the part of the sinner, and that in included all of us.

"She would at that," he said, giving me one of the mischievous smiles I had loved as a child. It always meant he was planning something he knew my parents would not approve of, like eating ice cream before bed or running around outside without my shoes on.

"What woman wouldn't want to marry an old teddy bear like you?" I said, hugging his arm close to me. I had found a new source of strength to help me through the difficult hours and days ahead.

Chapter 3

LeAnn's knock on my bedroom door before dawn the next morning brought me from a troubled sleep to near terror. I jumped out of bed, entangling myself in a sheet in my hurry to get to the door. My heart was pounding so rapidly I felt as if I might be on the verge of fainting. Had yesterday been too much for my father? I nearly tore the door off the hinges in my hurry to get it open. LeAnn was wearing a robe and looked even more tired than she had the day before.

"I'm sorry to wake you up so early, but Trevor has been throwing up most of the night," she said. "Too much cake, ice cream and excitement, I guess. He has finally gone to sleep, and I was wondering if you could listen for him, just in case he needs someone again?"

"I can do that," I replied, wondering why I hadn't heard anything if my little brother had been so sick. The bathroom was just across the hall from the guest room. "How is father doing?"

"He has been up most of the night too, but when I ask him if there is anything I can do to help, he always says no.

Sometimes I just lay quietly beside him so he won't know I'm awake. He feels guilty enough as it is."

"But he has nothing to feel guilty about. He hasn't done anything wrong."

"True enough, but sometimes he feels he is being unfair by asking to spend his last days at home. He knows it isn't easy for any of us to watch him die, and it is only going to get worse."

I sank back against the doorframe for support. Now that I knew my father was okay, at least for the moment, the rush of adrenalin was subsiding. "We wouldn't consider having him anywhere else."

"Most certainly not," she responded, not even attempting a smile. "But he has always been such a strong and independent man. This slow dying is incredibly painful for him, and not just in a physical sense. He always planned on his demise coming in a much more spectacular way, if you know what I mean?"

"You don't think he would do anything foolish?" I asked as my thoughts flew to the gun cabinet in the den. He kept it locked for Trevor's safety, but the key was always within reach.

"He most certainly would not! Suicide is a coward's way out, and your father is anything but that. He will fight this thing to the bitter end."

"I didn't mean to imply anything," I said, regretting my outburst. "He loves his family too much."

"Your father always puts other's needs above his own. That is one of the things I love most about him. But right now, he needs us to take care of him. I am sorry for being snippy. I'm just tired."

"No worries," I told her. "We're all running on a sleep deficit. I wll make sure Trevor's okay. Just try to get some rest. I know you are exhausted."

She smiled wearily. "I have never been so tired, but almost hate to sleep. I have so little time left with your father."

"But you have to take care of yourself, or you won't be able to take care of him."

"I know that logically, but my heart doesn't see it that way. I want him to live forever, or at least until we are able to go together."

"I wish I could tell you that everything is going to be okay."

"Me too! I have known this time was coming for over two years, but it is still hard accepting that your father and I won't be growing old together. Can I be honest with you, Brylee?"

I nodded. My heart went out to her more completely than words could ever express. If Ben were dying, I would do anything in my power to keep him alive, but God gave life and knew when it would end. And thanks to Ben, I now understood that we had agreed to everything before taking our mortal journey. Nothing happened by chance, but we could no longer see the entirety of God's beautiful plan.

"I have prayed so much the past few weeks that God would allow your father to stay with us for a while longer—years, if that was even an option. I know that is being selfish because he is in constant pain and so weak he can barely sit up in bed, but I can't deny how I feel. I really do wish I could pray that God's will be done, but I simply cannot accept this challenge. I haven't been to confession since I moved out here, but I still believe in God's mercy and goodness. Do you think I am a horrible person for not wanting to let your father go?"

"You're the most compassionate, loving woman I have ever known, LeAnn, and it is only human not wanting the person you love to die. I find myself fighting the same thing, but it really is out of our hands. Maybe Trevor is the lucky one because he doesn't fully understand what is going on yet."

"He will soon enough," she said, shivering, and then pulling her faded pink robe tighter around her slim frame.

Father wasn't the only one who continued to lose weight. LeAnn was beginning to look like a skeleton, but I knew she would not take time for herself. Maybe I could do more to help. Most of my time was spent trying to keep Trevor occupied, but I could fix more meals and make sure everyone ate something.

"Trevor is strong, and we will all be here to help him through whatever comes next," I said.

"I know, but he is going to need more than our strength when his father is no longer around to teach him how to become a great man. When you first came back, I was worried that you would never get over hating me. And the truth is, I would not have blamed you. If we hadn't become involved your mother would still be alive, and you would never have felt like you had to run away. My guilt for the part I played in messing up your life has always been great, but never more than now. You should have been here with your father all along."

Her honesty brought to the surface once again the painful memories I had been trying so hard to rise above. If she had walked away, my mother would indeed be alive and maybe none of this heartbreak would be happening. But I wasn't the judge, and cancer was always a possibility when behaviors that supported it were indulged in.

"There is no reason to dwell on the past," I told her as a veil of Christian charity descended upon me. "We have all done things we wish we hadn't."

"So true!" she said. "I just wish some of them didn't have to catch up with us, but I am glad you are here and willing to give us a chance to be the kind of family we all need right now."

She gave me a kiss on the cheek and then retraced her steps down the stairs to the master bedroom.

Sitting on the edge of the bed in the soft, yellow moonlight coming in through the bedroom window, I realized that I didn't know half of what I thought I did. Life wasn't static, and it was meant to be lived to the fullest, even when the harsh and bitter times came. If I walked away now, I might never be able to return, and I wasn't prepared to do that.

But leaving Australia wasn't my only concern. If I decided to stay for any length of time after my father was gone, there would be momentous decisions to make about running the ranch and making sure Trevor's legacy remained intact. LeAnn would support anything that made her son's life better, but I feared Jake would be far less compliant with any of my suggestions.

He already detested my presence and had made it abundantly clear that no one would stand in his way regarding what he felt was best for his family. But if I thought about all the obstacles that lay ahead now, trying to rest would be impossible. Like Scarlett O'Hara in the movie *Gone With the Wind* that I had watched with my mother as a child, I would not allow myself to dwell on things that had not yet happened. I would leave all my worrying for tomorrow—and the beautiful thing about tomorrow was that it never came.

Trevor seemed to have suffered no ill effects from having been sick during the night. When he got up around eight, he and Copper came running down the stairs as if he had gotten plenty of sleep. I had been sitting at the kitchen table for over an hour nursing a glass of juice and a slice of toast.

"Hi, Brylee," he said. "What's for breakfast? I'm starving."

I looked at him and smiled. "What do you feel like eating? You don't want to make your stomach hurt again."

"It won't," he said. "I feel fine now, but maybe just some cold cereal."

He got a bowl out of the cupboard while I secured the cereal and milk. Copper sat on his lap while he ate. I noticed that he was feeding her bites of his food.

"Have you fed Copper her breakfast this morning?" I asked. She was jumping excitedly at his hand—obviously quite hungry—and I didn't want her to get sick.

"I forgot," he said, immediately leaving the table and going into the laundry room to scoop up some puppy chow and put it in her bowl.

While he was doing that, I refilled the small holding tank that dispersed the water she drank. The little ball of hair was soon eating voraciously.

"She sure is hungry," Trevor said as he returned to his own meal.

I put a glass of orange juice on the table beside his bowl.

"Aren't you going to eat more?" he asked me between bites.

"I have been eating all morning," I replied, indicating the partially empty juice glass and half-eaten piece of toast on the table.

Sleep had been impossible after LeAnn awakened me. There was far too much to think about, and none of it was pleasant. Father was losing ground daily. Ben was too far away to give me the comfort I needed. And in the morning, Jake and I would be rounding up sheep and then taking them to Uncle Ned's so they could be sheared.

Meanwhile, I was left on my own to figure out what I needed to take with me on a roundup. I had planned on asking Jake, but when he came into the house for his morning coffee, he was in a foul mood and did nothing more than grunt in my direction when I wished him a good morning. I let him drink his fill and leave without saying anything that might add to my discomfort.

I refused to feel sorry for him. He'd had plenty of time to find someone else to go with him. Maybe he liked the idea of being able to torturing me with his open hostility because we would be away from anyone who might take exception to it.

The phone rang while Trevor waited for Copper to finish eating.

"Morning, sweetie," Uncle Ned said when I answered. "How is everyone doing this morning?"

"Tired, but fine," I told him.

"That's good because I thought I might drive over so we could talk particulars about getting the sheep from the open range to my place. It doesn't take a genius to know that you and Jake aren't exactly loving the idea of spending any extensive time together."

"I'm sorry our feelings are so transparent," I replied, trying to keep my jaw from locking. "I try to be civil, but no matter what I do or say, he does not trust my motives for being here."

"Jake is a complicated man with a complex past, but your father and LeAnn would never have survived the past few years without him."

"Are you saying that gives him license to treat me like trash?"

His laugh was gruff but gentle. "No one has that right, but you may have to overlook some of his less desirable qualities if you want to keep that promise you made to your father. He doesn't need further drama is his life right now."

"Absolutely," I grudgingly admitted. "I want to make things as easy as I can, but a certain someone seems to bring out the worst in me."

"Jake does have a taciturn side, but I will do what I can to intervene," he responded. "Now dry those pretty eyes and put on a stiff upper lip. You have to let him see that you are a competent women who can take care of herself, or he will never let up on the insults."

"But I am not competent at all, Uncle Ned, especially when it comes to keeping a ranch running."

"It is just that kind of attitude that gives him the upper hand. I have complete confidence in you and so does your father. I will see you in under an hour."

"Who was that?" Jake asked, giving me an amused look as he reentered the kitchen with an empty coffee mug in his hand. It was impossible to tell just how much he had overheard since I had been facing away from the back door, and he always moved stealthily.

"Uncle Ned thinks it would be a good idea to discuss things before we leave in the morning."

"Ned knows I can handle most anything," he said, his eyes narrowing to mere slits. "This is about something else. Have you been talking to him about our lack of communication."

"Why would I?" I asked, looking over to where Trevor was sitting on the floor next to Copper. He may not have understood what Uncle Ned and I had been discussing, but a disagreement between Jake and me would not be overlooked.

"Then why all the concern about the roundup? I have been doing it since I got here."

"Perhaps he just cares about his family like you do, but we will know soon enough because he is on his way."

That wasn't exactly true, but spending time with Jake right now wasn't advisable, so I asked Trevor to take me to see his animals—something he was more than happy to do. We put Copper in her kennel to rest so she would not get underfoot. She had barked incessantly the day before when Trevor took her to meet his orphaned animals. I hoped he would soon learn that Newton and the others would accept the active puppy more readily if they got used to her in very small doses.

When I heard Uncle Ned's pickup truck pull into the driveway, I knew it was safe to return to the house. Trevor took my hand as we walked through floating particles of dust that had yet to return to the ground. This would not be a peasant meeting. My father was much too weak to attend, and Jake would make sure his opinions were heard. But I knew Uncle Ned would protect everyone's interest. My father had given him the land he lived on, and he would not want to see anything happen to the old homestead and the ground that went with it.

LeAnn came out to the veranda to greet all of us. "Jack is waiting for everyone in the den. I told him we could handle things on our own, but he insisted."

"I would expect no less of my big brother," Uncle Ned replied, putting his arm around her shoulders. "He's been the boss since the day I was born."

"What's going on?" Trevor asked, nudging me. "Uncle Ned never comes to the house in the middle of the day."

"I think we are going to have a family meeting about getting the sheep sheared."

"I wish I was going with you," he pouted as the screen door swung shut on its hinges.

"Me, too, but your time will come soon enough."

Father was leaning back in his office chair, and LeAnn was standing behind him when Trevor and I got to the den. Uncle Ned was resting his shoulder against the gun case with his arms folded, chewing his bottom lip, and Jake was sitting on the sofa in front of the window looking his usual surly self. Trevor gave me a confused look before sitting on the floor in the middle of the room.

"I know all of you think this is unnecessary, but we are doing things a little differently this year since it's the first time we have had Brylee with us," father said in a very controlled voice. "Ned and I want to make sure we are all on the same page. A lot that can go wrong, even under the best of circumstances."

It was apparent that he and his brother had talked since my brief conversation with Uncle Ned earlier that morning. That didn't surprise me, but my father should be resting instead of conducting family business.

"Ned consented to join us because he grew up out here and knows the property almost as good as I do." He smiled fondly at his brother as I leaned into the door frame. It was impossible to go any further. "And there is no one I trust more to make sure things go as planned."

I thought Jake might pull one his tantrums and storm out, but he simply looked down at the floor and let my father continue.

"I mean no disrespect to anyone. Each of you is capable of running the operation, but emotions are heightened right now, and Ned can view things a little more objectively. All I ask is that you look to him if you have any questions. We have run our operations side-by-side for decades. He knows me better than I know myself most of the time."

That was the perfect introduction to a very unsavory issue. Uncle Ned and my father were as close as any two men could be.

LeAnn massaged his shoulders while they talked about the most likely places the sheep would be grazing, and the easiest way to force them out of mountain crevices to Uncle Ned's place. With the limited amount of water available on the flatlands, they would be higher up than usual and less likely to go willingly into the valleys below where it was much drier and the temperature considerably warmer.

We would ride the motorbikes on available trails and travel the rest of the way on foot, scouring the brush as we went for any sheep that had wandered away from the herds. There were plenty of open meadows where we could keep them at night if necessary. Our main concern would be providing safety from dingoes and other wild animals that prowled after dark looking for food. A herd of sheep in the open would be too much of a temptation for them to resist.

The entire ordeal sounded awful—the uncooperative sheep, the underbrush, the dirt, the bugs, the possibility of more snakes and having to fight off wild animals, but none of that compared with the horror that filled my soul at the thought of being alone in the middle of nowhere with Jake.

We would stay connected with each other and Uncle Ned by two-way radio as much as possible. Signals were easily lost in the outback, and he would be at his ranch organizing the shearers once his own sheep had been gathered in. He had far fewer than we did and could have them in the pasture by his barn in less than a day. It would take Jake and me considerably longer, possibly up to 72 hours if we had any problems.

I listened without saying much. There was nothing of value I could add. I might have lived in the outback for fourteen years, but I knew absolutely nothing about it. Jake really was taking a chance by allowing me to go with him, and I was most likely the biggest fool alive for agreeing to do it. But watching my father talk about the life he loved made me want to learn more about it. I might not make it out of the mountains alive, but at least I wouldn't disappoint him by refusing to go.

"I'm taking the plane up," Jake announced as we finished a late lunch. I almost asked if he wanted me to come along so we could talk, but decided against it. He was in no mood for conversation, especially one with me. It had been made perfectly clear during the hour-long family meeting that everyone knew what they were doing but me.

"Are you sure you still want to do this?" LeAnn asked me as she sat down at the table after checking on my father for the third time in less than an hour. He had gone to bed directly after Uncle Ned left. "Your father will understand if you change your mind. This isn't exactly what you signed up for when coming home."

I swallowed back the lump of trepidation in my throat. Nothing had gone as expected since coming home, but I couldn't back down. I wanted to be as brave as everyone else who was trying to prepare for the unpreventable.

"I'll be fine," I told her. "I just thought we would be home at night."

Ben had been none too excited about me going into the outback with Jake when I emailed him about what my father had asked me to do.

"It's too dangerous, Bry," was his instant response. *"You know absolutely nothing about this man, except that he's dangerous and doesn't approve of you. I'm really surprised your father would even allow it. There has to be someone out there who could go in your place. Australia is a massive continent just like the United States. Please tell me you have reconsidered and will be staying at the ranch where you belong.*

"Strike that! You belong here with me. You are only on loan to your family. Just give me the word, and I will be on the next plane to get you. I miss you so much. Sometimes I wish I had never asked you to go home to straighten things out with your father. I know it was the right thing to do, especially in light of the situation now, but you have been gone for over two months, and my life is completely empty without you.

"Did I tell you Becky and I have been looking at apartments? There are some pretty nice ones fairly close to my work. I can't wait for you to see them. Heck, I can't wait to be your husband so our real life can begin . . . ."

Recalling those words, I knew Ben would be more than disappointed that I was even considering sleeping under the stars with Jake around. We had promised to be faithful to each other in word and deed, forever and always. But what other choice did I have if we couldn't come home at night? I had to make good on my pledge to my father. He was dying, and this was his final request.

"So it's sleeping arrangements you are most worried about," LeAnn was saying as my mind spun back to the present. "Spending the night in the outback isn't at the top of my priority list either, but Jake will not let anything happen to you. This isn't the first time he has gone after sheep, and he's the best shot I have ever seen, even better than your father."

Her words were meant to be reassuring, but as kind and understanding as she tried to be, she adored her brother and knew very little about what I believed. Besides in all fairness, Jake had never laid a hand on me. I couldn't count him grabbing my arm after our picnic because I had provoked that, and I could deal with his constant unpleasantness and occasional threat.

"Of course, you are right," I told her, pushing my chair away from the table. "It's just fear of the unknown that has me feeling as if I am sitting on pins and needles. Why don't you tell me what I need to take? There's no way I will be able figure it out on my own."

"Getting ready is the easy part," LeAnn said, rising to her feet. "Jake usually packs all the pots and pans, and takes jerky, coffee and beans. But if I were going, I would pack my own supplies. Guys tend to be a little more self-reliant in the outback. They don't even need a bush most of the time."

LeAnn loaned me a warm jacket, raincoat and sleeping bag. She suggested I take toilet paper, sun block, a small first-aid kit, granola and candy bars, a couple of apples, hot cocoa for the morning since coffee wasn't my thing and additional water in case it was needed.

I secured all of the smaller items in the packs that hung on each side of the motorbike I had been riding, and she showed me how to tie my sleeping bag over the back of the seat after putting it in a large garbage bag that could be used as a barrier between the bag and the ground. Other than apprehension and a little well-founded fear, I was ready to go.

"I guess that does it," I told her as I tied off the twine that was holding the sleeping bag in place.

"Not quite," she said with a frown. "You might not like this, but your father made me promise."

I felt another clutching knot of alarm. "What kind of a promise?" I asked, glad that Trevor was in the house sitting with him.

She pulled something from her pocket—a small pistol with a silver barrel and ivory handle.

"No," I told her, forcefully shaking my head as I backed away. "I won't use a gun."

"My feelings were exactly the same when I first came out here. But your father convinced me it was a necessity, and I agree with him. He gave me this gun because I refused to use one of the bigger ones in the den. It is easy to keep hidden, and I have learned that it isn't dangerous as long as the safety lock is in place. Jake is an excellent shot, but what if he isn't around when you need him?"

Her logic did nothing to lessen my concerns. "I have never even held a gun."

"Then it is a good thing we have a few hours to practice before morning. Jake told me what happened the night you took Trevor into Edna. He won't force the issue again, but your father is adamant that you know the basics when it comes to handling a weapon. He asked me to teach you."

I wanted to run away, back to Ben's arms where I would be safe and free from making decisions that could jeopardize everything we had been trying to build. Knowing how to use a gun wasn't inherently right or wrong, but what if I were forced to use it?

"Don't look so horrified," LeAnn said. "Even Trevor knows how to handle a gun. Your father thought it would be safer than trying to hide them from him since they can be found all over the property."

"But he's just a little boy."

"Kids grow up fast out here. It's not like they have the luxury of learning about life and death in a civilized manner because they are surrounded by it every day. You have to let go of the fact that you were raised by a mother who wanted to protect you from every unpleasantness. You will be useless to Jake if you aren't prepared."

"Do you really think I will have to know how to use it?" I asked.

"Hopefully not! I never have, except for target practice— something we are going to have right now, unless you refuse."

I wanted to do just that, but knowing that my father was depending on me made me reconsider. So I followed her to the open field behind the barn where she had already set five empty bean cans along the top of the fence. I looked around to make sure no animals were near before she showed me how to load bullets and release the safety. Then she demonstrated how to hold the gun with both hands so it would be steady and how to look through the small "v" on top to line up my target. She knocked one of the cans off with her first shot.

"You're good," I said.

"I've had some practice and so has your little brother. He is just as good with a gun as he is riding a four-wheeler."

It took several tries before I was even able to hit the fence, but LeAnn seemed satisfied with my progress when I finally knocked a can to the ground.

"Just keep this with you and don't be afraid to use it if you need to," she said. "I keep it in a little case in the nightstand by the bed all the time. It makes your father feel better, and in a way, it makes me feel safer too. I know I can protect myself if I have to."

When I emailed Ben that night I didn't say anything about rounding up the sheep, or the fact that I had learned how to shoot a gun. I simply told him about Trevor's birthday and how rapidly Copper was becoming the center of his life. I didn't want him worrying about me any more than I knew he already was. It was going to be a long three days, but with any luck, I would survive it.

Chapter 4

I set my alarm for 4:30 a.m. I knew Jake would be in the house by five for his coffee before we left. I wondered why he didn't make it in the bunkhouse. He had everything he needed there. Maybe companionship was more important to him than he wanted to admit.

He was finishing a second cup when I walked into the kitchen wearing the only pair of jeans I had brought with me and my father's old shirt—the one LeAnn had loaned me on the Sunday I had learned to ride the motorbike. There was something comforting about wearing it. It made me feel a little closer to the man who had given me life and would not be with us much longer.

"I would offer you some coffee, but know you don't drink it any more," he said. "I have no idea why or how you gave it up, I'm just glad I don't have to. There is nothing more satisfying than a quick jolt of caffeine to get a person going in the morning."

"I remember those days, but some things in life are more important than a satisfying beverage," I replied.

He gave me an incredulous look. "You're a funny, girl. How could anything hold more importance than taking care of your needs and a few of your wants along the way?"

There was no point in trying to explain the Word of Wisdom or the law of chastity to him, but fortunately I didn't have to.

We both turned our heads when LeAnn joined us. "Do the two of you have everything you need?"

I felt so sorry for her. Her eyes looked almost as big as her face she had lost so much weight, yet she still presided over her house with precision, always taking care of the people she cared about.

Jake set his coffee cup on the counter, walked over to her and put his hands on her shoulders. I watched as he looked down at her.

"We're fine, Lee, and we have everything we need."

"At least let me fix you some breakfast," she volunteered, breaking away from him and moving towards the refrigerator. "I could have some bacon and eggs ready in ten minutes. You need something nourishing before you leave."

"Quit being a mother hen," Jake told her. "In case you haven't noticed, Brylee and I are adults and can take care of ourselves. Now go back to bed and quit fussing. You look like hell."

"Thanks a lot, little brother," she retorted, but I could tell that she appreciated his concern. "I would like to see how you look when you haven't slept in weeks."

She suddenly started to cry, and Jake moved towards her again, taking her in his arms and giving her the comfort she seemed to need so much.

"I'm sorry, Lee. I don't know how you have managed to keep it together this long. Jack is lucky to have you. You are the best woman I know."

"I'm not good," she whimpered. "I keep praying for a miracle, but God seems to have forgotten me."

Oh, how my heart ached for her. What comfort she would find in knowing that she could be with my father again someday, but she hadn't even accepted his approaching death yet. I didn't want to lose him any more than she did, and I knew without a doubt that this life was not the end. She only hoped it wasn't.

"Now you are being ridiculous," he told her. "You have done everything humanly possible to take care of Jack, and that has to be enough in anyone's book."

"I've tried! I really have, but promise me that you will keep Brylee safe, Jake. Jack si ply could not handle it if anything happened to her."

"She'll be fine, LeAnn. She is not as helpless as she looks."

I didn't know if it was a put-down or a compliment, but either way, I decided to let it go. Now wasn't the time to invent more trouble. I was already going to spend the next few days alone with Jake.

After LeAnn went back to bed, he sat down at the table where I was drinking a glass of orange juice and eating a toasted whole-wheat bagel.

"You don't have to go with me today if you have any reservations. Lee's right in saying there is enough drama around here already. I can handle things by myself. It just might take a little longer."

Part of me wanted to stay right where I was in the safety of the ranch house, even though it was impossibly hard watching my father fight for every breath. But a greater part of me wanted to prove how much I loved him. I could only do that by following through with the things I had already promised to do. Going with Jake would let him know that I was fully committed to taking an active role in making sure the ranch was preserved for Trevor.

"I want to go," I answered him. "I may not be much help, but I need to know about every aspect of ranching if I am going to be a part of it."

"You are not much good at lying, but I won't try to change your mind. So here is what I need you to do . . . ."

I took a deep breath and a bite of my bagel and tried to calm my racing heart. Jake could definitely be charismatic, even sensitive when he chose to be. But I wasn't sure I could ever get past his taciturn, aggressive behavior towards me, or his earrings and tattoos. Still, there was something appealing about him that made me want to move beyond his less than desirable outward behaviors so I could better understand the man beneath the surface.

Quite suddenly, I realized how desperately I needed to get back to Ben. I was feeling vulnerable because I was on my own trying to face the death of my only serving parent, and that was dangerous to more than just my physical life. It could affect my eternal salvation.

Jake unexpectedly slapped his hand down on the table so hard I thought it might bring LeAnn back to the kitchen to find out if something awful had happened before we even left the ranch house.

"Are you listening to me?" he demanded. "You have the annoying habit of checking out mentally every time I talk to you."

"I'm sorry!" I responded, unable to recall a single word he had said. "I've had a lot on my mind lately, and sometimes it does tend to wander."

"We all have a great deal on our minds, but that irresponsible approach to what we are about to do will get you killed. You can't afford to be daydreaming once we leave the house. I don't want to be scraping you off some mountain."

"I will pay attention," I promised. "Just go over it one more time, please."

He inhaled deeply before responding.

"I will find the herds. All you have to do is help me get them to Ned's. Just ride along the outside edges and make sure none of the animals get distracted. Sheep are notoriously stupid. They would follow each other into a pack of dingo's if something didn't keep them headed in the right direction."

"Is there anything else I should know?" I asked.

"Just watch where you are going and pay attention to everything around you. The terrain is rough in places, but we should be able to get the first herd rounded up and over to Ned's by early afternoon—if we don't have any unforeseen problems. We will leave in ten minutes. It should be light enough by then."

He got up from the table and left the kitchen through the back door. He didn't even put his coffee cup in the sink. I did it for him—all the time wondering what was wrong with my head. I had never been a risk taker, aside from running away from home. My mother had raised me to play by the rules of decorum and common sense. But all of that had changed now. She was gone, and I was on my own.

Still, I couldn't help wishing I knew more about men. Ben was open, honest and easy to read. Jake was an entirely different story. While most of our interactions had been borderline hostile, he had made a few comments that gave me cause for concern. But instead of going out to the barn and telling Jake I had reconsidered, I simply gathered up the few supplies that were still in the house and joined him by the motorbikes a few minutes later.

This was simply seventy-two hours of my life that would be over before I knew it. Jake Johnson, for all his animal magnetism and questionable charm, could not make any of my dreams come true.

The morning ride across terrain that was dry, barren and bumpy was not pleasant, and the flies and other biting insects that flew from the underbrush were prolific. But I had slathered insect repellent over every uncovered part of my body, and they didn't seem to bother me much, as long as I did not remain motionless for too long. I watched Jake's movements carefully when he began whistling and waving his arms at the first group of sheep that had sequestered themselves in a valley less than ten miles from Uncle Ned's part of the ranch. I tried to imitate them, but when it was time for me to ride along side the animals that moved at what seemed a snail's pace, I felt somewhat better about my decision to go. Maybe sheep weren't so stupid after all.

I hadn't been to Uncle Ned's since returning home. His house wasn't as large as the one I had grown up in, but it was definitely newer. He had added a veranda to the front and repainted. It looked clean and lived in. I remembered when my own childhood home had looked like that, but a lot can happen in five years.

I climbed off my motorbike feeling rather proud of myself. I hadn't become lost, tipped over, or let any of the sheep out of the lined formation they had fallen into once the lead sheep started to move forward. If it was this easy getting the rest of the scattered herds to Uncle Ned's, we might be completely done by dark. Then I would not have to spend the night in the open with Jake, and Ben would never have to know that I had done anything more than help drive a few head of sheep to my uncle's.

"It's good to see you again," Aunt Nora said, placing a tray of sandwiches, iced tea and lemonade on the veranda table so we could have lunch. "How is your father doing today? I wish there was more time to spend with him, but getting ready for the shearers is a full-time job while it lasts."

"I'm sure he understands," I told her. "And I know he is grateful that you and Uncle Ned have made all the arrangements for getting the sheep sheared this year."

"We're family, and that is what families do." She wiped at her eyes with a hand that had seen far too much hard work and sun. "Besides, your father has helped us out plenty of times. We wouldn't even have this house if he hadn't given us the land it sits on. He even helped us build it, but you were too young to remember all that."

I sat down on a wrought iron chair. "It was really nice of you to fix lunch."

"It's nothing fancy, but I did bake some shortbread for dessert. You used to love that when you were little."

"Still do," I told her. "And nobody makes it quite like you do."

She blushed and tugged at the faded, green apron she was wearing over her work clothes. "It's nothing, really, but I will wrap some up for you. It might be a nice treat after your beans tonight. I don't know why men can't be more creative when it comes to what they eat on trail drives. Ned would live on beans and jerky if I let him."

"I guess they have more important things on their minds than fine dining."

"I doubt they're more important, but they are definitely different. Ned has been driving me crazy with all his last minute plans."

"I have," Uncle Ned said as he stepped onto the veranda. "And here I thought you liked being kept on your toes. Be a real shame if I have been misinterpreting things all these years."

"Hush up," she scolded him as we sat down at the outdoor table. "Brylee was just telling me all about her morning."

"And a very productive one it had been," he responded. "Jack would be mighty proud of her."

It was my turn to blush, but I did't say anything because Jake had joined us.

Besides eating good food, the meal was spent talking about the shearing that would begin the next morning. Uncle Ned's sheep were already in the pasture closest to the barn, and the shearers would be there by sundown. They would stay in his bunkhouse until they were finished, and Aunt Nora would make sure they were adequately fed. It was an exciting time of year.

I helped Aunt Nora clear the porch table while the men went to top off the gas in the motorbikes so we wouldn't run out somewhere in the brush.

"You're awfully quiet," Aunt Nora said as we stacked the dishes in the sink. "Did someone say something to upset you?"

I shook my head. "No! I just keep thinking about all the things I missed out on when I was a child. My relationship with my father was so different from the one he has with Trevor. It's hard not to feel a little bit jealous."

"I might be speaking out of turn," she said, turning around with a look on her face that gave me a moment of anxiety. "But it wasn't your fault you spent so little time with him. I loved your mother dearly, but anyone could see how much she depended on you for everything, especially her happiness. Your parents were very much in love when they first married, but your mother just wasn't suited to life out here. She was like a fragile flower that needed shade and nourishment—things that could not be supplied in the outback."

I chewed at my bottom lip. It was becoming a habit I didn't much like.

"But I still don't get it, Aunt Nora. Love should last forever if it's real."

"That's what the song writers and poets would have us believe, but your mother was only sixteen when they met, and your father was ten years older. He'd had plenty of lovers, but had never been in love until they met. It was the classic example of forbidden romance, and your fraternal grandfather was a cold and heartless man. All he wanted was for his daughter to marry into some rich family where fortunes could be combined. I ought to know. Ned and I spent a lot of time with them."

"So you knew my grandparents on my mother's side?"

"No, dear, I never met them. Ned and I were just getting to know each other and weren't much interested in anything else. Your mother always met us at the pub on Westley Street. I'm not sure your father ever set foot in the ancestral home, but I drove past the estate once just to see where she lived. It burned to the ground nearly two decades ago. There was a big story about it in the Edna paper. I don't know what became of the family."

There were so many questions I had for Aunt Nora, but Jake didn't give me the chance to ask any of them. I saw him standing outside the kitchen door motioning for me to join him.

"We'll talk again soon," she said, giving me an affectionate pat on the hand. "And don't worry your pretty head about anything. Your parents loved you very much—both of them."

I was afraid Jake might ask what we had been discussing, but his mind was occupied with other things.

"I put petrol in the bikes. They should be good until we get back," was all he said when the screen door slammed shut behind me. I chided myself for not being more attentive.

"Where are we going this afternoon?" I asked as I straddled my bike and put on my helmet. It was feeling a little bit achy after my morning ride but knew it would only get worse as the day went on.

His eyes were fixed on the gas gauge in front of him. "We're heading up Devil's Peak. That's where we will spend the night. I hope you brought enough warm clothing. It's going to get cold."

He didn't wait for my reply, but it didn't matter. Thanks to LeAnn's careful packing, warmth and food were two things I didn't need to worry about. Spending the night alone with him was an entirely different matter.

We rode for close to an hour in silence, not that we could have carried on a conversation through the noise the bike's motors made. The ground was hard and uneven, but I managed to stay comfortably behind Jake. I knew he could have taken me over much rougher terrain, but for some reason he was following what could have once been a stream-bed. I thanked heaven for that blessing. My arms and legs were stiff with tension from fear of crashing.

But my thanks became premature as we turned into the thick brush and shrubs that covered the side of the mountain. Logs and fallen branches covered the ground that obviously had not been ridden over since the previous year. The bugs were horrid! They flew right into my goggles, and I had to keep my mouth closed, or they would have caked my teeth as well.

I had no idea how we were going to get to our destination as we zigzagged back and forth trying to stay clear of any obstruction that lay ahead. I could sense the movement of animals in the brush and every so often saw a flash of rust, brown or tan that let me know we had disturbed something other than a domesticated sheep or cow. I didn't have to be afraid of large predators because Australia didn't have any, and the wild dingo wasn't particularly dangerous unless it was running in a pack. Still, in an odd sort of way, I was glad LeAnn had insisted I bring her small revolver with me. I didn't want to be forced to use it, but at least I knew I could protect myself if given enough time to retrieve it.

Worrying about running into small rodents and reptiles was useless. They lived everywhere, and their colouring helped them blend into their natural surroundings so completely that most of time humans didn't even know they were there. That was one of the reasons I was glad Jake was riding in front, even though eating his dust was unpleasant. It gave me a few seconds to steady myself if he ran into something that could not be seen until he was riding over it.

This truly was *no-man's land*. It was rough, waterless and untamed, and the trees and undergrowth were so dry and thick they either crumbled or poked at the skin like cactus when we rode through them. I could see spots of blood on my shirtsleeves. It would take weeks for my scratches and bruises to heal. I just hoped I would live through this nightmare so Ben and I could be reunited. He had never seemed so far away.

Nonetheless, I couldn't help but feel that I deserved the bug bites, scratches and dusty dryness that burned my lungs and made me gasp for air. Pride and the desire to prove myself to the father I'd never really known had brought me to one of the most primitive places on earth, and with a man who held me in complete contempt. I had no one but myself to blame for anything that happened. I had been given plenty of chances to stay behind, and Ben had repeatedly told me not to come.

When the fine powder coming up from the ground in front of me finally cleared, I saw that Jake had come to a stop and was taking his helmet off. I pulled up behind him. There was no reason to say anything. He would tell me what he wanted me to know.

"This is going to be a hell of a lot harder than I thought," he said as the tracks between his eyes deepened into a frown. "We should have gotten Trevor a sheep dog instead of that sissy house dog that will never work a day in her life."

"We used to have a sheep dog," I said, thinking about the Blue Healer named Lola that had intimidated me with her playful snarling and growling.

"And how does hat helps us?" he asked.

There was no use trying to explain myself. He didn't want to understand. He just wanted to make me feel stupidly useless.

"I was just making a statement," I replied. "What do we do now?"

"We find the sheep on foot! They usually divide into two or three smaller herds. We will most likely have to flush them out."

"Wonderful!" I thought as I looked around at the desolate mountain crags and crevices. They could be hiding anywhere, and I would be lucky not to have an appendage torn off trying to find them, or worse, come upon another Eastern Brown snake that would not be as content at keeping its distance as the one Trevor and I had seen a few days earlier. I shuddered almost imperceptibly, but his next words let me know that he had finally taken notice of me.

"It's not as bad as it looks or sounds. I pretty much know where they are. I scouted them out in the plane last week. We just have to get them into the main gully over that clump of brush." He nodded towards the west.

At least I thought it was the west. It felt like I had been turned inside out and upside down during the past hour or so, and there were no distinctive landmarks to tell me where we were or how we were going to get back. I wished again that I hadn't come. I was woefully unprepared for this venture and would have to rely on Jake for just about everything.

"We can drive them down to Ned's in the morning," he was saying when my mind came back to the unpleasant situation I found myself in.

I had been praying all day that we would make it back to Uncle Ned's before nightfall so I wouldn't be forced to spend the night alone with a man I didn't trust But it looked like that wasn't going to happen, even if there were several hours of daylight left.

"Why won't we have time to do that before dark?" I asked.

"Look around you," he mocked. "Do you see any sheep just waiting to be led away? We will be lucky to find half of them before nightfall, and just to answer your next question before you feel compelled to ask, it would waste too much time to come back tomorrow for any stragglers."

He gave me a sudden sardonic smile that sent chills down my spine as he climbed off his motorbike and secured a helmet I had not seen him wear until today. "I just hope we don't have any trouble with dingoes. We're invading one of their prime hunting grounds, and they are not going to let two measly humans stop them from getting a tasty meal."

I felt a chill envelop me again. He might just be baiting me to get another reaction, but common sense told me he wasn't. Wild dogs had to eat just like everything else.

"Have we lost a lot of sheep to them up here?" I asked.

"More than I would like, but that is to be expected when everything is running loose. It's impossible to keep track of the number of sheep there really are until we have them rounded up for shearing. And there are always some we never find, even if they are still alive."

"Then why don't you stop them from coming up here if the loss is so great? There should be plenty of feed in the lower valleys."

"Are you bloody loco?" Jake asked as he took a cigarette from his pocket and lit it. "You saw what feed was like lower on the mountain. Sheep may be able to live off foliage cattle would never touch, but that doesn't mean they are going to do it if another option is available."

"I'm sorry for being dense," I replied, wishing I could stop myself from asking so many dumb and useless questions.

"It's not being dense, it is being inexperienced. I applaud your desire to honor your father's last wish, but bringing you up here was a mistake. You really should have stayed at the house."

"Then why didn't you take a stand and make me do it? No one would go against what you wanted, even my father."

"Because I could see how much it meant to him to believe you would really embrace the life he was offering."

"You still don't think I am going to stay, do you?"

"What I think is irrelevant. But just in case you're wondering, I truly believe you will go back to that bloody bloke in the states as soon as an appropriate amount of time has elapsed after the funeral. I've watched you closely since you got here, and you have lost every outward connection to the land and the people. I can see the disgust, disillusionment and unrest in your eyes, even if no one else can. Why would you even want to remain and live under that cloud?"

I watched him for a minute or two, turning away when he exhaled so I wouldn't get so much of his second-hand smoke. My father was dying because he refused to quit, but the people around him still didn't get the message that the same thing could happen to them.

Jake could accuse me of anything he liked, but he couldn't see into my soul. If I left Australia, it wouldn't be because I had lost touch with the land and the people. It would be because I chose to marry Ben. He was offering me everything I had ever wanted.

After finishing his smoke and making sure the remains were extinguished, he broke two long limbs from a nearby tree. I watched as he removed the shorter branches and then handed one of them to me.

"Use this to beat the bushes. It drives a lot of insects out, but it can also save your life by warning snakes and other dangerous things that you are on your way. We will work together today, but tomorrow you are on your own."

I was too frightened about the rest of this day to worry about what tomorrow might bring, so I took the limb he offered without comment. Traipsing through the outback looking for animals that didn't want to be found really wasn't the kind of life I wanted to live. I wanted to be home with Ben in a city where the world lay at our feet. I could find a job like he had in an air-conditioned building, and together we could find a place to live with an open floor plan that looked out on a park with Palm trees and plenty of green grass and colorful flowers. We could eat at a restaurant if I didn't feel like cooking, and attend family gatherings where I wouldn't have to worry about offending anyone because I no longer smoked or drank. But best of all, we could attend church together and make our home a place where the Holy Spirit could always dwell.

I really would be living under some cloud if I stayed here—a cloud that could be avoided if I just had the courage to tell my father that I would do as he asked, but he couldn't expect me to stay indefinitely when the man I loved was half-a-world away.

I heard some twigs in front of me snap. Jake was leaving me behind, so I wiped away the tears that were starting to form and fell into step behind him. I was miserably hot, cranky and scared, but I had no one to blame by myself. Not seeing Ben again for a few more weeks wasn't the only way to lose what we had. If he couldn't trust me to honor and respect him and his wishes when we were apart, he might not want to risk a thoroughly committed life with me.

Chapter 5

It was one of the longest afternoons of my life. The main body of sheep was easy to find, but the real work would be securing all the ones that had wandered away. I had no idea how much area we covered, how many times insects bit me or how often I looked down to make sure my footing was safe and some poisonous reptile wasn't about to attack. I even lost count of the number of sheep Jake had to wrestle free when they got tangled in creeping ground branches as they tried to get away from us. It seemed that the more he tried to help, the more agitated they became and the harder they struggled. He swore profusely, but I tried not to listen. I just hoped I wouldn't run into the same issues when I was left on my own the next day.

But as the sun began its decent, I found that his ability to work with unruly sheep surprised me even more than his ability to work with cattle. He knew instinctively which animals were the leaders and how to get them moving towards the clearing where we would be spending the night. All I did was walk around the edges of the herd we were gathering, waving my arms and hollering when one of the heavily laden animals decided to separate itself from the rest of the group.

Once we got them into the clearing we could only hope they would stay put while we went looking for more of them.

It was easily the second worst day of my life. The worst was being told by the headmistress at the boarding school that my mother was dead. The third would be losing my father. LeAnn was constantly adjusting his morphine, and he was becoming less lucid each day. There were times when I looked at him, and his eyes almost seemed glazed-over. I didn't know if it was just part of dealing with the pain, or if he was just too tired to care if he lived or died any longer.

I didn't want him to die, but I didn't want him to suffer any longer either. My respect for LeAnn had grown considerably over the past few weeks because she had been forced to make impossible decisions about the life and death of the man she loved. I would never be able to do that with Ben, and I knew the truth about our journey through mortality and the life beyond. LeAnn believed she would see my father again, but their marriage would be over the moment he took his last breath. That had to be a very bitter bill to swallow.

It was hard not thinking about my father and what was going to happen, regardless of the fact that I was kept busy trying to keep the sheep we had already gathered from scattering. There had been times over the past few days when all I wanted to do was hold him in my arms. Despite his apparent strength and lucidity in holding the family meeting the day before, it was taking him longer to find the words he wanted to say. And when he did speak, it was often in little more than a whisper. It was impossible to understand how LeAnn could spend all of her waking and sleeping moments with him without falling apart, but she was doing it.

"What's got you so quiet?" Jake asked? We were sitting around a small campfire, and he was opening a can of beans for supper. It was just after dark. "You did better than I thought you would today. We have all the sheep from this corner of the ranch pretty much secured. All we have to do now is keep them together until we drive them to Ned's in the morning."

"I wasn't thinking about the sheep," I told him.

"Then you must have been thinking about your father."

I looked at him through eyes that were narrowed from lack of sleep and the smoke that was drifting into them from the fire.

"It's hard not to! I should be back at the ranch with him instead of sitting on some God-forsaken mountain in the middle of nowhere with a man who detests me."

"I don't detest you, Brylee. Far from it! I admire your spunk and determination. I'm just not into forming more than casual attachments to women. It's far too much work."

"Really," I retorted, thinking about Janet at the airport and Beth at the diner. Heaven only knew how many others he was leading along. "Just because you've had one bad experience, it doesn't mean that all women are evil. Both Janet and Beth seem to be able to look past your considerable number of flaws."

His eyes became mere slits in his face, and I realized I had gone too far. If something happened to me out here in the woop woop no one would ever know it wasn't an accident. He could say anything he wanted when he took my lifeless body back to the ranch and people would believe it, as long as there wasn't a bullet in my back.

"I don't know what my sticky beak sister has been telling you, but she should learn to keep her bloody mouth shut. My personal life is no one's business but mine."

He went back to stirring the beans, and I pulled a heavy woolen blanket closer around my shoulders. It was going to be a long, miserable night, and I would do best to keep what little I knew about him to myself, but apparently he wasn't going to let me off the hook that easily.

"Just what did LeAnn tell you?" he asked a few seconds later without looking at me.

"Nothing, really!" I countered, breaking my promise about no further talking. "Only that you were engaged once."

"Did she tell you that my fiancé ran away with my best friend right before the wedding and got herself killed in the process?"

LeAnn had only mentioned his sad tale in passing as a way to help me understand her brother's often-erratic behavior, but I wasn't about to betray a confidence. I wanted my new stepmother to trust me.

"Not exactly," I replied.

He snorted his distain. "I'm not sure I believe that. I just hope the same thing doesn't happen to you with this bloody bloke you seem so determined to marry. Men, and I suppose women, have primal needs that cannot be denied for long. You've been away for weeks, and I am more than certain there are as many opportunities to find another playmate in the United States as there are here."

The tightness forming in my chest was making it hard to breathe. "Ben isn't like that," I said. "He is the most honorable and decent man I have ever known."

"He may be all those things, but men are not monogamous by nature."

"That's not true for all men!" I defended the man I loved. "Ben would never have an affair."

"Spoken like someone who has never been there. I used to feel the same way, but I learned that everyone cheats if given the chance. It's in the genes."

"No, it's not! It's a conscious choice people make. They could walk away if they wanted to."

"Are we speaking about you and this Ben or your father and my sister?" he asked.

"They're not the same thing."

"Aren't they?

I was feeling both flustered and angry. "You don't know anything about Ben and me. We love each other, and have promised to remain faithful. We haven't even slept together yet."

I regretted my words the moment they slipped out. How could I have told a man who hated me something so personal and private? Jake would only poke fun at something I considered sacred, and he didn't disappoint.

He rocked back on his heels and laughed. "Sounds like you've got yourself a pretty boy to me. No guy is celibate by choice, unless he hasn't admitted the truth to himself."

"You're disgusting," I spate the words at him. Jake could take all the pot shots at me that he desired, but I drew the line when he started to talk about the man I loved and was going to marry.

He just sat where he was looking at me with amusement while I jumped to my feet thrusting the blanket to the ground. "Not all men are pompous, skirt-chasing animals like you. There are still some who respect the virtue of women."

I was shaking—not with fear this time—but with righteous indignation.

He got to his feet too, but he was no longer laughing. "So you think I am some kind of deviate because I like sleeping with women? It's perfectly natural, and there isn't a single thing wrong with it as long as both parties are willing. I would never take advantage of a woman."

"Well, bully for you," I shouted, wishing I had the courage to slap his smug-looking face. He didn't know anything about morality, or if he did, he chose to dismiss it. The Ten Commandments had given me everything I needed to know before Ben came into my life and reinforced them. I would never give Jake more ammunition with which to ridicule me, and I would never allow him to mock what I now believed.

Suddenly he started to laugh again. The raw sound stopped the formation of tears in my eyes.

"You really are something," he said, his dark eyes dancing in the firelight. "You are either some kind of born-again

Christian, or you are living in complete denial. Just don't come crying to me when your little bubble bursts because it will. Men are pigs! They would just rather not admit it."

I clenched my jaw until my teeth ached. It was the only way I could stop the desire to tell him what I really thought about the kind of life he had chosen to live.

"I'll take the first watch," I said, wanting to put as much distance between us as possible. It had been a long day and I was exhausted. But I still needed time to clear my head and let some of the rage go. "You can relive me in a few hours."

"You can't change reality by running away," he called after me, but I didn't turn around and he didn't follow.

Maybe I was living in a bubble, but it was my bubble, and Ben was right there with me. I couldn't let Jake make me question my new beliefs, or the man I was going to marry. He had drawn me out of a world of darkness and had given me something to believe in. I would not betray his love or his trust again by discussing anything about him with a man who had no concept of what I was taking about.

I wished I had brought the blanket I'd tossed to the ground with me a few minutes later as I sat down on a log in the small meadow and watched the sheep mill around until most of them appeared to be sleeping. It was a clear night and the only sounds I heard were the occasional *woo* of an owl, and the grunts of sheep as they moved in their sleep. I wondered if the small fire Jake had made would keep the dingoes away as the night wore on. I had left the gun LeAnn loaned me in the bag on the side of the motorbike. I might be able to hit a tree trunk, but using it on a breathing creature was entirely different. Even wild dogs had the right to eat. They were God's creatures too.

A million tiny stars flickered overhead. I watched a few of them soar towards earth before their light went out. I thought about Ben and what he might be doing. It would be the middle of the day for him. Was he at work, eating lunch, making new friends or visiting old ones? Was he thinking about me and longing for my return, or was Jake at least partially right? Ben would never cheat on me, but I had been gone for what seemed like forever and had no idea when I might be returning. He wanted a wife and a family and wouldn't wait around for me indefinitely. But how could I leave when my father lay so close to death, and when I had promised him that I would stay and help out for as long as I was needed once he was gone?

And what about Trevor? He had stolen a huge part of my heart. I finally had a real family of my own and was beginning to see why Ben's family meant everything to him. I hadn't wanted to think about it before, but what if we really weren't meant to be together forever? Our relationship was still so new, and there was so much about each other that we didn't know. I had eagerly joined his world when being baptized and wanted every promised blessing, but then I had come home because he wanted me to. And instead of taking the return flight as planned, I put a hold on my ticket because I had discovered an entire other side to my life that could no longer be ignored.

I loved my father and my little brother. I even loved LeAnn, though I still occasionally wondered why. It was hard forgiving others for their weaknesses, but I knew it was necessary if I wanted to be forgiven for mine.

I heard a rustling of dry leaves behind me, and jumped to my feet as fingers of terror made my heart race and my head feel light. How foolish I had been not bringing something along with which to defend myself.

"It's only me," Jake said as he took a few more steps until he was standing in the dark beside me.

"You startled me," I managed to say, even though the hair was standing up on the nap of neck. "You could have said something instead of just sneaking up."

"I wasn't sneaking," he replied. "You should have heard me coming unless you were asleep or daydreaming again. I believe

I have already told you that is a good way to get yourself killed."

"I wasn't asleep," I countered, trying to steady myself by relaxing some of the tension in my knees. "I was thinking."

"You do a lot of that when I'm around. Does that mean I am getting to you, or are you just cursing my very existence?"

"You get to me all right," I retorted. "Just like a root canal."

"Are you that cheeky with your boyfriend? He must like feisty women as much as I do."

"I'm not going to discuss our relationship with you any further since you don't believe it is going to last. I think you just like tormenting me because it gives you some kind of sadistic pleasure, but since you are here, I might as well head back to camp and see if I can get some sleep."

"Running away again," he said. "That seems to be a habit with you. Do you really hate me that much, or are you just afraid to be alone with me for fear you might give in to your passions?"

"I'm not one of your flings, Jake," I said, wishing I could stop myself from sparring with him. I knew it took two people to tangle, but he seemed to know exactly the right buttons to push. "I simply choose not to be around you because it always ends up in some kind of power struggle, and I am sick to death of playing your games."

"Is that what you call it," he said, taking a cigarette from the pack he always had in his shirt pocket and lighting it. "I think most people would call it foreplay."

"You never give up, do you?" I retorted, turning to make my escape as quickly as possible. "Besides, foreplay only happens when two people are interested in each other. It seems very clear to me that we only promised to try to get along because it is what LeAnn wants, and we both know it's the right thing to do for my father."

"I think you protest too much, Brylee. I don't detest you. I find you both interesting and complex. You are torn between two worlds and haven't quite decided which one you want to live in. What you need is a man who understands you, not some boy who is totally inexperienced with life."

I turned back around, my eyes blazing like the fire we had both left behind.

"Ben isn't a boy! He is the man I am going to spend the rest of my life with."

"Does he understand how conflicted you are? I bet you haven't said one thing that would lead him to believe you might not be coming back."

My heart constricted. I was going back to Ben. I just didn't know when that would be, and I was terrified that Jake might be right about him finding someone else. Ben was a handsome, righteous, intelligent man with a golden future. He was exactly the kind of man most Latter-day Saint girls dreamed about meeting. I had seen the way they reacted to him when they thought I wasn't looking. If I didn't get home soon, he would have a dozen of them lining his parent's driveway for a chance to talk to him.

"You're not answering me," Jake said, taking one last drag on his cigarette before rubbing it out with the sole of his boot.

I coughed to hide my embarrassment. Why was this man able to see things in me that no one else ever had, including Ben?

"Ben and I trust each other," I told him. "That is the most important part of any relationship."

"That's a little naïve, don't you think? Sometimes, even I wish life could be that simple, but it never is. If we don't do something to mess it up, someone else will. I would hate for you to become disillusioned like me."

"I won't," I assured him as I watched him kick at a dry leaf on the ground. "I know where I came from, why I am here, and where I will be going when I die. This life is just a test to see if we love God enough to do what is right, even when bad things happen."

"That is choice," he said with another attempt at forced laugher. "It's just religious speech-making used to make people comply. We're human! We don't just sit there when something bad happens and say, 'It's okay! God knows what is best for me.' I'm surprised you can even speak such nonsense in light of what is happening with your father."

"I love my father dearly," I said as fresh tears clouded my vision.

"Yet, you still maintain that God knows best? He could have stopped your father's cancer any time he wanted to."

"We've had this conversation before," I told him.

"I suppose we have, but you couldn't give me a satisfactory answer, so I am asking it again."

"My reply isn't going to change."

"Give it to me anyway."

I allowed the night air to fill my lungs before speaking. Jake might be looking for an answer, but I couldn't be sure it was for the right reason. That meant I needed to be very careful with what I said because I didn't want him to ridicule Heavenly Father again.

"Yes, God could take away all suffering, but we wouldn't learn very much that way."

"I could do with a little less learning in that department."

"I suppose we all could, but we aren't on this earth just to have fun."

"Why not? It sounds like a pretty sweet existence to me."

I wished I had the words to explain what I now believed, but while my testimony was strong, it was still in the fledgling state. Perhaps I had relied on the testimonies of others too much, and now it was time to find my own voice. But doing it around Jake was impossible because he didn't really care what I believed. He just wanted to make my life as miserable as possible.

"You can't argue religious beliefs," I finally said, trying to look into his eyes without flinching. "I only know that God loves each one of us and will give us the strength to make it through anything we have to."

"Well, I hope he comes through for you since you claim to believe so strongly."

"He will," I said. "And he would help you get over all your bitterness if you would just give him a chance."

He gave me one of his all too familiar cold looks.

"I'm not bitter about anything. I am simply a realist, and you had better become one too because you have no idea what is going to happen when your father's gone."

He turned away from me and began walking back towards the campfire. This time, I heard every crunch of dry grass and twigs. I was shaking, but it wasn't from the cold. What Jake had said frightened me. Was he planning some kind of a takeover, or did he simply know something I didn't? Either way, one thing was certain, he already knew I would oppose anything I didn't believe was right.

There was no rest for me that night, even after Jake came to relieve me a couple of hours later. I wanted to go home, and not just back to my family at the ranch. I wanted to return to my happy, safe life with Ben where I didn't have to worry about conflicting religious beliefs, unnecessary bickering and my father's impending death. Why couldn't I just pack a suitcase and take him back to the United States with me? The very thought was both selfish and irrational, but I wasn't sure I could deal with any more trauma, and one member of his new family was really starting to scare me.

There was something dark and disturbing about Jake that countered everything he said about loving his family, but I couldn't ask my father or LeAnn any questions that might dissuade my fears. Our last few days together should be as pleasant as possible. Still, there was one person I could talk to —Uncle Ned. I would make time to discuss my concerns with him once I was off the mountain. Certainly he would be able to give me the direction and answers I needed.

Chapter 6

It was nearly dawn when Jake walked back into our makeshift camp. I shot to my feet the minute I heard him coming. I hadn't climbed inside my sleeping bag, but I had certainly wrapped it around me as I lay against a log to rest.

"It's almost light," he said in a voice as cold as the morning as he rubbed his hands rapidly together and blew air into his cupped palms. "And where the hell is the hot coffee? I'm half frozen to death."

I kept my steady gaze fixed on his face. I would not let him get the upper hand again. "I didn't know when you would be coming back."

For once he let my comment go without a snide remark, no doubt realizing that another confrontation would only waste time.

"Then we'll start down the mountain right now before the sheep have a chance to start grazing. I assume you are ready to go."

"Give me five minutes and I will be," I said as I started to roll my sleeping bag up while he dumped the remainder of the coffee from evening before and gathered together the few items that had been left on the ground. All I wanted was to get away from this desolate place and him. Maybe then I would start to feel safe again.

It took hours to get the sheep down the mountain and across the dry grasslands to Uncle Ned's ranch. They were hungry and when one of them bent over to pull some yellow fodder from the earth it seemed as if all the others followed. I was kept busy just watching my side of the herd and trying to anticipate when an animal might get spooked or decide to separate and get caught up in the brush that became less dense and green the further down the incline we went.

My voice was becoming hoarse from continued shouting in the hot, dusty and dry air that slowly sucked the moisture from everything. My eyes burned for the same reason, and with the bloodthirsty insects swarming my head, it was an utterly horrid morning.

I heaved a giant sigh of relief when I saw Uncle Ned riding out on his horse to meet us. He was a big man, much taller and wider than my father, and his horse looked almost small beneath him. But I knew Old Soldier was strong and perfectly capable of carrying his load.

"You guys made good time," he said as he rode up beside me.

I planted my feet firmly on the ground. My legs ached from the intense pressure and abuse they had endured from riding the motorbike over uneven ground.

"I wasn't expecting you until later today. It looks like we will be really to start shearing your sheep tomorrow like planned. The blokes I hired have been working on mine all morning and should be done by nightfall. I don't have nearly as many as you, but their wool helps pay the bills."

"We've been lucky," I replied over the noise of my bike's motor. "We didn't have any trouble rounding them up or getting them down the mountain. I thought it would be a whole lot worse."

"Not me," Uncle Ned said as he kept a tight hold on his horse's reins. Old Soldier was prancing in place, a reaction from standing so close to a noisy motor. "Jake's just about the best sheep man in all of Australia. Your father is very lucky to have him. If he says he is going to do something, you can count on it getting done."

"Does that go for threats?" I asked, but Uncle Ned had already ridden off.

I helped the men drive the sheep into a fenced pasture not far from where we had put the small herd the night before. I had never really paid attention to Uncle Ned's homestead, always thinking it was nothing more than a replica of the place where I had grown up, and where the buildings simply seemed to expand as the need arose. But looking at all the order around me, I realized that my uncle had planned his operation with a great deal of thought. The barn stood separate from the rest of the outbuildings, and the dirt connecting them was not filled with ruts.

There were a number of vehicles parked in front of the bunkhouse, and I could hear the sound of cursing and laughter coming from the open barn as the men inside sheared the sheep and then shoved them outside. A large semi-truck stood ready to haul the wool to town.

Aunt Nora greeted us warmly, and after a quick lunch of meat loaf and mashed potatoes, I volunteered to help my uncle with the dishes while she cleared the table and visited with Jake. It warmed my heart to see them sharing the housework. It was exactly what Ben and I were planning to do.

"Uncle Ned," I said, walking up beside him with a handful of silverware as he was stood loading the dishwasher. He refused to wash anything by hand the way Aunt Nora did.

"What is it, love?" he asked, giving me one of his broad smiles that made him look more like Santa Claus than a rancher from the Australian Outback. "You were quiet all through lunch. Are you worried about your father? I talked to LeAnn a couple of hours ago. She said he is holding his own but is very frustrated because he can't be out helping us."

I couldn't stop my brow from creasing. "No, Uncle Ned, it's not father, although I will never stop worrying about him. It's Jake."

"What about him?" he asked, turning his head to face me. "If he did something to hurt you, I will break his damned, bloody neck."

He looked so ferocious I almost laughed.

"He didn't hurt me physically, but he did say something that has me concerned."

"Jake's a man! That means he says exactly what's on his mind. It may not be pleasant to hear, but I know for a fact that he would never hurt a fly."

I knew that wasn't true. I had seen his volatile more than once, but I couldn't make my uncle believe something he didn't want to see.

"I know you like Jake, Uncle Ned, but I'm not sure he is being honest with us."

"He has no reason to lie about anything. He's family."

"Maybe so, but he told me I had no idea what was going to happen when father is gone, and it's got me worried. He could be planning something."

"Oh, Brylee," he said, tilting my chin upwards so I would have to look at him. "I don't think he said it to frighten you. Life is uncertain, and your father's ranch hasn't been doing well since he got sick two years ago."

"But I've been over the books. Everything is in order. I know there isn't a lot of extra cash to work with, but we are not that far in the red. Father said the money from the wool should put us in fine shape again."

"I certainly hope that is true, but the economy hasn't been strong here for years, and with big corporations still trying to buy us all out, it is only going to become harder to make a living."

"That may be true, but we can still do it. I can work harder and not just at keeping the books."

It was a grand show of bravado, but I would do anything to save the ranch for Trevor, even if it meant staying away from Ben longer.

"I know you have great intentions, but you have to be realistic. You've never had any experience running a ranch. It's all well and good that you know how to work with figures and round up sheep, but that is just the beginning of what you need to know."

"Father thinks I can do it, or he wouldn't have made me promise to stay."

"I agree with him, but you have to be able to work with Jake to do it."

I shook my head at him and frowned. "How can I work with Jake? He hates me! He does nothing but make me feel like a pathetic, little schoolgirl. He thinks I am utterly worthless."

"That's because he likes you. Do you really think he would spend so much time tormenting you if he didn't? He could have any girl in town he wanted, but I think he wants you."

"That's preposterous, Uncle Ned!" I replied, feeling the bile rise to my throat. He wasn't the first one to make a comment like that, but I refused to believe that he was actually serious. "Jake knows I'm going to marry Ben."

"A ring doesn't stop a man from wanting a beautiful woman."

"I'm not beautiful!" I told him, looking down at my filthy clothes. My hair hadn't been combed since I had braided it the morning before, and I hadn't even washed my face. "I look absolutely horrid."

"Only to yourself. You are the kind of woman a man wants to protect and to spar with."

"But I don't need protection, and I am tired of having to prove that I care about my family. Why can't he just accept me as a competent person?"

"He torments you because you let him. It's good to have your own opinions. But as well-intentioned as they might be, he has far more experience than you do when it comes to ranching and surviving in the outback. He's spent his entire adult life doing it, and you have to face the fact that at some point men like to fix things even if they aren't broken. And they never like having their authority questioned. Show him that you respect his judgment and are willing to do what he says without engaging in some battle of wills. It might make a huge difference in how you get along."

I opened my mouth to protest, but Uncle Ned silenced me with another look. I did let Jake get under my skin and that gave him the upper hand. I would start asking questions—lots of them—and I wouldn't let my beliefs, theories and opinions get in the way unless it was necessary. I would quit being his doormat and show him just how eager I was to help keep the ranch operating, but I would do it in a way he wasn't expecting. That way, he would be the one on the defensive instead of me.

I was hoping we would find the last of the sheep so we could go home that night, but it didn't happen that way. Jake rode up to me on his motorbike about dusk when we had what I thought was a pretty good band of sheep already gathered into a clearing.

"Those damned, stupid animals," he muttered, rubbing the sweat from his forehead with the sleeve of his filthy shirt. "There's a whole flock of them scattered in a ravine. It will take hours to flush them out."

"I could drive these back to Uncle Ned's while you look for them," I volunteered, nodding my head towards the not-so-white fluffy animals a few yards away.

"You would never make it before dark, and you don't want to be herding anything when you can't see what's in front of your face. Take my word for it."

I was about to tell him I could do anything I wanted to when I remembered Uncle Ned's advice. Ask questions and listen before challenging him.

"What would you suggest as an alternative?" I asked, forcing just the tiniest smile.

He looked at me with surprise. "What, no smart comment? That's got to be a first."

Oh, how I wanted to say something cutting, but I held my tongue.

"I accept that you know more than I do about what goes on out here. I would be foolish not to. Now, what do you want me to do?"

His jaw dropped as if I had slugged him.

"What I would really like you to do cannot be said in polite society," he smugly replied, and I could hardly miss the wicked glimmer in his eyes. No wonder he had all the girls in Edna waiting around for him. He knew just how to undress a woman with his eyes and make her feel desirable—even when she felt she looked no better than a dropped pie—but his subterfuge would not work on me.

"I thought we were talking about the sheep," I replied in a smothered voice, my face hot with embarrassment.

The look of amusement dropped from his face. "Leave it to you to kill the moment, but I suppose you could set up camp. It won't be as cold down here as it was last night, but we will still need a good fire. Have you ever built one before?"

"No." I admitted. "But I can gather kindling and dry logs."

"That should do it if you add some dry leafs. You can use this to light it." He tossed his cigarette lighter towards me, and surprisingly, I caught it.

"Do you want me to heat up some beans? I could have them ready any time you like."

"Why are you being so agreeable?" he asked. "You usually rip me a new one every time I say something you don't like."

"Why should I question your directives out here? I have only spent only one night in the outback where you have spent years."

"I would hardly say years," he admitted, pulling a couple of pots and a few cans out of the pack he had been carrying and setting them down on a nearby log. "But I have seen dingo's attack at night and what they leave behind isn't pretty."

"I bet you saw a lot more than that when you were flying supplies into the interior. My father told me about your former life as a bush pilot. He wanted me to understand you better."

"Did he now," Jake replied, looking away, but not before I saw the lines on his face harden. In my exuberance to do what Uncle Ned had suggested, once again I had gone a too far by bringing up another subject he obviously didn't want to discuss with me.

His voice was deep and low when he swung around to face me. "I have seen enough to know that this land can be ruthless, and anyone who thinks otherwise is a damned fool."

I knew he was referring to me, but I was not going to get caught up in his games again, at least not tonight.

"Do you think we will be bothered by wild animals before morning?" I asked.

"Probably not! Most packs hunt higher up like where we were last night, but I wouldn't be complacent about anything. Just stay close to the fire until I get back."

"I won't wander off," I responded, biting the tip of my thumb even though it was so dirty I should never have put it into my mouth. "No heroics for me."

"That's good. I should be back in an hour or so. I just want to see how many more I can find while there is still some daylight left. You're sure you can handle things here until I get back?"

I looked across the meadow at the sheep that appeared to be contentedly grazing, although the grass in the clearing looked anything but palatable.

"Most certainly! I will have everything ready so you can eat when you get back."

He shook his head and took a few steps away before turning back to face me with a skeptical look on his face. "Are you sure you're okay? You are acting very strange."

"Never better," I told him with another forced smile as his eyes narrowed again.

Maybe Uncle Ned knew what he was talking about. If I didn't act defensive, Jake wouldn't have any reason to put me down or make me feel useless or uncomfortable. I liked the feeling of being in control around him.

I dragged my foot through the dirt until I had cleared a large, bare circle around the place where I was going to build the fire. The last thing I needed was to start a brushfire, and the tiniest spark gone astray could do it.

The taller grass and low-growing shrubs around the edges of the clearing were so brittle and dry it only took a few minutes to gather what I needed to start a fire, and a few minutes more to get enough larger pieces of wood to keep it burning. After an hour had gone by without incident, I opened a couple of cans of beans and put them into a small Dutch oven to heat. I also put water in the coffee pot so it would be hot when Jake got back. I wasn't sure I could make a decent cup of coffee any longer, but if the water was boiling Jake could fix his own.

I moved around the small herd of sheep one last time before the sun disappeared. They had settled down considerably, and I hoped they would stay that way until morning. I was tired both emotionally and physically, and I wished Jake would hurry back so I could close my eyes. My night without sleep and all the stress of the past thirty-nine hours had finally caught up with me.

While I was waiting, I took the wool blanket I had carelessly tossed to the ground the night before and wrapped it around my shoulders. I wasn't a fan of wool. It was too scratchy and still smelled faintly like sheep, but it felt oddly comforting tonight. The wool had come from Hawkins' sheep. My father had several new blankets made each year with different markings—usually a band of strong colors along the top edge. There had to be a huge pile of them somewhere. I would look for them before I went home. Ben might not want to use them for anything other than camping, but they were a part of my heritage, and I wanted to preserve that for our children.

My stomach growled for a second time. The lunch we had eaten at Uncle Ned's had definitely worn off. Even the beans heating in a pot over the fire sounded good. I stirred them with a sturdy stick I found on the ground, and then opened one of the granola bars LeAnn had suggested I pack for additional nourishment.

It seemed like I had been away from the ranch forever. All I wanted to do was take a shower and climb into a nice, soft bed for hours of uninterrupted sleep. My neck was stiff from resting my head against a log the night before while I waited for the sun to come up. And my entire body ached from the mistreatment it had suffered throughout the past two days as I rode and walked to find sheep. I had ducked to keep from getting hit in the face by overhanging brush and twisted my head to discourage pesky insects that wanted to bite or simply annoy me more times than I could count. But I was still alive and that had to count for something.

The evening air was still except for the occasional croak of a frog or the chirp of a cricket as it came out to play. That meant we were fairly close to water, even though I wasn't exactly sure if it was a running steam or simply a muddy bog. Either way, that meant we were in more danger from predators than we had been the night before, regardless of what Jake had said. Water was the one thing every creature hurried to for survival. I was rather surprised he had decided to set up camp so close to such a potential threat, but then maybe I was being overly cautious. Uncle Ned had said to trust him, but despite my resolve, I was having trouble doing it.

I stoked the fire once or twice more while waiting. The beans were hot so I moved them to one side so they wouldn't burn. I already had tin plates, cups and spoons out so we could eat the minute Jake got back to camp. He had to be every bit as hungry and tired as I was.

It was nearly eight by my watch when he returned with less than a dozen sheep. He looked both angry and frustrated after putting out so much energy for such a small return, but I was still relieved to see him. The thought of spending the night alone in the mountains with nothing but sheep to keep me company was terrifying.

"Is everything okay," I asked as I walked away from the fire to meet him.

"Damned, stupid animals," he mumbled through clenched teeth as he lifted his left arm and grabbed his wrist. Even in the semi-darkness I could see that his shirtsleeve was torn and caked with blood.

"You're hurt," I said.

"Just a scratch, but it wouldn't have happened if those bloody sheep weren't the stupidest animals on the face of the planet. Half of the ones I tried to rescue are still rummaging around in the undergrowth. They will be lucky if they aren't carcasses by morning."

"You saw predators?"

"Heard them howling in the distance. I'm surprised you didn't hear them too."

"It's been quiet here. Even the sheep have settled down."

"Let's hope it stays that way because I'm tired and hungry as hell. Where's that food you promised?"

He started off towards the small fire that was in need of another log, and I trudged along behind him.

"I took the beans off the flame so they wouldn't burn, but I'm sure they are still warm."

I watched as he sat down on the log I had pulled close to the fire and picked up the pot of beans. He was about to put a spoonful of them into his mouth when he asked me if I had eaten.

Instinct told me to tell him I had, but then I remembered my resolution to advocate for myself and not react negatively to anything he said or did.

"No, I was waiting for you," I said.

"Why?" he asked with a shrug of his broad shoulders. "You could have eaten hours ago."

"And let you starve! I might have eaten everything."

He laughed, and this time it wasn't mocking. "Not a tiny thing like you, but I am glad you waited. I see you have the plates and spoons out. Do you want to serve or should I?"

"Go ahead." I said, holding one of the tin plates in front of him. "I am sorry I didn't make coffee, but I don't know how you like it."

"Hot and black," he replied, pushing a heaping portion of beans onto the plate I held in my hands. "I'm sorry I don't have better silverware, but I usually eat alone."

"It's all good," I said, extending the other plate in his direction. He filled it with the rest of the beans and put the pot on the ground. "LeAnn sent some granola bars. We could have one after the beans if you like."

I lacked the courage to admit that I had already eaten one, but I still a few left so it didn't really matter.

He rubbed his hands along the bottom of the warm plate he was holding.

"Along with some hot coffee?" he asked. "Not that it's all that cold yet, but old habits die hard, and the night is still young."

I smiled, and for the first time it seemed almost real.

"I would like to look at your arm after we eat, if that's okay with you. LeAnn sent a few medical supplies along. I know you don't want it to get infected."

"Probably not the best idea," he said, taking a bite of beans. "I'm not even sure what I cut it on. When the sun goes down all you ever really see are shadows until you run into something."

I took a bite of my own beans. They weren't bad, but I wished I had some warm French bread to go with them. When I looked up from my plate, I saw Jake watching me.

"You never cease to amaze me," he said. "I thought you would be mad as hell because I was late getting back and jump right down my throat."

"Why should that make me mad? You gave me the easier task. I got to stay here by the fire. You were the one trudging through the brushwood in the dark."

Lines of concern creased his forehead, and it caused me to frown. Doing what Uncle Ned had suggested wasn't the least bit easy.

"I didn't want you to get lost or hurt."

"Thank you," I replied, looking down at my plate. This was the most civil conversation we'd ever had. It might be unnerving, but I didn't want to ruin it by saying anything that would send us back to hostility and name-calling.

"This is nice," he said a few moments later as he scraped the last of the beans into his mouth from off the side of his plate. It wasn't the way I was used to seeing a man eat, but it suited the situation.

"What is?" I asked.

"The two of us being in the same place and not fighting."

"Maybe I'm tired of fighting," I told him as I finished the last of my own beans. "It takes too much energy, and I am running low on that right now."

"You didn't sleep last night, did you?"

"Not much, but then you didn't either."

"I don't need a lot of sleep, but I am sorry for the things I said that made it so you didn't feel safe enough to close your eyes."

"It takes two to argue. I only got what I deserved."

"You deserve to be happy, Brylee, and to have a man around who wants to love and protect you, even when you think you don't need it."

I felt my cheeks blaze scarlet, and it wasn't from the heat of the small fire in front of me. Jake had given me an honest compliment and it unnerved me considerably.

"Ben does love me, despite what you might think. He even told me not to come with you he was so worried about what might happen."

"And just what was he the most worried about," Jake asked. "The wild animals, the deadly terrain or me?"

"Ben knows he can trust me. I have never given him any reason not to."

"Then I would say he's one lucky bloke, but I really am surprised that he isn't here with you. I know if I really and truly loved someone—and she was going through what you are —I would move heaven and earth to be with her. Nothing else would be more important than that."

His admission surprised me as much as it confused me. He had seemed so bitter and against love the night before, but maybe there was a modicum of humanity left in him —if one was willing to dig deep enough to find it.

"Ben asked me if he should come, but I told him he didn't have to, at least not yet. There isn't much he could do but wait around for the inevitable. Besides, he just started a new job, and it is not exactly the best time to take a leave of absence."

"If that makes sense to you," he said. "I only know that if the woman I loved needed me, nothing would keep me away."

My breath scraped the ragged edges of my emotions. Maybe I was more needy than I thought. What Jake hinted at actually made sense. If Ben really wanted to be with me, he would have come no matter what I told him. Even new bosses understood the need for bereavement leave when it involved family. What if we had gotten engaged before we really understood each other's needs? But I couldn't afford to start second-guessing our relationship now. We loved each other, and we would have plenty of time to learn the nuances of each other's personalities when I returned to L.A.

"Let me take a look at your wound," I said, putting my plate on the ground and walking around the fire until I was standing next to him. He unbuttoned his shirt and began taking it off.

I tried not to stare, but it was useless. His upper body was tanned and well-defined with muscles that seemed to glisten in the glow of the firelight. He had tattoos on his shoulders and a large one of an eagle across his back. The tattoo on his injured arm was covered in blood. I wondered if the gash would leave a scar once it had healed.

"Let me get the things LeAnn sent," I told him, forcing my eyes away from the sinewy muscles I so much wanted to touch. Butterflies were doing fast-moving summersaults in my stomach. Satan certainly knew how to insert temptation into a situation when the defenses were down. I might feel an attraction to Jake right now because we weren't fighting, but I would dislike him just as much as I always had once daylight came again.

I washed the grime away from the wound with warm water from the coffee pot. Then I patted his arm dry with a clean cloth LeAnn had sent along for just such an emergency.

Jake never said a word, but I knew when I was hurting him because the muscles in his arm constricted at my touch. I applied some antiseptic and taped a gauze dressing in place.

"There," I said, stepping away from him so the pounding in my head would stop. I understood the reason I was feeling so drawn to him. It was a combination of a night filled with stars, the lack of incessant fighting and the intimate circumstances we were in, but I also knew that there was a morsel of truth behind very temptation. I liked the way Jake took charge, but I loved Ben now and for always. Nothing would ever change that.

"You have a very soft touch," he said as he reached for his shirt that had fallen onto the log he was sitting on.

"You are just grateful the worst of my nursing is over," I replied.

"I wouldn't be so sure of that."

His comment reminded me once again of how much I had to live for—both in this life and throughout eternity. One night of need and desire could ruin everything. Jake and I were better off fighting.

"Why don't you just lie here and rest? I'll take the first watch," I said. But in my hurry to get away, I kicked over the coffee pot and would have fallen into the fire if he hadn't caught my arm.

"Are you okay?" he asked as the pressure of his fingertips seared my flesh. "You could have been badly burned."

I struggled to stand on my own.

"Thanks to you, I'm right as rain," I replied as another surge of adrenalin caused my heart to race. I had never acted so carelessly around a man before. Maybe Uncle Ned's suggestion about listening instead of reacting was nothing but hazardous for me. "I didn't mean to kick over all the hot water. Let me refill the pot so you can have some coffee."

"Forget the coffee," he said, dropping his hand to his side. "You have been acting strange all night. Would you mind telling me why? All this sweetness is giving me a sugar high."

"It's been a long, tiring couple of days."

"That is certainly true, but it doesn't explain the change in you."

I glanced over at his lips, which had always seemed so hard and cruel. They appeared soft and inviting. All I wanted was be held and comforted for just one moment. It didn't need to turn into anything else, but with Jake that would be impossible. He was used to getting his needs met and then walking away. I didn't need that complication when I had Ben waiting for me. I just needed to be strong for a while longer, and then I would be back in his arms for good.

All the tension in my body suddenly seemed to be centered in the back of my neck. I squeezed it long and hard. Jake must never know I had felt a moment of attraction to him.

"But you still haven't answered my question," he said, starring at me with a quizzical look but not making another move towards me. "Why haven't you been attacking me like you usually do?"

"I could ask you the same thing," I replied, glad that there was no longer any physical contact between us. I could still feel the hardness of his muscles as they rippled in his arm when I was trying to take care of it.

Jake slowly let the air out of his lungs. "Since neither of us seems willing to come clean about what is really going on, I suppose we will just have to conclude that we are having an off-night, and things will be back to normal in the morning. You'll be irritating me, and I'll be annoying you. But you have to admit that tonight has been a rather pleasant diversion. I rather like not fighting with you all the time."

"You would be bored in no time at all if our hate-hate relationship changed."

"Then heaven forbid we call a truce," he said as he reached out and ran his fingers across the knuckles of my hand. It made the blood rush to my head again. "You're really quite beautiful in the firelight."

My heart screamed out to be kissed. His touch was intoxicating, but one moment of passion would ruin my eternity with Ben.

"Your wound must be making you delirious," I said, pulling my hand away. "Why don't you crawl into your sleeping bag and get some shut-eye?"

"I could sleep better if you joined me. The sheep aren't going anywhere for a while. We could zip our sleeping bags together so we would have plenty of room. Or even better, you could share mine with me."

"I don't think so," I told him, both shocked and a little excited about what he was proposing. But if he thought I would fall into his arms like all the other women he had ever known did, he was sadly mistaken. I had the man I wanted and wouldn't do anything to mess that up. "I'm an engaged woman, or have you forgotten?"

"How could I?" he asked, sinking back onto the log. "You bring it up often enough, but I have noticed that you haven't been wearing his ring much the past few weeks."

I looked down at the hand he had just touched so tenderly. "I haven't wanted to get it lost or ruined. I came close to doing that the day you delivered Newton."

"That must have been quite an ordeal. Not only did you have to go up in a plane with me, but you had to get your hands mucky doing the despicable tasks I demanded."

"It wasn't just my clothes," I reminded him.

"I suppose it wasn't, but living out here requires sacrifice and doing unpleasant things. I can understand your aversion to most aspects of it, but what I will never understand is why the man you love isn't here with you. That would never happen with me."

"We talked about this last night, and nothing has changed since then," I said, swallowing back tears of frustration. I wanted to be strong, but I was tired, scared and desperately wanted to be held. Maybe I should tell Ben that I needed him here, but I didn't want to seem needy or clingy. And what could he really do if he came? He couldn't reverse my father's cancer. It was just a waiting game, and I might need him far more later on. I just needed this roundup to be over so my life could get back to its sad and depressing normal.

Jake was acting different tonight because I was. Uncle Ned certainly knew what he was talking about when he advised me on how to handle him, but I could ill afford to follow that advice any longer. Jake thought I was warming up to him, and I had done little all evening to prove otherwise.

I took the gun LeAnn loaned me from the side holder on the motorbike before making my first round along the outside of the pasture where the sheep were resting. Thank goodness the intense heat of the day had subsided, as had the constant buzzing of hungry insects around my bare skin. At least I had been wise enough not to scratch. That would have drawn blood and caused more of the insufferable beasties to attack.

Sitting down on the ground in front of a tree, I sighed heavily and drew my knees up so I could wrap my arms around them and rest my chin. I had no idea how I would ever make the decisions that were facing me. I could still see Ben's face when I closed my eyes, but I had to concentrate to remember the smooth timbre of his voice and how it felt to have his arms around me. That shouldn't have happened in just a little over two months.

Maybe we had become engaged too fast. Maybe we had been so caught up in the idea of being in love that we had missed what falling in love was all about. It was spending time getting to know everything we could about each other. Not just likes and dislikes, but how our very dissimilar pasts might affect the future we hoped to share. That meant blending my very dysfunctional family with his well-adapted one since I no longer believed I could live without them.

But it was hard imagining what that relationship might look like. My father would be gone soon, but I still had Trevor, my uncle and aunt and their family. There was even LeAnn and her horrible brother, Jake, to consider. I still hated him with his arrogant attitude, tattoos and earrings. He was everything I detested in a man. So why had my body responded to his touch? And even worse, had he noticed? Was that why he had suggested sharing a sleeping bag, or were all of his come-ons just part of some sick plan to keep me from guessing what he was really after—my father's ranch?

About two a.m., I walked back to the fire that had all but gone out. I added a couple of small logs and sat down to stare at Jake who was enclosed in his sleeping bag like a moth in its cocoon. He had cleaned up the remains of our supper, except for the pot that sat by the edge of the fire. I wondered if he had filled it with coffee, or if there might still be some water in it so I could make a cup of hot cocoa. I rubbed my hands together like he had done earlier, in hopes of restoring some feeling before reaching for the pot.

"What the bloody hell," Jake shouted as he bolted upright.

I let the pot's lid drop back into place. There was coffee in it anyway.

"I didn't mean to disturb you," I said, surprised at his sudden outburst. "You were sleeping so soundly."

"I never sleep soundly," he retorted, stretching his shoulders. "What time is it anyway?"

"About two. I just came back to get something warm to drink."

"And here I thought you had changed your mind about sharing my sleeping bag."

"You're impossible," I said.

"And you are irritatingly naïve."

I shook my head in the near darkness. "It sounds like things are back to normal with us."

"I guess they are," he replied, unzipping his sleeping bag and rising to his feet. "I'll take my turn now. Just make sure you are up and ready to leave by first light. I even warmed up a nice place for you to sleep, and you claim I don't know how to be a gentleman."

He sauntered away, leaving me fuming with indignation. He was incorrigible, insufferable, and I hated him. Yes, things were definitely back to normal because there was no way I would climb into a sleeping bag he had been using. I would freeze to death first.

Chapter 7

I was dozing when he came back to camp and kicked the log I was leaning against. It was still dark, but I knew the sun would be up by the time camp was broken, and we had our gear stored away.

"Time to get up," he said, staring down at me. "I see all that righteous indignation you are so fond of proclaiming kept you from using my sleeping bag. It's a pity the warmth left over from my body had to be wasted."

I didn't reply. I simply got to my feet and began folding the wool blanket I had used to keep me warm. I felt and looked lousy, but I was too tired to care. I needed a bath, a good meal, and a warm, comfortable bed. But mostly, I needed a return to the sanity of life without Jake Johnson in it.

He ignored my less than pleasant behavior. "I'm heading back into the brush to get the few stragglers I had to leave last night. It should take less than an hour. Do you think you can keep the other sheep here until I get back?"

"Gee, I don't know," I shot back, unable to stop myself. "According to you, I'm pretty much useless as both a person and a rancher."

"Just keep your eyes on them," he said with contempt. "And see if you can't get everything put on the bikes while you're at it—including my sleeping bag. I guarantee you won't catch anything from it."

"That is the least of my concerns," I replied, kicking at the innocent piece of fabric and goose feathers that was lying on the ground near my feet. "Anything else you want me to do?"

"You made it perfectly clear last night what you will and will not do. I never beg for a woman's attention or approval."

"Lucky you," I mumbled as he turned and walked away through low-lying brush that crackled and broke with each step. I must have been suffering from sleep deprivation to think I could ever be attracted to him. He was the most insufferable man on the planet.

I ate a granola bar while pushing dirt on the embers of a fire that had been cracking with energy the night before, and then rolled up his sleeping bag. I would have preferred burning it but was too practical. Besides, I didn't want to give him the satisfaction of knowing just how much his attitude offended me. I had spent five years proving that I could take care of myself, and his contempt was undermining everything.

He was back in less than forty-five minutes with half-a-dozen sheep. By that time, the ones in the clearing were beginning to mill around and nibble at the dry, yellow grass they had been sleeping on. I hoped we wouldn't have to sell many of them to make ends meet. Even if Jake thought they were stupid, my father loved them. And because he did, I loved them too.

"You take the lead," Jake said, removing his canteen from one of his side packs and taking a drink of tepid water. I wondered if he was just trying to make me feel guilty for not heating up the leftover coffee before covering the fire, but he didn't even look in my direction. He just climbed on his motorbike and started the engine.

"I'll make sure they don't wander," he shouted. "The trail is narrow, but if we don't allow them to stop and graze we should be to Ned's before ten."

I didn't like the idea of being in the lead where he could watch me, but I disliked having a conversation with him even more, so I circled around the sheep on my own motorbike and managed to get the lead sheep headed in the right direction. I knew I should be grateful that we hadn't had any problems, but herding animals had to be one of the worst jobs ever, especially when it had to be done with Jake.

"Rough night?" Uncle Ned asked me after we had driven the last of the sheep into the holding field. He was leaning over the fence looking at the hundreds of wool-heavy animals. There were far too many to count as they milled aimlessly around, bleating loudly. I wondered how long it would take the shearers to compete their job and how many of the sheep would be sold—with or without my father's consent.

"I could use a warm shower and a good night's sleep," I admitted. "But we have been lucky. Two nights without any real trouble."

"Somebody must be watching out for you," he responded. "I have never heard of anyone rounding sheep up without at least one major incident."

"Jake did get his arm torn up on something last night. Does that count as a major incident?"

"Depends on how bad it is."

"I cleaned it up when he got back to camp but haven't checked it today."

"Why not?"

"We had some personal issues that made checking his arm a little uncomfortable, that's all."

"So I wasn't off base when I told you he was interested in you."

I looked around to make sure no one could hear overhear our conversation. Uncle Ned certainly didn't pull any punches.

"Interested in tormenting me! He said all kinds of crazy things like suggesting we share a sleeping bag."

"That doesn't sound like such a bad idea. It's gets mighty cold up there in the mountains."

"But it's not me, Uncle Ned. I'm engaged."

"That doesn't mean you can't be attracted to someone else and decide if you're going to do anything about it."

"But I'm not attracted to Jake," I insisted.

Why did he have to keep pressing the issue? Hadn't last night proven that anything personal between Jake and me would only lead to disaster? Perhaps the only reason I had momentarily lost emotional control while tending to his abrasion came through the power of my uncle's suggestion. He, like my father and Trevor, might want me to stay here permanently, but marrying me off to Jake Johnson wasn't the answer. I had already chosen the man I intended to be with forever.

"If you say so, but you certainly aren't indifferent to him."

"It's rather hard to ignore Jake since we live on the same ranch, but I suppose I could have asked him how his arm felt this morning."

"That would have been the usual thing to do, but not to worry, you will be home before nightfall, and LeAnn is one of the best nurses I have ever seen. She's tended everything from stinging insects to snake bites."

"Who got bitten by a snake?" I asked, remembering my own encounter with an Eastern Brown the day before Trevor's birthday.

"Your father. It was a red-bellied black as I remember. He was in a whole lot of pain, but LeAnn just stepped right up and took care of him. If she hadn't been around, I'm not sure your father would be walking around on two legs today. She really is an amazing woman."

I bit my bottom lip. Why hadn't I been prompted to come home so much sooner? There was so much I didn't know about my father and so much I wanted to learn.

"How is he doing today?" I asked.

"Not well," Uncle Ned said. "I saw him a few hours ago, but that reminds me, LeAnn wants you to come home as soon as possible."

Sickness engulfed me as my hand flew my mouth. Bright colors were dancing in front of my eyes, and I had no idea how to stop them. I should have stayed home with him instead of trying to prove what an independent and capable woman I was.

"Now don't go borrowing trouble. He is still hanging in there, but he's been asking if you made it back yet."

"We tried to hurry. There was just so much ground to cover."

"And your help was greatly appreciated, but Jake can take over from here. There aren't that many sheep left to find."

"You mean we didn't get them all?" I asked, feeling a sense of disappointment after all I had endured in showing my father how much I cared.

"You got the two biggest herds, but there are a few smaller flocks scattered around in the brush where no one likes to go."

"Just how many sheep does father have?"

"Last year, we counted nearly ten thousand head between the two of us."

"That's a lot of wool."

"And a lot of work. We sold off a good number because there just wasn't enough for them to eat. We haven't had a good rain in over four years. That's the biggest reason most of the smaller ranchers have sold out to the demon named Tucker. They felt it was better to make a little than lose everything."

"But that's not going to happen to you and father."

"Hopefully, but we' have already discussed selling more animals this year. You saw what the ground is like. We're just heading into summer, and there is nothing for any of them to eat."

I looked out across the holding fields. The number of sheep was incalculable, unless they were being counted during the shearing process, and they definitely could not survive without feed and water. Jake was right about far too many things. I had no idea what was going to happen when my father was gone. I didn't even know what was going on while he was still alive.

I had been so smug sitting at his desk and crunching numbers, but I was a dullard when it came to knowing anything about ranching in the outback. No wonder Jake was always mocking me. My own sense of reality was far different from what was being experienced out here. How could I ever learn what I needed to know if I refused to get along with the one man who could help me?

"Don't look so distressed, Brylee. We've been doing this our entire lives. One or two bad years isn't going to bankrupt us, but we have to cut potential losses. We can always rebuild if we have a little capital to work with, but dead animals won't do us any good. You may not like Jake much, but he has been a Godsend for your father. In a few hours, he can cover ground in his plane that used to take us days on horseback or motorbike, and he is one of the hardest workers I have ever seen. He is young and experienced in so many different areas that I am more than surprised he has stayed here this long. There are plenty of blokes willing to pay him more than what Jack can and for half the amount of work."

"I never thought about it like that before," I reluctantly admitted. "I guess I'm not as smart as I thought I was."

"You are plenty smart, and will learn what you don't already know. Believe me, as long as we Hawkins' stick together there is nothing we can't do."

"I hope you're right," I said as fresh tears of bitterness and confusion stung the inside of my eyelids. "I can't believe I ran away from home and from everyone I care about. I should have been here helping out all along."

Uncle Ned put his arm around my shoulders. "You've got to put the past behind you and concentrate on the present. It's not like the rest of us haven't messed up occasionally."

"But you never ran away."

"Oh, but you're wrong about that. I must have been about the same age you were. I got this hankering to see the big city, so I told your father I didn't want anything to do with ranching. I wanted my part of our inheritance so I could go to school and become some rich yuppie who lived in Sydney and vacationed in the outback."

"I can't see you wearing a suit or working in an office."

"Neither can I, but I was pretty sure that was the life I wanted back then."

"What made you change your mind and come back?"

"A couple of years of drinking and chasing women! Then I began to see that there was no substance to what I was doing, and I was just lucky enough to meet the most fantastic woman in the world."

"Aunt Nora?"

"The love of my life! She let me know I was acting plain loco and refused to have anything to do with me until I came to my senses."

"That sounds like her. She's the most down-to-earth person I know."

"And the smartest. I came back to the ranch and begged your father's forgiveness for wasting so much time and money. And do you know what he said?"

"No."

"He said it was all forgotten—that I was back and that's all that mattered. He signed over a good chunk of the ranch to me and helped me build a house. A year later, Nora moved out here with me."

"That's quite a story."

"We all have stories," he said, giving me one of his warm and inviting smiles. "I had to learn how to forgive myself for acting a fool, just like you do."

"So a parent's love really never dies, no matter how harebrained a child is."

"A sibling's love doesn't die either. You have a great new family, Brylee. Just don't take anyone in it for granted. Nothing lasts forever."

I rested my elbows on the top board of the weathered, wood fence. It was a dull, dusty-looking gray-brown—not much different in color than the hard earth it had been constructed on—and studied the herd of milling animals in front of me. We humans might like to believe we are in charge, but God controlled everything, even the number of breaths we were allowed to take before our allotted time on earth was over.

"I guess I should be getting home," I said a few moments later, as I tried to internalize what he had told me about families and forgiveness. I wanted to see my father, but I was afraid. Our time together was almost over and nothing would make the final transition easier for any of us.

"Tell your dad howdy for me. NJ got in late last night to help out. I think it's about time he got out of bed. I swear he would sleep around the clock if I let him. I'm not so sure all that book learning is good for him. It's making him soft."

"He's a good guy, just like his dad," I said, pushing myself away from the fence.

"I certainly hope so," Uncle Ned replied as I walked away.

When I turned to look at him again before making the ride home, he was still leaning on the fence. His eyes were focused on something I likely could not see because my understanding about life in the outback still left a great deal to be desired.

Chapter 8

Trevor was playing in front of the house when I got back. He came running towards me with Copper at his heels as I pulled to a stop in front of the shed where the bikes were stored. I looked more like a vagabond than the sister who had only been gone for two days.

"We have been waiting ever so long for you to get here," he said breathlessly as he reached out to take my helmet. "Did you have fun?"

I had to laugh. Fun was not an adjective I would use to describe the past two days. Pure torture was more like it.

"Let's just say that it was an experience I will never forget."

"But you got to ride the motorbike and sleep in the mountains and cook over a campfire. I can't wait until I am old enough to do that."

"And when you are," I said, removing my gloves and running my hand over the top of his head. "I will be the first one to help you pack for the trip. You can have all that fun and the bugs too. But right now, why don't you tell me what you and Copper have been doing while I was gone?" I didn't have the heart to ask him about our father, although that was exactly what I wanted to do.

"We just played and took care of Newton and the others. They are getting used to her now like you said they would. Father was too tired to even play checkers with me."

I felt the air rush out of my lungs and had to steady myself on the bike's handle. No wonder LeAnn wanted me home. Our father's condition must have deteriorated rapidly while I was gone. He had never been too tired to play with Trevor before.

"I'm sorry about that," I said, trying not to overreact and cause my little brother any additional worry. "How is he feeling today?"

"Okay, I guess. I only talked to him for a few minutes before mum sent me out to play. Can you do something with me now that you're home?"

"Most certainly, but right now I need a shower, some food and couple of hours of sleep. Would that be okay with you?"

He looked sad but didn't complain or ask any questions. He simply shrugged his shoulders and picked Copper up so he could kiss her soft head. The tender way he held his new puppy made more tears surface, but I brushed them away. He was such a sensitive and amazing little boy, and I was incredibly lucky to have him in my life. But right now, I just needed to find out what was going on with our father.

LeAnn looked up from where she was sitting at the kitchen table drinking a cup of coffee when I walked into the kitchen and put the remainder of my supplies on the counter. It seemed that was all her diet consisted of lately.

"Can I get you something," she immediately asked.

"No, I'm fine," I replied, joining her. "How is father?"

"Not good, but thank God for morphine. At least it allows him to sleep. How did things go with you?"

"Great," I responded. "Except for Jake getting a gash on his arm."

Her brow creased into a frown. "How bad is it?"

"I don't think he'll need stitches, but he might have a small scar running through one of his tattoos."

"I hate all those tattoos," she sighed. "I told him before he got his first one that they were a turn-off to most women, but he didn't believe me. And maybe he was right. He has never had trouble getting women interested in him."

"Well, I don't like them either. Why would anyone want dragons with ugly heads all over their arms?"

"Men," she retorted. "I don't think I will ever understand any of them, except for your father. He is the most unpretentious man in the world, and I love him so much. I don't think I can go on without him."

She put her head down on the table and began to cry—great sobs coming from deep within her soul that she had not allowed to come to the surface before—at least not in my presence.

I felt helpless watching her. She loved my father so much, and there was nothing I could do except put my hand on her shoulder as she cried. Life simply wasn't fair. So many people relied on my father and would be lost when he was gone. Why couldn't we have just one little miracle? Was it really too much to ask? But it was useless to play *what if* or *if only* games. He was dying, and that was all there was to it. The question was whether or not we could be strong for each other when that time came.

I was so tired that evening that I crashed right after my shower and slept clear through until morning. I'd had every intention of visiting with my father when he woke up and recapping the highlights of my adventures in the outback, minus a few details. There was no need for him to know about the issues Jake and I had with each other. Things would work out the way they were supposed to anyway.

I simply had to believe that God would not have orchestrated my trip back home when he did if there wasn't a reason for me to be here. I'd had time to talk most everything over with my father, and learning about my little brother had literally changed the focus of my life. I wanted to take care of him and shelter him from as many tough lessons as possible. Losing our father would be a horrible shock, but losing each other after we had just met would be intolerable.

Ben and I had emailed daily before I went into the outback with Jake, but when I got back things slowly started to change. There simply wasn't time to accomplish everything that needed to be done. While I missed him dreadfully, I couldn't just pack my bags and leave. I needed to stay where I was until I had made good on my promises. But how long could I really expect Ben to wait for me?

Father was soon too tired to get out of bed for more than a few minutes at a time. He no longer worked in his den or joined us at the table for meals. He was relying on morphine completely to control the pain and barely ate or drank enough to keep his organs working. He spent most of his time sleeping and seldom had enough strength to carry on even a short conversation.

LeAnn spent most of her time in the master bedroom with him. That left me to take over the cooking, cleaning, laundry and spend whatever time I had left doing things with Trevor. He never asked me about what was going on and slowly stopped going to our father's door and knocking. I suspected that such drastic changes frightened him but felt it unwise to exert any pressure. He would come to terms with his loss when the time came, and nothing about the situation could be rushed.

As for myself, I would slip in to check on my father whenever an opportunity arose. LeAnn would assure me that he was still with us, but it was hard looking at him when he was too weak to even open his eyes. Occasionally, I would hold his almost lifeless hand and watch as each labored breath became more difficult. But mostly, I left LeAnn alone because she didn't feel like talking and my presence felt like an intrusion.

Hospice was coming out daily in spite of the two-hour drive both ways. I knew they were helping LeAnn prepare for my father's death. There were times when he seemed incredibly far away, but that was all part of the dying process— something I was trying to come to terms with myself.

I had the chance to sit with him for more than my usual amount time two days after I returned from gathering sheep while LeAnn took a much-needed nap. She had slept so little the past month that I was beginning to worry about her becoming too sick to help him when he needed her most.

"I'm glad you're here," father said in a voice that was barely audible.

I sat down on the blue and red fabric-covered chair that had been placed as close to the bed as possible and took his hand. It was limp and white.

"You don't have to talk. I just want to sit with you for a while."

He gazed out into the room as if he was seeing something I couldn't. His breathing was slower and more relaxed than it had been the day before.

"I saw your mother last night," he said.

"Was it a happy dream?" I asked.

"It wasn't a dream, Brylee. She was standing at the foot of the bed. She looked wonderful—so peaceful and calm—just like she did before all the disillusionment set in. She said she had forgiven me and would be back to get me soon."

I felt convulsions of cold ripple up and down my arms as fear settled in. I knew what her visitation meant, although I doubted that anyone else would agree. My mother would be the one coming when it was time for him to pass through the veil of mortality into what lay beyond.

"Did she say anything else?" I asked, trying to choke back the tears.

He breathed deeply, and I was afraid I may have pushed him too hard, but he rallied. "She said to tell you that she was ready for a new start, and then she smiled that beautiful smile that made me fall instantly in love with her. It will be good to be with her again."

"You have so many people who love you," I said, putting his hand to my lips and kissing it. "I don't know if I can make it without you." Tears were falling, but I didn't try to stop them. God had granted me a tender mercy letting me know that everything would be oaky.

"This wasn't how I planned it," he said, and I knew he was offering the only comfort he could. "I wanted to grow old and see you happily married with a lovely family, but I don't have much to say about that now. I abused my body and have to pay for it. I'm just glad you didn't pick up all the bad habits I did."

I forced a wane smile. "Not everyone who smokes gets lung cancer. Why did it have to happen to you?"

"Just the luck of the draw, I suppose. I have lived a full life in many ways, but I still have a great many regrets."

"We all have regrets, father. I will never forgive myself for running away."

"Maybe you had to get away so you could learn how strong you really are. I am so proud of you. You have turned into the lovely young woman I always knew you would be. And that young bloke who has stolen your heart needs to know just how lucky he is. My biggest regret now is that there wasn't time to meet him, but at least I know that you won't be alone."

"I am grateful for him and love him very much, but it just isn't the same. I still need my father."

"And I wish I didn't have to leave you, but death will be easier for me knowing that you will always have someone to look after you. I wish I could say the same about LeAnn and Trevor. We don't have many friends, and I can't expect Jake to stay here forever."

"I'm sure he doesn't mind," I replied, remembering our conversations about the future, and the threats he had made about me wanting an inheritance I didn't deserve. "And just so you can rest more easily, I really do plan on being here for as long as I am needed or wanted."

"It was a very selfish thing for me to ask, but Trevor will need his big sister when I'm gone. And I do feel more at peace knowing that you've had time to get better acquainted."

"Me too. Never in my wildest dreams did I ever think I would have a little brother."

"You have handled everything with so much grace. You get that from your mother."

"I miss her," I told him.

"So do I, and a day never ends without me regretting all the pain I caused her. If I could live my life over again . . . ."

"We all wish that, father, but mother has forgiven you and you have forgiven me."

"How could I not forgive you, Brylee? You were not responsible for anything that happened."

His eyes closed, and I knew he was drifting off to sleep again. I held his hand for the longest time as his chest moved slowly up and down. It wasn't supposed to end like this, but I wasn't the only one whose heart was breaking. After everything was said and done, I had Ben waiting for me. LeAnn and Trevor would only have Jake. That seemed more like a penalty than a blessing.

There had to be some way to help ease their pain and loneliness even after I was gone. I didn't like how I felt about Jake, but he hadn't made it easy for me to view him as anything but a volatile man who was willing to take any risk necessary to get what he wanted. What if they couldn't handle all the challenges of life without my father, and what if they decided to sell the ranch because Jake wasn't around to help them?

I was so lost and confused. I wanted to keep the promise made to my father, but I also wanted to be Ben's wife. Having both seemed impossible. Emails from half a world away would do little to help my family in the outback when what they really needed was another hand to help with the work. And asking Ben to leave his family and come to Australia to live wasn't right either. I had prayed ceaselessly for an answer, but had begun to believe that I was asking the wrong questions.

While I was still deep in thought, LeAnn returned to the bedroom.

"Did you get any sleep?" I asked because she still looked as if she could barely put one foot in front of the other.

She placed her hand lovingly on my father's cheek before responding. "A little, but it's hard to rest when I know Jack won't be with us much longer. He is so weak, and his moments of lucidity are becoming less frequent. I just want to spend every moment with him while I can."

I watched her kiss his pale lips and brush the hair from his forehead before saying anything more. "It kills me that he has to go through this, but I can't seem to do anything about it?"

I wanted to offer her words of encouragement and hope, but it was too late for that. Death hung like a silent visitor in the room, and I knew my father would not want me to tell her about him having seen my mother. Still, knowing what I did about the connection between this life and the next, it was impossible to discount his vision.

"He looks almost peaceful," she said as her hand rested on his head. "I'm always grateful when the morphine kicks in, and he can sleep."

"I guess there are some things to be thankful for," I said as I watched her caress his hair. It was longer than I had ever seen it, but then it hadn't been cut since my return.

"Do you think you could take Trevor for a ride this afternoon? I would do it myself, but don't have the energy. I just want to sit here."

I wanted to sit with my father too, but Trevor needed a diversion from all the silence and gloom in the house. He had to be so confused by what was happening, but he never cried or made a fuss. His eyes just became large and filled with fright whenever our father had one of his coughing spells that could be heard throughout the entire house.

My heart ached for him, but it wasn't my place to tell him that the end was very near. That was his mother's responsibility, and thus far, she had refused to do it. In some ways, losing my mother in a car accident had been easier because I hadn't been forced to watch her die. My grief came from the suddenness of her passing.

"I'll take him," I finally said, although my heart wasn't in it. "Maybe it would do both of us good to get out of the house for a couple of hours. Where is he?"

"I sent him to the barn so Jake could help him saddle the horses. He thinks he is big enough to do it himself now that he is eight, but he is only a little boy who is going to lose his father."

She started to cry so I reached out and placed my hand over hers. "It's going to be okay," I told her. "Father believes in all of us. He knows it won't be easy, but he also knows we can make it if we stick together as a family."

"I hope you are right," she said. "We've had a lot of good years together, but they will never seem like enough. Your father and I are soul mates, and when you've had the best, no one else will ever measure up."

I didn't know if the same thing applied to Ben and me. I only knew I wanted to be with him forever. I just wished he was with me now, but even if I asked him to come to Australia today it would likely be too. Besides, what could he do other than offer me a shoulder to lean on? He didn't know what my new family had come to mean to me. I had accepted LeAnn and Trevor at first because of what they meant to my father. I loved them now because of what they meant to me.

"We won't be gone long," I told her. "I am sure Trevor will be anxious to see father when he gets back."

She shook her head and looked at me through narrowed eyes. "I'm not sure it is good for Trevor to his father the way he is now. He needs to remember Jack as the hero he was a few months ago when he was still strong and healthy."

"Have you talked to him about how serious father's condition really is?" I inquired, already knowing the answer.

"We must have hope," she replied. "There is still a chance he could go into remission again. His breathing has been a lot better the past few hours."

Father's breathing did seem less labored, but I knew he wasn't going into another remission. The Hospice workers had told us that sometimes terminal patients almost seem to be getting better, but that was the last thing they did before passing.

I forced that thought from my mind before giving LeAnn a quick hug, kissing my father's cheek, and then leaving the room. I leaned against the closed door for a moment or two, fighting the desire to return to their presence. But then I remembered how proud my father told me he was of the woman I had become. I would not give in to my fears and disappoint him now.

Trevor was feeding the horse he was going to ride a carrot from the small garden plot behind the house when I walked into the barn. Jake was saddling my horse, Rupert, so I could ride him as I had been doing since Trevor returned him to me. My little brother had the biggest heart ever, and I wished there was something I could do to keep it from breaking when our father was gone.

"I'm surprised you haven't checked on how the shearing is going, or even asked if I got the rest of the sheep in," Jake said as he tightened the saddle around Rupert's flanks and looked at me with his dark, cold eyes.

"I have been somewhat pre-occupied," I told him, trying not to sound as cold and bitter as he did. "I figured someone would tell me if any serious problems arose."

"You're right," he replied. "I was just trying to make conversation. We seem to have so few of those that aren't hostile."

I looked over at Trevor. Fortunately, he seemed to be concentrating on the tan mare with the dark diamond-shaped marking on the upper part of her nose rather than listening to us.

"It's not an easy time for any of us, Jake. You should know that."

"I was going to stop in and give your father an update once I finished up at Ned's. I just came back to get another set of clippers. An extra guy showed up this morning, and we decided to use him. If he's any good, we should be finished with the shearing by tomorrow. The sheep still waiting in the pastures are more than restless to be set free."

"Do you need me to help?" I asked, deciding that avoidance of difficult topics must run in the Johnson family. "I'm sure Trevor would understand. He could even go with us."

"That's not a bad idea, for Trevor anyway. He needs to know as much as he possibly can if he is going to be the big boss in a few years."

Taking his comment personally was futile. Father had made it perfectly clear that the Hawkins' ranch would someday belong to his son.

"Then that's what we will do, but can I ask you one question before we leave, Jake?"

"I suppose," he said, running his hand down Rupert's neck. "It's a free country."

"I want to know how many sheep you are planning to sell. Uncle Ned said it might be necessary, but I'm not sure it is what father would want."

"Your father wants what is best. Just leave it at that. The truckers picked up one load yesterday, and they will be back for another one tomorrow."

I fought back feelings of disappointment and anger knowing that while I might be in charge of keeping the books, my input would never betaken seriously when it came to how the ranch was being run. "Will you get a good price for them?"

"We won't know until the sale on Tuesday, but Ned says he isn't worried. Some things have stabilized, even if we are still technically in a recession."

I sighed as I looked into Rupert's large, black eyes, more grateful than ever that he had been returned to me. He was my only real link with a past that suddenly seemed quite foreign to me now.

"Then I guess it can't be helped," I sighed. "If there is nothing for them to eat, we don't have much of a choice."

"I think I heard a 'we' there. Does that mean you have decided to stay? I thought you couldn't wait to get back to wonder boy in the states."

I bit my bottom lip to keep from spewing forth any anger. "You know what I promised my father. I won't go back on that."

"Perhaps I should consider that a good sign, but I am fairly certain if you knew what was going on in my head you would be on the next plane out of here."

He waited for my reaction. I decided not to give one. Even thinking about what might be going on his head made me nervous.

"Well, at least you care enough about LeAnn and Trevor to consider their feelings. They are the ones who need you right now, not that bloody bloke you plan on marrying some day."

"My relationship with Ben isn't open for discussion," I said, taking Rupert's reins from his hands. "I simply came out to take Trevor for a ride."

"Then I guess I will see both of you at Ned's."

He turned his back on me and walked away, but I noticed that he stopped long enough to say something to my little brother that made him laugh.

What had happened in his life to bring him to such a desolate place? I knew he loved his sister and nephew, but he certainly had more aspirations than being a hired hand for the rest of his life—specially when knowing a little boy of eight was destined to become his boss some day. Still, his personal life wasn't any more my business than mine was his, and asking questions only made our relationship more tedious.

Trevor was so excited at the prospect of helping with the sheep shearing that he pushed his horse harder on our way to Uncle Ned's than I felt was prudent on such a hot day, but I decided that chastising him would only ruin his day. Besides, it wasn't a long ride, and I would make sure the horses got plenty of water and a shady place to rest once we got there.

Watching the shearers would be as much a novelty to me as it would be to him, although I was fairly certain this wasn't the first time he had witnessed it. While I had spent my entire childhood and youth growing up on the ranch, I had never paid much attention to anything my father did unless my mother approved it first, and that seldom happened. She wanted me to become a lady fit for the grandest lifestyle. I couldn't help but wonder what she would think of me now. I was hardly that pampered child she had raised to become a part of polite society. My face and arms were sunburned and dry, my clothes dusty and worn and my spirits about as low as they could possibly go.

But this outing was for Trevor, and I would not allow myself to give in to despair. So, once we had given the horses some water and led them into a side pasture, we walked to the shed where heavily muscled men were throwing sheep to the ground and holding them with one hand and a knee while they ran the shears next to their bodies in long, masterful strokes. They were hot and dirty, and the sweat ran in streams down their bodies, soaking their already grimy, sleeveless, once-white t-shirts. It was truly amazing how fast they worked and how rapidly the wool came off in nice wide pelts. The sheep looked almost puny as they scurried out of the barn with a few bloody nicks on their skin.

"This is a good crew." Uncle Ned said as he walked up beside us and rested his arms on the top board of the fence that separated us from the shearers. "We will be finished with your father's sheep by tomorrow night."

"I can't thank you enough for helping us with all of this," I responded.

"Your father has always been there for me, even when I didn't deserve it. Our parents left everything to him because he was the eldest, more responsible son. I walked away and blew every penny he had given me on nothing short of riotous living with my mates. Yet, he forgave me when I came back. He is the most generous bloke in the world, and I hate like hell to lose him. How is he doing today?"

I shrugged my shoulders before answering. "More weak than ever."

I couldn't exactly tell him my suspicions about how little time my father really had left, but my mother would not have appeared to him if the end wasn't near. It touched my heart deeply knowing he cared enough to share that sacred experience with me. It was further confirmation that death was merely the doorway into another part of living.

But standing there with the sun beating down on the top of my head, I wished I could be more certain that my parents would work through their differences and regain the love they had once shared. I desperately wanted to believe that we would be a real family again one day. But that was out of my hands, and there was more to consider than just the three of us now.

While I was still lost in my musings, Uncle Ned turned his attention to my little brother who was becoming fidgety watching the same process over and over again. "Say, Trevor, why don't you help NJ push the animals into the barn. All good ranchers need to learn how to do that."

"Can I really?" he asked with a broad and expectant smile.

Uncle Ned assured him that he could before I had time to object, and he ran off to join his much-older cousin.

"Are you sure it's safe?" I asked as I saw NJ help him over the top of the fence and into the pasture.

"Perfectly safe. NJ won't let anything happen to him. Sheep are docile creatures, and they are packed too tightly together to get into any mischief."

"That's what I am afraid of. What if he gets caught between some of them?"

"Quit worrying! Trevor has been around animals since the day your father brought him and LeAnn out here, and NJ is a responsible bloke, even if he doesn't want to be a rancher."

I wasn't sure I agreed with him, but then I didn't know anything about my cousin, except that he had been a little boy who liked to push limits.

"I haven't seen Jake," I said without thinking as I continued to watch what was happening in the outside pasture. "He should have been here long before us since he came back in father's truck."

Uncle Ned chucked. "He's in the far end of the barn working with the shearers. I am surprised you didn't notice him the moment you got here."

The color shot to my cheeks almost instantly. Why did I have to mention Jake? He was the bane of my existence, and Uncle Ned already thought there was a mutual interest between us.

"I guess I had other things on my mind, and I certainly wasn't aware that he knew how to shear sheep," I responded, fixing my eyes back on Trevor who was patting the head of the one of the animals that stood near him. He wasn't afraid of anything, and I wished I was more like him.

"This is his second season. He is young and strong and learning fast. He could get work as a shearer any time he wanted to."

"Do you think that is what he wants to do? He doesn't seem like a man who would stay in one place for long."

Unwittingly, my gaze returned to the barn where the shearers were working, but there was no illumination except for the light that came in through the open doors. All of the men were muscular and had tattoos. It would take more than a cursory glance to distinguish one from another. Still, my stomach lurched at the thought of Jake's taut upper body glowing in the firelight when he had removed his shirt so I could take care of his arm. It was an image I was trying very hard to suppress.

"Most men like adventure," Uncle Ned was saying as I forced my thoughts back to the present. "But all it takes is one good woman, and they will move heaven and earth to make her happy."

I wished my uncle could understand that I wasn't interested in Jake Johnson, not now, not ever. But he seemed to like the man who could so easily make my blood boil as much as my father did. Maybe it wasn't so unreasonable that most everyone thought we should be together. It would certainly make the transition easier when the time came. But Ben was the man I had chosen to marry, and I would not let anything ruin that.

"Is what happened with you and Aunt Nora?" I asked, hoping to push him away from a very disagreeable subject. "I wish I could say the same thing about my parents."

"Your parents were in an impossible situation. She was little more than a child when they fell in love and not the least bit prepared for marriage, especially to a rancher who couldn't give her any of things she was used to having. I am not saying they didn't try, but some relationships just become too broken to fix. Everything might have different if she had It been able to adapt the way LeAnn has, but those two women were cut from very different bolts of cloth."

"Maybe they were, but I think my parents have finally forgiven each other."

"What in the world makes you say that?" he asked.

"I sat with father earlier today. He said my mother had come to him to say that it wouldn't be long now, and she was going to help him make the transition."

"Rubbish!" he shouted, pushing back on the board fence. "It's just the medication talking."

I knew better than to push the truth on unbelievers but couldn't seem to stop myself.

"I don't think so, Uncle Ned. He explained the visitation in detail."

"But your mother, Brylee. They weren't exactly on good terms when she died. In fact, most people still blame Jack for the accident since they don't know what really happened."

"Then someone should tell them."

"That's your father's call to make, not mine."

"But the fault lay with more than him, and I know my mother no longer blames him for anything."

"So you're a visionary too?" He looked at me with mocking eyes. "You will have to excuse me for not believing in all this religious nonsense. I'm not even sure I believe in life after death, even though the good book seems to indicate that it exists. Maybe the cold ground is where all of us will spend eternity."

His admission saddened me, but I could tell from the hard set of his jaw that he believed everything he was saying—if only to protect himself from more uncertainty and pain.

"You can't really believe that, Uncle Ned. Why would we have families here that we love if we only say goodbye to them forever when we die?"

"I'm not saying it makes any sense, but dying never does, especially when it's too soon like it is with your father. Do you really believe his time for leaving us is drawing close?"

"He is so tired, and morphine is his only relief from pain."

"That is precisely why we have drugs. No one needs to suffer needlessly." He suddenly looked down at me and smiled. "You do know that I am only talking about the legal ones. Your father and I never got involved with anything really addictive like meth or cocaine, but we did smoke our share of pot when we were young."

I frowned. Why was he telling me this now? I didn't want to hear anything negative about my father. I wanted good thoughts to be the only ones I remembered.

"Don't give me that look, Brylee," he said. "I know you have given up all the vices, but you need to understand that your father and me were never saints. We lived our lives just like everyone else in the outback, and he would never want to be put on some pedestal just because he is dying. Still, despite our many obvious flaws, I think we turned out pretty good."

I forced a weary smile. "Yes, you did."

"Then quit worrying about things that can't be proven. I guess the bottom line is that we will all know what happens after we die when we get there."

His attempt at levity was meant to make both of us feel better, but it wasn't working. Nonetheless, rather than belabor the issue, I turned my attention back to what was going on in the barn.

I knew little about what happened to the wool after shearing except for my father telling me that it was bundled in bails and sold to the highest bidder. He and Uncle Ned had been using a small wool company in Edna the past few years and had been dealt with fairly. I assumed the same thing would happen now.

"Need to get back to work," Uncle Ned said, no doubt sensing that my mind was no longer focused on continuing our conversation. "We have a good crew this year, but someone still needs to crack the whip occasionally."

"I'm sorry I can't help," I replied.

"Nonsense, love. Your very presence will give all the blokes in the barn a boost. Molly used to drive both them and me crazy with her playfulness. I am more than grateful she is at the university now. Wouldn't want her involved with any of the drifters I hire. It would break her mother's heart."

He didn't expect an answer and I was glad. My cousin was young and beautiful, and I doubted she had any plans to keep her virtue intact until her wedding night. No one out here viewed marriage and family the way I did. Perhaps I was a little too old-fashioned and naïve, but I liked the me that Ben loved. Our life together was going to be wonderful.

I fought back tears as my thoughts drifted back to the present. I was hopelessly ignorant when it came to the daily operations that kept the ranch running, and there was no way I could fulfill my promise to my father unless Jake and I were able to trust each other enough to become partners for the greater good instead of adversaries. LeAnn would defer to him in everything once she was left on her own.

I finally saw him as he threw a sheep to the floor of the shearing shed. He had moved into the sunlight, and it danced off his sweaty muscles as they bulged and throbbed with exertion. He wasn't smiled, but I could tell he was enjoying the experience. It was a release from whatever continued to bother him. He had never said a word about how my father's death might affect him personally, but he was a man who would have his ducks in a row when that time came.

And while he might love his family and the outback, he certainly wanted more from life than a meager existence away from the rest of humanity. I didn't believe it when he said he would never get married. He might claim to be passionately indifferent to the women he slept with, but he needed love and security just as badly as anyone else. Someday, he would make a move that needed to be stopped. My father's legacy was far too important to be lost.

Chapter 9

Trevor chatted enthusiastically about his adventures herding sheep with NJ all the way home. It was good to see him so happy, and I hoped he would have many more fun experiences in the future. Once again, I could see why our father had promised him the ranch when he was older. He loved everything about it. I could see it in his eyes when he talked about all the things he and our father had done together. But his joy always brought with it a certain amount of pain because I had missed out on so much as a child.

We got back to the ranch house several hours later than anticipated. Trevor had been so engrossed with a task he had never been allowed to do before that I hated taking him back to reality any sooner than necessary. But once the shearers had finished their work for the day, it seemed pointless to hang around Uncle Ned's any longer.

So, we climbed on our horses and rode away, but my hopes for additional happy times were shattered the moment I saw LeAnn sitting on the porch swing. She would never leave father unattended unless . . . . All the air went out of my lungs as I looked at her face.

"Hey, little brother," I called out to Trevor who was sitting on his horse beside me. "Would you mind taking the horses to the barn and giving them some water? I will help you with the saddles in a few minutes."

"But I wanted to tell mum what I did," he protested.

"Just do what Brylee asked," LeAnn told him. "I need to talk to your sister for a few minutes alone."

It was a lot to ask of him when he had something important to say, but he had been taught to obey his parents, so I handed him my reins and watched while he turned the horses in the direction of the barn. LeAnn kept her eyes on me as I climbed the three steps to the veranda. Her eyes were wide and glassy-looking, but she hadn't been crying—at least not recently.

"He's gone, isn't he?" I asked as I sat down beside her on the swing.

"Yes!" she replied in a voice without emotion. "He died right after you left! I was sitting by his side holding his hand and watching him sleep when he opened his eyes just long enough to say that he loved me, and then he was gone."

I sat still as waves of sorrow, regret and anger washed over me. I shouldn't have gone to Uncle Ned's! I knew something was wrong, but I had allowed my stepmother to dictate my actions because it was what she wanted. Now my father was gone, and I hadn't been there to tell him goodbye.

I stared numbly at the whitewashed boards of the veranda's floor. There was so little paint left, and the weathered wood underneath seemed to be telling me that a person could cover old things with all the color and beauty of the world, but underneath they always remained the same. It was that way with family.

My new life with Ben was like paint. It covered all of the scars and pain of childhood and losing my mother because it was wonderful, but underneath the new life I had found, I was still a child who needed to be part of her roots. What was I going to do now that my entire foundation had been ripped away? I couldn't possibly stay in a house with people who didn't really want me there.

"Can I go in and see him?" I asked as I continued to stare at the wooden floor. If I looked at her, I might say something unkind that couldn't be taken back. She hadn't known how quickly the end would come, but she could have called to let us know it had happened.

"He's already gone. I had the mortician from Edna come for him. They left about twenty minutes ago."

I felt like I had been gut kicked by a wild brumby from the outback, and the air came out of my lungs in one big blast of pent up anger and pain. How could she have had my father's body taken away without telling any of us? I was his daughter! I had a right to be included in whatever decisions were made, but I didn't say anything. I just sat there clenching and unclenching my fists.

"I thought about calling or waiting for you and Trevor to get back." I heard her say through the heavy fog that continued to settle over me. "But I didn't want my little boy remembering his father that way. Kids are impressionable. He might never be able to go into our bedroom again. I am sorry you didn't get to say goodbye."

I watched Trevor climb down from the mare he'd been riding and then lead both horses into the barn. My voice was hushed when the words came out. There was plenty of time for the anger to emerge once this awful moment was over.

"You should have let me know, but I understand why you didn't. Father knew what was going to happen. He told me it wouldn't be long when I talked to him earlier today, but I didn't expect it to come this soon."

"Me either."

I glanced sideways at her. The lines between her eyes were furrowed deeper than I had ever seen them, and her hands were wrapped tightly together in her lap.

"Would you mind if I told Trevor alone? I don't know how he is going to react," she said. "I should have prepared him better, but I didn't want to accept the truth myself. Do you think he is going to be very angry?"

"I don't know how he is going to feel, except lost, alone and frightened." I told her as I rose to my feet. I had to get out of there before I told her what my father had said about my mother being the one to come for him. It would hurt her immensely and would only prove how little I understood about the Savior's compassion for others—even when they hurt the people they claimed to love. At that moment, I hated both LeAnn and my father because she was the last person he had thought about before dying.

"I will unsaddle the horses and take a walk. I need to clear my head anyway," I told her.

But it wasn't a clear head that I needed, I realized while walking away on legs that were none too steady. I had to release all the pent-up rage and grief before it consumed me. Both of my parents were gone, and I had never felt so betrayed and unstrung. How could I be expected to put aside personal feelings and be a support for LeAnn and Trevor after what I had been through?

I wanted both of my parents to be proud of me when I saw them again, and knew that running away again wasn't an option. But I had made the biggest of mistakes by not asking Ben to come. He would never meet either of my parents now, and once I left Australia I would never be back. When the grief finally settled, Trevor would be the only one on the ranch who would even want me there.

I don't know how LeAnn explained our father's death to Trevor. After I put the saddles away, brushed down the horses and gave them water to drink and oats to eat, I went to the cemetery to talk to my mother. I was too numb to cry until I reached her grave and realized that my father would soon be resting beside her.

"I can't believe he's gone, mother," I cried out as I sat down on the dry grass in front of her headstone. "That you were the one to come for him should bring comfort, but it doesn't. I want him to hold me in his arms again and tell me that everything will be okay, but all I see is gloom and darkness ahead, and I'm not sure I will ever be able to forgive LeAnn for not giving me a chance to say goodbye. It was a horrible and mean-spirited thing to do. I just want to scream and break everything I can get my hands on."

That was certainly true. I would claw at the tree bark until my fingers bled and bang my head against its rough surface if I thought it would do any good. I had truly believed that I was prepared for this eventuality, but preparation was never equal to the moment of loss and privation. I was alone in a frightening world and had no one to blame but myself because I had been too short-sighted and proud to ask Ben to come.

I wiped the sweat from my brow and the tears from my eyes with the backs of my hands, and then buried my head in my arms. There was little shade in the family burial plot and the sun was still hot, even though it was late afternoon. Still, cold chills traveled through my body like ice cycles falling from a tree and piercing anything they landed on.

Prayers for my father's extended life had not been answered, and that shook me considerably. I appreciated the fact that he was no longer in pain, but hated the grief and sting in my heart. It was like my own cancer gnawing away at every new belief I had acquired. In that moment, I wasn't sure that the emptiness I felt inside could ever be filled, even by marrying Ben.

And how could I leave Australia? Despite the sense of disloyalty I felt over the way LeAnn had handled things, I didn't really hate her, and I certainly loved my little brother. In fact, I loved everyone here, except Jake. I didn't even like him, but I knew that without his help and expertise the ranch would never survive. Why couldn't father have been given a few more years to live? We all needed him so desperately.

I don't know how long I sat there as wave after wave of sorrow and regret washed over me. I knew my parents were enjoying a heart-felt reunion in heaven where all past feelings of hurt and infidelity would soon be resolved. But what was I supposed to do without them? I would soon be twenty-five—a grownup about to be married—and still felt like a child who needed to be held and comforted by her parents.

Theoretically, I understood that God would be always be there, but my knowledge of his complete love and devotion to his individual children was still very new. I had relied on Ben's testimony while being taught the gospel of Jesus Christ and prepared for baptism because he knew who he was, why he was here and where he was going when he died. But there were still times when I questioned if I would have joined The Church of Jesus Christ of Latter-day Saints if he had not been part of the equation.

I wanted to believe as he did because I had fallen in love with him the moment we met. He was strong and capable, yet tender and understanding. He was everything I had ever dreamed of in a man, and I knew the girl who married him would experience all of his goodness. I felt so blessed to be that girl, but the long weeks away from him had convinced me that I could no longer rely on his strength or his testimony to get me through the rest of my life any longer.

I had to know for myself if what I professed to believe was in fact the truth. For if God loved each of his children equally, why had some of them been given the gospel while other hadn't? My family members were good people and loved each other deeply—even if they smoked and drank and cussed and lived together outside of marriage. They conducted their lives based on what they knew just as I had done before I was introduced to the gospel, so how could I condemn any of them?

"Oh, Father in Heaven," I thought as I sat there so completely alone and frightened. "How can I know for sure that what I have embraced is true? I want to have faith and be strong, but I just don't have anything left inside to fight with."

I'm not sure what I thought would happen, an epiphany, a great rush of heavenly wings. But only these simple words came into my mind. *"You will find peace."*

Peace! What did that mean? The way things stood right now, I would never know peace again for as long as I lived. No matter which life I chose—the one with Ben or the one here—I would have to give up something I desperately wanted. How could peace ever come when I was being torn in two like that?

LeAnn and Jake were sitting at the kitchen table drinking one of their endless cups of coffee when I got back to the house. I wondered what they would do if that beverage was suddenly banned like it had been when I joined the church.

I felt like I had been dragged through a wringer, but I simply didn't care what other people thought about me right now. All I could think about was the pain in my heart, and the prayer that I would be able to make it though the next few days without destroying the fragile relationships I had worked so incredibly hard to create.

"How's Trevor doing?" I asked when they glanced up from their conversation.

Jake looked like he always did—cold and unruffled—but I could see concern in his eyes. He might treat me with contempt, but when it came to his sister and nephew he would do anything to see them happy. I wasn't entirely sure what that meant for me. It was like everything else right now and only time would tell.

"He's asleep after crying until his little body gave out," LeAnn said. "I left him on the sofa in the den. I thought it might help being surrounded by his father's things when I told him, but he is very mad at me. He wanted to see his father, and

I had to tell him that I had already sent his body away. I really messed things up."

She began to cry, and Jake put his arm around her shoulders.

"It doesn't matter, Lee. There isn't anything that would have made this easier on him. He will come around. Just give him some time and space."

"But a mother is supposed to protect her child!" she protested. "How do I ever get him to accept that his father isn't coming back and forgive me for keeping so much from him?"

Jake sat quietly at the table with her. He hadn't showered or changed clothes since coming back from Uncle Ned's. I wondered if LeAnn had called to tell him and if Uncle Ned knew what had happened. He would be more than furious if he did.

I might have replied to her question, if only out of consideration, but my own grief was too raw, and I was still afraid of saying something I might regret. A wave of bitterness stole over me. Life wasn't fair! It never had been, and it never would be. Even knowing that Ben was waiting for me back in the United States brought no solace. It seemed like we had been separated forever. I couldn't even remember what his kiss felt like.

"What about services," Jake was asking her. "I suppose there are a few things we should be doing."

I stood silently in front of the kitchen window that overlooked some of the land my father had loved so much, my hands clutching the edge of the countertop. I wished I could rip it right off. I wanted to be a part of what was going on but hadn't been invited into the conversation. Jake and LeAnn knew they were in charge.

"There isn't much to be done, Jake. Jack took care of all the arrangements when he first got sick. He wants a small graveside service with family."

"That should be easy enough. It's not like we have all that much family. Have you told Ned?"

LeAnn placed her coffee cup back on the table. "No, I've been avoiding it. I guess I was too worried about telling Trevor to think about anyone else. Will you do that for me? I can't break the news to him after what happened with Trevor."

Suddenly, I no longer wanted to be included in anything that was going on. I just wanted to be by myself, but I wasn't fast enough in beating a retreat to my room.

"Why don't we have Brylee do it?" Jake said, stopping me in my tracks just as I got to the swinging door that led into the front hallway. "He's her uncle, and I am quite certain it would come better from a blood-related member of the family."

He looked at me with his cold, dark eyes as if challenging me to decline his suggestion. I wanted to swoop across the room and claw his eyes out for being so unfeeling and cruel, but I would not give him the satisfaction of knowing that anything he said could adversely affect me after what had happened on the mountain.

"What about it, Brylee?" he continued to prod. "Could you help LeAnn out with this?"

I bit the inside of my bottom lip. This was an impossible situation, and no one could really blame me for being waspish, but I knew that wasn't why he continued to goad me. He wanted me gone for good.

"What am I supposed to say?" I asked him in the calmest voice I could muster. "He's just lost his only brother."

"We have all lost someone close to us. I simply think this news would be better coming from you. It isn't entirely unexpected. Of course, I can do it, if you won't."

I wanted to retaliate—to tell him what an insufferable, arrogant, horrible man he really was—but it would only upset LeAnn, and she had enough to worry about in trying to smooth things over with Trevor.

"I'll call him," I relented, but I wasn't about to do it from the kitchen where Jake and LeAnn could hear. Some conversations needed to remain private. "Do you think it would wake Trevor if I used the extension in the den?"

"Why can't you use the phone hanging right here on the wall?" Jake asked. "No one is using it, and you wouldn't risk waking the poor little lad, if he is still sleeping."

"Don't argue about something as stupid as a phone," LeAnn snapped. "You can get back to your constant bickering later. Right now we have more important things to worry about."

She looked totally whipped, and I momentarily wondered who would become the real boss once my father was laid to rest. The dynamics in the house were already starting to change.

"I'll be as quiet as possible," I said. But when I opened the door to the den, Trevor sat up on the sofa and looked at me.

"It isn't true," he said. "Please tell me that what mum said isn't true. Father just has to be here."

I walked across the worn carpet and sat down next to him on brown, leather sofa.

"I wish I could, little brother," I responded as he snuggled into my arms. "Father was very sick, and God decided it was time for him to come home."

"I don't like God," he whimpered. "Why couldn't he just make him well again?"

"That's something I can't tell you. I only know that God loves us and will help us get through this."

"But father said the ranch would be mine when he died, and I don't know what to do."

I brushed his hair away from his forehead and pulled him even closer. "You don't have to worry about that for a very long time. Your mother and Jake will be here to help you until you are old enough to do it on your own."

"What about you? You promised both father and me you would stay."

"And I will stay for as long as you need me."

My commitment had always included remaining with my little brother for as long as it took for him to adjust. The questions that needed answers were whether Ben would understand why I had made such a promise and if he would be willing to wait?

"But I don't want you to go, ever!"

"You know I have someone very special waiting for me in Los Angeles."

"I don't care! He doesn't need you like I do. You are my sister."

He started to cry, and I knew with faultless clarity that I could never leave until he was ready to let me go, even if it meant giving up my dream of marrying Ben and having the beautiful life we had planned on sharing.

"You know, Trevor, I have something really important to do and would like you to help me since you know what it means to have a sister."

He looked up at me with tear-filled eyes that were red and swollen from crying.

"What is it?" he asked.

"Uncle Ned doesn't know about father yet. I think it would be a good idea if we told him together. We could drive over in the jeep."

He breathed heavily for a moment or two, and I wondered if I had suggested the impossible. After all, he was only a little boy whose world had just been shattered.

"I will go with you," he finally said, wiping the tears away and rising to his feet. "But I have to tell mum where we are going so she won't be worried."

"That's a good idea. Why don't you do that while I get the keys? I will meet you outside."

I simply couldn't face Jake again until I had done what he asked. His eyes would only show his disapproval, and I didn't need any more reminders of my inadequacies and how they could be used against me.

It was well after suppertime when we got to Uncle Ned's. He and Aunt Nora were sitting at the table eating cold apple pie with clotted cream.

"This is a real surprise," Aunt Nora said when she opened the kitchen door to see us standing there in the dark. "You should have told me you were coming, and I would have prepared something special. NJ went into Edna with the rest of the shearers. I guess he felt like he needed a break."

"This isn't exactly a social call," I told her.

"Oh, my," she said, looking at our ashen faces and red-rimmed eyes. "Please come in. Ned, Brylee and Trevor are here."

I didn't know what to expect, but one look at my uncle's face let me know it was okay to give in to my grief. I rushed into his open arms. Tears were falling, my chest was heaving with sorrow, and I could barely breathe, but he just held me in his strong arms until I quit shaking and was able to speak.

"I should have called first," I said.

"Nonsense!" he responded. "When did it happen?"

"LeAnn said it was right after Trevor and I left to come here. She had his body taken away while we were gone."

"Damn that woman," he said, and then remembered that Trevor was in the room with us.

My little brother looked confused and hurt, but Aunt Nora hustled him into the dining room for cookies and milk while Uncle Ned and I continued to talk in more subdued voices.

"I didn't mean to say that in front of the boy. I'm just upset because none of us got to say our goodbyes."

"I guess I was luckier than you because at least I got to talk to him this morning."

"You aren't going to bring up all that nonsense about him having a visitation from your mother again, are you?"

"Not unless you want me to," I replied.

"Well, I don't! Although I do believe that some people can have premonitions. I just can't understand why LeAnn didn't call us. I know there would not have been time to get there before he passed, but damn it all, we are his family and deserved to know before she had his body whisked away by the undertaker."

"Maybe she thought she was sparing us by taking care of things herself," I whimpered. "She said father has the arrangements for a simple graveside service already made."

"I'm sure he has. My brother was never one for leaving details unattended to, but I am still mad as hell about not being told sooner. LeAnn may have been his wife for a few weeks, but I have been his bother since the day I was born."

I didn't want my uncle's attitude to affect me, but maybe it was okay to lash out at the world right now. I wasn't just mad at LeAnn and Jake. I was mad at my father for leaving us.

"Why couldn't he stay with us longer, Uncle Ned? Maybe we should have looked harder for alternative treatments."

He patted my hand affectionately. "I wish like hell that would have been a viable option, but your father still got to die on his own terms—relatively speaking. He was in his own room when he drew his last breath instead of some bloody hospital. I just hope I am as lucky as he was when my time comes."

"I can't see anything lucky about this. He's gone and nothing is going to bring him back. I was standing right there in the kitchen while Jake and LeAnn discussed his funeral arrangements, and I wasn't even included in the conversation. Why can't they understand how wrong it is to leave us out of everything? We're his real family, not them."

Uncle Ned looked at me while he sniffed away more tears. It was hard watching a grown man cry, but it helped sooth my tortured soul to know that someone who really mattered knew exactly how I felt.

"I guess there is no wrong or right way to handle things when someone dies, and I should have known how LeAnn would react. She is a very private person who knows how to take control when the need arises. More than likely, they went over every detail long before his final hours arrived, and she was just complying with his wishes the same way you are."

"My decision to stay hardly seems relevant now. Everything will go to Trevor eventually, and I could keep track of the finances from Los Angeles as well as from here."

"You aren't going to renege on your promise so quickly, are you?" he asked.

"I may not be left with much of a choice, but now isn't the time to be thinking or acting alone," I retorted, not wanting to talk about something so frivolous as my staying or going when we should be discussing what we would do if we were left out of anything else. "All of us should be part of this."

"Maybe LeAnn will be more forthcoming in the morning, once the initial shock has settled a bit. And a simple graveside service doesn't sound so bad, as long as we have a wake to go with it with plenty of booze where we can remember the good times. That's how I want it when I pass—nice and easy with no pretense."

My tears had slowed almost to a trickle, but my emotions were still very raw. How could Uncle Ned even joke about dying right now? I couldn't bear to think about losing anyone else.

"Don't say things like that, Uncle Ned," I told him. "You are the only real family I have left."

He reached out and took my hands. "I didn't mean to upset you, love. I plan on being here for a very long time, but the truth is that none of us know if we will be here tomorrow. Would it help you to know that your father asked me to watch out for you when he was gone?"

"He did?"

"I think his exact words were, *don't let anything happen to my little girl.* I mean to keep that promise, Brylee. I am here for you whenever you need me."

I stood on my tiptoes and kissed his weathered cheek. I wasn't alone! I had my Uncle Ned—a giant of a man with a gentle heart. I knew I could come to him about anything. We walked into the dining room together.

"Would the two of you like some cookies and milk?" Aunt Nora asked, linking her arm through Uncle Ned's and giving me a warm, reassuring smile.

Trevor was sitting at the table. He sill looked sad, but the anguish was gone from his face.

"You are a miracle-worker, Aunt Nora," I said as I watched him take another bite of a cookie.

"Not at all," she quietly replied. "All I did was give him something to eat."

"You let him see that parts of life can still be normal. I have no idea what is waiting for us back at back to the ranch."

"I am afraid normal won't be very pleasant for awhile, but I don't want you to worry about anything. I will prepare all the food for after the service."

"You don't have to do that," I told her, wondering how anyone could think about food at a time like this. "I doubt anyone will feel much like eating. Besides, there will be so few of us there. Father only wanted family."

"And those wishes will be respected, but I know he had a lot of friends who will want to know of his passing."

Uncle Ned cleared his throat. "Why don't I take Trevor into the den while you talk. I'm sure I could interest him in one of the games NJ set up on my computer."

Aunt Nora looked over at him and frowned. "I'm sorry, Ned. I wasn't thinking."

"No worries, love. I think we are all a little rattled right now. How about it, Trevor, could I interest you in a video game?"

My little brother just shrugged his shoulders and followed him.

"I feel like I should be doing something but don't know what plans LeAnn and Jake are making, or what my father has already set in place," I told Aunt Nora once they were gone.

"There's time to take care of anything that may have been overlooked, Brylee. I heard what you and Ned were talking about, and I do understand your frustration and pain, but try not to lash out at LeAnn too harshly. She has been under so much stress lately it's a wonder she is still standing."

I was glad Uncle Ned had taken Trevor into his den. He shouldn't have to overhear emotional conversations about his father or his mother. We would all have to be very careful not to confuse or upset him any further, while still acknowledging his feelings.

"Do you think LeAnn loved my father more than my mother did?" I asked my aunt.

It was a stupid question under the circumstances, but I suddenly felt the need for reassurance. My parents were now reunited and had a chance to sort everything out, but there were no guarantees when it came to us becoming an eternal family.

"It is hard to define what love is because it's different for everyone," Aunt Nora said. "But I do know that your parents were completely devoted to each other when they got married. They just didn't know how to converse once the newness wore off. Hawkins' men are notorious for wanting to hide their feelings. They just want to fix things, and don't seem to get it that some things can only be fixed with conversation. If your parents had been able to see past their differences things might have turned out very differently."

"It's just so sad," I said. "I can talk to Ben about anything."

The moment the words slipped out I knew I was being less than truthful. The secret I was keeping from him would come out eventually. And when it did, the fallout could be catastrophic. Not that being sexually assaulted was something to be ashamed of. It happened all the time on university campuses, but my life had definitely been altered because of it.

"Then you are very lucky, Brylee. Ned and I have a wonderful relationship, but it took years of training to get him to hear what I was saying instead of just trying to fix what he thought was wrong."

"I wish I had known my father better. It was such a horrible mistake to run away."

"You did what most young people would have done, and your father understood. He forgave you ages ago."

"But forgiving myself isn't quite as easy. Do you think he really can see into my heart now that he is gone."

Aunt Nora shook her head. "I'm not sure I am the right person to ask about that. Ned and I haven't attended mass or confession for a very long time, but I am sure your father knows exactly how you feel about him. His biggest wish was always that his family could be together and happy."

That thought stayed with me on the short drive home. We were together, but I wasn't sure any of us would ever be truly happy again.

LeAnn had food on the table for us when we returned, not that any of us felt much like eating a meal that should have been served hours earlier. Trevor asked to be excused since he'd had enough cookies and milk at Uncle Ned's to fill his knotted stomach. He wanted to spend time with Copper.

It would have been easy for LeAnn to insist that he eat something healthy, but she seemed to know—as did the rest of us—that we would each find comfort in our own way. Right now, Trevor would find that with Copper. Maybe someday, one of us would be able to reach him in a human way.

There was an awkward silence as three adults sat around the table trying to eat cold cuts and fresh vegetables. Jake had showered and changed clothes so the smell of wet wool and sweat wasn't nearly as strong. LeAnn had also showered and changed, but she hadn't bothered to fix her hair or put on any make-up.

They were exact opposites, I decided as I cautiously glanced from one face to the other. LeAnn was small-boned and blond with big blue eyes and very fair skin. She looked incredibly young in spite of her 44 years. Jake's skin had been tanned by the sun and his eyes were often as dark as coal. He was strong and muscular and almost ten years younger. I could not imagine how difficult it must have been for her to raise such a powerfully independent, younger brother. I wondered what my relationship with Trevor would be like when we were older. Nearly sixteen years separated us in age, but I hoped we would always feel like we belonged together.

I pushed the food around on my plate not daring to say anything that could not be retracted. LeAnn had been wonderful to me, but perhaps that would change now that my father was gone and she no longer felt like she had to please him. As for Jake, he hated my very existence and would gladly facilitate my leaving.

Had I still been the person I was when coming home, I would have my bags packed so I could leave the moment the graveside service was over. But something inside of me had changed since my unexpected arrival. I had learned to see my birthplace like my father did—a place of memories, life and death experiences and great beauty. I wanted the ranch to flourish. I wanted my little brother to be able to run it when he grew up, and I wanted it to stay in the family. I knew how to handle the finances and make decisions based on what I knew, but that was only part of the whole experience. Without Jake and LeAnn backing me up I would never be able to follow through on anything my father has asked me to do.

"Brylee," the sound of my name broke into my disturbing thoughts. LeAnn was speaking to me. "I would like you to say a few words at your father's service. I have already talked to Father Frederick. He will officiate, but I thought it might be nice for a family member to say something planned. That might help others say a word or two."

"I can do that," I told her, wishing I didn't have to attend the interment at all. It would be hard enough saying goodbye to my father in private. How could I ever do it in public?

"Good! We will have the service at ten on Thursday. It should be a little cooler that time of day. I thought about playing a couple of songs from his favorite CD if you don't have something else in mind."

"He would like that," I told her, wondering why I was suddenly so complacent after my outbursts at Uncle Ned's, and why I was being included as part of what they were planning now. Maybe I was just scared of the finality it would bring and of not having a place on the ranch once the funeral was over. The less I cared, the easier it would be to leave if that was what was asked of me.

"I need to order some flowers and get your father's suit cleaned. I wanted him to have a new one when we got married, but he insisted that the money could be used better elsewhere. He was always so practical."

Her bottom lip began to quiver, and I wondered if she was going to break down again, but she regained her composure almost instantly.

"Jake has offered to fly me into town first thing tomorrow, and I was wondering if you would be willing to stay with Trevor? I know you should be included more, but there really isn't much to do. Your father had everything planned. I just need to spend some time at the mortuary."

"Sure," I told her, closing my eyes against the brightness of the fluorescent kitchen lights. "Have you thought about putting a notice in the newspaper? Aunt Nora said there would be lots of people who would like to know of his passing."

"I'm sure the mortuary will take care of things like that," she immediately responded, and then seemed to check herself. "But I know that nothing specific has been written up yet. Maybe you could take care of that for me. I have a phonebook here somewhere. You could call and ask how it is done."

She got up from the table and began rummaging through the drawer where she kept all her correspondence.

"I'm sorry for your loss, really I am," Jake said, staring at me almost apologetically while she was looking. "It isn't easy to lose a parent or a good friend. Your father was one of the finest men I have ever known. He won't be easily replaced."

"He can't be replaced at all," I shot back through clenched teeth so as not to upset LeAnn again. "He had the biggest heart of any man in the outback."

"You're not giving the rest of us much credit. We might not have been born out here like you were, but it has been my sister's home for the past few years, and it is Trevor's birthright. Are you still willing to do your part, even knowing that everything is being left to him?"

His question and assumptions should have angered me, but I was way past feeling temperamental. My head seemed to be floating somewhere outside my body, and my limbs seemed too heavy to lift. I knew those feelings would pass, and when they did, I would be angry with everyone and everything again. But I could never take my frustration and sorrow out on Trevor. He was the only truly innocent person in all of this.

"I haven't forgotten my promise," I told him. "I just hope we can all work together like he wants us to."

"Here it is," LeAnn said, walking back to me with the thin Edna phone directory in her hands. "They will want a picture. I don't really have one except for the wedding photo you printed and framed for us, and I won't let that out of my sight."

"I will find another one," I promised. "I still have plenty of them on my phone."

I took the phonebook from her and turned to the yellow pages. Tears were swimming in front of my eyes making it difficult to read the small print. Why hadn't God allowed my father a little longer at life? It would have meant so much to all the people who loved him.

Chapter 10

I remember very little about the days immediately following my father's death, but perhaps survival is all one can really ask for when the world turns upside down. LeAnn moved around the house her face a study of pain and misery, but I never saw her cry. Perhaps she did that when she was alone, but during the day she completed her tasks with all the precision of a robot. Given time, she would be able to move through all the stages of grief I had studied about in a psychology class at UCLA. But for now, she was simply doing what needed to be done, and I was trying to follow her example.

I wasn't so sure about what was happening with Trevor. He was too young to understand the finality of death and spent most of this time in his room with Copper or out in the shed with his other animals. When I asked him if he wanted to go for a ride or play one of the games he had gotten for his birthday he declined saying he didn't feel like it.

Living in a fog was pretty much the state I found myself in. LeAnn and Jake flew into Edna to pick out flowers for the casket and get father's suit cleaned while I stayed at home with Trevor and tried to keep from worrying about how I was going to make ends meet until my life was back on track again. I wouldn't have missed this time with my father for anything, but now that he was gone, decisions I was unprepared to make hurled themselves into my mind the moment I was left with any time to think.

Having been on my own since running away I knew the value of money, and the less-than $800 in my checking account would not last long if I was going to do anything more than live off the charity of others. My ticket for flying home was already paid for—with the exception of a fee for changing the date and flight number that had yet to be determined—but I still had to provide for myself until Ben and I were married.

Nonetheless, even with that worry, it had never occurred to me that things would not happen as we had planned, or that I could actually become destitute until I picked up the weekly mail from the box at the end of the dirt road leading to the ranch house while LeAnn and Jake were gone.

I walked there during the heat of the day, leaving Trevor to play with Copper for the few minutes I would be gone since he didn't wanted to come with me. I understood his need to process what had happened in his own way since heartache was a very private thing, but it still frightened me. Children should not be left alone when they were as confused and frightened as he was, but there was nothing I could say that would make him feel better.

There was the usual assortment of monthly bills. My father had explained in detail how much money LeAnn was given each month to run the household and what bills had to come directly from the ranch's account. I had tried to convince him to modify his accounting practices so he could take advantage of more small business tax breaks, but he wasn't interested in changing anything. I wondered what would happen if I suggested the same thing to LeAnn, but it was much too soon to be thinking of doing that yet.

I was surprised to see a brown manilla envelop with my name written across the front in very familiar handwriting. Unless it was important, I had told Ben to keep all my mail until I came home. This was the first time he had forwarded anything to me, and it had been sent by overnight express. The letter inside had not been opened, and for that I was grateful because it was an overdraft notice from the bank telling me that my account was in the red. I hadn't returned the jeep to the airport, and rental charges had been withdrawn from my account at the end of every week since I had come home.

I sat down in the middle of the road and let the tears flow. How could I have been so obtuse? I was a business graduate. I knew all about compound interest and credit scores. I had even been smart enough to put overdraft protection on my bank account, but where would I come up with the amount I now owed? I couldn't ask Ben for it, and I didn't have a job. If father were still alive, I might have asked for his help. But I couldn't just take money out of the ranch's account to make up for my gross negligence when I was supposed to keep it afloat for Trevor.

Oh, what fun Jake would have if he found out. He already thought I was incompetent, and this would just prove he was right. My credit would be ruined if I couldn't fix the problem quickly, and I was in debt for the first time in my life.

But after my tears were spent, and I had called myself stupid for the twentieth time, I pulled myself to my feet and retraced my steps to the ranch house. If I ever needed God's help, it was now.

I hadn't even put the mail on the kitchen table when the phone rang. My fingers were cold when I placed the earpiece next to my cheek.

"Good morning, Brylee. This is Uncle Ned. I just had the strangest feeling that I needed to give you a call. Is everything all right?"

I choked back tears of gratitude for tender mercies in the face of adversity. In light of what we had all been through, Uncle Ned would not chastise me for overlooking the obvious. "I've done the stupidest thing, and I don't know how to resolve it."

"There! There!" he comforted. "Nothing is impossible if we take care of it together. Now, tell your Uncle Ned just what's bothering that pretty head of yours."

"It's my rental car. I forgot to return it to the branch office in Edna, and I owe the bank oodles of money I don't have. I can't even put it on a credit card because Ben and I decided it was best not to have one so we would not be tempted to buy things we couldn't afford or didn't need. I have been so dense! I should have taken the jeep back weeks ago."

"It's going to be all right," he said. "I've had plenty of dealings with rental companies over the years, especially since Molly went away to college. I swear that girl would forget her head if it wasn't attached. I will just call them and get the whole thing straightened out. They overcharge anyway, so quit worrying."

"But I wanted to order flowers from Trevor and me for Father's service and now I can't even do that."

"Have them charged to me for the time being."

"I can't do that, Uncle Ned."

"And why not? I know you're good for the money. And even if you aren't, I will just have you help Nora with all the painting she's been hounding me to do. It would be a small price to pay. I hate her redecorating projects, regardless of the fact that the end results are always worth the effort."

"I'll do it, Uncle Ned. All you have to do is tell me when."

"I know you will, but let's just take it one step at a time. I will call back as soon as I know something."

I thanked him profusely before hanging up my end of the conversation. God had come through for me again. How could I ever doubt his goodness and love? I went to my room, knelt down by my bed and offered a prayer of thanksgiving, but even as I rose to my feet, I felt the weight of responsibility descend on my shoulders again. I was destitute for a second time in my life. Uncle Ned might be able to help solve the problem with my rental, but what about all the other things I needed?

I felt incredibly exposed and vulnerable. I could use my father's illness as an excuse for not returning the jeep if I wanted to, but that didn't help with the other necessities of life. My toiletries were running out, and my clothes were becoming threadbare I had washed them so many times since coming home. And what about money for food and board? I couldn't expect LeAnn to take care of my expenses now that my father was gone.

There simply had to be some way to get back on my feet again financially, but until that happened, I would have to find a way to exist. Then, without conscious thought, I remembered the things I had left behind in the room that now belonging to Trevor. They might still be in the house. I had only brought my white sundress with me, and that was hardly appropriate for a funeral that was being conducted by Father Frederick.

I knocked on Trevor's door.

"Is it okay if I come in? There is something I need to ask you."

I heard the creak of the bedsprings as he got to his feet and crossed the carpeted floor to the wooden door that had many scratches running across its surface, some of which I had made myself.

He pulled it open, and I stepped into the room that still looked much as it had when I was a child—the same paint and furniture. Only the bedspread and curtains had been changed from frilly white to a more masculine brown and green print.

Trevor looked up at me with sad eyes, and then went back to the bed where he took Copper in his arms again. The puppy obviously knew something was wrong. Instead of being her frisky and playful self, she seemed perfectly content to sit quietly and occasionally lick his face.

"How's Copper doing today?" I asked him, not really knowing how to begin this particular conversation with him.

"She is tired and sad," Trevor replied. "She just wants to sit on the bed and do nothing."

"I guess we all feel a little like that." I replied, knowing that Trevor's remarks about the puppy's feelings were just a reflection of how he felt himself.

I sat down beside him on the bed and stroked Copper's soft hair.

"Have you been out to the shed today to check on your other animals?"

It was hard pretending that everything was okay when the weight of sorrow hung so heavily in the house, but for my little brother's sake, I had to try.

"We went out earlier. They are all sad and tired too."

"I can understand that. It is hard not having father in the house, isn't it?"

"The hardest," he said, as he wiped away the tears that had suddenly erupted. "Why did he have to die?"

"I'm not sure I can answer that, Trevor. He was very sick and in so much pain. Maybe God felt it was time for him to come home so he could be well and strong again."

"Is he well and strong again, Brylee? I wouldn't mind it so much if he was."

"I think he is, and I also think that he knows how much we miss him."

I was having trouble keeping my own tears in check, but maybe it didn't matter. Maybe Trevor needed to see that someone else was in as much pain as he was.

"You know, Trevor," I continued. "I have been doing a lot of crying myself, and I think I need to be held for just a little while. Do you think you could do that for me?"

He didn't even give me an answer. He just put his little arms around my neck and crawled onto my lap. We stayed that way for the longest time while I gently rocked him back and forth. It didn't exactly heal our wounds or take away any of the pain, but it certainly felt good to feel his heart beating next to mine and know that I wasn't as alone as I believed.

"I love you so much, Trevor," I finally said. "I can't believe how lucky I am to have you in my life. And if you ever need anything, all you have to do is ask."

It was exactly what Uncle Ned had said to me, but then that was the way it should be with families. They needed to rely on each other in both the good times and the bad. Maybe we were learning a crucial lesson about love and loyalty, even if it had to be the hard way.

He suddenly pulled away and kissed my cheek. "I love you too," he said.

I fought back a fresh onslaught of tears. Being told I was loved still moved me beyond belief it happened so rarely.

"I was just thinking that we could go on a scavenger hunt, if you wanted to."

"What's a scavenger hunt?" he asked, looking at me from beneath his long eyelashes.

"It's where you look for things on a list."

"What things?"

"In this case, the things I left behind when I went to the United States."

"Oh, those things."

He leaned back against the bed's headboard. "Mum boxed them up when we moved out here. I remember because I wanted to play with some of your toys, but she said we needed to save them in case you came back."

"Do you remember where she put them?" I asked, breathing a momentary sigh of relief since it appeared that they hadn't been thrown out or given away.

"Probably in that place where I am never allowed to go. That place where all the secret things are kept."

"You mean the attic?"

"I guess so. Mum keeps the key to that room in her jewelry box and told me never to take it without asking first."

His admission surprised me. The attic had not been the locked the day I had been left alone to amuse myself while everyone else went riding. Perhaps I should be more careful in my wanderings. The house was legally my stepmother's now.

"Do you think she would mind if I did? There are a few things I need to find from when I lived here before."

"I don't know," he said. "Why don't you just ask her?"

"Because she and your Uncle Jake went into town this morning, and I'm not sure when they will be back. It's going to take some time to find what I am looking for."

"Then I guess it would be okay since you are a grownup."

I wasn't sure he really believed what he was saying, but I needed something more appropriate to wear for the service that was to be held on Thursday morning, especially since I had been asked to say something.

Just thinking about going into the bedroom where my father had so recently died left a knot of misgiving and dread in my heart, but I couldn't ask Trevor to get the key for me. LeAnn would understand when I explained the situation, but there was no way I could tell her I was worse than broke. It would get back to Jake, and he would make my life even more unbearable than it already was.

My father had been a man of few words, but his presence was so strong in the master bedroom that when I opened the door I almost believed he was still there. The room itself looked just as it had when I had talked to him the day before, except that the bed had been made and the curtains closed. It hadn't occurred to me until then that LeAnn might not be able to sleep in the bed they had shared. Had she tried to rest on the sofa in the den without telling anyone? I had been in too much personal turmoil to give much thought to anyone other than myself.

"Are you're sure it's here?" I asked Trevor, but when I turned around he was still standing in door's threshold, unable or unwilling to go any further.

"I saw it there when mum was getting ready to leave."

"You saw her this morning?" I asked.

"Only for a moment. She didn't want me to come into the room because father isn't here anymore, but I couldn't help looking."

His lips were quivering, and I almost forgot about my mission to find something more appropriate to wear than my white sundress. What did I care about strangers coming to pay their last respects anyway? There was little doubt that many of them had negative opinions about me for running away. Edna was a very small town.

I might have left the room without the key if it hadn't been sitting on top of her jewelry box where Trevor said it was. It seemed an odd place to keep something like that, but perhaps she had visited the attic the night before to get something she needed too. I would return it before she got home, along with an apology for entering her bedroom without permission to get it.

The key turned easily in the lock, but my entering the attic this time was far different than when I found myself there simply because I had been left alone and was bored. The first thing I saw this time was the old treadle sewing machine my mother told me had once belonged to my great, great paternal grandmother. She had sewn all the clothing her family wore on it. The second was a white wicker baby carriage that had been handed down for several generations. I had taken my first stroll to the barn in it at my father's insistence.

I walked past the large trunk where everything my mother had brought with her when she married my father had been stored. I would go through it at some point when I was alone. Surely no one would take opposition to the fact that the things it contained now belonged to me. I could only hope there would be no unpleasantness when I asked if I could take a few small mementoes that had belonged to my father when I finally returned home to Ben.

There were old toys and dress forms, boxes filled with linens and crystal, faded newspapers, books and magazines, and trinkets I knew had belonged to my grandparents and all the greats. There was much to remind me of a past that had long been forgotten, but I would share everything I knew with Trevor before leaving.

He found our father's old tin soldiers and immediately collected them into his arms. I had tried to do the same thing as a child, but had been told by my mother that little girls did not play with boys toys. It hurt that he had gravitated to them so easily when I had been afraid to even pick them up.

"Do you think father would mind if I took these to my room to look at?" Trevor asked. "I would take really good care of them."

I wanted to tell him to wait until we could discuss it with his mother, but that seemed both cruel and unnecessary when they might be just the lifeline he needed to help him through a very difficult time.

"I'm sure he would want you to have them," I replied as the lump in my throat thickened. But Trevor didn't give me a chance to change my mind, and maybe it was better the way.

"I am going to put them the dresser right now," he responded, running towards the door that was supposed to stay locked. Copper followed him wagging her tail. It took so little to please him. How I wished it could always be like that.

After he left me alone, I spent a few minutes searching before locating the boxes labeled with my name. They contained few earthly possessions, but I was soon carrying my boom box, a clock radio and some of my favorite dolls, books and toys to the guest room where I was now sleeping. It made me wonder if my mother had packed away some of my baby clothes instead of giving them to a charitable cause. If I could find them, I wanted to take them with me when I went home to Ben. My own little girl could wear them when I had her one day.

The boxes containing my own clothing and shoes brought deep sighs of despair. Everything was dated and many items too worn out to wear, but I did find the black suit Aunt Nora had bought for me to wear to my mother's funeral. I hadn't taken it with me, even though it was new. I had wanted to leave all the sad reminders behind, but had soon learned that sorrow goes far beyond clothing and surroundings. It is something that begins deep in the heart and never completely goes away—even when other life events cause momentary gladness—like my meeting and falling in love with Ben.

I took a couple of boxes with me when I locked the attic door. It would be nice having a few additional items of clothing to wear. I doubted that anyone I would meet during the time I remained on the ranch would notice that they were more than a five years-old—except for my socially-minded cousin, Molly, who wouldn't really care what anyone was wearing as long as she was the center of attention.

I put the key back on LeAnn's jewelry box before heading to the den to see if Ben had answered the email I had sent the night before telling him of my father's passing. There had been no reason to suggest that he come for the short graveside service. It would be over before he got here, but I needed to know he was thinking about me, even if he couldn't be standing by my side.

His reply was sweet and dear. He told me how much he loved and missed me and how he wished he could there, but he knew that my inner strength would help me survive until we were together again. He also said that my name had been put on the prayer list at the Los Angeles Temple and that his family had sent flowers.

The only disturbing thing he brought up was that Jennifer, his high school sweetheart, had moved back to L.A. They'd had lunch together on two separate occasions—for old time's sake. She had been working as a legal assistant at a law firm in Salt Lake City before requesting a transfer to their hometown. I could only hope Ben was not the reason she had done it.

I decided to wait until after the service to respond. I needed time to determine just how I felt about his lunch dates with Jennifer before saying anything. I believed their meetings were innocent, but according to Jake, men had undeniable needs that couldn't be put on hold indefinitely. Just how long could any guy, even an amazing man like Ben, be separated from his girlfriend before old friends became romantic interests again?

Uncle Ned called while I was still trying to convince myself that Ben would not have said anything about Jennifer if he had something to hide.

"Just wanted you to know that everything has been resolved. The bloke at the rental office decided to refund last month's payment on the jeep so you will have $500 back in your account within the next 48 hours. But there is one catch, you have to return the jeep by the end of the week."

"I can't believe it," I said, as tears began swimming in my eyes making it hard to see the speckles of color on the linoleum floor beneath my feet. "You are a miracle worker."

"No, I'm just a bloke who has given them plenty of business over the years. Besides, he knew your father and was more than willing to work with us when I explained what had happened, but he still wants the jeep back. NJ is picking Molly up at the airport about noon tomorrow. You could drive into Edna in the morning, and he could swing by the rental agency to collect you. Would that work?"

"Absolutely," I said, as another wave of relief washed over me. "I can't thank you enough for taking care of this for me."

"Hey, I made a promise to your father. I am here for you, Brylee, and will be until the day I die."

His open show of love and charity made it hard for me to speak. "I love you, Uncle Ned."

"And I love you, Brylee. If there is anything else I can do all you have to do is ask."

"I will remember that," I said. "And thank you again. There is no way I can ever repay what you have done."

"I like to pay it forward once in a while. Your father taught me that. He was one of the most generous blokes in the outback, and you don't have to take my word for it. Just ask any of his neighbors."

Our conversation ended and I placed a call the florist who had been so generous with the flowers for my father's and LeAnn's wedding. He had chocked up when I talked to him earlier and told me he knew exactly what my father would like from his children—a flowering indoor plant that could be enjoyed long after he was gone.

I had wanted something more elegant to stand beside his casket, like daisies and chrysanthemums with greenery and baby's breath and a big ribbon that read, *With eternal love. Your children, Brylee and Trevor*, but I appreciated his honesty and went with his advice. Cut flowers would have difficulty staying alive for an entire day in all the heat even if the funeral was held in the morning. He was happy to send the bill to me instead of Uncle Ned and promised I would not be disappointed with what he selected if I could not come in to pick it out myself.

It was after five in the afternoon when Jake and LeAnn got back. They had been gone the entire day. I offered to fix them something to eat, but LeAnn said she wasn't hungry, and Jake said he had eaten in town. But they did sit down at the kitchen table and drink coffee while reviewing the highlights of their day.

Father Frederick had agreed to conduct the service, telling them that he was glad there would be a day or two to alert the congregation so they could be present if they felt so inclined. Although my father never attended mass or confession, he was a baptized member of the flock who always donated to service projects and activities when asked. He was also a respected member of the business community whose absence would be greatly felt.

Jake had arranged for the picture I had found and brief obituary notice I had written to be printed in Edna's only newspaper while LeAnn picked out flowers and took my father's suit to the cleaners. It had been necessary for them to wait until it was ready so it could be taken to the mortuary. They had remained in a room set aside for family members until he had been dressed for burial before flying back to the ranch.

"He looked so peaceful lying there in his suit and the shirt and tie you got him for our wedding," she said. "And when I leaned over to kiss him I almost believed he was going to kiss me back."

Jake cleared his throat, but LeAnn didn't seem to notice.

"I just can't believe he is gone," she continued. "This house is filled with his presence. If I had better eyesight, I think I could actually to see him sitting here at the table with us like he always did."

"Now, Lee," Jake scolded. "Don't beat yourself up like that. It's not going to bring Jack back."

"Maybe not, but it feels so real."

"You're not the only one who feels that way," I told her and heard Jake's snort of disapproval. "I believe the ones we love stay around for a period of time after they have passed. They want to make sure we are going to be okay."

"As if they could do anything about it," Jake muttered. "I miss Jack too, but he's gone, and we have to figure out how to do things without him."

I knew he was only trying to force reality, but it was too soon. We needed time to process our loss and the emotions that seemed almost impossible to deal with right now.

Aunt Nora called later that night to say that she'd had several calls from the women at church who wanted to help supply food for the wake that would be held after the interment.

That was something we hadn't discussed yet, and LeAnn was reluctant to agree until Aunt Nora assured her a wake was for the living, and she would be sorry one day if she didn't allow the people who cared about my father to pay their last respects. I remembered the one we'd had for my mother. I had stood on the sidelines hoping no one would talk to me. This one would be no different.

I lay in bed without sleeping most of that night thinking about my father and all the things we had missed doing together. I had no real memories of him except for the time we had spent together since I had come home. How could I write something to say at his service when I had so little to draw from? Most everyone already knew that we had never been close.

Chapter 11

I purposely got up early the next morning so I would not have to ask for permission to drive into town or run into Jake. He would have a field day knowing I had lost all the money I had left—and more—because I hadn't returned the jeep on time. The amount Uncle Ned had been able to get refunded was all that stood between me and living on the proverbial street. I would guard that carefully until I knew where my life was heading.

I also needed time alone with my father since I hadn't had that yet. I left a note on the kitchen table explaining where I was going and that I would be back early in the afternoon to help out with anything that needed to be done. There was no need to mention the jeep. My returning it would be abundantly clear when NJ and Molly brought me back to the ranch without it.

I arrived at Edna's only mortuary shortly before nine. I had pulled off to the side of the road to close my eyes for an hour or so since I had left the ranch before the sun came up to avoid another confrontation and had slept very little the night before. Decisions about my future had been swirling around in my head incessantly since my father's passing. Some of them would come about naturally, others would be forced, but there was no way I could adequately prepare for any of them.

Since I needed guidance no one in my family could give, I decided to call Ben. At least my cell phone still worked since we had put the contract in both of our names when we became engaged, and he was paying the bill. It was late evening in L.A., and he should be home. But he didn't answer the phone when it rang and after a few seconds it went to voice mail. There was nothing I could do but leave him a message.

"Hi, honey," I said. "I was hoping you would answer because I really need to talk to you. I can't believe my father is gone. I drove into Edna so I could say goodbye since I haven't been able to do that yet. The funeral will be held on Thursday at ten. There will be a wake afterwards. I know that's a little foreign to how things are done in the church, but no one I have met since coming back seems the least bit interested in what I believe or how I feel. I know I should have no regrets because we were able to make amends, but I feel very lost and alone right now. Anyway, I will be in town for the next three hours if you get this. I love you and miss you dreadfully."

It was true that I felt lost and alone. I also wished that Ben was here to comfort me, but I wasn't angry and filled with hate like I had been when my mother was taken from me and I wasn't planning to run away from anything. I had embraced most all of the people God had brought into my life because I knew it was the right thing to do. What I didn't know was which of the two lives I had been offered would be the one I ended up living—the one with Ben or the one with my family in Australia.

An older lady looked up at me from behind the stack of papers on her desk when I walked into the mortuary and let the door close softly behind me. After telling her who I was, she escorted me to a private viewing room where my father's casket had been displayed.

"Mr. Hawkins' has had a few visitors already. They signed the guest registry. Perhaps you would like to see it."

She motioned in the direction of a small pedestal table that had a thin book, a pen and a lamp attached to it.

"Thank you," I said as she walked away, but I didn't take time to read the names of people I wouldn't know. I had come to spend a few quiet moments with my father.

Complete sorrow and devastation took the air from my lungs as I looked down at his motionless face. The deep furrows on his brow and the lines around his mouth and eyes had almost disappeared, making him look more like I remembered him as a child. I wanted to put my arms around him and feel his love radiate until it took away the emptiness I felt inside. But such a gesture was futile, if not impossible. So I settled for placing my hand over his and just talking to him.

"I don't even know what to say," I began. "I'm confused and more than a little scared, and it's not just because you are gone. I feel like my life is falling apart, and my alternatives are drying up as rapidly as the morning dew on a Mulga tree. Ben's old girlfriend is back, and they have had lunch together a couple of times. I don't want to lose him because I am so far away, but I don't want to break my promise to you either. What am I supposed to do? When I ran away, I never thought I would want to come home to stay, but I am discovering that I have more roots here than I ever imagined possible. I really want to stick around and see the ranch prosper so Trevor can run it someday.

"But I also want to embrace the life Ben and I planned because I love him and will never have to be alone again. I know you weren't happy when I told you I had joined a new church, but how could I not accept what was being taught when it assured me that I can be part of a forever family? I want that so much and so does mother. I think that's what she meant when she asked you to give me that message. I have promised to do her temple work as soon as I possibly can, and

I am going to have Ben do yours—with LeAnn's permission of course—because I know that is what you will want as soon as you understand.

"I have no idea what that means for LeAnn and Trevor, but I will find a way to share the gospel with them, and I need you to promise that you will find our stubborn Hawkins' ancestors and make them listen. I can take care of all the work that is necessary here if you and mother can just help me locate the information I need. I know it can be done if we work together."

I wiped at the tears that were flowing down my cheeks in rivulets. It was a crazy way to say goodbye to my father, but it offered me hope that the separation between us now would only be temporary. His untimely death was just another part of the amazing, but difficult, journey of life that had been planned specifically for me by an eternal, loving Father. I just hoped I could finish what I wanted to start. I had never met anyone on my mother's side. I only knew that her maiden name was Olsen, and she had been born in Brisbane before moving to Edna as a child. That wasn't a whole lot to go on.

At least I still had Uncle Ned who could help me with Hawkins' family line. Certainly he knew something about his parents and grandparents, and if I could find the old family Bible it would contain many names and christening dates. That would be huge in trying to build a family tree, and the research could be done from anywhere now that literally millions of names had been entered into Family Search—a huge genealogical database. Besides, members of The Church of Jesus Christ of Latter-day Saints weren't the only ones who wanted to find out where they had come from. People all over the world wanted to check their DNA and connect with their ancestors. They already had the spirit of Elijah. They just didn't know it.

"Oh, my gosh!" I thought as the enormity of what I was planning to do washed over me like a cold shower on a hot summer day. I did have a reason for being here, and maybe my father's death was all part of the eternal plan to bring our family together in both this life and the next. It was a weighty responsibility, and there would be opposition. Satan would do anything within his power to keep people from coming to Christ.

I heard a footstep behind me and turned to see Brother Downing watching me. I had no idea how long he had been standing there.

"I didn't want to disturb you," he said, closing the distance between us with giant steps for he was a very tall man.

"How did you know I would be here?" I asked.

"I didn't," he said, extending his hand for a warm handshake.

"I don't understand," I replied as his fingers closed over mine. I hadn't been in the church long enough to fully comprehend how the Holy Ghost worked, or how people could recognize its promptings.

"Well," he continued. "I thought you had gone back to that young man of yours since you hadn't been back to church, but I was glancing through the paper last night and saw your father's obituary. I realized who he was and wanted to pay my respects. I didn't know I would be lucky enough to find you here."

"But you only met me once."

"We have a very small branch here, Brylee, and when someone new comes to church they become instant family. Is there anything I can do to help?"

"I think we have everything covered, but your coming here when you didn't even know my father means the world to me," I replied, once again realizing how much God's presence could be felt in my life even when I wasn't expecting it. "I was feeling very much alone."

"What about your fiancé? He is here with you, isn't he?"

"There wasn't time for the necessary arrangements. It happened very suddenly, even though we had been expecting it."

"That's understandable. You do have other family here?"

"I have an uncle and aunt and two cousins. I guess I also have a half-brother and a step-mother now."

"So they got married. I know how distressed you were about their living arrangements."

"I can't judge anyone, Brother Downing. My life certainly hasn't been without sin."

"Nor has mine! We just have to keep doing our best. That is all God requires. The atonement takes care of everything else, if we allow it to."

"I'm beginning to understand that," I replied. "Just like I am learning how much missionary work needs to be done if I want to be with my family again."

"Does that mean you are staying, at least for awhile?"

"I promised my father I' would help run the ranch for as long as I'm needed."

"That's a pretty big sacrifice for a young woman who is in love with a man thousands of miles away."

"And therein lies my greatest turmoil. I want my life with Ben more than anything, but I want to be here with my own family too. How do I make that decision? No matter which I choose, I will be giving up something important to me."

He smiled reassuringly. "If I had the answer to that I would be a multi-millionaire, probably even a billionaire. That is why we have to trust the Lord. He will send the answers we need when the time is right."

"But what if we don't recognize them? And what if we don't like the answers we are given?"

"That's where faith comes in, Brylee. We have to be ready to accept God's will, even if we don't understand it. He knows what we can eventually become. We have the tunnel vision of mortality and usually only see what we want to."

"But I want two things, and I don't want to give up either one."

"That's a tough place to be in alright, but I have learned over the years that things have a way of working out. Sometimes we just have to sit back and let God take charge. He will never guide us in a direction where we won't be happy."

"You're sure about that?" I questioned.

"As sure as I can be about anything. Our hearts tend to change when we are going in the right direction. I am not saying it is easy, but the rightness can be seen once the haze of confusion clears."

I thought a lot about Brother Downing's comment about hearts changing when one was headed in the right direction as I drove the streets of Edna to the rental car company near the small airport Jake used. Maybe I was over-thinking everything and not listening enough. I had always been guilty of that—even as a child—but how could I decide between two things I so desperately wanted? There simply had to be a way to combine both of my lives because I could not see myself ever giving up on either of them. One had what the other one lacked.

No one asked any questions when I returned the keys. The man working at the desk simply handed me a statement marked paid in full. The money for the previous month had already been returned to my checking account.

"Thank you," I told him.

He looked at me from over the top of his reading glasses. "It was our pleasure, Ms. Hawkins. I have worked with your father and uncle for many years and am very sorry for your loss."

"Thank you again," I said as I opened my purse and put the paper he had given me inside. Things like this would never happen in L.A. where the cost of living was high and most people didn't even know their neighbors. But everyone in Edna seemed to be part of the same big interconnected family. It was a small town thing, and I had forgotten how much I missed it.

It was twelve-thirty when NJ drove up in front of the rental office and nearly jumped out of his car.

"Hi, cuz," he said, once I had stepped through the glass door that had been tinted brown to help keep the hot rays of the sun out. Molly was looking in our direction and did not appear the least bit happy. Perhaps she was upset being summoned home in the middle of a school week. Nobody liked funerals, especially for family.

"I am really sorry about Uncle Jack," NJ continued, unexpectedly giving me a bear hug that only made the tears return. He was going to be just like his father when he got older—all cuddly, warm and toasty. Any woman would be lucky to get him. "He was a good bloke who was always there when I needed him."

"Thank you for saying that," I said, wishing the next few days were already over. I didn't like falling apart every time I saw someone who cared about my father, but I would never let grief drive me away again like it had after my mother's death. " And thank you for picking me up."

"My pleasure. You know I am here for you if you ever need me," he replied, holding the door open for me.

I touched his arm and looked up at his face. It was filled with kindness and concern. Why couldn't Jake be a little more like him? It would make what time I had left at the ranch far less threatening.

"I know you are, NJ, and I love you for it."

"Hey, don't say that too loudly," he countered. "I don't want to ruin my reputation with the ladies."

"And what reputation would that be, brother dear?" Molly asked as we both climbed into the fancy car Uncle Ned was helping him finance. "You're a nerd, and you know it."

"Even nerds have girlfriends!" he retorted. "Not all of us get through school with passing grades by showing a little too much cleavage."

"I hate you," Molly said, slumping down in the passenger seat without saying anything to me. She was incredibly lovely with her dark, auburn hair and creamy, white skin. I was starting to feel jealous of her all over again.

"Don't mind her," NJ said as he turned the key in the ignition. "She is just upset because her latest fling dumped her for some sleazy waitress who works at the club they are always at."

"That's not true, NJ, and you know it. Nate and I are just taking a little breather. We were getting way too serious, and neither of us were ready for that."

"You girls have it so much easier than we do," he told her as he pulled onto the street. "You just have to find some love-sick bloke who is willing to take care of you. We are the ones who end up working for the rest of our lives, whether we want to or not."

"Don't tell me that daddy has been giving you grief about settling down and moving back home. I can't imagine anything worse than living in the outback for the rest of my life. I want a rich bloke from the city to take care of me."

"It's not that bad," NJ replied. "In fact, I rather enjoyed wrestling sheep this past week. Manual labor keeps the body strong."

"Maybe it will keep your body strong, but not mine. I prefer to do my exercising in an upscale fitness club where I don't have to get all stinky, and the juice bar serves what I want."

It was almost refreshing to lean back and listen to my cousin's bicker. It reminded me that life goes on even in the face of tragedy and loss. They'd had a love-hate relationship for as long as I could remember. It was a bond no siblings could understand unless they were twins. At least that was what they always told me.

A few miles outside of town, Molly turned her head and looked at me.

"I am sorry about Uncle Jack, Brylee. You must think I'm the shallowest person on the planet talking about my guy troubles after what you have been through. But the truth is, I don't know what to say. I couldn't bear it if something happened to mum or daddy. Is the bloke you are going to marry coming for the service?"

I shook my head. "It all happened so suddenly there wasn't time to make any plans. He sent flowers."

Molly turned around again, and I leaned back against the headrest and closed my eyes. I hadn't even looked at the flowers that had been sent to the mortuary to see if his were there. I had been too preoccupied thinking about my father and decisions I did not want to make, but Ben should be here with me. If he was the man I was going to spend the rest of my life with I should have been able to ask him to come weeks ago, and he should have volunteered to come for the same reason. He hadn't even returned my call, and I had been in town for the promised three hours. What if he and Jennifer were on an actual date, and that was the reason he had not contacted me?

I couldn't believe how much I needed him right now. Molly had NJ and Uncle Ned had Aunt Nora. LeAnn had both Jake and Trevor. I was the only one who would be standing alone in the family graveyard on Thursday when my father's body was laid to rest. Life couldn't get much more lonely than that.

Jake was walking out of the bunkhouse smoking a cigarette when NJ pulled up in front of the ranch house. He looked like he had just climbed out of the shower. His dark hair was still damp and combed away from his face so his earrings were clearly visible. He was wearing a white, sleeveless undershirt, and I could see the long scab that had formed on his arm where he had caught it on something the second night we spent in the outback looking for sheep.

He threw his cigarette in the dirt and walked over to the driver's door just as NJ opened it and got out.

"It's good to see you again, mate," he told my cousin, giving him a manly hug. "What brings you over here today?"

"I do," Molly said, slamming the car door shut and pretending to shake wrinkles from her pale green, sleeveless sundress. After doing that, she smiled demurely up at him.

It was infuriating! Why did all the women around him think he was so wonderful? Maybe I was the only one who knew the truth about him. He could be just as ruthless as he was charming, and he had a mean streak a mile long.

"If it isn't the most beguiling, Ms. Hawkins," he said, giving her a toothy grin that made him look more like a predator than the pictures I had seen of dingo's stalking their prey. "It was good of you to come home for the service. It will mean a lot to both Trevor and LeAnn."

"How about you?" she asked. "Aren't you glad to see me too?"

"It's always a pleasure to see you, Molly. Have the blokes in Sydney been treating you okay?"

"They are just boys. I'm much more interested in a real man like you." She ran her finger lightly down his arm.

Jake appeared to be enjoying the attention.

"You've been hurt," she said as she took a closer look at the long, red wound that was starting to heal.

"Just a little run in with some undergrowth."

Her eyes filled with concern. "Did it hurt a lot? You are going to have a nasty scar."

"I'm used to it by now, and your cousin is a good nurse."

"Brylee was with you?" she asked.

"Of course she was, Molly," NJ responded. "The sheep won't herd themselves."

"You could have gone with him instead of Brylee," she pouted.

"I wasn't asked, and she did a bloody fine job for her first time."

Molly flicked her head just long enough for me to see a look I remembered from our childhood—a look of almost anger because I hd been in a place she wanted to be. I was glad I hadn't climbed out when she did. Despite her many social graces and incredible beauty, she had an insatiable need to be admired by men—all men—not just the ones she thought of as being interesting, dangerous or attractive. I was the exact opposite, and right now I just wanted to disappear.

"I would never have agreed to help round up all those nasty, smelly sheep," she told her brother after recapturing her momentary loss of composure. "It's not ladylike."

"You are the picture of perfection," he retorted. "I have never seen you break a sweat in your life."

"And I don't intent to start breaking one now, unless I am doing something far more entertaining than work. But I'm sure I could be just as good a nurse as Brylee." Her finger trailed along the healing wound again.

"I don't need a nurse any longer, but I appreciate your concern, Molly," Jake said, taking a step away from her. "And just for the record, I think you are still a little young for me."

"That's enough, sis," NJ said, moving quickly to her side and almost pushing her towards the house. "Jake isn't one of your schoolmates."

"But heis just so tantalizing," she sighed, looking over her shoulder and giving Jake another beguiling smile.

The inside of the car was getting hot since the AC had been turned off, but I didn't want to talk to Jake. I was hoping he would follow NJ and Molly into the house, but he just lit another cigarette and leaned back against the Dodge to smoke it.

I sat there for a couple of minutes longer, but the heat was beginning to make me sick, and beads of sweat were forming on my forehead. Besides, it was ridiculous to think he hadn't seen me through the tinted windows. He knew where I had been and when I supposed to be getting back.

"I was wondering how long you were going to sit there and make me wait," he said as I opened the back door and reluctantly climbed out.

"I was thinking," I told him, daring myself to glance in his direction without flinching. He could say whatever he wanted about my childish behavior. We'd already had that discussion numerous times in the past, and I would not change who I was simply because he thought I should be like every other woman he knew.

He blew an almost perfect smoke ring into the air.

"That's a lie, and you know it. You were trying to avoid me like you always do."

"Have it your way," I said. "But I do need to figure out what I am going to say at the service."

"Good on ya, but I figured you didn't want to own up about that jeep you rented. It must have cost a small fortune keeping it parked out here in the sun without using it. Wasting money isn't much of a recommendation for someone who is supposed to be so good at finances."

"It has been taken care of, so you needn't worry about it," I told him, not wanting to be the first one to look away. I could not afford to let him get the best of me again if I wanted to keep the promise I had made to my father.

"I wasn't worried, but I would have picked you in Edna any time you needed me to." He took another drag on his cigarette. "All you had to do was ask."

"I'll try to remember that," I said, wondering how he could be so condemning and yet so accommodating at the same time.

"You do know that neither one of us will be able to keep the promises we made to your father if we don't at least try to get along."

It had never dawned on me that my father would ask him to do anything besides be there for LeAnn and Trevor.

"What promises have you made?" I asked.

"Don't look so shocked. I have been here for years, and I knew him long before then."

I deliberately looked beyond his insinuation. "What does he want you to do?" I reiterated as the bile in my throat plummet downward until it hit my stomach.

"He asked me to look after LeAnn and Trevor naturally. Is that so hard to believe?"

"No! They're your family."

"So are you, indirectly." He threw his cigarette on the ground and put his hand lightly on my cheek before his index finger began traveling slowly down towards my neck.

I had never felt anything so sensual, yet so terrifying. I wanted to pull away, but something in his eyes held me mesmerized.

"You are a very beautiful woman, Brylee, and beautiful women need to be loved in just the right way."

"How do you know what I need?" I asked in a voice that was a little too husky.

"Because I have watched you grow from the scared little girl of your arrival into the strong-willed, independent woman you are today. Some men would find that threatening, but to me it is practically mesmerizing."

What was happening? I knew from the look in his eyes that this wasn't part of the game of wills we were always playing.

"Jake, I can't do this right now," I said, taking a step away from him and his electrifying touch. "I have just lost my father, and the man I intend to marry isn't here."

"I am fully aware of that, and maybe this isn't the best time, but it might be the only time you let your guard down enough to let someone else into your life."

"And you would take advantage of the situation knowing how vulnerable and lost I am right now?"

"I would never hurt you, Brylee. I just want to help you through this."

"Well, you aren't helping me by suggesting I hurt the man I love."

"I am not suggesting that you do anything you don't want to do, but you cannot tell me that you don't need and want someone to hold you, especially now."

"What I want and what I need are two very different things."

"So you do want to be held."

"Of course I do, but it would be a mistake."

"I'm not asking for a lifetime commitment, Brylee. I just want to give you a little comfort."

"And if it went farther than that, you wouldn't mind it at all."

"I can't say that thought hasn't crossed my mind."

"But it is wrong! I am not like you, Jake. When I make a commitment to someone I really mean it. I am going to marry Ben."

The intense desire to have his strong arms around me and feel his heart beating as rapidly as my own was beginning to consume me, but a hug could easily turn into something else. If only Ben had returned my call I wouldn't be feeling quite so needy, but I was terribly afraid that he was with Jennifer and might already be moving away from me in his heart.

"I am sorry, Jake. It isn't you, it's me."

I turned away from him and ran straight towards the house without looking back. The front door slammed shut behind me as I rushed blindly up the stairs to my room. I was both confused and frightened. How could I not have seen what was going on between Jake and me? We were attracted to each other, and all our fighting and name-calling was just a way to keep from admitting that truth.

But why was that revelation coming to a head now? I loved Ben. He was the best part of my life. He had shown me nothing but love and respect, and I believed God had brought him into my life to protect me from myself and because he could give me what I desired most—an eternal marriage and family.

Jake could bring me nothing but heartache. He knew exactly what most women wanted—what I had wanted before my innocence and dignity was stolen through sexual assault. But everything was different now . . . .

I lay down on my bed and closed my eyes.

"Please protect me, Father in Heaven." I silently prayed. "I don't want to lose what I have worked so hard to find."

Chapter 12

I must have fallen asleep for when I looked at the travel clock beside my bed it was six o'clock in the evening. I had been in my room for over two hours.

"This can't be happening," I told myself. "I promised LeAnn I would help her when I got back."

I swung my legs off the bed and plated my feet on the floor, but when I tried to stand the pain inside my head exploded. I was getting a migraine—one of those horrid headaches where bright lights flashed across my vision and even the ticking of the clock became magnified to an almost unbearable pounding in my temples.

Pushing my hands into my forehead, I sank back on the bed and tried to force the nausea away. There was so much to do, and I still hadn't figured out what I was going to say at my father's graveside service. I had to be prepared because LeAnn was counting on me.

Then I remembered that I still had a few of the pills Dr. Levens had prescribed when I'd had my first migraine nearly eight months ago. The missionaries had challenged me to be baptized, but while I believed they were honest, young men who really believed what they were teaching, I was having trouble accepting the Joseph Smith story. It seemed preposterous when I thought about it logically—a vision, a golden book buried in a hillside for centuries, and people who were willing to kill to get it. It sounded like a plot for an action movie, but when I had knelt down to ask God if it was true there had been such a burning in my heart that I couldn't deny it.

But that was when the migraines started. Every time I made an appointment with the missionaries to set a date for my baptism, the lights started to flash and the noise reduced me to tears.

I had talked to Ben about it. He said it was Satan's way of keeping me from coming to Christ, and I just needed to work through it. But he also gave me a Priesthood blessing where I was promised that the Lord had a great work for me to do within my own family, and I would have the strength and wisdom necessary to make it through any of the challenges that threatened my eternal exaltation.

I hadn't thought about that blessing for months. But as I lay alone on my bed with my eyes closed and my hands still pressed to my temples, I knew that God really did have something important for me to do. But if I did not make the right choices . . . .

My insane attraction to Jake was nothing more than one of the adversary's tactics to help me lose sight of what was most important in life. He had plenty of women to fill his needs. I would just be another notch in his belt of conquests if I gave in to what he was suggesting, and I had too much self-respect for that.

So I got off the bed and fumbled my way across the guest bedroom to the dresser. It took me a few moments to find the small bottle of pills and get the lid off but when I did, I put two of the tablets on the back of my tongue and swallowed. Amazingly, they went down without any water.

Then I retraced my steps to the bed and knelt down beside it. I prayed that my headache would go away, and I would know what to say at my father's service. It had to be something that fit with my beliefs and brought comfort without upsetting anyone who might be in attendance. In many ways, Catholics and members of the Church of Jesus Christ of Latter-day Saints were the only main Christian religions that still valued the traditional family. Every other church seemed to vacillate on doctrine if it meant more money in the coffers and more people in the congregation. That was certainly not the way God meant for it to be.

"You look like hell," Jake said when I walked into the kitchen a few minutes later to get some juice and soda crackers. So much for him wanting to comfort me in anything but a physical way.

"Thank you," I said, resting my hands on the kitchen counter. They were shaking, and I was afraid I might drop a glass if I reached up to get it.

I could feel him looking at me, and that made my head pound even harder. Why couldn't he have been in the bunkhouse instead of the kitchen?

He cleared his throat before speaking. "I wasn't trying to be mean, but you are white as a ghost. Are you sure everything is okay?"

"It's just a headache. I took something for it a few minutes ago. It should start taking effect soon."

But that wasn't what happened. Instead of starting to feel more in control, I felt the world reeling, and the next thing I knew I was lying on the floor. I could hear Jake moving towards me, along with the words he spoke, but there was no way I could move on my own or open my eyes. I even felt him cradle my head in his arms.

"You really know how to make a statement," he said as my eyes started to flutter after what may have been moments or even hours. I could feel his breath on my face and vaguely make out his form, but everything else was swimming so fast I closed my eyes again.

"What happened?" I heard LeAnn ask as the air moved around me again. "I heard the commotion clear from the master bedroom where I was trying to put a few things away."

"Brylee fainted—said her head hurts."

"This can't be happening, Jake. Carry her into the den. She shouldn't be left on the floor. Do you think we should call the hospital?"

"How the hell should I know," he replied. "She didn't hit her head or anything because I caught her as she went down."

His words drifted to me as I felt him slip one hand beneath my back and the other one behind my knees. Then he got to his feet, and I could feel my head resting against his chest as I listened to the thumping of his heart. I wanted to tell him to put me down but couldn't form the words, and then I was resting on the cool, leather sofa.

"Brylee, can you hear me?" LeAnn was asking.

I tried to nod my head, but reality was the last place I wanted to be. I liked the idea of floating way above the clouds where everything was sun-shiny and blue. My head didn't hurt. I had no worries, no responsibilities, and no hard decisions to make. But I knew I couldn't stay there, and with that realization I opened my eyes.

LeAnn was kneeling on the floor by the sofa, one hand brushing the hair from my forehead, and one holding my very limp hand.

"You nearly scared us to death," she was saying. "I couldn't bear it if something happened to you. I promised your father I would always look out for you."

What was happening? Four times since my father's death people had told me they had promised him to be there for me—

Uncle Ned, NJ, Jake and now LeAnn. Could it be that they really cared about me? During all the confusion and heartache had we somehow managed to bond? I really wanted to believe that I had finally come home.

"I'll be okay," I managed to whisper. "I don't know what happened. My headaches have never gotten this bad before."

"When was the last time you ate something?" she asked.

"Last night, I think. It's been a long day."

"I should have made sure everyone was eating," she scolded herself. "I was just so caught up in my own worries, I wasn't thinking like a mother. Has Trevor even eaten today, Jake?"

"A big bowl of cereal this morning and some mac and cheese for lunch. I fixed it myself so you wouldn't have to worry about feeding him when you have so many other things on your mind."

"Oh, Jake," she lamented. "I think I'm losing it."

He pulled her to her feet and into his arms. "Go ahead and cry, Lee. You have every right."

She buried her face in his white undershirt. "I have been trying so hard to be strong so I won't disappoint Jack and make things even harder for Trevor."

"You will only make things worse if you get sick like Brylee."

I wanted to protest, but it took too much effort so I closed my eyes again. I was back in the reality of the day, and on Thursday we were going to bury my father.

LeAnn opened a couple of cans of soup and heated them on the stove for dinner. I didn't know what had happened to NJ and Molly but could only assume they had gone home long before my fainting spell.

I could feel the medication starting to do its job, but I was still incredibly weak so she had Trevor bring my supper into what had once been our father's den.

"Are you really sick?" he asked, setting the tray containing soup, crackers and juice on the coffee table in front of the sofa. Copper had followed him and jumped up beside me. She was trying to nuzzle her head into my arms.

"I am doing much better," I told him. "And I can't thank you enough for bringing me something to eat. I think I was just overly hungry."

He simply stood there staring down at me, his brow wrinkly. He looked so much like our father, except for the coloring. Hawkins had dark hair and olive skin. Trevor was fair like his mother.

"I got scared when mum told me you were sick. You aren't going to die too, are you?"

"No," I said, forcing myself to sit up. "It was just a headache."

"Do you want me to rub it? I used to do that for father sometimes."

"That would be nice," I told him as he sat down on the back of the sofa behind me and placed his small hands on my forehead.

"Father liked me to rub his eyes like this." Trevor's fingers began pushing in a circular motion around the corners of my eyes. I just sat there and let him do it. The pressure wasn't hard enough to make much difference, but there was a world of healing in his touch.

We had both lost our father, but we had found each other. Like the famous writer, anonymous, once said, *there is always a silver lining if you look for it,* and that was exactly what Trevor had become to me—a silver lining at the end of a very dark tunnel.

I woke up the next morning to the sound of birds singing in the trees that grew not far from my bedroom window. I couldn't remember hearing them before, but my senses seemed heightened. Perhaps it was the illness I'd had the night before that made me so aware of how easily a body can be ravaged.

Standing in the sunlight coming in through the window blinds, I knew it was going to be another long, stressful and emotional day, but there was plenty of work to do, and that was a blessing. I wanted to help LeAnn make sure everything was ready for the service and wake that would be held in the living room the following day. But by the time I made it down the stairs to the main level of the house, I saw that she had already cleaned the entire area and gathered up all the chairs in the house—except for the ones we were using in the kitchen for meals.

I had to bite my knuckles to keep from crying when I walked past the door leading into the front room because it had been set up the same way it had been for the wedding, leaving plenty of room in front of the fireplace for the casket.

LeAnn was loading the dishwasher when the swinging door leading into the kitchen opened inward.

"I am sorry for sleeping so long," I told her as I sat down at the table. The clock on the wall said it was nearly ten in the morning. "I had every intention of getting up early so I could help you get things ready for tomorrow."

"It's okay, Brylee. You needed your rest. How are you feeling this morning? You gave us quite a scare yesterday."

"Much better, but it was a stupid thing to do. How can someone forget to eat?"

"I suppose it's easy when the mind is occupied with other things. Jake wouldn't leave the kitchen this morning until both Trevor and I had eaten something."

"Where is my little brother?"

"Jake took him over to Ned's in the truck to pick up plastic silverware and paper plates and cups so there won't be much cleanup tomorrow. Your Uncle Ned even arranged for a cask of beer to be delivered along with the flowers."

"That was nice of him," I said.

A wake seemed such a strange ritual now. What was so healing about standing around and getting drunk while swapping stories about all the escapades one could remember about the deceased? I much preferred the Latter-day Saint way —a beautiful, calm service in a ward building, with a viewing the night before and a luncheon for family and friends after the interment. There was no weeping and wailing and lavish ceremony like in some other churches. I had learned that much when attending Ben's grandmother's funeral a month before we became engaged.

I liked how the family all sat together after eating and shared fond memories, but I mostly liked the idea that death was not the end. It was simply a passageway to the next phase of living. I wanted so much for my new family to learn that we could be together again, but not without effort like Father Xavier claimed when I attended daily mass—a requirement of Catholic Boarding Schools most everywhere.

He always assured his congregation that going to confession and admitting sins, even on the deathbed, would assure them a place in heaven. But being saved was not something I had understood before leaving my old beliefs behind. I now understood that it take more than just a pardoning of sins to make it back to our Heavenly Father. It takes a great deal of work, patience and faith. I just hoped I could make it through the day of the service and wake with an open mind so I wouldn't offend anyone.

I contemplated what I was going to say at my father's service all afternoon but couldn't come up with anything concrete. I even found the old family Bible on a shelf in the den, but it wasn't much help when it came to learning more about his life, except for recording his christening date. Still, there were other names and dates that would help me later on when I tried to construct a family tree. The last notation was my own christening date.

"Have you figured out what you are going to say tomorrow?" LeAnn asked me when I joined Trevor and her for dinner early that evening. The table had been set for three. Apparently Jake would not be joining us.

I must have looked either confused or relieved.

"Jake flew into town," she said as she placed a crock-pot filled with meat and vegetables on the table and sat down with us. "He said he needed a break."

"I wanted to go with him," Trevor volunteered. "But mum said he had grownup things to do."

I didn't want to think about the grownup things he might be doing. There were plenty of girls in Edna like Janet and Beth who would be more than happy to comfort him, whether he needed it or not.

"Your mother's right," I said. "Your uncle Jake needs his own space."

"But why?" Trevor asked. "He likes being with us."

"Most certainly, he does," LeAnn told him, giving me a conspirator's wink that I chose to ignore. "Someday you will understand."

"You mean girls," he said.

"Yes, my darling, girls. Someday they won't seem quite so dreadful, will they, Brylee?"

"I'm sure they won't," I responded. All this talk about Jake and his female admirers was making me feel nauseous again, so I turned my attention to my little brother. I had allowed my own problems to consume me for the past two days without thinking of the burden he carried.

"I might not be able to entice you with a plane ride, Trevor," I said, trying to assuage my guilty conscience. "But maybe we could take Copper for a walk after we eat."

"I can't," he said. "I promised mum we would play games after supper, but you could join with us if you want to." He looked to his mother for approval.

"Most certainly Brylee can play with us, but she might need more time to prepare. I asked her to say something at your father's service tomorrow."

"Can I say something too?" he asked.

LeAnn smiled at me and then looked fondly at her son. "I think your father would like that, but there will be a lot of people—even more than there were at the wedding."

"Oh," he said, slumping down in his chair. "I thought it was just going to be us."

"It will be us, but your father had a lot of friends. We don't know who might want to come and pay their respects."

He looked at me for clarification, but I didn't know what to say about people coming to pay their respects. It was quite apparent he had never been to a funeral before.

"What would you want to tell other people about our father?" I suddenly asked without really knowing why.

He gave me a very thoughtful smile. "I would tell them that he was big and strong and brave and he took me everywhere with him. I got to ride horses and four-wheelers and take care of animals and go places with him in the Land Rover."

Suddenly, he quite talking and buried his face in his arms. The sound of him crying tore at my heart. I should never have asked him such a difficult question.

"I'm sorry," I whispered to LeAnn.

"It's okay," she responded. "He needs to cry."

She rose to her feet and walked around the table to where Trevor was sitting. When he felt her near, he climbed into her arms and buried his face in her neck.

I had never felt more awful. I should have known that talking about our father would upset Trevor, especially since he didn't understand things the way grownups did. But after a short time he quit crying and excused himself from the table. LeAnn let him go.

"I'm so sorry," I told her again after he had left the room. "I thought it might help for him to talk about father."

"I'm sure it did, but this is the first time he has really cried since it happened. It isn't good for him to keep everything bottled up inside."

Her words were meant to be reassuring, but I still felt hopelessly angry with myself for not being more insightful. I loved my little brother so much and hated the fact that I could only learn to relate to him through trail and error. There were no how-to manuals for complex relationships, especially for a family as mixed up as we were.

Chapter 13

I dreaded the coming of morning, but it arrived anyway. I was no closer to knowing what I was going to say at my father's funeral than I had been the night before when asking Trevor what he would say if he spoke to the people who were going to be there.

After a quick shower, I returned to my room to apply some makeup—that would only come off in the heat of the day—and curl my hair. The black suit I had worn to my mother's funeral had been hanging in the closet for the past two days, and when I took it out to get dressed I noticed that most of the wrinkles had fallen out on their own so it wouldn't need to be ironed.

I held it up in front of me without taking it off the hanger. The skirt had a slit up the right side that made walking in it easier, and the jacket had a V-shaped neckline with lapels, long sleeves and a fitted bodice. It was made of a lightweight fabric. Otherwise, it would have been too hot to wear.

But even though I knew it enhanced my figure and other people told me I looked good in it, the thought of having to put it on again made the tears fall. Once this day was over, I would put it back in the attic where I would never have to see it again.

The house appeared to be silent, and I couldn't understand why. On this of all days, people should be up early, but how could I have negative feelings towards anyone who might be getting a little extra rest just because I hadn't been able to sleep? Throughout the long night, my mind had replayed every interaction I'd had with my father since coming home. Our differences had been resolved, but that would never be enough.

As long as his body was still in Edna, we could all pretend that things really were not as bad as they felt. But once he was laid to rest, there would be no denying that life, as we had all known it, was over for good.

I would be a woman without a home, relying on the generosity of a family I barely knew for sustenance until I went back to Ben. No matter how I looked at it, I was stuck in a place no one should have to be in. How I wished Ben were here. I needed to know that our life together was still real. If it wasn't? Well, I couldn't think about that now, or I would never survive the day.

I heard a car door slam shut, then the squeaking of the hinges on the kitchen door. The day I had dreaded for over two months had begun.

On my way down the stairs, I heard Aunt Nora's voice in the kitchen.

"How are you holding up this morning, LeAnn? I can't imagine how hard this must be for you. I just wish I had something comforting to say."

"Your being here is comfort enough, Nora," she said. "We're family, and we have to stick together."

I braced myself against the staircase wall wishing I could avoid the entire ordeal, but I couldn't feign another migraine, even though people might actually believe I was having another one.

"Put those things on the counter," Aunt Nora said as the back door slammed shut again and my foot found its way to the next stair.

The table in the dining room had been polished, and a bouquet of flowers sat in its center. Stacks of paper plates, cups and napkins were sitting on one end along with an assortment of plastic cutlery. I wondered why so much care had been taken when only family and a few close friends would be attending the service and wake. Someone had even taken the chairs from the kitchen and put them in the living room facing away from the baby grand piano. I wondered where Trevor was. He hadn't seen our father yet.

I stood at the bottom of the stairs not knowing which way to turn. If I went into the kitchen I would have to accept what was happening. If I tried to run away, there was no place to go. And if I went back up the staircase, I would just have to come down again.

The choice was made for me when Trevor walked through the front door. He was dressed in black pants and the white shirt I had gotten him for the wedding. His hair had been brushed neatly down instead of standing up just a little in the front like it usually did. We had the same cowlick only mine wasn't so noticeable because I was a girl.

"A big, black car is coming up the driveway," he said, when he saw me standing immobile with my hand clutching the banister. I could tell from his expression that he was scared but a little excited too. Very little company came to the ranch and it was always enticing, even if it brought something bad with it.

I just stood there looking at him while the growing discomfort in my stomach became so large I could hardly get enough air into my lungs to facilitate breathing.

"Maybe we should go into the kitchen," I finally said. "I'm sure your mother has something she needs us to do."

I reached out to take his arm, but he stepped away from me. "What about the car?" he asked.

"Has your mother explained what is happening today?" I asked, wishing with all my heart that I wouldn't end up being the one with him when he finally understood that our father's body was in the car, and he would never be able to speak to us again.

"She said people would be here to pay their respects to father. Then we would all go for a walk to the graveyard where our grandparents are buried. After that, we would have sort of a party."

I bit my lip and tried to understand why LeAnn had been so vague about the day's proceedings with Trevor. Didn't he know that his father would be lying in a casket? And the walk to the family cemetery would be anything but pleasant. I wasn't a mother, but if Trevor were my son, I would have prepared him so much better.

Uncle Ned came running up the steps. I heard his feet pounding across the veranda before he pulled open the front door. When he saw both Trevor and me standing in the entry, his concern was obvious.

"I think it would be best if you took Trevor into the kitchen with the others. I'm sure Nora and Molly could use some help with the food."

He was doing what I had been able to, assuring Trevor in a very firm way that it was best for him to be away from what was happening now, even though I knew my little brother was more curious than ever about the big, black car that was now parked in front of the house.

"Come on, Trevor," I said, gently taking his arm so he would not became scared. "Let's see what everyone is up to."

LeAnn was standing in front of the stove, looking as if she had no idea what she should be doing. Aunt Nora was placing a large bowl covered with tin foil in the refrigerator, and Molly was standing with her hands on her hips in front of a small mountain of Aunt Nora's homemade rolls.

"Hey, little cousin," she said to Trevor. "How about you and I sneak a fresh roll with some peach jam. I'm kinda hungry, and I bet you are too. You could show me your new puppy while we are eating them."

Without waiting for his reply, she cut two rolls in half and generously applied both butter and jam. Trevor watched her, a look of confusion on his face. Apparently, he wasn't used to having so much interaction with his much-older cousin, but he didn't refuse or complain. She was able to whisk him up the stairs before Uncle Ned had time to return to the house with the mortician and the casket.

"I think Molly is going to be a great mother someday," Aunt Nora said. "She claims to hate kids, but she is really good with them."

"I'm glad she was able to come," LeAnn said. "Trevor is going to need a lot of diversion. There is just so much he doesn't understand."

I was going to ask her exactly how much she had told Trevor about what was going to happen today when I heard Uncle Ned swear.

"They must be having problems," Aunt Nora said, dropping a hand towel onto the countertop. I followed her back into the entry hall. Uncle Ned had a carpenter's measuring tape in his hands.

"What's all the fuss about?" she asked him.

"It's this damned, bloody door," he told her. "I was hoping we could get the casket through without having to take it off its hinges, but the handles stick out too far. Why does an inch have to be so much trouble? Jake is on his way to the shed for some tools."

I walked over to the doorway and peered around Uncle Ned to see what was going on outside. The mortician's helper was leaning against the front of the hearse smoking a cigarette. I wondered what kind of a man could be in the funeral business. There was definitely job security, but watching death and sorrow on a daily basis while dealing with distraught families sounded just plain morbid to me.

I stepped back into the cool hallway when Jake ran up with an electric screwdriver and an extension cord in his hands.

"I'll do that," Uncle Ned told him.

But Jake just brushed his hand away, and I wondered how he could be so rude considering the day.

"There is no sense in both of us getting overheated," was all he gave as an explanation.

Overheated was an understatement! It must be a hundred degrees outside already, and it was only a little after eight-thirty in the morning.

The next few hours were nothing more than a blur of faces, colors and emotions. Jake got the front door taken off its hinges and then helped Uncle Ned, NJ, the undertaker and his assistant carry the casket into the living room where it was placed on an expanding metal base so it would be the right height for viewing.

The mortician's wife, the woman I had talked to in the foyer of the mortuary, brought the flowers and plants in a small air-conditioned van.

LeAnn had chosen chrysanthemums in shades of brown and gold for the spray that lay on the casket. The potted, flowering plant I ordered ended up being something big and tropical with bright orange blooms, but the florist said it would thrive with a little sunshine and water. There were flowers from the church congregation, Uncle Ned and his family, the auction yard where the sheep had been taken only a few days earlier, the city council, my church branch in Edna, a few from individual friends and a stunning bouquet of yellow and white roses from Ben and his family.

How I wished he could be with me today, but he would find the service strange and have no idea what to say to any member of my family. I was grateful I had been given time to know them on a different level before my father's passing. If I hadn't, I might have lived my entire life not understanding how intricately our lives had been woven together as part of God's plan.

Trevor hung back when LeAnn took his hand and led him to the casket. He looked so small and scared and helpless, and the top of his head was barely higher than the opening. He couldn't see in on his own, so Jake picked him up while LeAnn encouraged him to look at his father. It was more than a tender moment when Trevor placed one of our father's tin soldiers next to his hands and then turned away. I knew this was the defining moment of their relationship. They loved each other, and not even death could destroy that.

Oh, how my heart ached for him. I wanted to hold him in my arms and shield him from the awful truth of knowing that he would never see his father again in this life, and he would have to learn from others how to take care of the legacy he had been given. But then Father Frederick arrived with a dozen or more of his parishioners and the moment was over. I had no idea who any of them were but they were genial and kind, especially to LeAnn whose tears had been held in check all morning and started flowing like water that had been let out of a dam. She accepted condolences in between wiping her eyes and blowing her nose.

The funeral director informed me that I needed to be standing next to my stepmother as we greeted the people who came to pay their last respects. I did as he asked without protest. Trevor held my hand tightly the entire time.

In all, there were less than thirty people who walked towards the small cemetery where several of Uncle Ned's hired hands had just finished digging the grave. They were wiping their brows with handkerchiefs and leaning on the handles of their shovels in the shade of the only tree in the enclosure when the rusty-hinged gate was pushed open so the funeral party could enter. Heavy straps had been placed across the opening in the earth, and I could see a metal crank that would be used to lower the casket into the ground once the family had gone.

All the words I had thought about saying went flying from my head as I looked around the small company of people standing there in the hot morning sun. The women wore crucifixes around their necks and fingered them while I spoke.

It was a surreal situation. I wanted to tell everyone about the Plan of Salvation and the redemption of all mankind, but that was impossible with Father Frederick standing there in his fine robes and jeweled crucifix. No one would understand what I was saying, and they would only think—as my own father had done at first—that I had joined some religious cult and needed to be exorcised so my soul would not be lost forever.

So I talked about the ranch and the oldies that had settled there. I talked about the new family I had found, and the old one I had been reunited with. I talked about my father's dreams for the future and how each one of us had been assigned a particular task. I talked about the family reunion we would all have one day. And then the tears started to fall, and I couldn't say anything more.

NJ stepped from the circle and put his arm around my shoulders while Father Frederick asked if there was anyone else who wanted to say something. When no one volunteered, he began my father's last rites.

While he was doing that, I looked around at the people who were standing closest to the casket. Uncle Ned and Aunt Nora were both crying. He had his arm around her waist, and Molly was clinging tightly to his other arm. Jake had one arm around LeAnn and was holding Trevor in the other. I was glad Trevor had him. Jake could never take the place of our father, but my little brother needed him, and that was good enough for me. When I went back home to Ben, he would have people around to help him adjust and learn how to be the kind of man my father was.

And then the service was over. Each of us took a handful of soil and dropped it onto the casket as we said our final goodbyes. Rationally and even spiritually, I knew things had turned out the way they were supposed to, but emotionally, my heart was still asking why something could not have been done to save both of my parents. I didn't want to be an orphan, even an old one. I wanted my parents to dance at my wedding reception and be there when my babies were born, but life would never be like that for me. Death had seen to that.

When we got back to the house, several of the ladies from the parish had already set the food out on the dining room table, and the large container of beer with its spigot was sitting on a small table close to the front door where it could be easily changed and accessed. It wasn't even noon yet, but I knew that wouldn't matter to the people who were there.

Both Janet and Beth were waiting for Jake on the veranda. They hadn't made it for the service—perhaps it was too early in the day for them—but they both had glasses of beer in their hands. I couldn't help but wonder which one of them he had chosen to be with the night before. Certainly that had to spawn rivalry, but they were acting like best friends.

"It is just so sad," Janet said, putting her hand affectionately on his arm the moment he was close enough to hear. "I still can't believe Jack will never be flying into the airport with you again. He was such a good man."

"He was the best," Beth from the diner said, reaching for his other arm. If Jake was uncomfortable, he didn't let it show. But then he was used to having women fawn over him. "I baked his favorite chocolate cake for today even though he won't be able to eat it."

She broke into tears, and Janet reached around Jake to put a comforting hand on her arm.

It was an odd scene since I knew both of them were interested in Jake, but maybe they were just practicing the wisdom of keeping your friends close and your enemies even closer.

I left Jake in their capable hands and went inside with the rest of the mourners without saying a word to any of them. Work was always a blessing when one didn't know what else to do, so I went directly to the kitchen to see if I could help.

The church ladies told me they had everything under control, and I should be with family so I returned to the living room and sat down on the bench in front of my mother's baby grand piano. I ran my fingers lightly over the ivory keys being careful not to make any sound while people filled their plates with mutton, pork, potatoes, casseroles, salads, rolls and cake. Once that was done, everyone gravitated to a frothy glass of beer.

Several other men had arrived, and I learned while listening that two of them were from the stockyard in Edna. Then of course, there was Buck Henry and his wife who had chosen to join him for a funeral after being too ill to attend a wedding.

Trevor was sitting in a corner of the room picking pieces of lamb off his plate and feeding them to Copper. I hoped the little puppy's stomach could tolerate the added grease. My little brother looked sad, confused and lonely, but he hadn't cried all day. I knew his time would come, and when it did, I would be there to help him through his misery. There would not be another blunder like the one I had made the night before.

Aunt Nora and LeAnn were talking to some of the church ladies, and Uncle Ned and NJ had joined a conversation about ranching that was becoming louder with each glass of neck oil consumed.

I looked out through the window to the veranda where Molly had joined Jake and the two girls from town. They were all laughing and putting a frothy cold one to their lips whenever they were not speaking. It made me feel more like an outsider than ever.

Who were all of these people who had likely never been to the ranch before? How many of them were actually friends, and how many had just come because it seemed like the right thing to do? If only Ben were here, I wouldn't feel like the world was closing in on me. I had nothing to say to any of them, and I had never mastered the art of polite social conversation, despite my mother's efforts at home and the class on decorum I had been forced to take while attending boarding school.

When I saw Father Frederick heading my way, I maneuvered myself around the edge of the gathering before he could ask me about going to confession or attending mass. I didn't want to lie, so I went into the den, closed the door and turned the computer on. The good father would not be bold enough to follow me there. Then I waited for it to boot up before opening my email account to see if Ben had written.

"Hi, honey," I read as I opened the small envelope next to his name. *"I'm so sorry I wasn't home when you called, but Jennifer and I went to a movie. Nothing great, but it helped pass the time."*

I felt my cheeks grow hot. He had been out on a date when I needed to talk to him about my father.

"I know what you're thinking, but you don't have to worry," he continued. *"It wasn't a date. Jennifer and I are just very good friends. Heck, we grew up together, so she's more like family than anything else.*

"I wish I could be there with you, but it happened so fast. You'll probably be getting ready for the service when you read this. I hope you can feel my love from across so many miles. I think about you all the time and hope the flowers got there. I picked ones just for you. Yellow roses because they remind me of the sunlight you bring into my life even when

*it's cloudy outdoors, and white ones because of the purity I see
every time I look into your eyes.*

*"I can't wait for you to come home. We have so much to
look forward to. My job is going well, and I have been able to
put aside more money that I anticipated. Of course, it helps
that I am still living at home, and we won't have to pay for a
separate apartment until you get back. I want to get married
as soon as we possibly can after that. No more long
engagement, just enough time to set a date at the temple. I
have already asked Brother Young if he will do the sealing.
Just let me know what day you will be arriving, and I'll get all
the details worked out on my end.*

*"I want to be your husband and hold you in my arms all
night long. I want to kiss your lips and have all those children
we talked about. It's hard watching all of our friends make
their big announcements. We any luck, we'll be doing that
ourselves in the next few months. How great is that going to
be?*

*"The family sends their love. Always know that you are in
our thoughts and prayers. You are a strong lady, and I know
you will make it through this time of bereavement. Just rely
on Heavenly Father. He can comfort any pain, but then I'm
sure you know that just as I do. Be safe and know that I love
you with all my heart, Ben."*

So that was it! Ben was sorry he couldn't be with me, but
he knew I was strong enough to make it through anything. And
what was he doing while I was in so much pain burying my
father? Going on a non-date with his high school sweetheart. I
had to get home and fast before he was no longer there waiting
for me.

I put my head down on the desk and started to cry. Life
simply wasn't fair! Why couldn't I have just come home for two
weeks like planned? I had felt so safe, secure and confident
about where my life was heading when I had stepped on that
plane nine weeks earlier, and now I was faced with two life-

altering choices—staying here while Bed married someone else, or going home and losing the family I had just discovered and the ranch my father wanted me to help keep in the family.

It was an awful situation? No matter how I sliced or diced it, one part of my life would be over for good as soon as I chose the other. Could this day possibly get any worse?

As if in answer to my question the door opened, and LeAnn stuck her head into the room. Her eyes were red-rimmed but dry.

"I was wondering where you had disappeared to. You really should come out and eat something. We don't want a replay of your headache."

"I'm feeling much better today," I told her. "And I promise to eat something soon. How are you doing?"

"Hanging in there! I just have to keep reminding myself that Jack isn't in pain any longer, and these people really cared about him, or they wouldn't have driven all this way to pay their respects. That should make me feel better, but it doesn't. I just want him to walk into this room so I can hold him in my arms again. That must sound very selfish to you."

"It's not selfish, LeAnn. I keep wishing for the same thing. It's because we love and miss him so much."

"We're quite a pair, aren't we?" she asked, dabbing at the inside corners of her eyes. "Father Frederick said I shouldn't be angry with God for taking Jack away, but I can't help it. He was my life, and I don't know how I will ever be able to go on without him. All I want to do is crawl into bed and never leave. I know that's not healthy or right, but it's how I feel."

"I think we are all pretty much in a fog, and I hate having people I don't even know tell me that time will heal. I'm not sure I believe that, but you have a son who needs you very much. That should give you some comfort, even if it doesn't seem like quite enough right now."

She looked at me blankly for a moment or two. "How can I be of any help to Trevor when I can't even deal with my own pain?"

I wasn't sure I had the right answer, but I told her what I thought she should do anyway. "You just hold him in your arms, let him cry, and tell him how much you love him."

"That's not going to do much good when what he really needs and wants is his father. They had this amazing connection, and I can't make it go away just because it might be easier for him."

"I suppose that's true, but he seems fond of Jake. Maybe that will help a little."

She sighed as she looked at the family picture I had framed for them after the wedding. "My brother's great, but he's not Jack!"

I couldn't agree with her more. Jake was headstrong and unpredictable. He might come through in a pinch, but I wasn't sure anyone should count on him longterm. My father was solid regardless of his indiscretions. I doubted he had ever been intentionally cruel to anyone, even to my mother when she had confronted him about his affair with LeAnn and the baby that had come as a result. That old familiar pain of losing her came rushing back. If I didn't stop it now, I would never be able to make it through the rest of the day.

"I saw Buck Henry. Do you think he just came to pay his respects? I noticed that his wife was with him this time."

I didn't like the man, and I certainly didn't trust him. But maybe that was just how most people felt about lawyers until they were needed.

"He's known your father since long before I did," LeAnn said. "So yes, he is here to pay his respects, but he also wants to go over your father's will. He said it would be a good time since everyone involved is already be here."

"Is that really necessary, today of all days?" I asked.

Suddenly, I was angry. How could this smug, unimpressionable man who claimed to be my father's friend suggest doing something for his own convenience rather than considering the needs of the family during their time of mourning? It was as if he just wanted to close his books on a client and get his portion of whatever my father had promised him. It was a totally reprehensible and unprincipled thing to do.

"I suppose he could come back at a different time, but it seemed to make sense when he suggested it," LeAnn said. "Nothing he says will bring your father back."

"But we already know Trevor is his heir."

I was more than angry now. I was furious and on the verge of a verbal explosion that could hurt everyone, especially myself. Why should I be forced to deal with my father's will on the day of his burial just because it was more convenient for Buck Henry? Yes, I had run away, but I was still his daughter. And even if he had left everything to my little brother, this was still my home until the final pronouncement was made. Maybe this was what Jake had been counting on all along, and Buck Henry was simply facilitating his desire.

"Your father talked to his attorney after you came back," LeAnn said, and I felt a sudden chill. "I don't know what transpired, but I do know that we need to honor whatever decisions he made, whether we like them or not."

My emotions were all over the place like a mad woman's breakfast. What if my father had made some changes they didn't like? We were family because of the wedding, but I was still the prodigal returned home. Did anyone really want me here now, except for Trevor? He was too young to know about jealousy and the concept of power and money. They were things people coveted in adulthood, but they seldom affected children.

LeAnn just stood in the doorway watching me. I was being irrational, I knew that, but who could really blame me? I wasn't part of the inner circle that had been in place for more years than I cared to remember, and I had no knowledge of what my father's will contained, except for what he ha already told me. Trevor was his heir. Not even my unexpected return would have changed that.

"Don't look so worried, Brylee," she continued. "I'm as much in the dark as you are. I have never even seen his will. All I can go by is what your father always told Trevor, that he needed to learn everything he could because someday this ranch would be his, if he wanted it. There was never any thought that he might not live to see his son grow up and inherit what is rightfully his."

"Rightfully his?"

The words screamed in my ears. What was right about any of this? My father was still a young man with a full life to live, and I had just come home. Maybe the ranch was never meant to be mine, but that didn't stop me from wanting to be included. I was every bit as much my father's child as Trevor was. It shouldn't matter who our mothers were, and whether he had loved one more than the other.

"I'm not worried, LeAnn. I am just afraid that we will never be able to teach Trevor what he needs to know when we are so ill-informed ourselves. And even with the best intentions wills have a way of changing things."

"Not for us, but we still have a long time before Trevor is ready to make decisions for himself," she said. "I don't have a head for business. I never have. That is why your father was so excited when he found out what you studied in college. He knew he could trust you with the financial end of the business while protecting all of our interests."

Her vote of confidence brought me back to a semblance of reality and humility. I had no claims on anything, and neither did Trevor, unless it was what our father desired. If he still wanted me to stay on and help out, I would. But it wasn't going to be easy if I had nothing but his wish to back me up.

"Father expects all of us to work together as a family," I finally responded, more befuddled than ever about what was going to happen before this day was over.

I was no longer even upset with my father for cheating on my mother. I now understood why he had done it, but I could not pretend that his decision didn't have repercussions. Even Uncle Ned had to be concerned about what was going to happen. He was part of the older generation and owned the most fertile part of it himself. My father had given that to him over thirty years ago. How was he going to feel knowing that our part of the family legacy was being managed by a girl who had no idea what she was doing?

Chapter 14

Buck Henry stood at the head of the dining room table with a stack of papers laid out in front of him. All signs of the wake had vanished, leaving only family there to muddle through the next few weeks without the man who had held them together.

Trevor sat in a chair between LeAnn and Jake. I wondered why he hadn't been allowed to go to his room to play with Copper. He was too young to understand the significance of reading a will, but perhaps LeAnn felt he would be better off in the company of family rather than off somewhere alone. He squirmed back and forth trying to get comfortable because his legs were too short to reach the floor. I couldn't imagine being eight and losing my father.

I listened while Buck Henry cleared his throat a few times. His fingers were busy shuffling documents around on the mahogany table, as if he was trying to decide which text he wanted to read first. My father had told me to contact him when the time came. I had been ready to do that, but the man standing in front of us had his own timetable. I resented him more than a little for overstepping what I thought were proper boundaries. I needed more time to come to terms with what might happen before part of my life was decided for me. I felt physically ill when he adjusted his glasses on his long narrow nose and began speaking. He could have made the trip back out to the ranch at another time. We would all have arranged our schedules so we could meet with him.

"I know this is a very difficult time, so let me begin by expressing my condolences to LeAnn and the rest of the family. Jack Hawkins was a good man and a great friend, and I'm glad I had the opportunity of marrying him and LeAnn just a few weeks ago. And I am glad to have met his daughter, Brylee, before this sad occasion. He will be greatly missed by the people in the community."

I kept my eyes fixed on the painting of daffodils on the wall behind him. My mother had painted it too, but for the life of me I couldn't remember when. How was I supposed to make it through the rest of my life with no one to turn to? Fortunately, I had Uncle Ned and Ben, but they were not the same as parents. Ben didn't know how really lucky he was to have both of his parents and the gospel. I couldn't begin to imagine what he had done in the pre-existence that made him so much luckier than the rest of us.

"Jack was very specific in his wants." I heard Buck Henry say as my mind returned to what was going on. LeAnn had her fists clasp tightly together as they rested on the tabletop. Uncle Ned and Aunt Nora were holding hands, and Jake had pushed his chair away from the table and was tapping his feet lightly on the floor. He looked out of place and uncomfortable, but then I already knew he felt more at home outdoors than confined inside.

"I'll skip all the legal jargon and get right to what concerns each of you. Ned, your brother would like you to have your great-grandfather's rifle."

Uncle Ned choked in a breath and began wiping at his eyes that had already teared up.

"Thank you," he almost sobbed. "You don't know how much that means to me."

Aunt Nora squeezed his hand and smiled tenderly at him.

"LeAnn," he continued, almost without missing a beat. "Jack wants you to have this house. Its title is free and clear, and he wants you to always have a home, but there are two stipulations."

LeAnn looked like she was in shock, and the knot in my stomach tighten uncomfortably. My father had given my home to someone else. I would never be free to live there again unless the new owner invited me to.

"What stipulations?" LeAnn was asking him.

"He wants to make sure it stays in the family. If you remarry and move, the house cannot be sold. It would pass to the next of kin which would be one of his children or his brother if the need arose."

"That's not even an issue," LeAnn responded. "Jack was the love of my life. There will never be anyone but him."

"And the second stipulation," he went on, not the least bit ruffled by her heartfelt outburst. "Is that his daughter, Brylee, will always have a home here, provided she wants to stay. The taxes and upkeep will be taken from the ranch's account just as they have been in the past, and you will receive a monthly cost of living benefit to be determined by the designated shareholders."

My head was swimming with information, but the only thing that truly registered was the fact that my father wanted me to have a place to return to if I so desired. LeAnn would never go against his wishes, even if someone who didn't want me there pressured her.

And then he turned his attention to me. The chill of previous moments returned. Part of my life had already been determined. Now I was to hear that my father had left everything else to my little half-brother. I wasn't sure I was ready to handle that yet, but his words literally took my breath away.

"Jack has left the ranch to his children, Brylee and Trevor, to be shared equally by them and their posterities. Since she is of age, Brylee can act for herself in any decisions that must be made. But as long as Trevor is a minor under the law, his mother, LeAnn, will represent his interests and his Uncle . . . . "

"Equally?" I was overcome with shock and trepidation. My father had included me as partial heir even after I had run away. This changed everything. The ranch was supposed to be Trevor's alone, now he was going to have to share it with me. How would LeAnn react once the news sunk in, and what would Jake do? This would only give him another reason to despise me.

I heard Jake clear his throat and could feel his cold eyes watching me. Did he think I was somehow responsible for the change my father had made? LeAnn just let out a sigh of surprise.

"I didn't know Jack had changed his will," she said.

Buck Henry took it from there.

"He didn't really change it, LeAnn. Brylee was the official heir until Trevor was born."

"But he always said the ranch would belong to Trevor someday."

"And it likely would have if Brylee had never come home, but since she did, he wanted to make sure there would be no misconceptions as to his wishes when he was gone. His children are to share equally in the ranch. I will leave a copy of the will for each of the beneficiaries to study, but I really hope there will be no problems. Jack was very specific about his wishes."

"Well, I for one, think it is a wonderful idea," Uncle Ned said. "Jack's children should share equally."

LeAnn looked at me and smiled, even though I wondered how she could really mean it after the blow she had just received. This was something no one could take lightly.

"Of course it's a wonderful idea," she said. "And exactly what I would have expected Jack to do. Brylee is his daughter, and she deserves to have everything that is rightfully hers. You will have no problems with me. I'm just glad she is here with us."

Jake had the good sense not to say anything, but I was still worried. He honestly believed that I had only come home to claim an inheritance, and what Buck Henry had just read only added fuel to that mistaken belief. I would have to be very careful until I figured out exactly what he was going to do, or what I was going to do. This new piece of information changed everything.

"Jack also left his horse Thunder to his son, Trevor, when he is old enough to take care of him."

I watched for my little brother's reaction. His eyes were bright and his mouth moved, but he didn't say anything. The number of people in the room was intimidating him.

"If I can have your full attention," Buck Henry said, clearing his throat again and looking around the table to make sure we were still listening. "Ned Hawkins, the beneficiaries' uncle—who has been a rancher his entire life, and who has a vested interest in the family property—will head a board of directors as specified and will be a valuable, neutral aide in any decisions that are made until both children are of legal age."

Uncle Ned looked both confused and surprised at the unexpected role he had been assigned, but I felt a wave of relief sweep over me. If he was involved, we might have a chance at survival. He had no ulterior motives. He loved his home every bit as much as my father had loved his.

Buck Henry licked his fingers and thumbed through a few more pages. "And to Jake Johnson, Jack's brother-in-law— without whom the ranch would not have survived the past three years—the horse, General, free room and board, and a monthly salary or 10% of the ranch's profit each year. This will be in effect as long as he decides to remain on the ranch and assume the duties of ranch foreman. He will also sit on the board-of-directors, along with Ned Hawkins, Brylee Hawkins, LeAnn Hawkins, and when he becomes of age, Trevor Hawkins."

I didn't know if I could take in any more legal jargon or surprises. I couldn't even process what had already been said, but Buck Henry just continued speaking.

"Jack called me a few weeks after his daughter, Brylee, came home and asked me to add a codicil to his will."

He drummed his fingertips on the table and looked directly at me through narrowed eyes. I felt the blood rush to my cheeks and had to grip the arms on my chair to keep from reeling over.

"Your father loves you very much, young lady. When he first told me about the changes he wanted to make, I questioned his sanity about leaving half of the ranch to you since you had already told him you were going to marry a man in the United States and had no intention of staying in Australia permanently. But, he assured me that you would change your mind. I hope you will not make a liar out of him."

My bottom lip was trembling, and I pulled it into my mouth so I could stop its movement. My father had never given up on me. That reality swept over me like a warm, hazy mist. Nothing else Buck Henry said would matter. What I couldn't understand was why he thought I would change my mind about going back and marrying Ben. That was all I had ever intended to do. I had only promised to stay here for as long as was absolutely necessary.

"So when you returned, Ms. Hawkins, he wanted to make certain you would be taken care of along with LeAnn and Trevor. You are to view this house as your home for as long as you decide to stay here, along with a monthly salary or 10% of the ranch's yearly profit for taking care of the finances and helping out as needed. You are also to receive all of your mother's and grandmother's personal effects and possessions of choice that can feasibly be taken with you should you decide to leave."

"And lastly," he said. "Should you decide to leave Australia permanently, your monthly income will stop, as will your interest in half of the ranch. It will revert to your brother, Trevor. If he decides to leave after becoming of age, his holdings will revert to Ned and to Ned's son after that.

"A trust fund is already in place for Trevor's education. Jack's greatest desire however, after making sure those he loved were taken care of, was to ensure that this ranch remained Hawkins' land. It was the legacy left to him by his father and grandfathers, and he wants to make sure that his posterity always has a home to come back to."

I followed his gaze as he looked around the table at the people who were sitting there. No one was smiling. My father's wish was for us to put aside personal differences and work together so his legacy would continue. But how could we do that when overt hostility raged between two of the principal players? I knew I was willing to give it a chance, but would Jake?

"Are there any questions?" Buck Henry asked. When no one spoke, he said he would leave copies of the documents for each of us to keep and study. If we had any questions we were welcome to call him. Father had put him on retainer for the next two months to help us transition.

We sat at the table in silence for what seemed an eternity after the outside door had closed behind him. I wondered if anyone felt my father's presence as strongly as I did. He had been more than generous to all of us, but he had put things together so our lives would be intertwined as long as we chose to stay on the ranch.

Trevor had fallen asleep in his chair, and LeAnn asked Jake to carry him to his room. She followed them. Some things in our lives were already starting to slip into place. Aunt Nora excused herself to return to the kitchen to take care of any details the ladies from church might have missed.

Uncle Ned leaned across the table so we could speak more privately, even though we were alone.

"Your father's will was as much a surprise to me as it was to you," he said, giving me one of his most paternal smiles. "I hope you're not upset that I have been asked to help out. I know you've been to college so you know lots more than I do about finances, but I know about ranching and have some good contacts."

"I am more than relieved that you will be around to help out, Uncle Ned. I had no idea he had organized a board of directors to run things, or that he'd left half of the ranch to me as long as I decide to stay."

"Surprises like this can be a little disconcerting, but it is a well thought-out plan," he responded. "It means no one can make a move without the other board member's consent. That should give you a some peace of mind. This is your home for as long as you need or want it."

"I suppose it should, but there is just so much to take in, and I wasn't prepared to do this today."

"I'm not sure there is ever a good time to hear the last wishes of someone we love and Buck's timing was unusual, but I have a feeling your father arranged for that too. He was always a man of action and never wanted to wait for either good or bad news. At least you didn't have to wait and worry until the next shoe drops. Everything is out in the open now and you have further proof that your father has always believed in you, or he never would have left you with a livelihood you could count on."

"I hope that belief hasn't been misplaced. I still have no idea what I am going to do in the long run," I said as I looked down at the stack of papers Buck Henry had left for us to read.

"That's one of the beauties of life. Few decisions have to be made on the spot."

"But half ownership in a ranch, Uncle Ned? I don't know anything about this lifestyle. You saw how miserably I fit in just trying to herd a few head of sheep."

"What I saw was a young lady who isn't afraid of anything when it comes to fulfilling a promise. You are a Hawkins, and Hawkins can do anything they set their hearts on."

"I wish I had your confidence in me, but I am still having trouble digesting even half of what Buck Henry said."

Uncle Ned leaned back in his chair and laughed. "Leave it to my big brother to stir up the pot even after he's gone. But the best thing either of us can do right now is to take a few days for things to sink in. Why don't you plan on coming over to the house some time next week, and I will walk you through the way I run things. Maybe that will give you a clearer picture of what you are up against."

"Thanks, Uncle Ned. At least I know that I have a place to stay for a few days, even if not everyone wants me here."

"Your father never meant to make your life more difficult by asking you to stay, Brylee, even after he found out you were engaged. He just believes in the power of family, and I hope you know by now that you will never be alone again, no matter what you decide to do with your life later on. We love you dearly and are very glad you decided to come home."

I pushed my chair out and walked around the table to give him a hug. I had always envied the relationship Becky and Ben had with each other and with their family, never believing I could have the same thing unless I married into it. But now I realized that I did have a family like that. I may have lost both of my parents, but I had gained my uncle, aunt and cousins. I had also acquired a new little brother and a special friend in LeAnn.

Jake and I might never get along, but he came with the package and I would just have to deal it as best I could.

Uncle Ned and Aunt Nora left, leaving me alone on the veranda. I waved as their Land Rover pulled away and then sat down on the swing to think. It had been an agonizingly long day, and I felt numb to my very core, but I couldn't think about any of that right now. I needed to concentrate on the blessings I had been given rather than on what I'd lost.

Leaning my head back, I looked up at the sky. There would be stars tonight, many of them. Perhaps even my parents would be looking down on me. Everything about life and death defied the science behind man's reasoning. God had created this world, and perhaps billions just like it. Yet, he knew each of his children personally, along with the challenges they faced.

I couldn't wrap my mind around how that could possibly be. It was just one of those truths that had to be accepted by faith. Just as I had faith that my parents had been reunited and somehow we would be a family again. Without that assurance, it would be nearly impossible to pick up the pieces of my shattered life and go on.

"You seem to have landed on your feet quite effortlessly after being given half of what had been promised to my nephew," Jake said as he stepped through the front door onto the veranda and then closed it behind him.

"I didn't know anything about the will. It was as much a surprise to me as it was to everyone else," I assured him, wishing he would even try to believe me. There was no energy left for an argument after the demanding day we had just endured.

"I seriously doubt that you had no inkling your father was going to make some changes that would benefit you. His guilt alone would be enough to warrant that, and the two of you spent literally dozens of hours locked up in his study with no one else around."

"We were talking about business and family. I don't want half of the ranch. What would I do with it once I am married? It was enough knowing his desire was for me to have it. I will sign papers to that effect if it will make you feel better."

"Like a signature is going to change anything," he scoffed. "Legally, you own half of everything here, except the house, of course. Though I suppose you could take exception to that if you really wanted to."

"Why are you being so hateful?" I asked. "I haven't done anything to deserve your wrath, especially today. I just buried my father."

"Perhaps the timing is unfortunate, but have you given any thought to how this must make LeAnn feel? She lost her husband, and now she has lost half of her security. It's not a very enviable place to be."

"I would never do anything to hurt LeAnn or Trevor. This ranch will always stay in the family. Father saw to that."

He leaned back against the house and took a cigarette from his shirt pocket, but he didn't light it.

"I suppose you're right," he finally admitted. "In many ways you are no better off than I am. If you decide to leave, you walk away with nothing, just like I will."

"You will have General," I said.

"And you will have everything that belonged to your mother and grandmothers. That could pretty much leave the house bare if you decided to take everything with you."

"There are very few things in the house I want. Just a few mementoes to remember my ancestors by."

"And I suppose that includes your mother's baby grand piano and a lot of other valuable antiques. Your father didn't stipulate which belongings could be taken and sold."

I was tired of his constant nettling and insinuations. I wasn't a bad person. I had just been put in a bad situation.

Why couldn't he understand that? I had no intention of selling anything that was part of my heritage, and it would cost a fortune to ship anything to the states. I hadn't even decided if there was anything worth causing a hassle over.

"What possible reason would I have for selling things that have been in my family for generations?" I asked. "They are part of this ranch as much as the land is."

"For money, naturally!" he said. "Why would you want to keep things that have no practical value?"

"I wouldn't! Most everything here needs to stay right where it is—not be put in someone's collection, and certainly not sold to make life easier for me."

"That's a little altruistic, don't you think? This isn't a museum, and the profit you would acquire from selling some of the larger items could mean a nice dowry for someone who is getting married and likely won't be back once her commitment to her father is complete."

"You think you know so much about me, but you don't, Jake? Not all of us are like your former fiancé. Some of us have scruples and values and believe in the sanctity of family, traditions and commitment."

I realized my mistake too late. Jake's hand shot out and gripped my upper arm with such force that it brought me to my feet in pain.

"You have no right to make assumptions about my former fiancé."

His eyes were blazing, and I was momentarily afraid he might hit me. I had been the recipient of his anger before, but not like this.

"I didn't mean it the way it came out," I said. Likening myself to someone he had once planned on spending his life with was a blunder anyone would take offense with. "I was just angry because you think so little of me. That's all."

He relaxed his grip on my arm but did not let go of it. I knew he was weighing his alternatives. His eyes were still narrowed, but after a moment or two, his breathing became more regular.

"Listen, I am sorry if I hurt you," he said, releasing my arm with such force it dropped to my side. "I shouldn't have grabbed you like that, but I don't like anyone talking about the woman I once loved, even if she did walk out on me. And quite frankly, it isn't any of your business."

"I agree," I said. My arm throbbed where his fingers had pressed into the flesh. I would likely have bruises, but at least his latest explosion was over. "We all have parts of our lives that we would rather no on talked about because it hurts too much."

He looked down at the worn wooden floor while my thoughts inadvertently flew back to that night when something so precious had been taken from me, but that was the last thing I would ever discuss with Jake.

"Still, I have to believe that even the most hurtful memories will lessen as time goes on," I quickly added.

"You almost make me believe you have been there."

"I know what it is like to feel betrayed by someone you trust," I said, rubbing the tender place on my arm where his fingers had been. "Surviving hard times is supposed to make us stronger, but I am not sure it always works that way."

"I don't suppose you would care to enlighten me about the secret you are trying to hide since you already know mine."

My face contorted with an expression I could not understand. If anyone, other than my bishop, learned my secret it would break my heart. It was one of the most vile things that could happen to a woman. I had despised myself for being in a place where it could happen almost as much as I despised the man who had so callously hurt me.

Jake was eying me curiously. "By the look on your face, whatever happened must have been pretty awful."

"Let's just say that I am a different person because of it. The old, trusting Brylee doesn't exist anymore."

"I don't know what the old Brylee was like, but I kind of like this new one who can be a little hell-cat when she wants to be, even if she did accept something that wasn't meant to be hers."

"What's done is done, and I had no part in it," I responded. "You have to know by now that money and possessions mean very little to me."

He shook his head. "That's the stupidest thing I have ever heard. Money can buy anything you want."

I looked at him with what almost felt like pity. He really had no idea who I was or what I valued, but that was the way most people felt who didn't know about the saving ordinances of the gospel. Eat, drink and be merry was a perfectly acceptable way to live if one didn't believe in forever the way I did. But I was too weary to even contemplate all the effort it would take to get anyone around me to listen to what I had to say about morality or anything else. I couldn't even get some of them to believe I had not been part of some master plot to take away half of my little brother's inheritance.

"I'm sorry for what happened today," I said. "It really was as much a shock to me as it was to you, but I will keep on assuring you that I have no intention of hurting anyone. I still plan to marry Ben, but I won't leave here until I am satisfied that things will run smoothly in my absence. I hope you can learn to live with that because it is just the way it's going to be."

"You are full of surprises," he replied, lightly touching my arm where he had grabbed it so roughly a few minutes earlier. "And I am sorry about hurting you, but your comment about my former fiancé caught me off guard. That relationship ended years ago, and I really need to quit being so prickly about it. But apparently I am not yet ready to let it go."

The honesty of his statement startled me.

"Holding onto the past only delays the inevitable," I told him. "You've seen what it cost me with my father."

The hard lines around his eyes and mouth softened. "It's hardly the same thing, but I will grant that you've had a tough time since you got here, and it has mostly been my fault. At least you have tried to make things right and forgive others. That is more than some of the rest of us can say."

"I deserved a lot of what I got," I admitted. "I am not much good at backing down when I feel threatened."

The porch light illuminated his face, and for the first time since our meeting, I could see something other than contempt for me. He looked almost human, and his dark eyes really were beautiful.

"I never meant to make you feel that way. I just wanted you to understand where I was coming from."

"Your feelings were abundantly clear from the moment we met, as I am sure mine were. We neither like nor trust each other. I can accept that. And If I hadn't promised my father I would help out, I probably would be on the first plane out of here now that he is gone. It's not pleasant staying where I feel like I have to watch my back all the time."

"You really feel that way?"

"Wouldn't you if our roles were reversed? I only came here because I wanted to see my father."

"And you got far more than you bargained for. Not many women I know would have accepted their father's mistress and illegitimate brother like you have."

"I could never blame Trevor for something that wasn't his fault, and LeAnn has been nothing but kind and generous."

He shook his head and laughed. "And I was just a big pain in your cute little arse."

I couldn't argue with him about that, even if I didn't like the way he phrased his assessment of my feelings for him. He had been tormenting me for weeks, but I had allowed it by not walking away.

"More like a thorn bush with four inch spikes, but you were just trying to protect your family. I get that. I just wish you could understand that they are my family too now. I would do anything to make sure their future is safe and secure."

"I can see you as a ferocious mother protecting her young."

"Is that a bad thing?" I asked, surprised that he suddenly seemed easier to talk to. Perhaps my father's death, and the reading of his will, would help heal the dark abyss between us. My inheritance was only valid if I stayed here permanently, and that would never happen as long as Ben was still in my life.

"Not at all!" he said. "I like a woman with fire and spunk. I hope that boyfriend of yours appreciates what he has in you. Not only are you beautiful and spirited, but you have a kind heart and are passionate about what you believe in."

He took a step closer to me, and I felt my head begin to swim. His piercing eyes found mine and for a moment or two neither of us spoke.

"You know what I want to do right now, don't you?" he whispered.

I stood without moving, but my knees still began to tremble as his hand touched my cheek. Jake was a dangerous man. He knew how to treat vulnerable women, and I was no exception, especially with Ben so far away.

"Yes," I whispered. "But it would be a very grave mistake."

His finger moved to my lips, and they began trembling too.

"Maybe so," he said, caressing them with his fingertip. "But you have to admit that it would certainly feel good."

"You know I am in love with someone else."

"Someone who should be here with you, giving you the comfort you both need and deserve."

"Ben would be here if he could."

"Maybe if you keep telling yourself that long enough you will actually begin to believe it. No real man stays away from the woman he loves when she is going through what you have the past few weeks."

My chest heaved with emotions I didn't understand. Why was this happening to me when my defenses were down? I loved Ben with all my heart, but Jake was right, I needed to know that I was still important enough that he would drop everything and come to me, even if I didn't ask. No job should be more important than love.

Jake seemed to sense the change in demeanor my thoughts had brought and moved away from me.

"Don't get me wrong, Brylee," he said. "I am no saint, and I don't think there is anything wrong with taking comfort where one can find it. But I have never taken advantage of a woman in pain and have no intention on starting tonight. You have nothing to fear from me."

He smiled sadly and then turned around and walked away. I sank back on the swing before my legs gave way. I wasn't indifferent to him! That much was abundantly obvious now. If I didn't have the gospel and Ben, I might be tempted to go after him. He knew exactly what I needed, and it would feel heavenly just to be held. But I had trusted the wrong man before and it had nearly destroyed my life.

Chapter 15

I slept fitfully that night. Mixed-up dreams of my father, Ben and Jake kept me tossing until the sun began to rise. Its pinkish hue saturated the frothy white curtains at my window, but I didn't want to face a new day without my father. I wanted to stay where I was and cry until there was no moisture left anywhere in my body. Talking about about feelings would only make the day harder because each of us would be dealing with grief in our own way, and I doubted anyone could understand how I really felt.

I had come home to make things right with my father, not bury him and have to accept that he had a new family—one he had been part of while his old one was still intact. I truly believed I had forgiven everyone involved, but realized as I lay beneath my light covering that forgiving and forgetting were two very different things. I wanted my old life back. I wanted my father to hold me in his arms, and I wanted to feel like I could stay in the home of my childhood for as long as I desired without feeling beholding to anyone.

But I didn't have my father or my home any longer. Perhaps this would be the last day I could realistically remain here. LeAnn hadn't said much about the contents of my father's will, but it was obvious that it had upset her. She had planned on having everything for her own family once my father was gone, and now that would only happen if I walked away from my promise.

I closed my eyes against the harsh reality that was now my life. What was the point of being part owner in a ranch where I might never feel truly accepted? My skills were not that important because LeAnn could learn to keep the books. As for the stipulated salary for basically doing nothing, they could hire extra ranch hands to help out. That was what was really needed, not some citified girl who had never been part of what was going on even when she was living here.

Maybe if I read the will myself, I would get a better idea of what my father really intended. Staying here for a short period of time seemed futile. I was going to leave someday, and everything would automatically revert to Trevor. Perhaps I was only making matters worse by trying to fulfill what had basically been a deathbed promise. I could return for a visit after Ben and I were married. We could come for our honeymoon. He could see the place of my birth, and I could make sure everything was still running smoothly. That plan seemed far more sensible than the one that had been devised for me.

But I realized—even as the thought crossed my mind—that it would never happen. Once I left, there would be no coming back. I did not have enough emotional investment in the ranch or the people to warrant it. My father must have known that I needed more time to connect with the land and my family— both the old and new. Perhaps that was his reason for including me in his will. I needed to make an informed decision this time around, not an impulsive one I might live to regret like so many others.

So I climbed out of bed and got dressed. I didn't have to decide anything right now. I could wait and see how everyone reacted to me after they'd had a night to reflect on my father's wishes. As things stood now, I was a financial liability. LeAnn would be my measuring rod because I already knew Trevor had completely accepted me.

My little brother was eating a bowl of cold cereal and Copper was drinking water from her bowl when I entered the kitchen.

"Where's your mother?" I asked him without really thinking. There was no reason for waiting to find out where I really stood.

He looked up at me, and I knew instantly that something was wrong. "She's sick and hasn't come out of her room," he replied. "She isn't going to die too, is she?"

"Most certainly not," I told him as I sat down beside him. "She's probably just tired. It's been long few days."

He put his spoon down on the table where it leaked milk. "But she never stays in bed! There is something wrong with her. I just know it."

He looked so lost and forlorn that it made my heart ache.

"Would it make you feel any better if I talked to her?"

"Yes!" He looked a little more hopeful. "I knocked on her bedroom door but she told me not to come in. She has never done that before."

I felt a sudden wave of unease. This was the last thing I expected. LeAnn was the most devoted mother I had ever seen, and she'd been an absolute rock since the moment I arrived.

"Try not to worry, "I told him. "Maybe she thinks what she has might be contagious, and she would never want you to get sick."

"I don't feel like eating any more," he said, climbing off his chair. He picked up his bowl and carried it towards Copper. The little puppy's tail began wagging in anticipation of a special treat. I reached out and put a restraining hand on his shoulder.

"Why don't you wait until I talk to your mother before giving Copper the rest of your breakfast? I don't think human food is very good for her. At least not cereal with a lot of sugar in it."

He gave me a defeated look and retraced his steps to the table, slamming his bowl down with a clunk that made the remaining milk spill over the sides. He was definitely upset. He had never acted out before.

"I will only be gone a minute," I promised.

LeAnn was laying in bed with the sheet pulled up over her head. It reminded me of the way I had acted as a child when things had not gone as I wanted. I had to push back feelings of impatience just looking at her. She had a child who needed her, but she had also lost the man she loved without the sure knowledge that she would ever see him again. I still had Ben. That awareness made me feel a little more generous.

"Trevor said you weren't feeling well. Is there anything I can do?"

She sighed and turned over so I could see just the corner of her face. She was as white as the petals on a Shasta daisy.

"I feel absolutely horrid. I never get sick, but I have thrown up three times already this morning. I must have eaten something bad yesterday."

I didn't advance any further into the room, just in case it was the flu and not a mild case of food poisoning or overwrought nerves.

"I could check around and see if anyone else is feeling unwell. Some of the food was transported a great distance in some very intense heat. It could easily have begun to spoil."

"I don't want you to do that. It might make someone who was only being kind feel bad. I will be back to my old self in no time. I just need some rest."

"Trevor's worried about you."

"Tell him I will be fine in a few hours," she said, pushing the sheet back and hurrying to the bathroom door.

I felt utterly helpless. Should I hold her hair back or let her puke in private? I wasn't ready to be left in charge even for one day, especially when I had so much to consider. My father hadn't even been buried for twenty-four hours, and I felt more ill-prepared to face life than ever.

"I will bring you some crackers and a soda a little later," I called out to her, though I doubted she heard since she was busy wrenching. "Unless there is something I can do now?"

"Just take care of everyone until I get over this," she managed to say before her sickness returned.

Trevor was sitting on the floor with Copper in his lap when I got back to the kitchen. He was talking quietly to her.

"How's mum?" he asked, looking in my direction, but I couldn't miss the fact that he was clutching the little dog harder than necessary, and she yelped.

"She said for you not to worry. She just needs some rest," I replied, crossing the room towards them. "Do you remember how you felt the night after your birthday party when you had eaten too much cake and ice cream? Your mother said you threw up several times, but you were fine the next morning?"

"I guess so," he said. "Will she be up later? I really need to talk to her."

"I am sure she will, but why don't you finish your breakfast. Then I could go out to the barn with you to check on your animals, if that's okay. I haven't seen them for days."

He set Copper on the floor and stood up without speaking, but I knew it was his invitation for me to join him. He was already dressed with his shoes on, so I followed him to the sink and watched as he fixed fix a bottle of formula. There was no reason to fuss over the remainder of his breakfast. We would be having lunch in a few hours, and I wasn't the least opposed to giving him a snack if he got hungry before then.

"How's Newton? I bet he's growing like wildfire," I said as we walked side by side in the hot morning sun. The sky was blue as always and the ground hard and thirsty. I wondered if it would ever rain, and if it did, would it bring life or destroy everything with a flood? I had never lived through one, but I'd heard stories and they frightened me.

"You guys are out early," Jake said as he rounded the corner of the barn and took several long strides towards us. I never knew what he did when he was away from the house, and I really didn't want to see him after what had happened the night before. But the only way I could escape a surprise meeting was to stay in my room and hope he didn't come looking for me.

"We were just going to the shed to see Newton, Sheba and the others." Trevor told him. "Do you want to come with us?"

"I would like that," Jake said, ruffling his hair. "Why should kids have all the fun?"

He winked at me, and I looked down at the ground. It was far better for me when we were fighting.

"You know, Trevor," Jake continued. "I believe it would be a good idea if you went with me in the plane this afternoon to check on the sheep we sheared last week. Do you think your mother would go along with it?"

"I don't know," he said. "She's sick?"

Jake frowned as his jaw moved back and forth.

"What's wrong with her?" he asked.

"She wouldn't tell me." Trevor replied. "She wouldn't even let me in her room."

"Is that so!" Jake turned his attention quickly to me. "Have you talked to her, Brylee?"

I looked at him from the corner of my eye. He was acting like our conversation on the veranda had never happened, but it had cost me a great deal of sleep.

"Only momentarily. She must have eaten something that disagreed with her."

We were in the shed by then and Jake knelt down beside Newton and ran his hand along the calf's back. Newton was a beautiful animal now that he was beginning to fill out. His coat was a reddish brown and he had a white nose.

"Perhaps your sister would consider asking for permission since your mum apparently doesn't want to talk to any blokes today." He smiled at Trevor, but I knew he was holding something back, and it bothered me.

"I will see what I can do, but I can't imagine she would have a problem with it," I told them. "I'm sure she could use a day of rest."

"I imagine an entire afternoon with no men underfoot might sound good to you as well," Jake responded.

Perhaps he was just trying to be helpful, but his words stung. I wanted men underfoot—the right men. I wanted to hear my father's laughter and see the way his brow furrowed when he was trying to explain something I couldn't understand. And I wanted Ben. No, I needed Ben. He could make my life seem whole again.

I pushed myself away from the calf's stall and was about to leave when Jake placed a restraining hand on my arm. His touch was gentle, not like it had been the night before.

"I'm sorry for being insensitive again," he said as we watched Trevor feed Newton the bottle of formula he had fixed in the house. He had to hold it with both hands to keep the calf from knocking it to the ground as he whipped his head back and forth. Some orphaned animals didn't thrive when they lost their mothers at birth, but Trevor seemed to have a magic touch.

"There is no need to apologize," I told him. "I know you are just trying to help Trevor. I'm not sure any of us understand how much father's death has affected him. He never says much."

"He doesn't have to," Jake said. "He says everything with his eyes, just like you do."

I felt heat rush to my face, and I had to look away from him. It would be good to have a few hours alone. I would spend that time writing to Ben.

LeAnn was back in bed when I returned to the house. I knocked three times before she told me it was okay to come in.

"I hope you weren't sleeping. There is something I need to ask you."

She looked more than sick. She looked wildly frantic, but who could blame her for that? She gave every ounce of strength to her family and must be completely lost now that my father was no longer here to worry about or share her troubles with.

"I can't sleep. I haven't done that for months now."

"Well, perhaps you will be able to once your stomach has settled."

"It is not my stomach I'm worried about," she said. "I need to see Trevor. Where is he?"

"He's in the barn with Jake."

"Well, go and get him."

"Are you sure that's what you want? You told me a few minutes ago that you were afraid you might be coming down with something and didn't want him to get sick."

"I'm his mum! I have a right to change my mind."

I was completely bewildered. This wasn't the LeAnn I knew, but I needed to be patient. People reacted to grief in their own way, and she had just suffered the biggest loss of her life.

"You do have that right, but I came to ask if it would be okay for him to go up in the plane with Jake this afternoon. He said he needed to check on the sheep, but I am sure he just wants to give Trevor something to do."

"Well, he's not going. It isn't safe. I need him to come to me right now."

I looked at her in absolute confusion. She had always trusted Jake when it came to Trevor. Why the about-face now?

"I'm sure Jake will be careful," I told her. "And Trevor really needs a distraction. He was so worried about you this morning that he couldn't even finish his breakfast."

She didn't answer. She simply started to cry.

"I can't do this any more," she wailed. "It's too hard! I want to go where Jack is. I don't want to be here without him."

I sat down on the bed beside her. She was really starting to scare me. Her emotions were all over the place, and the strange look in her eyes reminded me of someone who had lost the ability to maintain control.

"This isn't going to be easy for any of us, LeAnn, but you have a son who loves and needs you very much. He is devastated without his father and terrified that he is going to lose you too."

"But what about my loss?" she whimpered. "I have lost my soul-mate—the only man I will ever love. I just can't pretend that life is going to get easier someday because it won't. This ache in my heart is to big for anything to fill."

She rolled over and covered her head with the sheet again. I sat there for a few moments longer.

"What about Trevor?" I asked.

"You make the decision. I just want to be left alone."

I should have let it go, but this hysterical woman was a stranger. I understood her need to grieve, but she simply couldn't shut everyone out. It wasn't healthy, and it wasn't right. Trevor needed her more now than ever.

"But you just said that you needed to see your son. I will get him for you."

"I don't want to see him now. I am not sure I ever want to see him again. He reminds me too much of his father. I just want to forget everything and be left in peace."

"You don't mean that," I said.

She pulled her head out of her cocoon and glared at me.

"Who the hell are you to tell me what I mean and don't mean? You said you came here to see your father, and I believed you. When all you really wanted was to take my son's inheritance away."

Her outburst shocked me to the core. "You know that's not true, LeAnn. I never intended on staying here permanently. I am only here to help."

"Well, you can take your help elsewhere because I don't need it. Now, get out of here and leave me alone."

It was on numb legs that I moved away from her. She didn't mean what she was saying. She was just reacting to grief, but I was glad Trevor hadn't been in the room with us. It would have destroyed what was left of his fragile life.

"What's the verdict?" Jake asked, when I walked into the kitchen on my way to the back door. He was standing at the counter making sandwiches, and Trevor was helping him spread mayo on the bread, but he nearly dropped his knife when he saw my face.

"He can go," I said, biting down on my bottom lip and trying to smile. No one had ever acted the way LeAnn had in front of me before, and I wasn't sure how I was supposed to react. I needed to be alone and have a good try before trying to figure out what had prompted such erratic behavior.

"Did you hear that, Uncle Jake," Trevor shouted, jumping down from the stool he was kneeling on and rushing across the floor to give me a hug.

I kneeled down on the cool linoleum to embrace him as tears filled my eyes. How could LeAnn ever think Trevor wasn't enough to live for? I would give anything to have a son as amazing as he was.

"I want you to go with us," he said, leaning back so he could see my face. I forced my eyes wide open to stop the tears. "Uncle Jake said it would be okay if I sat on your lap since we aren't going very far. He's making sandwiches so we can have lunch."

"Did he really?" I asked, swallowing back the bile that was quickly rising to my throat. I didn't want to go any place with Jake—not today anyway—but how could I deny my little brother such a simple request when his mother was losing touch with reality? He didn't deserve any of this.

"He sure did," Trevor continued. "He said he is take us some place really special."

I managed to push my confusion and heartache aside. "In that case, it would be very impolite of me to refuse."

He kissed my cheek. "Did you hear that, Uncle Jake? Brylee's coming with us."

"I heard," Jake said.

It was obvious that he had been watching us and knew that something awful had happened, but I appreciated his composure. If he said anything to me about it right now Le Ann would not be the only one falling apart.

"Maybe the two of you could go into the pantry and look for some chips and cookies and a few cans of soda," he said. "And bring the picnic basket with you. I'll wrap our sandwiches."

We did as he asked, and nothing more was said as we loaded everything we were taking with us in the picnic basket we had used on Trevor's birthday. I glanced back at the house as we walked towards the small landing strip behind the barn. It looked the same from the outside, but everything behind the front door had changed.

Trevor literally had his nose to the window during our flight over the small mountains that made up most of the land on the ranch. We were flying close enough to the ground that I could pick out the places I had ridden on motorbike while rounding up the sheep for shearing. Every wash, rock and gully that had given me so much grief then seemed almost smooth from a distance.

"Do you see that little mountain over there, Trevor?" Jake asked his nephew. "That's where Brylee and I went to get the biggest herd of sheep. In a few years, you will be able to go with us."

"Could I ride the four-wheeler?" he asked. "I'm not big enough for the motorbike yet."

"You can ride anything you want to, sport. You will know this land like the back of your hand before you are ready to run it."

"Is that how you know it, Uncle Jake?"

He was thoughtful for a moment. "I guess it is. I fly over it often enough and have been most everywhere on foot."

I fought back my desire to tell him he was exaggerating. No one could know that many acres of land when it was mostly wilderness, but I had no right to take out my frustration and hurt on him. He had been a perfect gentleman all day. He had even saved me from acting like a fool and upsetting Trevor in the process. My little brother deserved a pleasant afternoon with people who could put their personal differences aside.

Besides, I had more to worry about than my relationship with Jake. LeAnn was acting loco. I needed to talk to him about what was happening with her, but it would have to wait until the time was right. I didn't want to make matters worse by saying the wrong thing in the wrong way. If my father was indeed watching over us as I believed he was, he needed to make his presence felt and help me know how to handle this latest dilemma.

I glanced over at the lean line of Jake's jaw as the plane hit an air pocket, but I didn't react to the sudden movement with anxiety or fear like I had in the past. He was one of the most tormented men I had ever known, and he could fly off the handle at a moment's notice. What if there was something in the Johnson genes that made both brother and sister act so erratically at times? Hereditary instability would explain a lot, but it wouldn't solve any of our problems.

I could try being more compassionate, but I wasn't prepared to deal with fallout that came from a past I knew nothing about. I was still reeling from losing my father, and the surprises and decisions the reading of his will had brought. But maybe Jake could do something. He seemed to have a sixth sense in knowing where and when he was needed, like the day he had delivered Newton. If I thought with my rational mind instead of my emotional one, it was quite evident that my father had been very wise in placing the two of us in basically the same situation when it came to running the ranch—if that's what we ended up doing. We needed each other whether we wanted to admit it or not.

"We will put down in that clearing," Jake was telling Trevor. "There aren't a lot of places flat enough to land a plane, but I have managed to scout out a few of them."

He handed Trevor a piece of gum. "I forgot to give you that when we went up, but it always helps keep the ears from popping and clogging up."

Trevor obediently put it in his mouth and began chewing. He really wouldn't have needed it since we weren't that high in the sky, but I was grateful that Jake was concerned about his nephew's welfare. We were all living in a state of limbo and shock, but we still needed to take care of the present and think about the future—uncertain as it might be right now.

"What's wrong with my sister?" Jake asked, after we had eaten our sandwiches.

Trevor was watching a small rodent burrow into the ground. There was a grove of wattle trees close by and plenty of bird life. A colorful flock of cockatoos was darting in and out of the branches, and the movement of their wings sent other smaller birds scattering.

"She said she isn't feeling well."

It wasn't a lie. LeAnn was in a horrible emotional state that had likely prompted her bouts of nausea more than any of the food she had eaten the previous day. But the directness of his inquiry made me hesitant to say anything more. He would only think I was out to criticize now that my father was no longer around to protect her.

"Look! I know you are covering for her, but we have to be honest with each other if we are going to make it. My sister has a history of instability when it comes to certain things."

I hugged myself, suddenly chilled even though it was well over 90 degrees in the mountains. "She seemed fine until today."

I knew I would crumble at the scrutiny of any look he gave me, so I turned my attention to the brilliant blue sky overhead. It stretched for miles in every direction, unbroken by even a tree line.

Jake's gaze followed mine.

"Listen, Brylee," he said. "I wish this didn't have to be said. LeAnn is the best sister in the world, but she suffers from severe bouts of depression. I almost had to have her institutionalized during that year after your mother died and your father stopped visiting her. She quit eating and sleeping, and began abusing both alcohol and pills. Even having Trevor to take care of didn't help. Why do you think I came to Edna? Being a ranch hand isn't my dream job. My sister needed me, and I couldn't just look the other way when she was the one who raised me."

"I'm sorry. I didn't know," I told him.

"How could you? I am a very private person and tend to lash out when I shouldn't, but that is what being part of a family is all about. They enjoy the good times, but more importantly, they support each other during the bad."

I felt the air go out of my lungs a little too loudly.

"Like I should have supported my father after my mother's death instead of running away," I said, wishing I had the luxury of allowing myself to cry.

"For once, I wasn't referring to that," he responded. "I know LeAnn said or did something that upset you this morning. You looked like you had lost your last friend when you came out her room."

"She's just grieving."

Now that the subject was out in the open, I wasn't sure what to say. What surprised me most was the fact that instead of picking a side or saying something that would only sound judgmental, I was trying to protect the woman who had brought so much pain and confusion into my life.

"Rubbish! We're all grieving, but we are not locking ourselves away, and reusing to take responsibility for our behavior. We are getting on with life because that is what has to be done."

"Maybe it's not so easy for her. She just lost her husband."

I looked over at Trevor who had wondered closer to the grove of trees. I wanted to call him back. Anything could be lurking beneath their branches. Wallabies and wombats and even Tasmanian devils wouldn't hurt him, but poisonous snakes and spiders would and they were plentiful everywhere.

"Don't worry about Trevor," he said, noticing my concern. "He's perfectly safe. I want to know what you are trying to hide from me."

"It doesn't really matter. We all say things we don't mean when we are upset and unhappy."

"But it does matter. You must think my sister and me are the dregs of society after what you have been through since coming back, but we are not always self-absorbed, irrational and explosive."

"I know that, but she didn't mean any of what she said."

"I think you need to let me be the judge of that. I told you what I did because I am worried about her too. I lived with her when she only thought she had lost Jack. It has to be a hundred times worse now that he is gone forever."

I wanted to tell him that he was wrong—that we would all see the people we had lost again some day—but he wouldn't take my word for it. He was a man who needed to be in charge, and right now he couldn't control anything.

"LeAnn said she didn't want to see any of us again. I can understand her hating and blaming me for at least part of what has happened, but she said she couldn't stand to look at Trevor because he reminded her so much of father. Is that what you wanted to hear?"

"Hell, no, but in her state of mind you had better believe she meant exactly what she said. I already told you how she dealt with Trevor when he was a baby."

"But he should bring her the most comfort of all because he is part of my father."

"Perhaps that is how you and I might see it, but she has never been able to deal with loss rationally. She had to grow up way too fast when our parents died, and she had to take on responsibility she wasn't prepared for—meaning a younger brother who was every bit as confused and angry as she was. I think personal survival is the only thing she can deal with right now."

"What she is doing is dangerous. Isn't there anything we can do to help?"

"Have you ever known anyone who accepted help before being ready for it? Well, and my sister is more than mulish when she makes up her mind about something."

"Then what do we do? We can't just sit back and watch her self-destruct. Trevor needs her."

"Did she say anything else? Think carefully. It might be important."

"She said she wanted to join my father."

Jake sighed deeply, leaned back against the trunk of a dusty green tree, and pushed his sunglasses to the top of his head. "That's just what she said about our parents while your father was grieving after your mother's death. I had to pay a lady to come in and take care of both of them when I had to be gone."

"It must have been very hard for you."

"You don't worry about yourself when the ones you love are in pain and need you. She will come around again. It will just take some time."

I was going to ask him just how much time he thought it might take when Trevor came running up to us. His hands were cupped together.

"Look what I found," he proudly announced, moving his thumb so we could see what lay inside. "It's a lizard. Can I keep him?"

A lizard was the last thing I wanted in the house. I hated creepy, crawling things, but how could tell him I didn't want the greenish, brown creature around when his mother was acting so strangely?

"Well, let's consider this," Jake said. "Do you think it's fair to take him away from his home? He has the perfect life out here, and I am not sure he would appreciate being kept in a box where he couldn't feel the sun, sit on his favorite rock, find the things he likes to eat on his own, or be around his family or friends?"

Jake's diplomacy when it came to dealing with Trevor amazed me. Maybe if I could look beyond the earrings and tattoos he might be a man worth knowing. He had certainly shown me today that there was more to him than I had originally thought. Not many men would walk away from their own lives to take care of a sibling. At the least, I had to give him credit for family loyalty. He was here where he needed to be and had given no indication of walking away when this situation could prove far worse than the last time he had rescued his sister.

"You're right, Uncle Jake," Trevor said, dropping to his knees and opening his hands. The black-eyed lizard with the darting tongue jumped to the ground and scurried away. "Copper would just scare him anyway."

"If I was that lizard and met Copper, I would get away from her as fast as I could. Now if you're finished eating, we should probably be getting back."

"What about the other sheep?" Trevor asked. "I know we haven't seen them all."

"We've seen all we need to," Jake told him, and I suddenly realized that this excursion had no practical purpose. Jake was just trying to divert Trevor from all the sorrow and confusion at home.

Chapter 16

LeAnn was still in her bedroom when we got back to the ranch. Trevor wanted to tell her about his outing, but Jake convinced him that his mother needed to rest. That seemed to satisfy him, at least momentarily, and he followed his uncle out to the barn to feed the horses.

Standing alone in the kitchen with just the ticking of the clock to keep me company, I suddenly felt a moment of near panic. What if LeAnn didn't get well? What if she chose to never leave her bedroom again? Who would take care of Trevor? I knew nothing about raising a child—even a child as well-mannered and easy to love as my little brother.

Jake seemed in a far better position to take over as a surrogate parent than I did since he had been around Trevor since he was a baby, but I couldn't expect him to shoulder the entire load. Losing my father had seemed like the worst thing that could possibly happen to a family who was still trying to connect, but this unexpected change in LeAnn's behavior could turn into something truly life-altering if what Jake had said about her ability to deal with loss was true. It could keep me from going home to Ben for a very long time.

I didn't have to worry about what to fix for dinner that night. Bowls and platters of food had been left in the refrigerator after the wake the day before. The thought of eating more casseroles or potato dishes was revolting, but our bodies needed sustenance, and life had to go on despite LeAnn's choice not to be part of it. So I pulled out the least offensive dishes and had them on the table by the time Jake and Trevor returned from the barn.

"This looks good," Jake said as he washed his hands at the kitchen sink.

Trevor was standing on a stool beside him, and I momentarily wondered if he really meant it, but after his show of love and support for his family that afternoon I had to start giving him the benefit of the doubt over some things. Without LeAnn around to run interference, we would have to do it ourselves, and that meant being on our best behavior and squelching the desire to retaliate every time something was said that made us angry or upset.

"It should be," I told him. "I didn't make it."

"Come on," he said, drying his hands on a kitchen towel and then tossing it to Trevor. "I'm sure you are a very good cook."

"Hardly! Although I am good at opening cans and nuking frozen entrees."

"What's nuking frozen entrees?" Trevor asked, looking quite perplexed.

"Let's just say, they are a low form of food in a cardboard box that doesn't taste much better than the box itself," Jake volunteered with a broad smile that made the corners of my lips turn up his description was so accurate.

"Then I don't want any! Will mum be ready to fix dinner tomorrow?"

"We certainly hope so, don't we Brylee?" Jake said.

I looked at him with appreciation. "Absolutely! Although I am sure I wouldn't poison you if I ended up fixing a few meals. Ben taught me how to make spaghetti and enchiladas."

"What about meat and potatoes?" Trevor said. "It is what mum always makes, and it's what I like best."

"I am sure that can be arranged, sport," Jake told him as we all sat down at the table.

"Can I say grace?" Trevor asked, and I nodded.

It was one of those rituals we had decided not to discuss, just like everything else of a religious nature, but I was glad my little brother seemed receptive to the idea of a higher power. So he bowed his head and repeated the short prayer I had learned as a child. Then both he and Jake made the sign of the cross. I didn't. My new beliefs had taught me there was a better way to honor our Savior and our God.

I fixed LeAnn a tray after the rest of us had eaten. Jake and Trevor were taking care of the dishes. I hated that she had taken to her bed without any warning, and if what her brother said was true there was no way of knowing when she might be ready to resume her responsibilities. It looked like we might have to figure out how to run the house on our own until she was well enough to take over again.

When I knocked on the door, she didn't answer. So I put the tray on the floor in the hall and told her it was there if she felt like eating.

Jake was sitting at the table drinking coffee when I returned to the kitchen. It had been a miserable day, and I wanted to escape to the den to write to Ben. The times I spent corresponding with him were my sanity hours because they took me away from all the chaos and turmoil of the unexpected life I had thrust into.

"Thanks for taking care of the dishes," I told him. "Where's Trevor?"

"He took Copper out to the barn to check on his other animals before bed. He said they were lonely."

"He has been saying that a lot lately." I sat down across the table from him and put my chin in my hands. "I am sorry dinner wasn't better."

"Dinner was fine, but I know funeral offerings won't last forever. Did you talk to LeAnn?"

"No, I knocked on her door and called out, but she didn't answer. Do you really think she is going into another decline?"

"All the signs are there, and it is not likely to resolve itself overnight. I did a cursory inventory while you were gone and noticed that we were pretty low on supplies. I can give you a rough idea of what we use, but LeAnn is the one who plans all the meals."

"And you think we had better do that without her?"

"Just for now. I can fly into Edna and get whatever you think we need."

"Gosh," I said with a heartfelt sigh. "I don't think I am ready for this. What if she really doesn't want to get better this time?"

"Then we will take over for her, for Trevor's sake. You did notice that he looked like he was actually having fun a few times this afternoon?"

"Especially with the lizard, but he is still one very sad and confused little boy."

"All the more reason for us to keep what his mother is going through from him. He doesn't need anything else to worry about. I'll go into town tomorrow if you would like. Shopping isn't one of my favorite activities, but it does beat driving in all this damned heat."

"Thank you," I told him, trying not to obsess about all the complications LeAnn's illness might bring. Even Jake, who nad been through it with her before, did not sound all that optimistic about a speedy recovery.

Why couldn't I just go home to Ben where I belonged and take Trevor with me? He would be so much better off around a normal, loving family that was not tortured by guilt and pain all the time. He could learn about the gospel and grow into the kind of man I knew he was destined to be.

Ben would help him. He was the one golden exception to nearly every rule about men I had ever learned, and he supported me in everything from deciding what kind of laundry detergent to buy to allowing me to lead out in scripture study when I felt ready to do so. My quad was sitting on my nightstand by my bed, but I had barely opened it the past few weeks. I was always too tired, sad or frustrated to read before going to bed. Maybe my neglect in that area was one of the reasons I felt so emotionally crippled right now.

"I will plan on leaving early," Jake said, interrupting my thoughts. "There really isn't all that much for me to do around here right now anyway. The sheep are back in the hills and the cattle can pretty much take care of themselves as long as they have something to eat and drink. It would cost a small fortune if we had to feed them hay like we do the horses."

"I saw that there wasn't much hay in the barn," I volunteered.

"You have been up t o the loft?" he asked.

"Only a couple of times. Trevor likes the swing, and I don't like having him up there alone."

"Did you go there as a child?"

"Not often," I admitted. "I was a houseplant. My mother didn't like me to get dirty."

"Sounds dull and boring."

"It was, but since I didn't know anything else it seemed perfectly normal to me."

"So much for happy childhoods," he mocked. "I would have ended up in a Catholic orphanage if LeAnn hadn't insisted that she was old enough to take care of me. Can you see me listening to the nuns and going to confession every week?"

I had to smile. I couldn't imagine him ever doing anything but live life on his own terms, except when it came to his family.

"I went to Catholic boarding school," I volunteered.

"Then all those teachings must not have taken since it was so easy for you to move onto something else."

We were on dangerous ground again, and I needed to retreat. My newfound faith was all that I had left to cling to now that both of my parents were gone.

"Have you spent much time on the swing in the loft with Trevor?" I asked, hoping he would be willing to return to a more neutral topic.

"I am not into that kind of motion, but Trevor seems to love it. So yes, I have been up there more than a few times."

"Climbing the ladder used to scare me more than the swing," I admitted. "I think I am a little leery of heights."

"Then I should feel honored you were willing to go up in my plane. I know it's not anything fancy, but it is my baby, and I do love her."

So Jake was capable of loving something besides his family. I wondered if that was how Ben felt about surfing. He was certainly good at it and went every chance he got. I seldom went with him. Besides having a healthy fear of the ocean, I had always worked evenings and weekends at the Outback restaurant since they were the busiest times of the week. I had been working there for nearly five years and had taken vacation time to come home and see my father.

Ben had talked to my boss about why I had not returned as planned, and thankfully, he had been assured that my job would be waiting for me whenever I was able to get back. I would keep it until I found something better—something my education had prepared me to do.

"Your plane is nice," I told him. "And you handle her like a real pro."

He laughed. "I should! I have been doing it long enough. Is there anything you really like to do?"

No one had ever asked me that question before, not even Ben, and I had no answer for him. I didn't have any hobbies. I had never had time to pursue them once I was old enough to understand what they were.

"I spent most of my childhood in the house reading books, doing embroidery, talking to Keida or my mother and trying to learn how to play the piano."

"I have never heard you play."

"That is because I haven't sat down at a keyboard since I left home. I wasn't that good to begin with never having the passion to play like my mother did. It was just one of the things we did together."

"I am sorry your life has been so hard," he said. "You have missed out on a lot not having a real childhood. At least I got to play in the streets with my matess after school. Not that it was always a good thing. I was lucky not to have ended up in jail."

"You mean you did things that could have caused that to happen."

"Hell, yes! I could steal whiskey and beer with the best of them, and I did my share of trespassing. I was just damned lucky I never got caught."

"And LeAnn knew what you were up to?"

"Not everything, but she did put up with more than she should have. She never had a life of her own once she decided to take care of me because our parents left nothing behind for us to live on when they were gone. That's why I was so glad when she met your father. He was very good to her, making sure she had help when she needed it. I don't know how many times he made repairs on her car and fixed the plumbing or electrical issues in the trailer where we lived. She didn't make much waiting tables at Emma's, and she did not have a chance for an education. She didn't even graduate high school. She was too busy working to take care of me. So you see why I cannot desert her now? I have to believe she is going to come around."

"Then we will both be here for her."

"You mean that?" he asked. "You are not on the next plane out of here?"

"I was under the impression that my leaving would make you very happy."

"As far as I am concerned, our feelings about each other don't really matter right now. We need to concentrate on Trevor. He is the one who needs to be protected from things he is too young to understand, but I am curious about what this means for you."

"If you are talking about my wedding. It is still going to happen. This might just mean another delay."

"I hope you don't wait too long if it is what you really want. I would hate to see you go through what LeAnn is. In many ways, I completely understand why she doesn't feel like getting up in the morning or talking to anyone."

I was sorely tempted to ask him about his fiancé, Wendy, again but decided against it. We had been civil to each other all day, and I didn't want to see it end.

"We certainly got off the subject, didn't we?" I said.

"What subject was that?" Jake asked, staring at me so intently I had to look away there was so much I did not understand in his eyes.

"We were talking about the little amount of hay in the barn."

"Oh, that," he said. "It's the reason Ned and I agreed that selling some of the cattle along with the sheep was a good idea. We haven't had much rain the past few years. You have seen how dry everything is. It's better to thin out the herds while we can still make a little money, rather than leaving their carcasses for the wild animals to pick clean."

The image of Newton's mother drifted into my mind—her bloated belly, her sad, frightened eyes. I didn't like thinking about what had happened to her once we left with her new baby in the plane. But the reality was that if Jake had not gone back bury her, predators would have devoured everything they could.

"I didn't know you were going to sell some of the cattle too," I said, trying to fight the image.

"Just a hundred head. They should bring in a little more than the sheep do, not counting their wool, and there is no sense losing any more of them."

"Have we lost more than the one I saw die?"

"Several, but you have to understand that raising cattle out here is a huge risk. They are not like sheep that can adapt more easily to hot temperatures and dry feed, although we leave them on their own most of the time because we have to."

"There is just so much I don't know," I lamented despite my desire to stay positive and strong. "Sometimes I wonder why father even wanted me to stay. It's not like I am a great asset for anything other than balancing the books and even a numbat could do that."

"Don't sell your father short, Brylee, or yourself either. He didn't make a mistake wanting you here. This is your home and apparently your legacy, along with Trevor. He just wanted you to decide how important it really was to you before you left again. There may be no coming back if you do."

His words made cold sense, and they chilled me.

"Why would you say there may be no chance coming back?" I asked, thinking back to my morning reflections. "Father said this was my home for as long as I wanted, even though the house technically belongs to LeAnn now."

"True enough! But once you go back to the states and marry that bloke, I doubt that you will ever return for more than a brief visit. Life out here is hard, and the payoff is unreliable, but it can be the best existence possible if you love it like your father did and like your Uncle Ned and Trevor do. With them, it is almost a religious experience."

"Are you telling me that you believe in God?"

He took another sip of his coffee. It must be cold and quite dreadful by now, but he didn't seem to mind.

"I believe in a higher power of some sort. I am just not sure what it means."

I thought it might be that magic moment when I could tell him about the gospel, but he didn't give me a chance. He was off on another subject.

"Once things have settled down a bit we need to start discussing necessary repairs to the barn, outbuildings and fences. I hated bothering your father with mundane trivialities once he got sick because he would have insisted on helping, but the fact remains that maintenance is required if we don't want every structure on the ranch falling down around our shoulders."

"Thank you for caring so much about him," I said as tears I would never allow to fall flooded my eyes. "I should have been here to help him instead living my own life somewhere else."

"You can't regret what you have done, or the guilt will eat you alive. I have learned that the hard way," Jake replied, and he wasn't smiling. "Now, why don't we write down all the things we will need for the next week or so? I know the staples LeAnn always asks me to get, but if you want something special for meals you will have to tell me."

He got a tablet and pen and began compiling a list that began with coffee, beer and cigarettes and ended with stuff like detergent and shower cleaner. I told him it would take a little time for me to figure out menus, but I would have the information for him first thing in the morning. He slapped both of his hands down on the table when he had finished and excused himself by saying he was going to check on Trevor.

I stared at the list he had made for the next few minutes, more than grateful he would be doing the shopping. Purchasing things I no longer believed in taking into my body would make me feel like a hypocrite betraying the God I had come to know and love.

LeAnn kept a few cookbooks in a drawer, so I pulled them out and stacked them on the table in front of me. I perused their pages for anything that might indicate favorite recipes and what everyone liked to eat—other than what I had personally observed—but there was nothing to help me. I could only assume that she must cook from memory or experimentation, and I wasn't ready to even attempt that yet.

When Trevor came back to the house, I asked him what some of his favorite meals were. Like most kids, he liked macaroni and cheese and pizza—things he rarely got—along with his favorite meat and potatoes. His favorite cereal was Captain Crunch, and his favorite breakfast drink was orange juice. Other than that, he seemed happy to eat anything his mother prepared. I wondered if my own children would feel that way when I had them one day.

There was plenty of meat in the freezer: lamb, beef, pork and chicken and I knew we got fresh eggs and milk from Uncle Ned and Aunt Nora. But Jake hadn't included any of the staples I always bought like cheese, butter, yogurt and fresh fruits and vegetables that could not be grown in a home garden in the outback without a great deal of effort. I would have to make my own decisions about things like that. If he didn't think they were necessary, he simply would not buy them.

I brought LeAnn's tray back to the kitchen before heading up to bed and dumped the food into the trashcan. A garbage disposal was one of the luxuries that had not yet come to the ranch. I knew she would be okay for a few days without food as long as she was drinking water, but she was was far too thin.

Why couldn't she understand that what she was doing wasn't fair to anyone, especially Trevor? He needed his mother. Jake needed his sister and I needed to grieve my father's death. Now, instead of being able to do that, I had to worry about her and figure out how to take care of her family. It was the last thing in the world I wanted to do, but I had been left with little choice since I refused to abandon ship until the promise I'd made to my father had been fulfilled.

Chapter 17

The next few days were more than hard. All I wanted to do was cry. The silence in the house was oppressive. Trevor spent most of his time in his room playing with our father's toy soldiers or out in the barn with his animals. I knew it was his way of coping with loss, but too much time spent alone wasn't healthy. I tried to get him to come outside with me each day to practice riding the skateboard I had given him for his birthday, swing in the hay loft or ride his four-wheeler, but he would lose interest after a few minutes and ask to be excused so he could be alone again. It was an incredibly sad and voiceless household.

Jake picked up the groceries and supplies I had put on the shopping list, and I had talked to Aunt Nora about the staples she supplied. There didn't seem to be much else to do except fix meals, keep the house clean, weed and water the small garden plot with its carrots and onions and potatoes and try to keep Trevor from spending too much time alone. LeAnn stayed in her bedroom. If I had a few extra minutes, I emailed Ben, but he was busy at work and couldn't return my emails as rapidly as I sent them.

Sometimes I wrote to him several times a day. They were basically filled with my day's experiences and how desperately I missed him, but since I had no idea when I might be coming back, I skirted that subject all together. I simply couldn't leave my little brother when his mother stayed locked in her room and had run out of excuses to explain her actions. But even at eight, Trevor knew something was dreadfully wrong, and there was little I could do to reassure him. His mother was the only one who could do that.

Jake came into the house for meals, but he rarely stayed to visit. My guess was that he felt guilty about his sister's behavior because he couldn't get her to come out of her bedroom either. She had begun locking the door, effectively discouraging us from even trying to make contact with her.

Still, I tried to get a response when I set a tray of food in the hallway, but her retort—when she did say anything—was always the same. "Go away. I don't want to talk to anyone."

I quit encouraging Trevor to even go near her room after his first unsuccessful attempt because he was completely crushed that she wouldn't let him in. It was a cruel thing to do to a child when he was in pain too, but she was the only one who could change how she felt inside and what she was willing to do about it.

A week after my father's funeral, I decided to saddle two horses so Trevor and I could ride over to Uncle Ned's. He had promised to walk me through how he ran his operation, and I needed to be doing something more constructive than household tasks and looking at the numbers I had put into an accounting program on my father's computer if I wanted anything to change. I had too much time on my hands to think and was beginning to feel almost despondent myself.

Jake made sure the synchs were tight enough so the saddles wouldn't slip but didn't ask me why we were going or suggest he come with us. In a way, that was a relief after the emotional ups and downs of our tenuous relationship. I still felt incredibly uncomfortable around him, even though we had managed several normal conversations during the time LeAnn had exiled herself away from the rest of us. He said he would keep an eye on her while we were gone.

Uncle Ned was nailing a loose board on a corral fence when Trevor and I reined in our horses and climbed off so we could give them something to drink. There were watering troughs placed strategically at both ranches. Water was the one thing no living thing could do without. But in the outback it wasn't always readily available, especially during long droughts like the one we had been having for the past few years. He turned around to greet us.

"How was your ride?" he asked, hanging the claw of his hammer over the top board so he could talk to us without the temptation to keep working.

"It was great," Trevor said with a broad smile that let me know just how much he had enjoyed getting back on a horse. "Uncle Jake let me ride Thunder, but only if we rode slow and Brylee was with me."

Trevor had been riding horses since our father had moved his new family out to the ranch and knew how to handle them to a certain extent. But Thunder was a man's horse, and regardless of the fact that he had been left to Trevor, I didn't think it was wise for him to be riding such a large and spirited horse by himself until he was much older. I believed we were only asking for trouble by encouraging it.

But Jake had dismissed my concerns as being irrelevant. Trevor had been on the horse hundreds of times with our father, and the animal was used to the sound of his voice. That fact should have lessened my concern for my little brother's safety, but with his mother acting so strangely I felt an added need to protect him.

"Sounds like a good idea to me," Uncle Ned was telling Trevor. "Our horses need to learn to trust us before we try anything fancy. Aunt Nora baked cookies just for you. Why don't you run on up to the house and get some while Brylee and I have a little sit down together?"

Trevor started off towards the house after securing Thunder's reins around a fencepost where he was close to water.

"How is he doing?" Uncle Ned asked.

"I'm not sure. He doesn't say much and spends most of his time alone. I keep trying to get him involved in other things, but I'm not very good at it."

"Trevor has always been a loner. That's just what happens when children grow up out here without siblings—as you well know—but that doesn't explain why he is alone so much with three adults in the house. Isn't LeAnn spending enough time with him?"

"LeAnn isn't spending time with anyone. She hasn't been out of her room since father's funeral. She says she can't live without him."

"That was a week ago!" His voice boomed, but his facial expressions turned to concern almost immediately. "I was hoping that wouldn't happen again."

"So you know about the other time?"

"I watched both of them live through it. Your father had put himself in an awful position. If he and LeAnn hadn't become involved your mother would still be alive. He blamed himself for her death, but he also blamed LeAnn. I wish like hell none of it would ever have happened."

"But they had Trevor to think about."

"I am afraid your father couldn't think about anything but his bottle of whiskey the first six months or so. He just sat in his office and drank. I could barely get him to talk to me, unless we were both drunk."

"He never told me any of that."

"He was ashamed of behaving like a damned toe rack in deceiving both his wife and his daughter, and when you couple that with pride, it becomes a real combination for disaster."

"That's basically what Jake said. He told me LeAnn even got involved with pills."

"At least your father didn't have those readily available! The alcohol abuse was bad enough. I am not sure any of them would have survived if Jake hadn't come back to take care of LeAnn and Trevor. It gave your father time to adjust to some of the devils that seemed determined to destroy him."

"Is that why he decided to bring all of them out to the ranch?"

Uncle Ned squinted in the bright sunlight. He was so much like my father, and yet so very different. He loved everything about the outback but wasn't afraid to talk about his feelings too. I imagined Aunt Nora was the reason for that.

"Your father had lost both his wife and his daughter, but he eventually realized that he would do the same thing with his son if he didn't snap out of it."

"But he loved LeAnn. Otherwise, he never would have cheated on my mother."

"Naturally he loved her! Men aren't monogamous by nature. They like to play around as long as they don't get caught. Your mother was his first love, and a man never really gets over that, even when they drift apart."

"Is that how you feel, Uncle Ned?" I asked.

"I sewed all my wild oats before Nora even entered my life. She is the only woman I have ever really loved, and I knew from the beginning that if I ever made a misstep with her there would be no going back."

I wished it had been that way for my father, but I could neither judge nor condemn him. Life wasn't black and white, and the shades of gray it produced were mind-boggling. Just when I thought I was starting to understand and accept my past some new information was thrown into the mix that altered everything. My father had walked away from Trevor just like I had walked away from him. No wonder they had become so close over the years. He didn't want to fail at being a parent for a second time, or fail at love like he had done with my mother.

"I never would have guessed what was going on while I was away if you hadn't told me," I said. "My father and LeAnn seemed very much in love when I came back."

"Love was never the issue between them. It was all the lies, secrets, guilt and betrayal. I can't imagine how hard it was for them to stay together after what happened, but somehow they made it work."

I shook my head and looked out at a new colt that was standing by his mother in the pasture. It was the color of soft, tan leather and had white spots like a fawn in a mountain meadow.

"I couldn't do what she did," I responded. "Moving out to the ranch and into the bedroom my lover had shared with his wife would be too weird. I would always wonder if he was thinking about her or me."

"Knowing my brother as I do, I am sure a lot of that went on. But you have to give both of them credit because they pushed through the tough times. I'm sure a lot of it had to do with Trevor. They wanted him to be raised in a home with two parents."

"That is one of the best gifts parents can give children," I said as the lines between my eyes deepened into a frown. "The other gift is the knowledge that their parents love each other. Father never showed affection towards my mother the way he did LeAnn."

"Your parents loved each other, Brylee, never doubt that. But they were both so afraid of being hurt they wouldn't allow themselves to be emotionally vulnerable once the newness of being married wore off."

"But what were they scared of? They had each other and me. That should have been enough."

"Your father was afraid your mother would leave him and take you with her because she was so lonely out here and had sacrificed everything she had ever known to be with him. And your mother was afraid your father would grow tired of her because she wasn't cut out to be a rancher's wife. I used to tell him that they needed to sit down and really talk to each other, but they never did."

I pulled my bottom lip into my mouth and bit down on it until the pain came. I needed to feel something other than sorrow for what might have been.

"It is just so sad, Uncle Ned," I finally said. "People need to be honest with each other or relationships won't work."

I thought about the big secret I was keeping from Ben. Was I any different from my parents, hiding something that had caused me anguish from the man I claimed to love? And why did I feel like he wouldn't understand my being sexually assaulted? Maybe it had nothing to do with him. Maybe I just felt too dirty and ashamed to share it—just like my father had done with LeAnn.

"We can't change the past," Uncle Ned was saying when I allowed my thoughts to drift away. "But we can work on the present. I know that must seem rather hard to do with LeAnn mucking around like some crazy loon who doesn't know which way is up right now."

"I'm trying, Uncle Ned, but there is just so much I don't understand, and I don't like being forced into trying to take LeAnn's place with Trevor. I just want to be his sister and friend."

"Then be that."

"But what about his mother?

"All we can do is hope she will come around."

"And if that doesn't happen? I can't stay here forever, and I doubt she will give me permission to take Trevor to Los Angeles."

Fear of the unknown was invading every cell in my body. Instead of the relatively positive and happy person I had been with Ben, I was returning to the sad, fearful child I had been before I left Australia in the first place, and I hated it.

Uncle Ned looked at me with genuine concern.

"Let's not get ahead of ourselves," he said. "We have to believe that LeAnn will get through this. You aren't planning to bail on us soon, are you?"

"I don't know what I am going to do, but I'm not sure LeAnn would really want me here if she were thinking rationally right now."

"That bloody will," he retorted. "As fair-minded and sincere as my brother was in writing it, I was afraid it might stir up some trouble. Has she said something I should know about?"

"Only indirectly, but it is apparent that she blames me for taking half of the ranch away from Trevor. That was never my intention. I don't know what I would do with it even if I stayed. I don't know anything about living in the outback."

"You've lived here most of your life."

"I lived in a house that just happened to be out here. I was never part of the outback in any way that really mattered."

"But that can change if you want it to. I think that is what your father was trying to tell you when he included you as part owner. Sometimes we just need to be reminded that the things we want aren't necessarily the things we really need."

"I want to be here, but I also want to be with Ben. I could manage the finances over the Internet from anywhere in the world if LeAnn would just come out of her bedroom and take care of her family again."

"You could do that," he responded. "But it's not what your father wanted. He was hoping you would grow to love this land

and your new family enough to want to stay here permanently. Why else would he have made provisions for a salary, and the stipulation that you couldn't sell your portion of the ranch?"

"I understand all of that on a logical level, Uncle Ned, but I made a commitment to Ben first. We were supposed to be getting married. How do I forget about the man I love?"

He put his arm around my shoulders, and I wished the weight of it felt more comforting.

"You don't have to convince me that you are in a tough situation. No matter which life you choose, you will be giving up something significant. I can only tell you that family is the most important thing in the world. Your mother learned that the hard way by leaving the life she had been born into to marry your father. I don't want the same thing to happen to you. Loving someone, even with all your heart, isn't always enough."

I thought about what Uncle Ned said concerning the idea of needing my own family to be happy as he escorted me around his ranch, explaining how he did things as we walked. His ranch replicated ours in almost every aspect, except that the buildings and fences were in better repair because they had been constructed 50 years later. He had stalls in his barn that were filled with baby animals who had lost their mothers, a loft partially filled with hay and straw, holding pens for sheep that had yet to be sent into the hills, and a large pasture for horses and other animals that were waiting to be sold. He also had a room in the barn for veterinary supplies and a small bunkhouse for the men who traveled the Australian Outback looking for work.

He didn't own a plane but told me that Jake was always available to help when help was needed. A portion of his ranch had been cleared and seeded with a hearty strain of alfalfa that was cut and bailed several times each year. It was watered with a sprinkler system connected to it's own well. He owned the bailer and the trailer used for cutting and hauling the hay, but he divided the crop with my father once it was harvested.

He explained that the land my father had given to him was flatter and more fertile than that of the original homestead because it hadn't been overly used. Sharing the hay was one of the ways he gave something back. Had my father not willed him a good portion of the family ranch, he never would have been able to stay in the outback and do what he most loved.

The more we walked and talked, the more I understood how important it was to keep the legacy our ancestors had left to us available to those who came after. It was a simple, hard life, and the elements were never predictable—leaving one constantly at their mercy. Herds had to be checked every few days during the birthing season to make sure they were safe from wild animals and no assistance was needed. Hay had to be bailed, sheep sheared and animals transferred to and from the stockyard in Edna when they were either sold or purchased. And that didn't include constant fence mending, searching for water and trying to subsist on practically nothing.

But mostly, everyone who lived there learned to understand and trust the land. Its vital clues were everywhere if one knew where to look—like the aborigines who had inhabited the land for centuries before the white man came and took it away. It saddened me every time I thought about them, but so-called progress demanded sacrifice. I just wasn't sure some of it was worth it.

"Do you know what happened to Asum and Keida?" I asked my uncle as we paused to look at the tractor he had been overhauling. He did most of his own work since he was mechanically inclined, and it was far less costly and time-consuming than relying on someone else who had to travel into the outback to do the work for him. "Father said they simply disappeared one morning without any warning."

My uncle looked at me with dancing eyes.

"They were a pair if there ever was one," he said. "Just like Asum's parents before them, Ishmael and Muga, who worked at the ranch when your father and I were ankle bitters. We had a lot of aborigines working for us in those days. You could never understand a thing they said unless they wanted you to, but they were smart as hell when it came to controlling fires, looking after animals and knowing where water could be found. They understood the nature of the land. To them, looking after their desert home was caring for their ancestors, and they took that responsibility seriously. If we were even half as smart as they were, we wouldn't be in the mess we are today. We would have all the water we need, and we wouldn't waste any of our natural resources."

"But do you know where they are, or why they left, Uncle Ned? I would really like to see them again while I am here."

"You could go troppo thinking about that long enough. They went a-walking not long after your mother died. Aborigines live by their own set of rules and don't always act like they understand what is going on, but they knew your father was cheating on your mother, and in their culture that never happens. Oh, it's not that they don't sleep with other people. That is part of their culture too, but when they are married it's forever, and they are never emotionally unfaithful."

"But that doesn't explain where they went, only why they left."

"I don't suppose we will ever know where they went for sure. There are still nearly 1300 communities of them in the outback. It would take a minor miracle to find them, or a bloody amount of good luck. Why are you so interested in them anyway?"

"I don't know," I admitted. "I guess they are just a part of the past that I would like to hold on to. In many ways, Keida was as much a mother to me as my own was."

"And I bet she could spin a yarn or two if the spirit moved her."

"She did tell me about the birds and the bees."

"They were never reluctant when it came to things like that. Old Ishmael took your father and me to see our first ritual-mating dance. I think he must have been all of ten, and I was a couple of years younger. Can you imagine any two young blokes more enthralled than we were watching those naked bodies gyrating around as the sparks from the fire shot up around them? I have never forgotten it."

I looked over at him and frowned. "I can't believe you just told me that."

I wasn't a prude by any means, but Keida's explanation of sex had been far less graphic, even though she explained everything more effectively than my own mother had. At least I had understood enough to know that storks did not deliver babies.

"I thought for sure your father had mentioned it to you. Trevor knows all about that story."

"Well, he didn't," I said, once again feeling a stab of bitterness for having been left out of so much. "But Asum and Keida were a very important part of my life. Other than my parents, they were basically the only people I saw growing up."

"It shouldn't have been that way, Brylee. Your dad and I were wrong for not insisting that our families spend more time together. But it seemed like there was always so much work to do. Not that we didn't squander a lot of time yakking to each other about things that didn't really matter, because we did. We saw each other nearly every day, but we didn't see to it that our families got to know each other. And now it's a little too late for that."

"It's never too late, Uncle Ned. Father may no longer be here, but that doesn't mean we can't become closer. Maybe that is part of the reason he put all of us on a board of directors together. It will force us to learn how to get along and work for the common good."

"I think there is a little more to it than that. But I want you to know that I loved my brother dearly and will see to it that his entire family is taken care of. I won't let anyone take advantage of anyone else."

"Anyone," I mused as we began walking again. Uncle Ned already knew about my toxic relationship with Jake and there was no reason to rehash it now.

He showed me around the rest of his ranch while explaining how his household operated on a monthly allotment that was taken from the ranch's account just like ours was. If the year was good, there was extra money to increase the size of herds, buy equipment or do necessary repairs. No one took a salary because Uncle Ned and Aunt Nora did all the work. NJ and Molly had helped out while they were living at home. They didn't receive an allowance but knew their parents would provide what they needed, including money for an education as long as they were committed to getting one.

The last stop we made was in his office where he explained his accounting system. It was similar to the one I had set up for my father. Aunt Nora kept all the records after taking an on-line accounting class.

"Unless you are a big rancher," Uncle Ned said, sitting down in a leather chair at his desk and drumming his fingertips on the smooth surface. "There really isn't much of a profit to work with. One bad year can affect us for the next five. That's why it is imperative that we keep a healthy balance at the bank. Your father and I have been lucky in the past because we haven't had to borrow very often, but if we don't get some rain soon that might be our only option left."

"Would getting a loan to keep going be a problem?" I asked him.

"Only to me! The property has been title-free for over forty years, and your father and I have worked hard to keep it that way. But this damned economy has hurt everyone but the richest ranchers. That's why most everyone else has sold out. They did it to survive."

"We won't let that happen, Uncle Ned." I said. "But what about the corporations who want to buy our land. Father said they were always circling around like vultures?"

His snort was anything but dignified. "Those damned corporation people think all they have to do is wave the right amount of cash around and anyone will cave, but they haven't dealt with Hawkins. Maybe it is that convict heritage, but our ancestors worked hard to give us a life where we wouldn't have to depend on others and we would die before letting that go. Out here, we are free to make our own decisions. It really is all about living life on our own terms."

"Freedom!" I thought about that concept as Trevor and I rode home. He was silent, except for an occasional, "Did you see that?" as we passed by small animals scurrying hither and yon.

Just how important was freedom to me? I had always considered myself free to do or be anything I wanted, but was it really freedom when I had to work for someone else and rely on their whims or even sound business decisions for the basic necessities of life? I really was at the mercy of others in Los Angeles, but that's where Ben was, and he wanted to stay there so he could be close to his family. If I wanted to be with him, that was where I would have to stay too.

Jake was in the kitchen stirring something on the stove when Trevor and I got back to the ranch. I had managed to get the saddles off the horses, and together my little brother and I had put them in their stalls and given them hay and water.

"Did you enjoy your ride," he asked, without turning around.

Trevor startled both of us with his response.

"Can I have Thunder for my own horse right now? I would take good care of him, and I rode him all the way to Uncle Ned's and back."

I swallowed back my uncertainty and dread. Father had indeed promised Trevor that the horse would be his, and my little brother was incredibly bright, pretty much fearless, and warm and loving too, but he was still just a little boy and Thunder was an unpredictable stallion.

"You did very well," I told him, and saw a smile brighten his face

"So can I have him? I won't ask for anything ever again if you say yes."

I knit my brow and looked across the room at Jake who appeared very out-of-place in the kitchen unless he was eating. I hoped he would side with me on this one, even if he didn't agree. I couldn't watch Trevor around the clock and knew he would want to spend every available moment with Thunder if we gave in.

"That is something all the adults here need to discuss," Jake told him. "Having a horse like Thunder is a big responsibility."

"But I'm taking care of Copper, and you said that was a big responsibility."

He was right on target with that. He made sure Copper had food and water and was played with every day. But a horse wasn't a puppy, and I didn't want to risk Trevor getting hurt just because he would be disappointed if we didn't give him the answer he so much wanted.

"Come here, Trevor." I told him, pulling out a chair at the kitchen table for him to sit on. It would be better if we were eye level when we had this discussion. Why couldn't LeAnn just come out of her room? It was her responsibility to take care of the parenting, not Jake's and certainly not mine.

"You love Thunder a lot, don't you?" I asked him.

"Yes," he said, looking at me with large, sad eyes. "He is father's horse, and we used to ride him together."

So that was why he wanted Thunder to be his now. It was a way of keeping our father alive.

"Riding him with father must have been a lot of fun."

"It was the best! We talked about the ranch and how it would be mine someday."

I looked at Jake for help, but he was back to stirring whatever it was he was cooking.

"Father loves you very much," I told him, and then watched as his eyes filled with tears. "But he knows that you are just a little boy right now and need lots of help so you will be the best rancher in the outback when you grow up."

"That's what I want to be! More than anything else, that's what I want to be," he gasp out.

"I know it is, but do you know what else father wants for you?"

"No," he sniffled.

"He wants you to be safe, and Thunder isn't a safe horse for you to be alone with right now."

"Why not? I know he likes me cuz I feed him apples."

"He likes you a whole lot, but he is really big and doesn't realize how strong he is. He's okay as long as he is in his stall, but what if you had him alone in the pasture or even in the corral and he got scared and kicked you, or reared up when you were riding? He wouldn't mean to hurt you, but he would because you are not physically powerful enough to handle him all on your own yet."

"But I did handle him today. You said so."

"Yes, but we went slow, and he had another horse to keep him company. Do you really want to know the truth?"

He nodded.

"Thunder could hurt me, and I am a lot bigger than you are."

"So I can't have him." The animation left his face, and he just looked incredibly miserable.

"Your sister's right," Jake said, turning the burner on the stove off and pushing the pot to a cool place. "Thunder can never be a pet like Copper. He is a big horse that has been trained to work hard, and you have to be strong enough to handle him in all kinds of situations. But that doesn't mean you can't be his friend or ride him as long as you are with an adult."

"If it would make you feel better," I told him, feeling just a tiny bit inspired. "We could draw up a paper—like a contract—for all of us to sign that says Thunder is your horse now and for always, but adults will help you take care of him until you are old enough and big enough to do it by yourself. It would just be an extra assurance that he will never belong to anyone but you."

"Can we do that, Uncle Jake?" Trevor turned to him and asked.

"I don't see why not as long as you understand that you cannot get in the stall with him, and you cannot ride him unless one of us is with you. But you can feed him all the apples and carrots you want."

"I promise," Trevor said. "Now can I go out and talk to him? I want him to know that he still has someone to love him."

"Sure, sport," Jake said. "But come back in half an hour because we are having lasagna for dinner. It will take me that long to put together and get it cooked all the way through."

So Jake was fixing dinner. He was certainly a man of surprises. I walked with him back to the stove after Trevor had left, even though I didn't understand why. He certainly hadn't asked me to, but he didn't seem to object either.

"It's hard watching him try to make sense of what has happened, isn't it?" he said as he spooned the sauce he had made over noodles that were already lining a glass baking dish.

"It breaks my heart. He is grabbing onto anything he can so he won't feel so alone."

"And it doesn't help that LeAnn has locked herself away from living again. He was only two when she did it before, so I doubt he remembers anything about it consciously. But he knows something is wrong now, and I am getting tired of making excuses for her."

"What else can we do?" I asked him while getting four plates out of the cupboard for dinner—three for the table and one for the tray we would fix for LeAnn, even if she refused to eat it.

"Nothing!" I could hear the frustration in his voice. "I love my sister dearly, but she is stubborn as a mule, and if you try to force anything she just digs in her heels more. She will come out of it when she's ready and not a moment before."

So there really was nothing we could do but wait. I hated it! LeAnn should be considering all the blessings she still had not just what she had lost. Trevor needed her desperately. Jake and I were trying our best to be there for him, but he needed his surviving parent, not an uncle and aunt who had little idea of what they were doing.

Chapter 18

It was 3:30 in the morning according to the travel alarm clock on my nightstand when I awoke with such a feeling of dread that I immediately bolted upright in bed. I had never been awakened like that before. My heart was beating furiously, and I felt like I was going to be physically ill. I couldn't remember having had a bad dream, but what else could explain the cold chills, and the knot in the center of my stomach? Something was very wrong, and I needed to figure out what it was and fast.

I listened intently for any sound that might indicate that all was not as it should be, but the house was silent and dark. I considered laying back down to see if sleep would come again but after fifteen minutes of tossing—and the threat of another migraine—I decided to get up and check things out.

Trevor was sleeping soundly when I cracked open the door to his bedroom and shinned the beam coming from my flashlight on him, and everything else appeared to be okay on the upper level of the house. I couldn't smell smoke, and there wasn't any thunder and lightening outside, so what had awakened me from such a deep sleep?

I crept down the stairs following the focused shaft of light I was carrying. The faces in the pictures that lined the staircase had never looked more menacing. I had forgotten how eerie a shadowy house had always seemed to me. There was nothing but darkness and quiet on the main floor either, but when I walked into the kitchen and flipped the light switch, I noticed that a folded piece of printer paper was sitting on the table. Picking it up, I saw that it was addressed to Jake and me and the handwriting belonged to LeAnn.

My hands literally shook as I read her brief message.

"I know what I'm doing is wrong, but I just can't be here right now. The memories are too painful, and I feel like I'm slowly dying. Take care of Trevor for me and let him know how much I love him. LeAnn."

I fought off the desire to sink to the floor and slip into nothingness myself. What was LeAnn saying? Had she run away? Did she plan on taking her life? I ran to the master bedroom, pushed the door open and turned on the lights. The bed was made and LeAnn wasn't there. She wasn't in the bathroom either. Her suitcase was gone from underneath her bed and some of her things in the closet were missing.

My knees were trembling, but I managed to make it out of the front door and down the veranda steps without falling. My father's Land Rover wasn't parked in the driveway where it should have been, and I was holding LeAnn's cryptic note in my hand. I had no choice but to wake Jake. He knew his sister better than anyone, and he was the only one I could turn to now.

I rapped loudly on the bunkhouse door.

"What the hell?" I heard him shout as the bedsprings creaked. He pulled the door open before I had time to knock again.

"Now, this is a surprise, but you should have given me some notice," he said when he saw me standing there wearing nothing but thin shorts and a t-shirt. I was holding the flashlight in one hand and the note in the other. "I'm not exactly in the entertaining mode, but I can adapt to anything."

But instead of refutation, I started to cry.

"Hey," he said, putting his hand on my shoulder. "I was just kidding. What's wrong?"

"It's LeAnn," I managed to whimper. "She's gone!"

I extended my hand in which the crumpled note lay, and he took it from me.

"Maybe you had better come in," he said, pushing the door back so I could walk into the room, but I stood just inside the doorway until he turned on an overhead light and motioned for me to sit on one of the two chairs at small kitchen table. He was wearing nothing but boxers, and the huge eagle tattoo on his back looked almost more threatening than the pictures of my dead ancestors on the walls had done.

He read the note quickly and looked down at me as I sat at his table, hating the fact that I had been forced to come to him in the middle of the night.

"It's bad, isn't it?' I said.

He ran his hand through his thick, dark hair.

"Well, it's not good. I knew she wasn't thinking clearly, but she has never done anything remotely like this before. When did you find the note?"

"Just now," I said. "Something woke me up and when I got to the kitchen I found it. She isn't in her bedroom and the Land Rover is gone. You don't think she would hurt herself, do you?"

"I doubt it," he said, but I could see more than simple concern in his eyes. "Do you have any idea how long she has been gone?"

I shook my head. "I only know that she was still here when I went to bed about eleven."

"That's good," he replied as he started to pace back and forth across the worm linoleum in the small kitchen space in the bunkhouse with his fingers locked and the palms of his hands beating together. "Maybe we can piece together what happened. I went out for a smoke about one. I'm pretty sure the Land Rover was still there. I would have noticed if it wasn't. That means she hasn't been gone for more than two hours. I just can't believe I didn't hear her. I'm not a sound sleeper."

"Should we call the police?" I asked.

"They won't do anything until she has been gone for twenty-four hours."

"But what if it's a suicide note?"

I started to cry again. This couldn't be happening? I had just buried my father. We couldn't lose someone else.

"It's not a suicide note," he replied, giving me an irritated look.

"How can you be sure? She didn't say anything about coming back."

"Because she is Catholic and knows that it's a sin. She may be mentally fragile right now, but she would never do something dim-witted like that."

"Then how do we find her? She needs us, even if she doesn't think so right now."

"I have a friend on the police force. I will give him a call and let him know what happened. He's known LeAnn for a long time and will be more than willing to help. He can have his people check along the road to make sure she isn't stranded somewhere."

"That's a start, but what can we do? We can't just sit here and wait for something else to happen."

"I am afraid that's all either of us can do right now. I will fly into Edna as soon as it's light. She has a couple of old friends from the diner she might contact. If she's not with one of them, they might know where she is."

"So call them! We have to know something before Trevor gets up."

"I will," he said. "I just don't want everyone in the country knowing our business until it's absolutely necessary."

I rubbed my hands together as I tried to think of something constructive to say or do to help find her, but it was the middle of the night, and she had taken the only reliable vehicle on the ranch. I might have no choice except to trust the man who had been more of an adversary than a friend until the past few days. He was the only one who knew his sister's friends and what they might be willing to do to help her.

But what was I going to tell Trevor when he woke up, even if we knew something by then? He was getting used to his mother staying in her room, but he would notice that the Land Rover was gone when he went out to feed his animals and would want to know why.

"Don't look so worried," Jake said. He had pulled on a pair of jeans while I sat at the table contemplating our problem. "LeAnn's not stupid, just confused. She will snap out of it and be home before you know it."

"I hope so," I told him. "But right now, I'm more concerned about Trevor."

He ran his hand through his hair again and sat down on the chair across the table from me.

"Poor kid! As if losing his father wasn't enough, his mum has gone bonkers. Maybe it's time we level with him. He hasn't seen or talked to her for over a week. That's a long time for a kid who is used to having his mother around every minute of every day."

"But what if she comes home on her own in a few hours? We would have worried him for nothing."

I was reaching for straws and knew it, but I just couldn't deal with any more heartbreak and confusion. They had been constant companions since the day I landed back in Australia.

Jake covered my trembling hands with his own.

"Listen, Brylee," he said. "I wish I could assure you that everything will be okay, but we don't know where this is going to lead. I'm not a religious person, but even I need hope."

"You're right," I said, surprised that I was letting his hands remain on mine, but I needed strength beyond what I could summon on my own right now.

"Maybe I can keep him occupied so he won't ask too many questions. He has been begging me to teach him how to cook—as if I know my way around a kitchen. You would be a much better teacher than me."

"You're selling yourself short again, Brylee. I happen to think you will make a great wife and mother when the time comes. You are a strong and determined woman."

"No, I'm not," I said, pulling my hands away so I could brush back the tears that were staring to fall. Jake was the second man to tell me I was strong, and it just wasn't true. "I'm acting like a child, but I never expected anything like this to happen."

"How could you," he replied, leaning back on his chair as if our moment of intimacy had made him as uncomfortable as it made me. "We are a complicated lot, we Aussies. Why do you think we drink so much? We're incapable of expressing our true feelings without something to help loosen us up. That is why we react instead of talking things out."

I had to smile despite the grave situation we were in.

"That explains our rash decision-making skills, but it doesn't help us right now, does it?"

"It made you smile. That has to count for something. Now . . . ." He looked at the clock on the two-burner stove. "It's after four. I will be able to take off for Edna in an hour. Until then, I suggest we both try to get a little rest. I'll keep you posted on anything I find out, and you can do the same. I have a feeling it is going to be a very long day."

Jake was right about that. I went back to the house and lay down on my bed, but when I closed my eyes, I had visions of

LeAnn lying in a coffin in the living room like my father had done just a little over a week earlier. So I slipped off the bed and onto my knees. I couldn't think of anything to say except, "Father, help me! I can't make it through this on my own."

After a few minutes of kneeling, my heart started to slow. I took a deep breath and prayed for LeAnn's safety and that Trevor would understand what was happening without feeling guilty or abandoned. I also prayed for the wisdom to make the complicated decisions that seemed to keep materializing from out of nowhere.

Since all thoughts of sleep had vanished, I took a long shower and dressed for the day. It was 5:20 in the morning when I re-entered the kitchen. LeAnn had been already been gone for several hours.

I sat down at the kitchen table and rested my head in my arms. Was this how my father had felt when I ran away? I had never considered how my leaving might have affected him until recently, but he must have been frantic with worry. That's how I felt right now. Was LeAnn safe? Would she come back on her own? Would we ever see her again? But one thing I knew for sure, I couldn't judge her for having to leave. Sometimes that seemed like the only alternative to stop a heart from completely breaking.

I heard Jake's plane take off a few minutes later. It was getting light. I wished there was some way I could reach LeAnn and help her understand that running away wasn't the answer. I had lost five precious years with my father by doing the very same thing. She didn't want to have that regret with Trevor. I contemplated calling Uncle Ned but decided it would be best not to sound any alarms in case she returned during the day.

Since there didn't appear to be anything I could do to help find my stepmother, I decided to email Ben. He was stable and logical and would just be getting off work, but maybe he would check his email before going home or doing something with friends.

It seemed like I had been away from him forever. How I missed the simplicity and predictability of our life together. I had done nothing for the past two and a half months except go from one upsetting situation to another with never enough time in between to get grounded before something even more traumatic happened.

I would be lucky if I didn't have a complete physical or mental breakdown myself before leaving Australia, but even the thought of a psychotic split from reality didn't frighten me as much as the fact that I was changing inside. I rarely smiled and had almost lost my belief in miracles and happy endings.

Life was just too hard and without Ben's support when I was vulnerable in so many ways. I had grown up in an environment where alcohol was used to dull pain and relieve boredom, and where people used each other for physical comfort without commitment or love. I simply had to make it through this latest challenge without falling apart like LeAnn had done, or allowing myself to become involved with something I would only regret.

I was looking through one of LeAnn's cookbooks when Trevor came running down the stairs with Copper close behind him.

"What are you doing?" he asked as he sat down at the table beside me. "Those are mum's books, aren't they?"

"Yes," I replied. "I thought today would be a good time for us to learn how to make a few things. I get tired of eating the same old stuff all the time, don't you?"

"I guess so," he said. "Maybe we could take something to mum. I know she would eat it if I made it for her."

"I'm sure she would love anything you made," I replied as I forced an unfelt smile. I wasn't exactly lying to him. It was more a matter of avoiding certain information, but Jake and I had decided not to say anything about his mother's disappearance until every lead came to an end.

"But first, I think we should eat a healthy breakfast," I continued before my courage waned. "I'm sure we will be making plenty of goodies and will want to sample as we go. So what do you feel like eating?"

"Toast and eggs," he said. "I haven't had that since mum got sick."

"Then toast and eggs it is," I quickly replied, knowing that I had to keep him distracted so he wouldn't ask me anything else about his mother. I didn't want to make matters worse by responding with more half-baked lies and avoidance.

Trevor and I ate while we looked through cookbooks that boasted glorious, color photos of myriads of pastries, cakes, cookies, candy, crock-pot meals, and a hundred recipes for cooking mutton and lamb—a real staple among the Aussies.

I had never been much interested in cooking until I met Ben, and we'd had so little time together before I came home that I'd never really had many culinary experiences. Today would remedy that. Trevor and I would be creating memories that either made us laugh or allowed us cry.

Jake called at a quarter past eight. I had looked at the phone and clock so often I was surprised Trevor hadn't noticed, but he appeared blissfully happy measuring sugar, salt and butter into a large mixing bowl that would soon hold all the ingredients for chocolate, chocolate chip cookies.

"Can you talk?" he asked me.

I willed my voice to sound as normal as possible, even though my heart was racing. I didn't want to be here any more than LeAnn did, but I would never leave my little brother. "Trevor and I are making cookies."

"Then just listen. I haven't made much progress yet, but my friend checked the road between here and the ranch and didn't see the Land Rover. We have to believe she made it to town. I talked to one of our mutual friends from the diner. You remember, Beth. She was at your father's funeral, but she hasn't seen LeAnn since then."

I didn't want to hear about one of his admirers, but I couldn't let Trevor know that anything was bothering me, so I looked over at him and smiled. He was pouring chocolate chips into the batter. I motioned for him to stop for a moment.

"I see," I told Jake. "What's the next move?"

"Beth told me that Emma still lives in town. She is the owner of the diner and was a great friend to LeAnn back in the day. I don't know why I didn't think about her myself because I used to hang out there as a kid when LeAnn was waitressing. Anyway, Beth gave me both an address and a phone number, but I decided this was something that needed to be discussed in person. I'm on my way over there now. Wish me luck. I am afraid I just might need it."

"Always," I told him. "You will keep me posted?"

"As soon as I know anything you will. I don't suppose she has managed to make it back there."

"Not yet. Is there a number where I can reach you?"

"Wish there was. All I can do is promise to call as soon as I know something more."

"We will be right here in the kitchen baking. Good luck."

"I wish I didn't feel like I needed it, but if she isn't at Emma's, I don't know where else to look."

I wondered how successful his latest venture in finding his sister would be, but Trevor didn't give me time for either worry or contemplation.

"Who was that?" he asked, after I placed the receiver back on the wall.

"Your Uncle Jake! He went into town on some business."

"Will he be back when the cookies are finished?"

"He's not sure when he will be back, but why don't we make an entire meal? I think that would be a pretty good surprise after a long day, don't you?"

Trevor was excited about the novelty of creating food of his own. He made comments about his mother several times as we worked throughout the remainder of the morning but seemed to be okay with my rather vague answers. I just hoped Jake would call with good news before our meal preparations were finished. I had no idea what we were going to do after that.

The distraction of teaching Trevor to make cookies, a pie, fudge and an oven-meal of pork roast, potatoes, carrots and onions did little to relieve the panic I felt growing inside. My mind was consumed with negatives and the only thing I knew for sure was that I would move heaven and earth to make sure I was the one raising Trevor if he was ever left alone.

"Brylee." The sound of his voice brought me back to a very precarious present. The timer on the oven had gone off.

"I'm sorry, Trevor," I told him. "I guess my mind was wandering."

He frowned as I opened the oven door and removed the pie we had made from a can of peaches I found in the pantry. It was perfectly browned. I just hoped the crust would be flaky. What a funny thing to think about when everything in our world was in such disarray.

"I haven't been very good company today, have I?" I asked him as I put the pie on a metal rack to cool.

"It's okay," he said. "I am worried about mum too."

"You're an amazing little brother," I told him. "I am so glad we found each other."

He was sitting on a stool next to the cupboard, and I pulled him into my arms and kissed the top of his head. How could LeAnn ever leave him? He would bring nothing but joy into her life if she would just give him a chance. He was so intuitive and loving and didn't deserve what had happened to his world.

Jake called again at 11:30. I was far from prepared for what he had to say.

"LeAnn is at Emma's, but she won't come out of the bedroom and talk to me. I tried every approach I could think of, but all she would say is that she can't come back to the ranch. It brings back too many sad memories."

"But what about . . . . ?"

"Trevor?" he finished for me. "She said he was better off without her because every time she looks at him she sees your father, and she can't take any more pain."

"But that doesn't make any sense."

"Nothing about this situation makes sense. Emma and I are trying to convince her to see a doctor. I know he could put her on something to help combat the depression. We think she needs some counseling too."

I felt Trevor's eyes on me, so I looked over my shoulder and smiled at him. How could I tell him that his mother was gone and might not be coming back? He was too young to understand.

"I agree," I told him.

"Is Trevor still with you?"

"Of course! We just took a peach pie out of the oven. I hope you will be hungry when you get back."

"Listen, I am going to stick around Emma's for awhile. She said LeAnn is welcome to stay with her for as long as she wants, but she is plenty worried about her too. She says my sister looks horrid and isn't the least bit rational. Emma is afraid she might do something stupid."

"So am I."

"Unfortunately, I concur, but let's try not borrow any more trouble than we have already got. We will discuss options when I get home."

I fought the tightness in my throat. How could I continue pretending that life would go on as usual when everything was so very wrong? I wasn't ready for the responsibility of trying to raise a child. That was supposed to come much later, after Ben and I had been married for a while and then we would start with an infant.

"Do you know when that might be?" I asked him.

"A couple of hours, probably. I can't leave Emma alone to deal with LeAnn quite yet. It really isn't her problem."

"Then I guess we will see you when you get here."

"I really sorry this happened, Brylee, but I can't begin to tell you how grateful I am that you are here for Trevor. I'm afraid he is going to need both of us to make it through this."

My heart was heavier than ever when I hung up the phone and turned back to face my little brother. He looked so small, lost and alone. How could I ever help him when I didn't even know how to help myself?

"Was that Uncle Jake again?" he asked. "Is he coming home soon?"

"He's not exactly sure but should be here in time for dinner. He's very excited to eat all the yummy things we have been making today."

"And mum too," he said, jumping down from the stool. "Can I go and tell her what we have been doing? She has been sleeping all day."

I thought my heart would break for him. There was no way I could continue to avoid his questions. He was a very smart little boy.

"Why don't we take a walk?" I suggested. I couldn't talk to him about his mother when we were in the house. He would just want to go to her room to see for himself that she was gone.

Trevor wanted to take Copper, but having an active puppy with us might prove a huge liability. When I suggested he put her in her kennel he didn't argue.

I prayed that the right words would come as we crossed the hard-packed earth of the driveway. Oh, how I wished Jake had been able to convince LeAnn to come back before Trevor had to know what was going on, but his last call had stripped away that possibility. And even she did come home, it wouldn't help Trevor any if she never came out of her room. He needed to know that there were still people in his life he could count on.

"Can we go swing?" he asked when we walked into the barn. "You could push me really high so my feet could go out the window."

"Why not!" I told him, looking around at all the ancient equipment that was covered in layers of cobwebs and dust. Boards were loose or missing entirely from the sections of the walls. No wonder Jake was already talking about the repairs that needed to be made. Everywhere I looked there were signs of decay.

The window Trevor was referring to was the opening in the barn's loft where the bales of hay were lifted on a derrick so they could be stacked away from the animals that would eventually eat them. There weren't many of them left, and that worried me almost as much as Trevor getting hurt by let go of the ropes that held the swing suspended from the rafters. I followed as he climbed up the boards that had been nailed less than two inches away from an outside wall. I had to turn my feet sideways to keep from slipping off, but there was no need for concern about getting slivers. The boards had been polished smooth from having been climbed so often.

Once our heads peaked through the hole in floor as we pulled ourselves into the loft. Trevor ran to the swing and sat down on the flat, wooden board that had been used as a seat for decades—probably from the time our first great-grandfather Hawkins had built it.

"Higher," he shouted as I pushed him from behind.

He was laughing. It was a sound I hadn't heard since he had gotten Copper for his birthday.

"I'm trying," I called out. "Just don't let go of the ropes. I don't want you to fall off."

"I won't fall. I just want my feet to go out the window so I can look at the trees and the sky."

I understood exactly how he felt. Being nearly twenty feet off the ground brought a different perspective to the land and blue expanse surrounding us. It also made us level with the upper branches and leaves of nearby trees. I could see a large nest nestled close to the trunk of the one closest to us as he moved back and forth. If I was a few years younger—and had no aversion to heights—I might be tempted to see what was inside.

He screamed with delight as I braced my feet on the floor and pushed him as hard as I could—running a few steps after him I had done it with such force.

"I can see! I can see!" he shouted. "Do it again! Do it again!"

So I did! I kept right on pushing him until my entire body gave out, and I sank down onto a bail of hay that had started to split open.

"I couldn't push you again right now if my life depended on it," I panted as I watched each repetition of motion make the swing move slower. "I'm too tired to move."

It wasn't long until he jumped to the floor and sat down beside me.

"That was fun, Brylee," he said. "Can we do it every day?"

"If I can find the energy," I told him. "You really made me feel my age today."

I ran my hand over his soft hair. It was damp with perspiration, but then so was mine.

"There is something I need to talk to you about, Trevor."

I waited for him to answer.

"It's about mum, isn't it?"

"Yes," I replied, wishing I had gone into child psychology instead of accounting. There was no easy way to tell a child that his mother had left home and might not be coming back, at least not any time soon. "She is going through a very hard time right now."

"She's sad because father's gone, isn't she?"

"Yes, and she has decided she needs a little time away from the ranch to think things out, but she's okay. She will probably be home in a few days."

"Where did she go?" he asked.

"She's in Edna."

"Then I need to go there too so I can take care of her. I promised father."

Dejection and confusion were etched into every feature of his face when he jumped to his feet, but I pulled him back down beside me.

"You don't have to worry about her, Trevor. She is being well taken care of."

"But I promised," he said as tears started to slide from the corners of his eyes. He was trying so hard to be a man.

"I know you did, but there are some things adults need to do on their own," I replied, wishing I knew the exact contents of the discussion he'd had with our father. "It doesn't mean they love or need us any less. Your mother spent all her time caring for father the past couple of months. It took a lot out of her. She just needs some time to rest and get strong again. You know how sad and tired she's been."

I pulled him into my arms. He didn't say anything. He just snuggled close to me, and I pulled a strand of hay from of his hair. He was so young and impressionable. Why had our father made him promise something that was so far beyond his capability? But then how could anyone have known what LeAnn was going to do? She had seemed so totally together when we met and had handled my father's illness with such compassion and courage that I had allowed myself to believe she could deal with anything.

That gullible premise had now been shattered, but I wasn't ready to assume any more responsibilities than the ones I already had. I just wanted to go home and marry Ben.

"Don't look so worried, Trevor," I said. "She has ask your Uncle Jake and me to take care of you while she is away and we plan on having lots of fun."

It wasn't a promise I should have made without consulting Jake, but it was the only thing I could think of that might make

Trevor feel a little less scared. Besides, Trevor was my family now, regardless of what his mother was doing, and it was my duty to protect and take care of him even if I didn't know how to do it.

Jake got home shortly after five that afternoon. He had been gone for twelve hours and appeared to have aged significantly during that time. I wondered if I looked much the same way. I certainly felt a lot older than when awakening during the night to find LeAnn gone.

"Something smells delicious," he told Trevor as he washed his hands at the kitchen sink.

"We made roast and potatoes," Trevor told him. "And we have cookies and pie for dessert."

"Well, I'm starved." Jake replied, wiping his hands on a kitchen towel and then joining his nephew at the table that had been set for three.

I was standing in front of the stove scooping vegetables onto the serving platter where the pork roast sat ready for carving. It was evident from Jake's demeanor that he had made no headway with his sister.

Everything tasted far better than I thought it would, and Jake made all the appropriate comments, but the uneasiness I felt inside kept me from enjoying a single mouthful. I was more than grateful when dessert had been served, and Trevor said he wanted to play in his room with Copper before going to bed.

I thought Jake and I might be able to talk while he was out of the room, but when I started to ask him a question, he put me off by saying we would talk later because he had a few things he needed do. So I cleaned the kitchen and then joined Trevor in his bedroom where we played a few games before I read him a story and pulled the sheet up to his chin.

"See you in the morning, little brother," I said, before bending down and placing a kiss on his forehead.

"Will mum be coming back then?" he asked.

"I'm not sure, but we will plan something fun, I promise."

I didn't wait for his reply. I simply turned off the light and slipped out the door. I couldn't play this pretending game any longer. I needed answers because the thoughts running through my head were driving me crazy.

Jake was on the veranda when I stepped outside to get some air.

"I'm really worried," he said, lighting a cigarette before sitting down on the wooden glider and motioning for me to join him.

I didn't want to be that close to him and I certainly didn't want to have smoke blown in my face, but given our rather precarious situation it seemed rather foolish to object. So I sat down beside him, folded my hands in my lap waited for him to continue.

"LeAnn wouldn't talk to me. I waited in that house for over five hours hoping she would change her mind and come home. She finally told Emma she would consider going to see a doctor when she felt stronger, but I don't know if she will actually do it. She may have just been trying to get rid of me. What are we going to tell Trevor? I'm afraid he is going to be without his mum for a very long time."

I sat for a few moments in stunned silence as the enormity of what he had just said swept over me. What did LeAnn's refusal to come home mean for Trevor? And what did it mean for Ben and me? I couldn't bear being away from him any longer, but my hands were tied unless a miracle occurred and I was beginning to wonder if they still existed.

"I talked to him about the possibility of his mother being gone for a few days earlier today," I said as my lungs constricted in a physical ache.

Jake blew a smoke ring into the air.

"I thought we were going to do that together."

"We were, but he was so adamant that his mother would come out if she knew he was the one fixing dinner that I felt it necessary to tell him as much as I thought he could handle. What if he had gone to her room and seen for himself that she wasn't there? He would think that in addition to both of his parents leaving him, he couldn't trust us either. He needed to know that there would always be someone in his life to love and take care of him."

He leaned back in the swing and looked up into the star-filled Australian sky. "You're right. How did he take it?"

"He said he had promised our father that he would take care of his mother."

"That is a mighty big promise for such a little guy."

"I don't think father meant for him to take it literally. He just wanted to give him something to think about other than his impending death."

"Adults can really screw kids up," Jake said with a sigh that suggested he was thinking about more than just the situation we were involved in right now.

"I suppose so," I replied. "You and I certainly seem to have our share of issues."

"The blind leading the blind, so to speak. I love being Trevor's uncle, but I'm not sure I am ready to take on a parental role."

"Me, either," I admitted. "But who will do it if we don't?"

"No one! So I guess that means it's up to us to make sure he has as normal a life as possible until his mum comes to her senses. I just can't believe LeAnn would walk out on him like she did. But then, I should have considered the possibility after what happened when your mother died."

Jake put his cigarette out on the sole of his boot and threw the butt onto the hard-packed, earthen driveway. Then he turned his body so he was looking directly at me. I felt a moment of alarm and wanted to escape, but I couldn't show my reluctance to be around him when Trevor needed both of us so desperately.

"What's the matter, aside from the obvious?" he asked as his eyes searched mine in the semi-darkness of the porch light. "This has turned out to be one hell of a vacation for you. I know we've had our differences since you got here, but I hope you will believe me when I say that I never wanted you to get caught up in all our family drama. I was really hoping LeAnn would be able to handle this, and there would be no more hard feelings between us."

"None of this is your fault, Jake, and I know we need to work together if we are going to help Trevor."

He placed his hand over mine, but I recoiled just enough for him to notice. The removal of that hand was instantaneous but our moment of closeness was over.

"I really thought you would turn tail and run back to that boyfriend of yours long before now," he said, after clearing his throat in the process. "It can't be easy staying here when your heart is somewhere else."

"Ben will understand."

Jake chuckled. "You've said that before, and I will continue to tell you that absence does not make the heart grow stronger, unless it is towards someone else."

"I really do wish you would quit saying that. Ben isn't like other guys. He would never cheat on me."

"Bull dust," he responded in a huff. "I thought the same thing about Wendy until she proved me wrong and we were even closer to our big day than you and surfer boy."

His choice of words when it came to describing Ben infuriated me. I didn't love and want to marry Ben because he was handsome and athletic, although that was a definite plus. I loved him because he loved me, and because I always wanted to be a better person when we were together. I didn't want to believe that God might have something different in mind for us, but everything surrounding me seemed to be falling apart right now.

I choked back a sob of bitterness and fear.

"I love Ben with all my heart, but I love Trevor too."

"And you are willing to stay here, even if it means giving up the man you love?"

My heart plummeted, and I tried to push the possibility of losing Ben away. It had never seemed real until now, but Jennifer was back in his life, and they had loved each other before he went on his mission. Was it possible that those old feelings were being rekindled because I wasn't there? Jake certainly thought that was going to happen, and he didn't even know Jennifer existed.

"I will stay for as long as Trevor needs me," I assured him.

"That could be a very long time. I don't mean to sound like a whacker, but we have no idea when, or even if, LeAnn will come back. Are you really ready to sacrifice your personal happiness for someone you barely know?"

I clasp my hands together again in a vain attempt to keep them from trembling. I had suddenly become very cold and very worried that my fragile world of happiness was about to explode.

"I have to believe that all things happen for a reason, and if Ben and I are meant to be together nothing will stop that from happening—no matter how long I stay here."

"Then you have more faith in human nature than I do," he replied, bringing his arm up and around my back to rest on the top of the swing. "I've noticed that you haven't been wearing your ring lately."

It wasn't the first time he had mentioned that, and his nearness made the fine hairs on the back of neck bristle.

"I have been doing a lot of cooking and cleaning. I didn't want to lose it."

"Are you sure that is the only reason? Long distance relationships are hell to maintain and rarely work out. Believe me, I know that from first-hand experience. People are always evolving. If they are not together geographically it is very easy for one or both of them to become disinterested—or in my case find someone else who could be there when I wasn't."

"Ben and I will be fine. He knows why I can't be there right now."

"If you say so." He stood up and stretched his back. "I really do hope things work out for you. Someone around here deserves to be happy."

I sat on the swing long after he had gone. Was I being unrealistic and maybe even a little naïve and unfair? Ben deserved to have someone in his life that was completely there for him. Even if I returned home and we got married, part of my heart would always be here on the ranch. I would never quit worrying about Trevor, even if LeAnn came back to raise him.

But what if she didn't come back? I would have no choice except to stay here or see if I could take him back to L.A. to live with Ben and me. That wasn't something Ben had signed on to do when he asked me to marry him, and gaining LeAnn's permission to take   her son away from his home would likely never happen. And even if it did, asking Trevor to leave the ranch when it was all he had left was selfish. He loved the land every bit as much as my father had.

Chapter 19

The next few days were overwhelming. I fixed meals, cleaned the house, and spent every moment I could with Trevor. Jake called Emma every morning to see how LeAnn was doing, but there was never much change. She mainly stayed in the guest bedroom, and when she did come out, she just sat on the sofa and cried. She was still losing weight and refused to see a doctor about the state of her physical and mental health.

Trevor asked questions about his mother a few times, but after being told there had been no change for several days he simply let the subject go. That worried me, but it seemed to be understood that as soon as we knew something, he would.

Jake joined us for meals and took Trevor up in the plane every day or so to give me some alone time. I appreciated his thoughtfulness and used those precious minutes to write to Ben. His replies to my emails were always positive and encouraging, but we weren't talking about "us" as much. He knew about LeAnn's absence, and the delicate situation I was in with Trevor. He suggested I bring Trevor to L.A. for a short visit. It was a wonderfully thoughtful idea, and one I had thought about numerous times, but Trevor didn't have a passport. It could take months, or even years, for him to get one because LeAnn would have to agree to it and right now she wasn't speaking to any of us.

I wished she hadn't taken the Land Rover. Without transportation, I felt incredibly isolated. I took Trevor on outings to Uncle Ned's so he could ride Thunder, but even those short trips were less than joyous. Aunt Nora fed him cookies while I talked to Uncle Ned about business. But when it came time to start home, I was just as empty inside as I had been when we were riding there.

One morning after LeAnn had been gone for ten days, Jake came into the kitchen for breakfast in the best mood I had seen him in since LeAnn pulled her disappearing act. Trevor noticed it immediately.

"Is mum coming home today?" he excitedly asked.

Jake squatted down in front of him. "I'm afraid not, but I had what I think is a pretty good idea if you and your sister agree to it."

That peaked Trevor's interest after another disappointment concerning his mother.

"What idea?" he asked in a very skeptical tone.

"Well," Jake continued, not the least ruffled by his less than enthusiastic response. "I don't have anything urgent to do on the ranch today, so I thought we could all drive into town, have lunch and catch a matinee at the cinema. I don't know what's playing, but we could be back before evening chores."

Trevor threw his arms around Jake with such force that it almost propelled both of them to the floor. "Oh, thank you, Uncle Jake! I haven't ridden in your truck for ages."

"Then it's about time that changed. It will take a couple of hours to get there, but there's AC, and it should be a pleasant drive."

This was the first time I had heard Jake talk about having a means of transportation other than his plane, but it didn't surprise me. He was a very private man, and keeping secrets appeared to be part of his genetic makeup.

My father's old truck, that had rarely been used even when I was a child, wouldn't make it any farther than Uncle Ned's ranch, and I was deathly afraid of trying to drive it, especially with Trevor sitting beside me.

Jake stood up, and Trevor looked at me for permission. "We can go, can't we, Brylee?"

I wasn't sure how I felt about spending a day with them away from the ranch, but if it made Trevor happy that had to be good enough for me.

"I don't see why not," I told him. "Cleaning can always wait. What time do you want to leave?"

"Around nine. That would give us plenty of time for lunch, and depending on what time the movie starts, maybe we can stop by the toy store in the mall."

"I will feed my animals right now." Trevor said, jumping from his chair and running across the kitchen floor towards the back door, but he wasn't fast enough. Jake caught him by the neck of his t-shirt.

"Back up a minute, young mate. Your sister has breakfast on the table, and we still have a couple of hours before we need to leave."

Trevor sighed and lowered his shoulders in defeat. "Okay, but if we get ready sooner can we go?"

"I'll tell you what. Eat your breakfast and feed your animals, and then you can help me with all the other chores. That will give you something to do while your sister gets ready. It takes girls a little longer than it does us—all the hair, makeup and stuff."

Trevor gave me a strange expression, but I was too stunned by Jake's show of understanding to react. He had been doing that quite often lately, and I had to wonder just how long the change would last.

It was nearly nine by the time chores were done and everyone had showered and dressed for an outing in town. I combed Trevor's hair so it wouldn't look like he had just climbed out of bed. I felt strangely uncomfortable. It was almost like we had become a family, only I wasn't sure how we fit together yet.

Purposefully, I wore my engagement ring. It made me feel closer to Ben, and less like I was cheating on him by going into to town with Jake and Trevor to see a movie. It was a ridiculous thought since he and Jennifer had done the same thing on several occasions, and they had been seriously involved once. Jake and I were somewhere between unwanted family and halfhearted friends.

I offered to sit in the back seat of his extended cab truck so Trevor could see more easily, but Jake insisted that there wasn't enough legroom. My little brother was so excited about going into town that I was sure he would have ridden in the truck's bed with the hot sun beating down on him if that arrangement had been opened for discussion.

"This is a nice truck," I told Jake after we had left the familiarity of the lane that led up to the ranch house. "I didn't even know you had one."

It was a new, gray, extended cab pickup truck, but I hadn't taken note of the model.

"I keep it in the shed by the bunkhouse. It's rarely driven, but I guess we will have to use it until the Land Rover comes back. I don't think that old truck of your fathers would make it very far with or without a serious tune-up."

I glanced over my shoulder at Trevor who was staring out the side window and didn't appear to have heard what Jake said. He didn't need to have his day ruined by talking about our father. Not that we would ever forget him but we still had to go on living, regardless of our loss.

"Sorry about that," Jake recanted. "Sometimes I have momentary lapses in judgment It's not like I have forgotten anything."

"None of us have, but this is our reality for now. Hopefully, it won't always be like this."

"I'm not complaining," he replied. "It has given me a chance to get to know the real you."

How was I supposed to respond to that without leading him to believe something that wasn't true? I was enjoying the time we spent together without fighting, but Jake could never expect more than friendship. My real life was with Ben. This was just something I had to do.

"Thanks for suggesting this trip," I said, without looking in his direction. "Trevor is so excited. It's almost like he has never been to a movie before."

If Jake noticed my evasiveness, he didn't let it show.

"I'm not sure he has, at least not since he was old enough to remember it. Living out on the ranch doesn't leave much time for what most people would call normal living."

"Perhaps the idea of normalcy depends on the person interpreting it," I responded. "I thought it was perfectly normal to be home-schooled and never leave the ranch when I was young, except for occasional shopping trips into town or going to Uncle Ned's to see my cousins."

"Ah, your cousins! I haven't seen them around lately. I suppose Miss Molly is back at school charming all the blokes there. She is a feisty little thing. Wouldn't want to be the man she reels in."

"Why not?" I asked him. "The two of you seem to enjoy bantering back and forth."

"She is a child, and a very spoiled one at that. I want a woman with substance—a woman who has seen enough life to be interesting, yet hasn't allowed it to take her sweetness away. There aren't many women out here like that."

"Even the girls in town?" I asked. "I am quite sure they didn't come to father's service to see the rest of us."

He shook his head and started to laugh.

"You refuse to give me a break, don't you? I wish you could learn to see yourself the way other's do, and quit hiding from experiences that make life really worth living."

His insinuation was insulting. I wasn't hiding from life. How could I be when I had been given more responsibility than I could possibly handle?

"Just because I don't grovel at your feet like other women, it doesn't mean I am hiding from anything. I know where I'm supposed to be. It's just taking a little longer to get there than anticipated."

"Is that why you're wearing your ring today? You need it to remind you that you belong to someone else? Life isn't horizontal! It is full of twists and turns, and we don't always end up with the first person we fall in love with."

Now he was just making me mad! Why did he insist on returning to the subject of my engagement when I had made it perfectly clear that it was none of his business? Did he honestly believe that every woman he met would find him irresistible? As much as I would like to set him straight, I wasn't going to do it now. I would bite off my tongue first. This was Trevor's day, and he deserved to spend it around adults who knew how to act civil, even when they didn't want to.

"Why don't we just agree to disagree," I told him. "Some things in life just are, and they're not open for debate."

I turned around and looked at Trevor again.

"Hey, little brother," I said. "Where would you like to go for lunch? It should be some place special."

Trevor squinted as if doing so would help him make a better decision. "Can't we just go to Macca's? I like it there, and maybe there will be other kids."

Oh, how lonely he must be surrounded by adults all day. Even Copper couldn't give him the socialization he needed. It had been different for me growing up in the outback. I had been content spending the majority of time with my mother because I didn't know there was anything else. Trevor had spent his first three or so years in town, and while I was sure he didn't consciously remember much of it, I was certain he'd had other kids to play with.

Jake just scowled at Trevor's suggestion, but went along with it because my little brother looked so happy being given the chance to make a decision that included more than himself. I pulled the debit card my father had gotten for me out of my purse as we stood in line to place our orders. It touched my heart with a sad kind of gladness every time I thought about the contents of his will, but I still felt guilty not using my own money for such a small thing as a meal away from home. There was no way of knowing how long I would remain in Australia, and when I returned to California and Ben, I would need something to live on until I was gainfully employed again. Less than five hundred dollars would not last long.

"Put that card away," Jake said. "This is my treat. I have never had a date pay for anything in my life and am not about to start now."

"This isn't exactly a date," I whispered, not wanting to cause a scene in a public place.

"Don't get all ruffled," he whispered back. "It was an unfortunate choice of words. I haven't forgotten where you stand on the subject of men."

Trevor was looking at me oddly, so I smiled at him instead of engaging in another verbal battle with his uncle.

"Thank you," I told Jake as I put the debit card away. I wanted to say that the next time the treat was on me, but there might not be a next time. I was going to marry Ben as soon as I possibly could. He was the only man I knew who could make my dream of having an eternal family come true.

We watched other customers come and go as we sat in a booth and ate. Trevor's eyes darted rapidly back and forth as each child arrived. It was evident that he wanted to join in their play but was hesitant to even try until we had finished eating and Jake had given him permission to climb through the assortment of colored boxes that made up the framework of the slides, shoots and ladders other kids were already playing on.

"I'm sorry for being difficult, Jake, " I said once my own burger and fries were gone. Trevor was looking down at us from the entrance to a slide that made several turns before reaching the floor. He looked happy and waved at us, but when two other children joined him, he hung back and his smile faded. My heart went out to him, and I wished I was small enough to climb inside some of the boxes too.

"No worries," Jake said, watching my little brother as intently as I was. "It wasn't my intention to make you uncomfortable. I just thought we could all use a break from the ranch. The past few weeks have been hell for all of us."

He looked so sincere I reached across the table and touched his hand.

"You're a good man, Jake Johnson, and I appreciate all you have done. Trevor needs you now more than ever."

He took his free hand and placed it over mine. The soft pressure made my head begin to swim, but the comfort of human contact prevented me from pulling away. How I missed Ben! I needed him in every way. He was my anchor, my iron rod. Without him, I was like a dry leaf being tossed to and fro in the dry, hot wind.

"Why are you so afraid of me?"

Jake's question brought me back to the reality of my life now, not the one waiting for me in Los Angeles.

"I'm not afraid of you," I retorted, jerking my hand away from his.

"But you are and just proved it."

My face flushed scarlet. "Just because I don't want to hold hands doesn't mean I am afraid of you. I belong to someone else."

"But if you didn't, would it make any difference?"

"I can't answer that because it won't happen. I am going to get married as soon as I return to the United States."

"And when will that be? You promised Trevor you wouldn't leave and you cannot keep one promise without breaking the other?"

Tears of anger and frustration formed in my eyes. "I'm just trying to do what is right for everyone."

"But what's right for you, Brylee?" He looked at me so intently I began to squirm and looked away.

"It doesn't matter what I want right now. My little brother has to be my main concern."

"That he does," Jake concurred. "I don't suppose any of us can go back to the way things used to be, but that doesn't mean we can't take what is right in front of us and enjoy it."

"You simply refuse to hear what I am saying," I responded, shaking my head with resignation. "You still think I am like every other girl you have met, but one-night stands with no commitment is not for me."

Jake leaned back in the booth and laughed. "So you think that's what my being nice to you is all about?"

When he said it like that, it sounded absurd, but I still looked around in embarrassment wondering who had heard. Fortunately, there were few people in the restaurant and they seemed to be involved in conversations of their own.

"Come on, Brylee," he said. "We're both adults who are capable of making decisions. We can do whatever makes us happy and right now, I think you need someone to hold and comfort you without any strings attached. That's all I am offering. If something were to happen in the future, it would come from a mutual agreement."

It took a few moments for me to order my thoughts. If I hadn't met Ben and joined the church things might be different, but I couldn't turn my back on everything I now believed? One moment of comfort was not worth risking an eternity with everyone I loved?

"I don't expect you to understand where I'm coming from, Jake. Maybe if we had met a few years ago things . . . . You're an attractive man, and I am not indifferent to you, but I made a promise to both God and Ben that I would be faithful to the covenants I made when I was baptized. I am a different person than I was even six months ago."

"So, now I'm a temptation!" He lifted his eyebrows in mock surprise. "I guess that is better than not being appreciated at all. But it really is too bad you didn't come home sooner. I think we could make quite a team."

"We can still be a team, but not in the way you're suggesting," I told him. "We have a ranch to run and a very special little boy to take care of."

"But you expect us to do that without indulging in any pleasantries when we both admit to feeling a certain attraction. Still, if that's the way you want to play it, I have no other choice."

His willingness to accept my position without making a federal case of it almost made me reevaluate my impression of him, but that would be a huge mistake since we were living at the ranch with only a little boy to run interference.

"It's the best way for everyone involved," I told him as Trevor ran up to me and put his arms around my neck.

"Are you having fun?" I asked.

"Yes, but those kids want to know if I can come back tomorrow to play," he said. His face was literally glowing. Their acceptance meant the world to him.

"We live a long way from town, but if they will point out their mother, I will see if we can set up a play date. I don't see why we can't come into town more often. I think your Uncle Jake would agree with me."

I smiled at the man sitting across the table, hoping he would be open to my suggestion since he was the only one with transportation.

"I think that could be arranged," Jake told him. "I have to fly into town every so often for supplies anyway. I don't know why you couldn't come along and have some fun with your new mates. Someone at the ranch should be able to enjoy life once in awhile."

His words were lost on Trevor but not on me.

Trevor kissed my cheek and hugged Jake before running off to rejoin his new friends. I spotted a woman sitting on the far side of the room watching the children play. Since she was the only other adult in the area, it was easy to make an assumption.

"If you'll excuse me," I said to Jake. "I think I will talk to their mother. Trevor really does need friends to play with."

"How can you be sure she is their mother?" he asked as he appraised the woman who looked to be in her early thirties and was rather pretty, if one liked the hardened type who had seen far too much sun.

"Because no one—other than a mother—would be hanging out here by choice."

"Point taken," he said, turning his attention back to me. "I'll get some coffee and wait for you. And just for the record, I know you're right about not pursuing any kind of a relationship right now. We have to concentrate on Trevor. The two of us becoming involved would only complicate everything."

"And how!" I muttered as I walked away. I would be safer being around another Eastern Brown Snake. It could only take my life. Jake could take my soul.

"Excuse me," I said to the woman in a tank top and a very short skirt. "I'm Brylee Hawkins."

I extended my hand in her direction like I had learned how to do at church when I was meeting someone new. She did likewise, but her fingers barely closed over mine.

"I've been watching your son play," she said. "You and your husband must be very proud of him. He has such charming manners. I can't even get my kids to say grace before a meal. They just want to shovel the food in."

"He is my little brother," I told her as I sat down in the booth across from her. "And the man with me is his uncle. It's rather a complicated situation."

"I'm sorry for getting it wrong," she apologized, looking rather pleased. "But you look like a family, and it's easy to see that the boy's uncle adores both of you. My husband walked out on us a couple of years ago, but I can remember when he looked at me like that. I'm Mary Jenkins, and my little rough necks are Veronica and Jesse. The kids seem to be getting along well."

I decided not to pursue her comment about the way Jake been looking at me. Our relationship was none of her concern anyway.

"That's what I wanted to talk to you about. We recently lost our father, and Trevor is having a rough time. We live two hours away in the outback so we don't get into town often, but I was hoping we could set up a play date for the next time we do. No other other children live near the ranch, and he gets very lonesome."

"I can see that," she said. "My kids are a product of divorce, and my ex spoils them. I think he is trying to win them back after cheating on me and then deserting all of us."

"I'm very sorry," I told her, trying not to think about LeAnn and my father and all the grief their affair had cost my mother and me.

"Oh, it's not so bad. I can date anyone I want to, and as long as my ex isn't late with child and spousal support we get along fine."

She looked past me at Jake who had returned to our booth to drink his coffee. "School's out, and I work in the cafeteria, so my time is free for pretty much anything."

"That's good, I replied, wondering if she was hinting that she would like to spend some of that free time with Jake. He seemed to have that effect on every woman who saw him— except for me.

"How about a week from Friday?" she asked when I didn't say anything more. "I'm taking the kids to the coast for a few days, but we will be back in town by then. We could meet here for lunch and go swimming at the city pool. It's the only way I can stand being outside in this heat, and I have the cutest bikini's." She looked over at Jake again, but if he noticed her interest in him, he didn't let it show.

"That should work," I told her. "But why don't we exchange phone numbers in case something comes up for either of us?"

She opened her purse and took out a pen and a piece of paper that had a child's drawing on it. She scribbled a few numbers and passed it to me.

"Why don't you write your number on the other half. Then I will know how to reach you and Trevor's uncle."

"His name is Jake," I told her as I wrote the telephone number at the ranch on the bottom of the paper and tore it in half. I wished there was some other way Trevor could meet children his own age. I didn't like getting involved with strangers.

"Then I will see all of you here next week at this time unless something changes for one of us," she responded. "Is there a cell number where I can reach you in case you're out of the house?"

I knew she was hinting at making contact with Jake, not me.

"Afraid not!" I told her. "We live too far out for that."

The rest of the afternoon went by without incident. We saw "Toy Story Three". I made sure that Trevor was sitting between us. We ate popcorn and drank soda and laughed. I hadn't laughed for such a long time that it was almost a cleansing experience. If real life were the least bit like it was represented in the movies, we would all be a whole lot happier.

But life was more than just having fun and eating popcorn. We were here to be tried and tested, and if we failed, we could loose everything of real value. I didn't want that to happen to me or to any of the people I loved.

At the toy store, Trevor saw a "Buzz Light Year" moveable toy. That was exactly what he wanted, so Jake bought it for him.

Once we were in the truck and on our way back to the ranch, I realized I hadn't even tried to call Ben while we were in town. That thought disturbed me. Why hadn't I excused myself to do it? I needed to hear his voice and feel more connected to him. I would send an email as soon as I got home and let him know about Trevor's playdate the following week so he could be near his phone.

We had a light supper of sandwiches and fruit. Then I went upstairs with Trevor to read some of his favorite stories before tucking him in bed. Lying beside him with my arm under his neck brought a sense of calmness because he snuggled right up next to me. Having children of my own would be a wonderful thing when the time came, but how could I ever consider having a life without my little brother in it?

"I love you, Brylee," he told me when it was time to turn out the lights.

"I love you too, little brother, now and forever," I said, suddenly knowing that I meant it with all my heart.

Chapter 20

Had I have known what the next morning would bring;
I might not have gone directly to my own room after tucking
Trevor into bed. But I was so emotionally and physically
drained I must have fallen asleep the moment my head hit the
pillow, and I didn't stir until the sound of rain pelting the
copper roof of the house woke me up. It was pitch black
outside, but I hurried to the window and looked out anyway.
The rain was sliding down the window with such force that I
could see nothing beyond the glass.

I hadn't seen rain like this since my childhood, and it
frightened me. I knew how much damage it could do from the
stories my father had told me about the great rains of his
youth. Rain that had filled the gullies, wiping out every living
thing in its path as it swept through the lowlands on its way to
the nearest riverbed or valley.

Suddenly, the door to my bedroom opened, and Trevor
came running in. "I'm scared, Brylee," he cried out. "I couldn't
turn on the lights. I tried."

He was sobbing when I took him in my arms.

"It will be okay. It's just a storm. I have a flashlight right here by my bed."

With one arm, I reached behind him and grabbed it.

"Here," I said, switching it on. "It's not so dark anymore. Why don't we go downstairs and wait for Jake. I am sure he's awake and will come looking for us."

I wasn't wrong in my assumptions. Before we made it to the top of the stairs, I heard the back door slam shut, and the sound of Jake's boots as they made contact with the linoleum-covered floor.

"Brylee," he shouted. "Where are you?"

"Up here," I called back. "We will be right down. I have Trevor with me."

"Not until you're dressed," he said. "And make sure you put something on your feet."

He took the stairs two at a time until he was on the second floor of the house with us. Water was dripping from every part of his body, but he had another flashlight with him. The two lights cast creepy shadows on the walls.

"I'll help Trevor," he shouted above the pelting rain. "Get dressed and don't take too long doing it."

I wanted to ask what was happening, but the urgency in his voice startled me into a fear-induced compliance.

"Please Heavenly Father," I silently prayed as tears slipped unceremoniously down my cheeks. I slipped a t-shirt over my head and pulled on the pair of jeans I had brought with me. My hands were shaking so hard I had trouble lacing my boots, but somehow I finally managed to get the job done.

Why was Jake in such a hurry unless we were in immediate danger? The ranch house had been built on an incline just below the side of a small hill. It would take a whole lot of water to reach us. Wouldn't we be much better off just staying where we were until first light when we could actually see what was going on and not just hear it?

"Are you ready?" Jake called out as he stuck his head inside my bedroom door. I could see from the light shimmering in front of him that he had Trevor by the hand.

"Where are we going?" I asked as I followed then down the stairs.

"I don't know, yet," he said, running his hand through his dripping hair. "I've been trying to get Ned on the CB radio, but no one answers. Their house sits a whole lot lower than this one, and they are closer to Hangman's Gulch than we are."

"Is it that bad?" I asked, and immediately wished I hadn't. No one could predict how much rain it would take before the gulch overflowed, except father and the aborigines, and none of them were around to help us any longer.

The rain was coming much harder and faster now, and the clamor on the roof made it impossible to hear what anyone was saying, so I didn't ask him if he thought Uncle Ned and Aunt Nora were safe. It seemed preposterous that the gulch could fill up with water in a matter of minutes and then overflow enough to reach them, but I knew Jake didn't share my naïve opinion. He had flown planes filled with supplies into areas of the outback that had been destroyed by too much rain.

"What do you want us to do?" I asked him as he strode into my father's office with Trevor and me trailing behind. My little brother was whimpering, and I took his hand when Jake relinquished it. He pulled back on my arm just as we were about to enter the room.

"We can't leave Copper alone upstairs," he said in a very frightened voice. "She's scared! We have to get her?"

I looked ahead to see if I could judge Jake's reaction to his request, but he had already disappeared into the dark abyss.

"Sure," I told him. "But she needs to stay in her kennel. We wouldn't want her to get frightened and run away. We would never find her until morning."

Since Jake seemed to have forgotten our presence, I took Trevor's hand, and together we climbed back up the staircase in the sinister dark. Copper was barking when we entered the bedroom. She usually slept with Trevor, but something had prompted me to put her in her kennel before going to bed. Divine providence people would likely say if they ever heard what had happened, but I knew it was just one of God's tender mercies.

"It's okay, Copper," Trevor said as he lifted the kennel with both of his hands. He could make it on his own, but I didn't want him tripping down the stairs. The sound of pounding rain was more than disconcerting.

"Why don't you let me carry the kennel, and you can guide us with the light."

He didn't object, so we retraced our steps to the office where Jake was waiting for us.

"Any luck getting through to them?" I asked without mentioning our return to the floor above.

"I haven't tried since coming inside! The CB radio is in the bunkhouse, and they are probably outside pushing the animals to higher ground anyway. Ned's lived through storms like this before. He knows what to do."

"Should we go and help them?" I asked as frightening visions of my uncle and aunt in the dark, foreboding rain brought tears of fear for their safety.

"Don't you think I would go out and look for them if I thought it would do any good? I got the truck halfway down the lane and had to turn back. The water has already washed away a big chunk of the road. I have seen storms before but never one like this that came without warning. There wasn't a cloud in the sky when I went to bed."

I sank down onto the leather sofa. So we were trapped here at the ranch with no way to get out. I had been worried before, but I was terrified now. My thoughts suddenly flew to the horses and animals that were trapped in their pens in the barn, but asking about their safety would only frighten my little brother more than he already was. He was curled up on the far end of the sofa with his new *Buzz Light Year* toy clasp tightly in his hands and Copper's kennel sitting beside him.

Jake seemed to anticipate the question I wanted to ask. "I don't think we have to worry about anything around here right now, but it might be a good idea to check on the animals again. We spend half our lives praying for rain, and the other half cleaning up after it comes. You stay here with Trevor. I shouldn't be gone long."

"But I want to go with you, Uncle Jake," Trevor said. "Newton needs me."

"Not a good idea!" Jake responded. "I'll take care of them for now. That rain is pelting like hail and has made the ground slippery. I will try to get the generator going while I'm gone. We still have a couple of hours until it is light enough to see anything."

"Be careful," I warned, not knowing what else to say.

"Always am," he replied. "Just stay in here where it's dry, and I will be back before you know it. If you want something useful to do, you might pull together some food and water that can be taken with us just in case we need it."

"We can do that," I replied, grateful that he had not used the word *evacuate*. If we couldn't get away in his truck that meant his plane was likely grounded too, and we would have to ride horses or walk. But where could we go to be safe? The animals stood a much better chance than we did if Jake released them from the confines of the pens and pasture.

"I'm scared," Trevor said the moment he was gone. "Why isn't mum here with us? I need her."

I knelt down in front of the sofa and pulled him into my arms. The rain didn't sound near so threatening on the main floor of the house.

"It's going to be okay," I told him. "We just need to have faith that God will take care of everyone, and that includes your mother, the animals, and all the people who are in the same situation we are."

But even as I was speaking those words, my thoughts flew to the family burial plot. Could the water reach that spot of land? And if it did, just how much damage could it do to the bodies of the family members who were resting there. Our father's grave had not even begun to settle yet.

"But what if God doesn't know we are here?" Trevor asked.

His timely question interrupted my disturbing thoughts. "God knows where all of his children are. Would you like to pray with me?"

"You mean *now I lay me down to sleep* again? Mum taught me how to say that."

"That's a good prayer, but since we are not going to bed, maybe we could ask God for something else."

"Like keeping Uncle Jake and my animals safe?"

"Yes, and asking that Uncle Ned and Aunt Nora are safe too."

"Okay," he said. "You say it. I will close my eyes."

And so we talked to God in that eerily dark room while the elements lashed out around us. The storm had come on so suddenly that people would not have had time to prepare for it. How I wished I had emailed Ben. That had become my nightly ritual, but I had been too tired after our long trip to town.

I don't know how many minutes passed while we waited for Jake to come back. Keeping an accurate accounting of time when fear is involved is nearly impossible, but I was almost certain I knew the exact place on the lane where the water had washed the road away. It was less than half a mile from the house. That wasn't nearly far enough, and a rain-induced ravine of any kind could take days to dry out before we could even attempt to refill it with dry dirt that had to come from somewhere.

And just how long would the rain keep falling? It had lasted for 40 days and 40 nights while Noah was on the ark. We didn't have an ark to take us to safety. We didn't even have a rowboat. We had never needed one before tonight.

Trevor's breathing slowed, and I knew he had fallen asleep. I covered him with the light blanket our father had often used during the last weeks of his life. It wasn't cold in the house but the air was damp, and I didn't want him to get sick. Copper had settled down in her kennel. Trevor had asked to hold her again, but I had been able to convince him that she would be safer where she was, even if she was whining. Maybe the worst of the storm would over be soon.

I tiptoed out of the room and went through the master bedroom and into the bathroom to get some towels. Jake would need them when he came back to the house. I wished there were dry clothes he could put on, but he was much taller than my father and outweighed him by a good fifty pounds.

Not knowing if he would use the front or back door when returning to the house, I stepped outside to the veranda. It was close enough to the den to hear Trevor if he needed me and kitty-corner to the barn. There was nothing but murkiness and water everywhere. I had never seen a night so forebodingly black and wet.

"Oh, Father in Heaven," I silently prayed as I wrapped my arms around my body. "Please help us make it through this awful night, and please keep everyone safe."

"You shouldn't be out in this." I heard Jake say as his flashlight illuminated the area around me a short time later. "You are going to catch a chill."

"Trevor fell asleep, and I was beginning to feel confined."

"It's just as well, I suppose. I couldn't get the generator running. It has been sitting idle for too long."

"What about the water? Is it getting any closer to the house?"

"A little," he said as it dripped over his face. "It is so bloody dark out here I can't see anything. Half the ranch could be a raging river, and we wouldn't know it until light. You think you feel confined. I feel like a trapped animal, and that is a damned pathetic thing for a man like me to admit since I have always been so fond of pushing limits."

My heart went out to him. Every man I knew liked to fix things, even Ben, but this situation was unfixable. God was in charge of the storm and everything it brought with it. All we could do was wait it out and attempt to clean up the mess it left.

"Why don't you come inside and dry off? I put some towels on the table in the dining room."

"Thanks," he said. "I don't suppose you have some hot coffee to go with those towels. I think my teeth would rattle out of my head if they weren't permanently attached."

"Sorry," I replied. "I can't even offer you a glass of water."

"This is a hell-of-a-way to be spending the night. I heard on the radio earlier today that we might be getting some rain, but I never expected this."

"Why didn't you tell me?"

"And let you worry for nothing? Do you have any idea what the odds are for having a downpour like this? It is once or twice a century. God-fearing people out here have spent the past two years praying for rain and by morning everything they own could be washed away."

"Do you really think it is going to get that bad?" I asked as my own teeth started to chatter.

"I didn't want to say anything negative Trevor might overhear, but we will be bloody lucky if there is any pasture land left after tonight. All the top soil on the ranch could be washed away for all I know. I have never seen rain like this before. I have only flown supplies into areas that have."

"What about the sheep and cattle? Do you think they made it to higher ground while they had the chance?"

"I am hope that's the case. They pretty much stay away from the lower elevations during the summer months since it is much too warm for them, but I can't say anything for sure until I can get the plane in the air. I will do that as soon as the rain lets up, and it is light enough to see anything."

I was surprised he thought his plane could take off. The tires might be completely covered with water by now.

"Can Trevor and I come with you?" I optimistically asked.

My request must have astonished him, but this was a desperate time.

"I thought that pesky attraction between us would keep you as far away from me as possible since you already know what you want and seem determined to get it."

"Can't we just let that go for now? Under the circumstances I feel much safer having you around."

"You have Trevor."

"And I am responsible for him on my own most of the time, but if what you said about the gully in the road is true, we are pretty much stranded here. I have watched documentaries about tsunamis and dams breaking and don't want Trevor exposed to anything like that."

"Neither do I, but there isn't much we can do about anything right now. I would suggest that you try to get some rest—at least close your eyes for a few minutes—but when have you ever listened to me? Tomorrow is going to be one hell of a day."

"It is already tomorrow," I told him.

"Then our waking nightmare has begun."

"Where are you going?" I asked as he moved towards the veranda steps when I had hoped he would come inside and discuss even partially viable options before Trevor woke up. I had already acknowledged my dependence on him. What else did he expect of me?

"I'm going back to the bunkhouse to see if I can get through to Ned yet. It would be much more convenient if the CB radio was in the house like it used to be, but that is the first thing LeAnn had moved when she came out here. She wanted your father's undivided attention when he was home."

"I can see where she was coming from," I replied, recalling my own childhood and how seldom my father had been available for either my mother or me. "But you can move it back whenever you want to now. It might seem outdated, but it gets the job done."

"That it does! You just might make a born-again Aussie yet," he said, squeezing my arm and then going back down the steps into the swirling inferno of water that had made its way to the parking end of the driveway.

The noise of falling rain had lessened considerably, and I listened to the sloshing of his footsteps until the sound disappeared. But when I went inside to check on Trevor, I was shivering uncontrollably. I stood beside the sofa and listened to his rhythmic breathing for some moments before remembering the promise I had made to Jake.

So despite the chill that seemed to have penetrated every cell in my body, I made my way to the kitchen and filled the picnic basket we had used on several occasions with granola bars, dried fruit and jerky from the pantry. I was glad LeAnn kept plenty of water bottles in the freezer. They would be easy enough to grab on the way out if we needed them.

I wanted to believe Jake's plane would be able to take off no matter what, but the pasture he flew from was lower than the ground around the house. If things went from bad to worse —as they had a habit of doing—we might be stranded for a very long time.

Trevor was still sleeping when I got back to the den, and Jake hadn't returned yet, so I sat down in the chair by the window to wait.

The rain was still cascading down the glass. What would I see when the sun came up? That thought was so distressing I closed my eyes, but my mind would not quit its circular thinking. Maybe my father was lucky to be gone. He wouldn't have to deal with whatever came with the dawn.

I must have dozed off from the metrical pounding of the rain because the next thing I was aware of was Jake shaking my shoulder and whispering in my ear. "Wake up, Brylee. We need to talk, but I don't want Trevor to hear."

I forced my eyes open. He was standing beside my chair and had changed clothes, but his hair was still wet. I noticed that it was somewhat lighter in the room.

"What time is it?" I whispered, trying to stretch the stiffness from my limbs so I could stand up. He extended his hand, and I took it.

"Let's not talk in here. It is going to be anything but a pleasant day, and Trevor shouldn't have to see all of it."

He released my hand the moment I was on my feet, and I followed him into the kitchen. It was one of the brightest rooms in the house because its windows faced east. I couldn't hear the rain pounding any more.

"Sit down for a minute before you topple over," he instructed. "Things look pretty different outside."

Cold chills swept over my body again as I slipped into a chair at the kitchen table. "The rain has stopped, hasn't it?"

"Pretty much, but it has certainly done enough damage. Many of my missions as a bush pilot were flying supplies to people who had been the victims of sudden rain storms like this, but I have never witnessed the immediate aftermath before."

"What have we lost?" I asked, wishing I could see his face clearly. His eyes would tell me if he was being truthful.

"The buildings are still standing, if that's what you mean."

"What about father's horses and Trevor's animals? They're still safe, aren't they?"

"For the moment, but there is at least a foot and a half of water in the barn. I need your help getting them to a drier place. I had hoped all the rain would sink directly into the ground as dry as it is, but it seems to have done just the opposite. Most of it came down too fast to be absorbed so it just went wherever it wanted to."

I took a deep breath of moist, dank air. Even in the house, I could feel the dampness. It smelled like dirt and moss and caught in my lungs, making me cough.

"Are you okay?" Jake asked.

"Just swallowed wrong! Can I go outside now?"

I didn't wait for his response. I just got up from my chair and headed towards the back door, slipping my arms through the sleeves of an old jacket before pushing it open. If we had sustained a lot of damage, I couldn't begin to imagine what had happened at Uncle Ned's.

But even with Jake's warning, I wasn't prepared for the reality on the other side of the kitchen door. Water was everywhere. It surrounded the house for as far as I could see— how deep it was I couldn't tell. Leaves and branches had been stripped from trees that had stood in the yard for decades. All the flowers, low shrubs and yard decorations were submerged, and it wasn't just any water. It was brown, filthy sludge that would soon carry diseases as it stagnated in the hot sun that would surely come.

I couldn't bear to think about what might have happened at other ranches in the outback. There were dry creek beds everywhere that would carry the bulk of the water towards the ocean, but that was 300 miles away and a lot of property could be destroyed before it got there. And if the town of Edna had sustained any damage it would be days, if not weeks, before help arrived for any of us in the outlying areas.

"Are Trevor's animals okay? Some of them are awfully small." I asked Jake as he came up behind me.

"I carried them up to the loft earlier and tied them to some of the beams, but they can't stay like that all day. Someone will have to take water to them and make sure they don't eat too much hay. They could easily bloat."

"I can do that," I said. "Do you want me to go with you now?"

"Only if you think Trevor will stay asleep. I don't want him leaving the house alone."

I went into the den to see if my little brother had awakened, but he was still peacefully sleeping on the sofa, and Copper was curled up in a ball in her kennel. If we hurried, there was little chance he would wake up before we got back. It was still. Early and he was exhausted after his adventure into Edna and his night of interrupted sleep.

The water in what was left of the driveway was about eighteen inches deep, and I felt my hiking boots being sucked into the mud with each step.

"I thought we could drive the horses to the pasture above the house," Jake said. "There should be plenty for them to eat, but I do worry about the water situation. I filled the troughs in the barn before I went to bed last night, but it won't take long for them to be drained. Then I don't know what we will do."

I hadn't thought about the amount of clean water needed for anything more than people. Slightly muddy water would be okay for the animals to drink since they did it all the time on the range. But if it became tainted it could kill an entire herd in a day.

"Maybe things aren't as bad as they seem," I said, trying to sound even somewhat hopeful when all I wanted to do was cry, but there would be plenty of time for that once we had accessed just how hard we had been hit. "At least the rain has stopped."

"There is that," he said. "But there will be some tough decisions to make before it's over and right now we need to take some counter measures to make sure we survive. We will start by draining all the taps in the house. That water can be used for drinking as long as it doesn't sit in the pipes too long, and there is an old outhouse in the trees behind the bunkhouse. We might have to wade to get there, but at least we wouldn't need any water for flushing."

"You think we might be here for awhile, don't you?" I asked, looking at him for reassurance, but all I saw was the hard contours of his face.

"I have no bloody idea, but without power things can get ugly fast. We need to prepare as best we can and then hope for the best."

"I will go through the pantry and cupboards to see what we have that can be prepared without water or heat. We could cook a few things on the grill, I guess, but I have no idea how to light it."

"That's my girl," Jake said. "We need to take inventory of what we have in the way of other supplies for both ourselves and others. If we keep the freezer lid closed, most of the meat should be good for several days. We will set the grill going as it unthaws and can start with the meat in the top of the refrigerator."

I breathed deeply of the moist, pungent air again. At least we had a plan. There was plenty to do before we started worrying about what might happen even an hour or two further into our day.

I followed Jake to the barn. It no longer mattered that the foul-smelling, muddy water had risen above the tops of my boots and seeped in between my toes. This was not the time to get squeamish. This was my home, and I needed to help preserve as much of it as I possibly could.

I looked around while Jake put bridals on all the horses— except for Rupert, whom I took care of myself. "I hate tying them to trees, but I don't want them running away. We would never find them again if they do."

He handed me the reins to Trevor's horse, Thunder, and took the rest. We walked slowly out of the barn as our feet made odious noises each time we lifted them. The horses were in a highly agitated state, and it took all my strength to keep the two I was leading from breaking away as they jerked their heads back and forth, snorting with what could only be described as anger for being tethered when all they wanted to do was run free.

"Talk to them like you did to Newton's mother," Jake instructed. "The sound of your voice should calm them somewhat."

I did as he requested, but it was hard to stay focused when I was so acutely aware of my surroundings. The sky was still dark, but the rain was no more than a gentle pitter-pat. I slipped on wet grass several times while pulling two horses up the steep incline behind the house but fortunately remained upright. I could easily have been trampled if I had.

The trees along the ridge looked every bit as bad as the trees around the house, and I wanted to cry out in anguish as I looked from them to the panoramic view of the valley below. There was nothing but water for miles in every direction and not a sign of life anywhere. The only things visible besides vile water were the roofs of the house and outbuildings directly below where we stood.

"Do you think anything is left?" I asked.

Jake waited until he felt certain that none of the horses could break free before responding. "I don't know, but I have to find out so I am taking the plane up. You and Trevor will have to stay here. It is much safer, and I don't know what I might find once I am in the air."

"I thought we were going to stick together," I said as my eyes filled with tears. Crying had become my constant companion for more days than I cared to remember, and it didn't appear that it was going to stop any time soon.

"Listen, Brylee," he said as we made our way back down the hill. "I got through to the tower in Edna before I came to get you. The air traffic controller said the town has sustained no real damage, just a lot of extra water in the streets. They are overseeing rescue operations and need every plane they can find in the sky. If there are survivors, we need to get to them as soon as possible. You and Trevor will be safe here, and I will be back before dark."

I bit my bottom lip to keep it from trembling. "What if you can't get your plane off the ground. There is so much water."

"I have flown it out of deeper water than this, but it is not a pretty sight. Trust me, you and Trevor will be safer inside the house and than in the plane with me."

He suddenly stopped walking and placed his hands lightly on my cheeks. They smelled like mud and barnyard animals. But it really didn't matter because I was trying so hard not to acknowledge how his touch made me feel, even when he tilted my face upwards so I would be forced to look at him.

"You can do this, Brylee. I would take you into town right now so I would know both you and Trevor are safe, but someone needs to take care of things around here. We don't know what the situation will be with the cattle and sheep that have been grazing. Worst scenario—most of them have floated away or been trapped in places where they can't get out."

"And the best scenario?" I asked.

"They are safe on higher ground until we can bring them home. I will look around while I'm gone, but my main concern is finding people who may be stranded. They need to be found before nightfall."

I knew he was right, and I was just being selfish by wanting him to stay with us. Trevor and I were safe and our home was still intact. Many of the other ranchers might not be so lucky, and that included Uncle Ned and Aunt Nora. I needed to know if they were okay.

"We will be fine," I told him, forcing an uncertain smile.

He leaned down and kissed my forehead as he might have done to a child, but it still made my heart race. "You're always fine, love," he said. "And never believe anything different."

I thought Jake was oversimplifying getting his plane off the ground, but apparently I knew very little about bush planes. They were made to withstand the worst conditions. I heard the sound of its engine turn over just as Trevor called my name.

"I'm on the back porch," I responded loudly enough to be heard. It was up to me to keep him from being worried about his animals, his mother and everything he saw once he left the house.

"Copper and I were scared when we woke up, and you weren't there," he said as the back door slammed shut behind him, and he carried the wriggling puppy outside.

"Well, I'm here now," I told him as I pulled my ruined boots from my feet using the side of the house for support. After wading through the barn and up the hill they needed to be tossed, but they were all I had besides sandals and a worn pair of tennis shoes. So I set them down on the back step hoping they would dry out a little before I had to put them on again. I also removed my socks and pulled up my pant legs. My feet were totally brown, and without running water there was no way of knowing how long it might be before I could mop the kitchen floor again.

"Would you mind getting my flip-flops," I asked as I stood on the rug just inside the back door. "They should be in the bottom of my closet."

"How come you're yucky and wet?" he asked.

"Because I helped take the horses up to the clearing above the house."

He looked down at the water that stretched from the bottom step onward.

"Are my animals okay? I couldn't stand it if something happened Newton."

"Newton's fine," I assured him, even though I had not seen the small calf for myself. "Your Uncle Jake carried all of them up to the loft. We will check on them as soon as we eat something and have a little talk."

"But I want to go now!" He crossed his arms defiantly across his chest. It was only the second time I had seen him take a stance like that, and it shocked me. He was usually such a quiet, well-behaved child.

"Come here," I told him.

He hesitated for a moment or two, but I put one knee on the linoleum-covered floor. And when I opened my arms to him, he ran swiftly into them. "I know this is hard to understand, Trevor, but the rain last night made an awful mess. You and I are going to have to work together to make sure all of the animals are okay for the next few days. With the power off, we won't be able to use any of the appliances or turn on the lights. We won't even have running water."

"I am sorry," he said as he started to cry. "I didn't mean to be angry."

"You just didn't understand," I replied, wiping the tears from his cheeks with the back of my hand. "I think we are both a little scared, but everything will be okay as long as we're together."

He put his arms around my neck. "I love you, Brylee."

His honesty brought tears back to my own eyes. How lucky I was to have a little brother.

"I love you too," I told him. "Now, if you wouldn't mind getting my flip-flops, and finding the oldest pair of boots or shoes you have, we will eat something quick and then check on your animals. I know Newton will be glad to see you. He has had quite a night."

While we ate cold cereal, I told him about draining the taps for drinking water and how we would have to use the old out house behind the granaries and bunkhouse. I tried to make it sound like a grand adventure, and to Trevor it probably was. But I didn't know how I would survive without my daily shower.

Before leaving the house, Trevor helped me fill all the empty pots we could find with water that was still in the pipes. What was left over went into the bathtub. I wasn't sure that we would really need it because Jake could get more from town if they had not been left without power too. But he might not have time, and I didn't want him to think I was being careless. Even growing up in the outback where the days were hot and the water always scarce, I had never really considered what it would be like without it until now. We needed to conserve every precious drop.

Trevor didn't seem to mind walking through the filthy water even though it came to his knees, and he had to hold my hand so he could make the dismal trek without falling. I knew his mind was centered on making sure Newton and his other animals were safe, but he wasn't happy when we reached the loft and he saw them struggling to get free from the ropes Jake had tied around their necks to keep them from getting too close to an exit and falling.

I assured him that they weren't in any pain, only frightened. While he tried to calm them, I lugged half-filled buckets of water up the board ladder. It wasn't an easy task. I had to hold the bucket behind me while I climbed, and then swing it over my head onto the floor of the loft because there wasn't enough room to crawl through the hole with it still in my hand.

Trevor had gotten two more calves since Jake and I brought Newton to the ranch in the plane and had named them George and Sam. The names stuck even when he found out that one of them was a girl. He also had two little lambs—both of them with black faces and the whitest fleece I had ever seen. Fortunately, they had all been weaned from bottles. With no way of heating water except for building a fire, mixing formula would be impossible. We would have to watch closely to make sure they were eating enough of the calf and lamb feed Jake bought at the feed and grain store in town and drinking plenty of water. Having one of them die would be devastating for my little brother.

Jake certainly knew what was needed around the ranch, I decided as I looked for the supply of feed and grain I hoped would last until the worst of the flooding and cleanup was behind us. Instead of leaving it on the barn floor like most of the outbackers did, he had attached wooden pallets to the wall three feet off the ground and stacked burlap bags on them by kind. It put less stress on the back when moving them, and meant that none of the feed had been exposed to the water so it would be mold-free and safe for all the animals to eat.

I swung the doors to the loft open and looked out over the southern exposure of the ranch while Trevor explained what had happened to his animals. It was a heart-wrenching sight. Trees that had sported gray-green leaves the day before had been stripped clean, and I could only hope they would eventually come back to life. Looking through their empty branches, I could see for miles in three directions. There was nothing but water. It could have been an inch or six feet in depth. It all looked the same from where I was standing.

But there was one thing I had never noticed before. Without leaves to block the view, the family burial plot was visible. It was submerged in water too and not a single headstone could be seen, just the top of the white picket fence that surrounded it. I bit   my lip to keep from crying out as I thought about our father's casket. It had been buried for less than a month, and the soil above it had not even begun to settle. We hadn't even picked out a stone for his marker, but a white cross had been pounded into the ground to mark his final resting place beside my mother.

"Oh, father," I thought as my eyes filled with tears for what seemed like the zillionth time since coming home. "Can you see what has happened to the land you loved so much? Earthly things can be taken away in an instant. All we really have is family, and ours is in a horrible mess right now. Isn't there some way you can reach out from beyond the grave and convince LeAnn to come home? Trevor needs her, and I don't know how to put anything right on the ranch again or raise him, even with Jake's help."

I turned around and looked at my little brother. He wasn't worried about himself or what was going to happen during the next hours or days. His thoughts were focused on his animals and making sure they were as comfortable as possible. If an eight-year-old could make the best of a very uncertain state of affairs, then at least I had to try.

"How is everyone doing?" I asked, walking back to the far end of the loft to join him. "Did they all get something to eat and drink?"

"Newton's being a pig," he said, putting his arms around the neck of the reddish-brown calf.

"It's probably because he is the oldest," I responded, running my hand across the calf's soft head. "You have done an amazing job with all your animals. Father would be very proud of you."

"Do you think he can see what we are doing, even if he isn't here?"

It was a golden, teaching moment—too perfect to miss. "I know he can, Trevor. Heaven is not so far away."

He gave me the most quizzical look. "Then why can't we see it?"

"Because we are mortal and must learn how to walk by faith."

Trevor looked even more confused.

"I don't know what that means," he said.

"Well, let's see if I can explain it a little better. I am not much of a singer, but I learned a little song before I came home. Do you want to hear it?"

He nodded his head, and I began to sing, *"I am a Child of God, and He has sent me here. Has given me an earthly home with parent's kind and dear. Lead me, guide me, walk beside me. Help me find the way. Teach me all that I must do to live with Him some day."*

I couldn't remember the other verses, but Trevor's heart was open, and he began to cry softly. "Does that mean we really will see father again some day? I miss him so much."

I wrapped my arms around him and kissed the top of his head.

"Yes, we will see father again, and we will see Grandpa and Grandma Hawkins, and their parents too. This life is not just about you and me. We have all these wonderful people who lived before us and who are hoping we will do everything we should so we can be a family again. No matter how tough it is right now, we can make it if we try. There is too much to lose otherwise."

"Can you teach me that song?" Trevor asked. "I want to remember it so I can sing it to my animals when they are afraid."

"I can do that," I said with a smile that tugged at my heart. "It is wonderful knowing we are never alone, even when it seems like we are."

And so the moments slipped by as I taught him the words to the first verse of "I am a Child of God". The sky was still dark outside the loft window and the small animals unhappy about being tied up, but I found that I was actually happy, regardless of the fact that the world around me was filled with both chaos and too much dirty water that might be around for days.

Before heading back to the house to check on Copper, we got the broom LeAnn used to sweep off the back steps and sloshed our way to the outhouse. It hadn't been used for years and I hoped it wasn't filled with spiders and bugs. I hated all of them and certainly didn't want to be bitten by anything—poisonous or otherwise, but without running water all of us were going to see just how some of our ancestors had lived.

The outhouse sat on a small incline in little more than foot of water. It was made of rough-cut lumber that had turned a dusty brown from age, sun and unrelentingly hot weather like most everything else on the ranch. It was approximately five feet wide and the roof had been covered with a sheet of once-silver tin. I didn't even want to think what it must look like on the inside, but someone had attached a cutout of a moon to door. That should have made the minuscule structure more inviting since it didn't need to be large to be functional, but all it did was make me want to run away.

"Do you think we should wait until your Uncle Jake gets back to see what it is like inside?" I asked.

Trevor just shrugged his shoulders. "I don't even know what a building that small is used for. The shed where mum keeps her gardening tools is twice as big.

"I guess I should have have explained," I said, trying not to fixate on just how long we might be without electricity or a way off the ranch. "Without running water there will be no showers or flushing the toilet."

"No way," he said, stamping one foot in the water and covering his legs with mud. "I don't like it out here any more."

"I suppose many of our great grandparents felt the same way at times. They didn't even have electricity until after our father was born and the power lines made it this far into the outback. They used kerosene and candles when it got dark and cooked all their food on a wood and coal stove instead of the nice electric one we have now."

"Did they do a lot of camping too?"

"Most likely. They still had the house, but it took a lot of work stringing electrical wires and adding pipes for plumbing. Perhaps it will even be fun living the way they did for a few a days. Not that I am thrilled about using an outhouse, but it will be huge adventure to tell your friends about one day."

"Maybe," he reluctantly said. "But you have to go inside first."

"I can do that," I responded, taking a deep breath. I really did want to make the most of my time while Jake was gone and prove to him that I was worthy of the confidence he had placed in me that morning. So I handed Trevor the broom, and told him to hold it above the water while I pulled on the door's handle. It wasn't exactly stuck but the hinges were rusty, and the foot of water I had to pull it through made my job harder. But I refused to give up and kept pulling on it until the door flew open and hurled me backward.

I was covered in mud from the tips of my boots to my armpits, but fortunately my head had remained above water. I couldn't tell if Trevor was going to laugh or cry so I made the decision for him. This would go down as one of the most embarrassing moments of my life, but we both needed some emotional release since this might be as good as it was going to get for awhile.

When I was finally able to pull myself upright—dripping from muddy water while Trevor was still trying to control his laughter—I saw that the inside of the outhouse door was covered with cobwebs, but that was nothing when compared to the white maze inside.

I felt a new kind of terror rise to my throat and unintentionally baked away, but I couldn't let Trevor see my fear. Jake had said someone needed to be here to take care of things, and since there was no one else to fill that role, I had make sure the outhouse was safe. I would wash away what I could with the broom, but the next time I came, it would be with a can of Raid in my hand.

Trevor stood a respectable distance from the door as I held the broom's handle and swept away at the sticky, white labyrinth forcing what appeared to be hundreds of scurrying spiders out of their home. But after the first few stabs, I decided to go for broke. It was either them or me, so I ran the broom's bristles back and forth in the muddy water until they were saturated and then began hitting at the cobwebs, watching carefully to make sure nothing menacing crawled down the handle.

I felt like I was whitewashing a fence as I attacked the spider population, but instead of using paint, I was layering every inch of the enclosure with muddy water. I was almost jealous of Jake and Trevor. They could relieve themselves wherever they wanted to. I had two options at present and neither one of them pleasant—squatting down behind a leafless bush or using the one-seater.

"Look out," Trevor cried out as I brought a particularly spider-filled broom out of the structure.

I looked down at the handle. Three huge, black, hairy specimens were running as fast as they could towards my hands. I dropped the broom in the water and screamed.

"I'm not going in there, ever," Trevor shouted as he backed even further away, looking down at the water as he did so. "Mum would hate it out here."

I couldn't agree with him more. Logic told me that the spiders, ugly and big as they were, were likely harmless and more afraid of us than we were of them, but I didn't want Trevor thinking of me as a complete coward after my childish outburst. He needed to know that I could protect him—even if it was only from spiders—so I took a deep breath and reached down into the muddy water to retrieve the broom.

"Those spiders aren't going to get us, Trevor," I told him as I brushed some of the mud from the broom's handle. There was no possible way I could get any dirtier than I already was. "I will get them out of the outhouse if it is the last thing we do."

There were dozens of species of spiders in Australia, most of them intimidating but not hazardous to anyone's health. I had learned that at boarding school in Sydney—home of the infamous Sydney Funnel-Web Spider, one of the most dangerous of them all.

Only six species of spiders were to be religiously avoided—the Red-Back Black Widow, the Lampona, the Mouse spider, the Wandering spider, the Australian Funnel-Web and any spider from the genus Loxosceles. I didn't know which kinds inhabited the outhouse or the black hole beneath it, but I wouldn't let Trevor know that I was terrified of being bitten by any one of them. I would simply get on the Internet to double-check what they looked like so the proper precautions could be taken, but then I remembered that we didn't have any power.

What would I do if something even more awful happened while Jake was gone? I was stuck in the middle of nowhere with a child and had absolutely no idea how to take care of him or keep him safe unless I confined him to bed, and that was never going to happen. There was simply too much work for one person to do.

So I closed my eyes and lashed out at the walls and the floor and the seat of the outhouse with more vengeance than before. I even coated the ceiling until mud was dropping onto the water that covered the wood floor. I would pour Clorox down the hole and hope it would kill anything remaining after my ferocious cleaning.

Then I tackled our next problem—or rather my problem since Trevor only had wet feet and legs. I had to find a way to wash all the mud from my body without using the clean water that might be needed for other things later. Jake had been gone for less than three hours, and I had already managed to terrify Trevor and fall into the mucky water. It was going to be an incredibly long, discouraging and unpleasant day.

"Any idea how I can get cleaned up before going back into the house?" I absentmindedly asked my little brother.

It was a silly question to pose to a child, but in addition to the mud that covered my body, and most of my head now, I could feel invisible spiders crawling all over me. I wondered if he felt the same way but wasn't going to ask.

He frowned for a few moments and then went sloshing off as fast as the standing water would allow.

"Hey, where are you going?" I called after him, but he didn't respond or turn around. I increased my own speed to keep up with him as I carried the muddy broom an arm's length away from my body. I would get a new one the next time I went into town—whenever that might be.

Trevor was in the back yard standing next to a wading pool when I breathlessly reached him. I was nearly exhausted after what would soon become known as my battle with the outhouse spiders.

"Will this work?" he asked, trying to catch his own breath.

"Oh, my gosh!" I exclaimed as I looked inside. It was filled with clear rainwater. The rim had been high enough to keep the mud from getting inside.

"You are my favorite person in the whole wide world, and the smartest one too!" I exclaimed as gratitude filled my heart once again for God's outpouring of love in even the most desperate and depressing situations.

I wanted to give him the biggest hug ever, but in my present condition knew it might not be appreciated. So instead of expressing my thanks in the traditional way I began looking around for a bucket or some other way to get the water out for us to use. It would best to save as much as possible since there was no way of knowing how long it would be until power was restored. Everyone had to be rescued first, and then it would take time for water to recede enough for crews to repair the roads and get trucks moving again.

"Why don't you just jump in?" he asked me, looking somewhat disappointed.

"There is nothing I would like more, little brother, but this water may have to last us for awhile."

"There is plenty more in the bathtub," he volunteered.

"I know there is, but we need to conserve every drop right now since there is no way of knowing how long we might need to make it last. Do you know where a bucket can be found so we can scoop some of it out?"

He was thoughtful for a moment and then gave me a big smile. "Mum keeps all of her gardening stuff in that little shed." He pointed towards a small wooden structure at the far end of the back yard. "Father built it for her because she was always losing things. I know there are some buckets in there because I use them sometimes to play with."

"You really are my hero," I told him as we made our way to it. I couldn't be sure, but it looked like the water might be receding around the house. Maybe it wouldn't be long until it did the same thing everywhere.

I sent Trevor into the house to bring me the bottle of Tide we used for doing laundry while I scooped a bucketful of water from the the pool and carried it to the back porch. Then I helped him take off his shoes and wash his feet and legs. The foul water had etched its way up his shorts, but other than a few splashes of mud above the waist, he was virtually dry. I told him to change his clothes and leave them in the laundry basket until we were able to use the washing machine again.

He brought me a bathrobe before going up to his room. I told him he could play with Copper once she was fed but to keep her away from any doors so she wouldn't try to escape. I assured him I would be in as soon as I was able to get the mud out of my hair.

I marveled at the stamina of our ancestors as I scrubbed my body and hair clean. They had sacrificed everything to leave us a legacy I had almost walked away from. This ranch might not appear valuable to anyone from the outside world—except for the corporations who wanted it for expansion—but my veins were filled with the blood of the people who had cleared this land and built the buildings we still used. It had been our home for generations. How could I not do everything within my power to keep it intact for the generations of Hawkins yet to come? Ben simply had to understand why I couldn't come back right now. My own family needed me every bit as much as I needed them.

JS Ririe

Trevor and I spent the next two hours reading and playing games on the veranda. With the A.C. off it was too hot to remain inside, though I had to admit it wasn't much cooler outdoors. We decided—with a little coaching from me—that it would be a good idea to get some sleeping bags from the attic and camp out in the dining room. It was the only room in the house with cross ventilation, and if we got any breeze during the night it would be far cooler than our bedrooms upstairs.

Trevor wanted Jake to camp with us. I hoped he would decline the invitation when it came, but we got a sleeping bag for him anyway. Then we scoured the house for flashlights, batteries, and old kerosene lamps. Most of them hadn't been used for decades, but the wicks were trimmed, and they were filled with kerosene. I didn't want to be caught in the dark again, so I tried to turn everything into a game so Trevor wouldn't realize the severity of the situation we were in.

We also made a few rules like not leaving the house unless we told each other where we were going, and that included the outhouse. I wasn't so worried about me, but I was terrified that something would happen to Trevor. Even a spider bite left untreated could mean pain and illness to him, if not death.

We talked about things like not opening the freezer or refrigerator without permission so the food wouldn't spoil so quickly, never turning on the taps until the power was restored, and never taking more water than we were going to drink at one time. I even quizzed him afterwards so he wouldn't forget.

I tried to remember everything I had been told at a preparedness fair sponsored by my home stake in Los Angeles several months earlier. It was my first introduction to just how concerned the leaders of the church were about our physical welfare. Our greatest fears in California were earthquakes and fires but while each disaster—natural or manmade—had its own procedures, they all shared the same basic guidelines.

Have enough food and water for at least 72 hours, a change of clothing, first aid supplies, and all valuables—like pictures and documents—where they could be easily found and transported. It was also advisable to have sleeping bags, solar blankets, water purification tablets, money and a way to stay in contact with the outside world.

But I had never been through a disaster before, and I had certainly never considered the emotional side to one. Ben and I had always talked about getting prepared as a family once we were married, but this experience was teaching me what many people already knew. If one was not prepared for an emergency before it arose, it was already too late. I hoped the other people in the outback, like Uncle Ned and Aunt Nora, were as safe as Trevor and me. The thought of losing them filled me with more dread than losing everything of a physical nature around me.

Once I was calm enough to think past our immediate needs and what might be happening in the world beyond our present confines, Trevor and I sat down at the table and made a list of everything in the house that might be useful—not necessarily for this emergency since our home was still standing—but for the future when we might not be so lucky. By the time we had found everything available, the dining room looked more like a Red-Cross Evacuation Center than a room where a family would gather for a Sunday meal.

I organized all the medical supplies by type, and then I hunted through the shelves of books in the den until I found the health reference book I had looked at with my mother when I was a child. It wasn't up-to-date, but it would be better than nothing if a medical emergency arose.

Before doing what chores we could, I pulled some lamb chops from the freezing compartment of the fridge and wrapped some potato wedges in tin foil so they could be put on the grill while the chops cooked. I had never lit a propane grill before and even though Trevor said he could do it, I didn't want to take any chances with him getting burned. I would have Jake show me how it was done when he got back.

We made one more trip to the barn to feed and water Trevor's animals and then walked up the hill to check on the horses. Trevor was mostly worried about Thunder and wanted to pet him, but I convinced him it was wise to keep his distance for now. They had calmed down considerably since morning and still had plenty to eat without moving them further up the hill, but I was very concerned about keeping them watered. The buckets Jake had left for them were empty and despite the rain and still cloudy skies, it was oppressively hot outside. When Jake returned maybe we could take them back to the barn. Most of the water had sunk into the ground, and if we spread out a few bales of straw they would have a dry place to rest for the night.

It was a strange sort of day with no sun, the possibility of more rain, and the air heavy and wet. But as the hours marched slowly onward, it became evident that the water around the house was indeed sinking into the ground. Our second great grandparents had chosen the plot for their homestead carefully. It sat high enough that most rainstorms would not affect it until everything else in the area had been washed away—including Uncle Ned's home. I prayed that would not be the news Jake delivered when he finally returned.

Chapter 21

When we heard the engine of Jake's plane, Trevor hurried onto the veranda to wait for him while I got a glass of lemonade using the last particles of ice in the trays to make it colder. I couldn't believe how anxious I was to see him. I didn't much like being left alone with responsibilities I was unprepared to handle. When things got back to normal, I would find a way for us to have greater contact with the outside world.

Jake was sitting on the porch swing when I brought him the glass of lemonade. He looked dirty and tired, and my heart went out to him. It couldn't be easy trying to find people when they lived so far apart and rarely saw their neighbors. No one—with the exception of their own families—would even know if they were at home. His muddy boots were on the step and Trevor was sitting on the wooden floor listening to him talk about his day's adventures, or so I thought.

"Trevor has been telling me about your day," he said when I handed him the cool glass. "It sounds like you had a little trouble with the spiders in the outhouse."

I smiled stiffly and immediately began scratching at my neck.

"It was an experience I will never forget," I told him.

"Trevor said you didn't even swear when you landed on your back in the muddy water with spiders swimming all around you. I'm impressed."

He took a long drink of lemonade as I continued to scratch my nose, my ears and my cheeks. I was afraid to close my eyes for fear vivid images would resurface. I hoped all the spiders I had washed away were gone now or even better, utterly and completely dead.

"This tastes good. Where did you get the ice?"

I forced myself to quit scratching. "It's all that was left in the top of the refrigerator."

"And you saved it for me." He gave me a very strange look that caused me to glance away.

"We knew you would be tired and thirsty when you got back, didn't we, Brylee?" Trevor explained.

I smiled fondly at my little brother for diffusing a potentially awkward situation. "Yes, we did," I responded. "It only seemed fair since you were gone all day helping other people."

I wanted to ask him directly about what he had learned but knew he had a reason for skirting the subject while Trevor was still awake.

"What else have the two of you been up to?" he asked Trevor, who was more than willing to share.

"We took care of the animals and then set up the neatest camp in the house. We are all going to sleep there tonight."

"Is that right?" Jake's voice betrayed his surprise.

I cleared my throat my loudly than necessary. "Don't you think we should allow your Uncle Jake to decide for himself where he wants to sleep? He might prefer his own bed in the bunkhouse to a sleeping bag on the dining room floor."

Clearly Trevor did not understand the dynamics of our relationship, but Jake certainly did, and I hoped he would respect my feelings.

"Why don't you show me this new kingdom you have created, and we can decide the rest later," he told Trevor once his lemonade was gone.

At least he had heard what I said, I mused as I fell into step behind them. As relieved as I was to have him back, I didn't want to be put in another compromising situation. Two nights on the mountain with him had been enough for one lifetime.

"You must be a disaster relief worker disguised as Trevor's sister!" Jake exclaimed as he stood in front of the dining room table that had been pushed to a side wall to accommodate the sleeping bags.

I felt my cheeks go red. There was a fine line between praising someone and making fun of them, and there was no way of knowing which side of that line Jake was standing on right now.

"Brylee said we should be prepared for anything," Trevor interjected.

Jake continued to look at me with studied admiration. "Well, I hope we don't need any of this stuff, but it's nice to know it is handy in case we do. I don't suppose the two of you have figured out what we are going to eat tonight, or where a guy could wash up without running water."

"Trevor has that all figured out," I said as I put my arm around my little brother's shoulders. "You wouldn't believe how hard he has worked today."

"Just looking around here, I can tell that both of you have been busy."

"I will show you where to wash up, Uncle Jake," Trevor volunteered, taking his hand and leading him through the kitchen to the back porch where a bucket of water, Lava soap and a dry towel were waiting for him.

A sense of pride and accomplishment filled my soul knowing that Trevor and I had been able to handle things, but tomorrow was another day, and there would be new challenges. I was more than certain of that.

Jake grilled the lamb chops while the foil-wrapped potatoes cooked closer to the source of heat. There weren't a lot of perishables in the fridge, and I was glad we hadn't gone grocery shopping the day before. Things like milk and lettuce would not last long without refrigeration.

We ate our meal on paper plates that had been left over from my father's wake. It hurt to think about his body lying in its watery grave, but in light of what was happening now, I knew he was better off in heaven. Seeing the land he loved immersed in water would drive him from his sick bed in more than just discouragement and pain.

After eating, we walked up the hill to lead the horses back to the barn. Jake was amazed that so much of the water was gone, but he didn't say anything about what was going on outside our shrunken world. He threw bales of straw from the loft to the ground so Trevor and I could break them apart and scatter small pieces in the horse's stalls.

Jake promised to bring Newton and the others back to their pens in the barn as soon as the ground was dry. He didn't want to risk them getting sick. Trevor and I both agreed that they were better off where they were, even though I hated climbing that ladder to the loft carrying half-full buckets of water.

I excused myself while they sat together in the loft talking. I needed privacy for my visit to the outhouse and wasn't sure I would have the courage to go there once complete darkness had fallen, no matter how much Mother Nature called out to me.

When we returned to the house, Trevor informed me that he wanted to sleep in his boxers since, according to him, no one took pajamas on camping trips. I lit a kerosene lamp while he slipped into his sleeping bag, more than amazed that he was willing to go to sleep without a fuss when he had been through such a bizarre day.

"Will you sing me the song you did this afternoon?" he asked me. "I like being a child of God."

Jake was outside on the veranda smoking a cigarette, and I hoped he would not overhear. He was a man who had shown that he wasn't religious and had no intention of changing.

"*I am a child of God,*" I began singing softly as I ran my hand across Trevor's soft, light brown hair. "*And he has sent me here. Has given me an earthly home with parents kind and dear.*"

The words were coming out of my mouth, but my thoughts were certainly elsewhere. What was Trevor thinking as I repeated the words of the song? Our father was gone and his mother had run away because she couldn't deal with the reality of being alone. So where indeed were our parents kind and dear?

"*Lead me, guide me, walk beside me.*"

Never had those words reached such a tender place in my heart. Without God's guidance none of us would ever make it back to him, just as we would not be able to navigate through any of the tough days ahead without his protection.

"*Help me find the way.*"

Would God really be there for me every time I knelt to pray?

"*Teach me all that I must do to live with him someday.*"

Was all this just part of the lessons I needed to learn to become more like him? I couldn't justify what was happening any other way. But if this was preparation for tougher things to come, I did not want to contemplate what the main event might be.

By the time I had finished singing the verse, Trevor was asleep. I sat by his side for a few minutes longer. I might not know where my life was going, but I had been given an extraordinary gift. My little brother was rapidly becoming the most important part of my life, and I could not imagine ever being without him.

"That was a nice song," Jake said when I walked outside to join him for a few minutes before trying to sleep myself. I had placed Trevor's sleeping bag in the middle so there would be no questions if he decided to join us.

Could he possibly be as tired and as in need of human contact as I was? I wasn't sure I had enough willpower left to push him away again if he approached me with anything even closely resembling compassion.

"It's just a little song I learned a few months ago," I told him. "It seems to calm him."

"You are doing an amazing job as his surrogate mother. I don't think I have ever seen him quite so content. I figured he would be completely lost without LeAnn and his father, but you have given him a reason to go on."

"I haven't done anything. Trevor is his own person."

"But you are molding him in a good way. LeAnn won't recognize him when she comes back."

"Does that mean you have talked to her?"

"I talked to Emma and told her to let LeAnn know we were okay. I really thought my sister would want to come home in light of all that has happened, but she didn't even get back to me."

"I am sorry. I think all of us need her right now."

"Well, I wouldn't hold my breath. LeAnn is the most mulish woman I have ever known—present company excluded. I don't know what it will take for her to wake up and smell the coffee, but peace will never be found as long as she refuses to face reality."

"Deep inside she knows how much Trevor needs her," I said.

"But that wasn't enough before! Like I told you, it took months for her to come to her senses, and that only happened because Jack came back into her life. Right now, I'm not even sure you will want to stick around to help sort out all the mess this rain has made. The flooding and damage to property is inconceivable unless you have seen it with your own eyes."

The light from the kerosene lamp on the other side of the window provided just enough light for me to see the rigid set of his face.

"I told you before that I am not going anywhere as long as Trevor needs me. Is there something other than property damage and what went on with LeAnn that I should know about?"

"I didn't want to worry Trevor, or you, for that matter."

"I am a big girl and think I have earned the right to know the truth," I responded. "Did you find Uncle Ned and Aunt Nora?"

He put his cigarette out before answering me. "No, but that doesn't mean they aren't okay. I flew over their ranch a couple of times and as close as I could tell, there seems to be about six feet of water running through their house. Only the upstairs was visible."

My heart sank as I sat down on one of the chairs that surrounded the small patio table. "Could you tell anything else?"

"Not really! I only know that if the animals are in the higher elevations they should be okay for awhile. I just hope Ned and Nora had enough time to drive their horses and milk cows to the mountains and get there themselves. I will head out again at first light and see if anything has changed, but I can't land my plane anywhere near their place until the water recedes far more than it has now."

My heart was filled with both fear and pain, but it would serve no purpose to fall apart until we knew something concrete.

"What about the other ranchers? Were they able to get to safety?"

"A few of them made it to town, but mostly they are stranded just like us, only with more water surrounding them. I dropped supplies to the ones who will be okay where they are for now. You wouldn't believe how many of them refuse to leave their homes, even when they are practically submerged."

"Father used to tell me stories about the old-timers who would rather be washed away or burned up than leave their homes."

"We are not so different," he said. "Do you really think you could have left this morning, even knowing your life might be in danger?"

"I believe life is far more important than possessions. I would make sure Trevor was safe, but after that I might be just as foolish as everyone else."

"At least you are honest," he said, sitting down in the chair opposite the table from me. "I am not sure how much sacrifice it will take for any of us to rebuild. Even if we don't lose a lot of animals it will take both time and money to put things back to the way they used to be both here and at Ned's. What about those who have lost everything?"

"We help them!" I responded.

"With what?" he asked.

"With whatever we have! I feel so incredibly blessed that we still have a place to live."

"Even if it doesn't offer all the niceties of life like power and water?"

"Anyone can rough it for awhile. I am more worried about getting enough clean water for the animals to drink."

"I have been thinking about that, so I did a little checking at the courthouse while I was in town. There is an old abandoned well out by the family cemetery. It hasn't been used since power was brought to the ranch, but if the shaft is clear we might be able to drop a gas-powered pump into it. Worse case scenario—other than it being dry—we have to draw it out by the bucketful once we have rigged up a pulley system that will work."

"Why can't we just access it from the well that feeds into the house?" I asked. "The water has to come from the same source."

If Jake thought my question was dumb, he let it pass without some snide remark.

"You're right! The water does come from the same underground river, but the pump in the well by the house uses electricity. It won't do us any good until the power is on again."

"And I don't suppose anyone knows when that might be."

"Not at the moment! The power lines are still above water, but no one can work on them until all the water is gone. That could take weeks."

"Then I suppose we just keep doing what we have done today," I responded. "The animals can't take care of themselves."

"Are you saying you want to stay out here?" he asked. "I could take care of the animals in the morning and at night and fly you and Trevor into Edna in the morning."

"To do what? I'm sure there are people needing assistance far more than we do right now are overrunning the town. Besides, we are perfectly safe right where we're at.

"You've got guts, Brylee, but I don't like the idea of you and Trevor being stuck out here with no way of getting off the ranch. I can be here at night, but during the day, you will be on your own. What if you needed me, and I couldn't get here in time?"

"We'll be fine," I told him. "And we do have the horses."

"I guess you do," he said with a shake of his head. "And after what you have been through today, I can no longer accuse you of being a city girl. You are one fine Aussie woman, Brylee Hawkins."

His compliment embarrassed me, and I looked down at the tabletop. Why was he being so nice anyway? He could have found at least a dozen things to chide me for, and I was beginning to feel lightheaded with his hands just inches from mine.

"Do you know where it is?" I asked, moving mine from the table and into my lap where they would not betray what I was thinking.

He frowned. "Where's what?"

I had definitely spoiled the mood and he did not appear to be happy about it.

"The old well! Do you know where to find it?"

"Oh, that," he said, tipping his chair backwards and putting a few more inches between us. "According to the plot diagram, it should be somewhere around the shed in the cemetery."

"But I have walked all over the land out there and have never seen a well."

I was thinking about the cute rock wells I had seen in books and movies. A well with a bucket attached to a wooden beam with a rope and a handle, but once again, Jake didn't correct my mistaken idea.

"It wouldn't be a working well. It has likely been covered up for years so someone would not fall into it accidentally. If you and Trevor could figure out where it is, I will get back early tomorrow with a bunch of rope and a pulley. Maybe we can rig something up so we can at least find out if the shaft is clear. It's a long shot, but it is the best we have right now. With the road washed out and most of the countryside covered with several feet of water, moving animals isn't an option."

"How long before the water turns septic?" I asked.

"If we have more cloudy days, it might be okay for a week. But once that sun comes out, everything that hasn't been washed away will start breeding all kids of awful stuff. Needless to say, it won't be a pleasant sight."

"You are talking about dead animals, aren't you?" I purposely didn't say people. I was not yet prepared to hear about human casualties.

"I can't begin to describe what I saw today, Brylee," he said as he lit another cigarette. "This whole area has become one huge river heading towards the coast and taking most everything with it."

"But you said Edna was okay except for a little water."

"It is. The water is running through the flatlands north of town. Fortunately, that area is not heavily populated, but that doesn't mean people haven't lost everything because they have."

"Then we have even more to be grateful for," I said. "What can I do to help?"

He took a long drag on his cigarette, but blew the smoke away from me.

"There isn't anything you can do right now, except stay safe so I don't have to worry about you and Trevor."

"That goes without saying, but there has to be something I can do to help relieve some of the suffering." Quite suddenly an idea popped into my mind. "What about all the supplies we gathered from around the house? Some of the blankets and sheets from the attic may smell a little like moth balls, but you could still take them into town. I am sure the Red Cross would appreciate any donations they could get."

"I am sure they would," he responded. "I understand that the Catholics, the Mormons and some other latter-day religion are all sending humanitarian aide. I heard it on the radio flying around today."

I wanted to tell him that the Mormons and the Church of Jesus Christ of Latter-day Saints were the same and that I was proud to be a part of all the good they did, but I wasn't sure he even knew the name of the church I had joined. Besides, we were both too tired to get into a philosophical discussion about religious conviction.

"I will help load what we have in your plane so you can get an early start," I told him. "And Trevor and I will look for anything else that might be useful once it gets light."

"You are an amazing woman, Brylee Hawkins. I hope that guy you are going to marry realizes just how lucky he was to find you."

I smiled to myself as he walked towards the bunkhouse, his feet making sucking noises in the brown, slimy mud. He might not know it yet, but he was starting to change. I was catching more frequent glimpses of a better man than the one I had met when I first set foot on Hawkins' land three months earlier.

That man would never have considered my feelings. He would have slept in the house with Trevor and me simply because he knew it would annoy me. The man walking away from me now with his head held high respected the person I was, and that made a world of difference in how I was beginning to view him.

To be continued. . . . .

Enjoy this excerpt from
Exposed

Indecision's Flame
Book Three

by JS Ririe

I waited for what seemed like the longest time on the veranda looking up at dark, cloudy sky and wondering if Jake would reemerge from the bunkhouse. It had been one of the strangest days of my life with all the rain, the destruction and the battle with the spiders in the outhouse. But what had kept me going through all the unpleasantness was knowing that the man I had sworn to detest would be returning at the end of each long, lonely and work-filled day.

That seemed very strange to me. I liked that he was beginning to understand, or at least accept, that my future was with Ben. I was committed to him, our marriage and our future children, but there was still something about Jake Johnson I couldn't shake. Maybe we had simply been through too many unsettling experiences together or perhaps I had just gotten used to our constant wrangling, but I relied on him to bring a semblance of normalcy to our otherwise scattered and unsettled lives.

I brushed my teeth with the smallest amount of water I had ever used for that purpose, and then slipped into a clean t-shirt and pair of pajama pants. My little brother might be able to sleep in his boxers, but I didn't have that luxury. I needed to be fully dressed and ready to move at a moment's notice. Last night's storm had taught me that.

Since there was little else I could do to prepare for bed without running water, I made my way cautiously down the staircase to the dining room where Trevor had set up our sleeping bags. I knew he was still asleep from the sound of his rhythmic breathing and was just about to lie down and turn off my flashlight when I heard a rustling beside him. It caused me to jump with fright.

"It's only me," Jake whispered. He was lying on the sleeping bag nearest the door. He he had extinguished the lamp, and the smell of kerosene suddenly invaded my nostrils. It was strong and pungent but almost a pleasant change after the musty, earthy smell outside. "I didn't mean to scare you."

"You didn't!" I said as my heart slowed to a more normal pace. "I just thought you had decided to sleep in the bunkhouse tonight, that's all."

"Maybe I should have. I know it is not the best situation having the three of us in one room together, but with everything that has happened the past few hours, I didn't think it was wise to leave you alone either."

The beam of light I was shining in his face made him look almost sinister, somewhat like an aborigine's native mask with hollowed-out, black eyes and lips curved into a sardonic smile.

"And would you mind shutting that bloody light off," he continued. "You are blinding me."

"I'm sorry," I said as his image disappeared into the darkness. "My nerves are a little ragged."

What I wanted to tell him was that we would be fine without him. But the truth was, I felt much safer with him around. My body was bushed, and I felt like I could sleep standing up, but I knew I wouldn't be able to rest worrying about Trevor and what might happen in the next few hours without him close enough to reach if the need arose.

"Whose aren't? It's been one bloody hell of day, and tomorrow isn't going to be any better," he responded.

"You're still going out at first light?"

"I have to, Brylee, much as I would rather stay here with you and Trevor. I know today wasn't easy for either of you."

"We managed!" I told him. "And even had a few laughs in the process."

"I wish I had been here for the outhouse incident. I could have used a little humor today."

"Then I am sorry you missed it, even though it was not one of my finer moments. There is always strength in numbers during both good and bad times."

"Strength in numbers," he reiterated in a lazy, quiet voice. "You are a very tactful woman when I am more than certain you would prefer me being half way across the country right now."

"That's not true," I replied as I lay down on top of my own sleeping bag in the dark, grateful that Trevor separated us, and that the expression on my face was hidden from view. I no longer understood my feelings for him. They were all over the place like marbles from a dropped jar that scurried so fast I couldn't begin to catch them. "I trust you with my life, Jake, and Trevor's too."

"But not with your heart."

"That is already taken as you well know. We can't control what happens when it comes to love."

"I suppose not," he admitted. "A woman would be crazy to get involved with a bloke like me anyway. I am not exactly the most honorable man in the world, at least you have certainly told me that often enough."

"I never meant to criticize. I have enough skeletons in my own closet."

He laughed and it wasn't comforting.

"We all have pasts, Brylee, and the majority of it we would like to forget. But life would not be worth much if it wasn't filled second chances."

His words caused added confusion. That's exactly what the gospel was—an opportunity for second, third and forth chances. We would get as many as it took for us to learn the lessons necessary to get back to our Heavenly Father as long as we never quit trying.

Oh, why had I ever encouraged his offer of friendship when I knew the kind of relationship he wanted would never materialize between us? Even if Ben wasn't in my life, Jake could never be a part of it that way. I wanted a marriage that would last forever, and he was about as far away from being an ideal companion as anyone could possibly be.

"I guess we never know what is going to happen," I said, wishing I did not need him so desperately right now. "And real friends are rather hard to find."

"Well, at least that is something," he replied. "Every relationship has to start somewhere, and we never know where a new day might take us."

"That's for sure," I said as I allowed my body to relax just a little. "The past few months have certainly been different than I ever thought they would be."

"And I suspect the next few will be the same."

I heard him roll over on his sleeping bag and knew he was facing me. "Have you ever wondered why things happen the way they do?" he inquired.

I shook my head in the darkness. Where was this personal conversation coming from? Perhaps our brush with the possibility of death had caused him to reflect on something more than the present, or the women who were such an important part of his life away from the ranch.

"I think we all wonder that, but I believe that nearly everything that happens to us is part of a bigger plan."

"You said 'nearly'. Is this one of those 'nearly' situations? I can't imagine what plan could include all this destruction."

"I was thinking more along the lines of personal choices that take us away from where we want to be."

"And I suppose you want to be back in Los Angeles."

"Part of me does but I also want to be here with my family, helping them continue the Hawkins' legacy for generations to come."

"So you really are caught between the proverbial rock and a hard place," he said. "Can't say that I envy you much. You do know that you cannot have both lives."

"So it would appear, but I have faith that Ben and I will be together, and that I will still be able to help my family. Don't you believe in God just a little bit, Jake?"

"I don't know," he said. "When you have seen as much of life as I have, it's hard to believe any higher power exists. Why would a merciful God allow good people to suffer as much as they do?"

"Maybe they need to learn just how strong they really are. I know we will never be given more than we can endure if we put our faith and trust in God."

"I tried that before. It doesn't work."

I looked out the open front door at the navy blue sky overhead. How could anyone not believe God existed? Evidence of his reality was everywhere from the depths of the oceans to as far into the universe as eyes could see and beyond. People couldn't live forever, and tragedies had to happen or people would never learn to depend on him.

"I know you have had a lot of disappointments, Jake."

"Don't go feeling sorry for me," he promptly retorted. "It is a waste of time and energy. I have learned to deal with whatever comes my way."

"That sounds like mere existence to me."

"Well, it's worked this far, and I don't intend on rocking the boat, but you could answer me one thing."

"What's that?" I asked.

See Book Three: **Exposed - Indecision's Flame** for more of Brylee's story.

About the Author

JS Ririe is the pen name for Jan Hill. She spent her youth in the country where she learned to appreciate solitude, making her own fun, and reading romance novels from some of the masters like the Bronte sisters, Louisa May Alcott, Victoria Holt and Phyllis Whitney. She penned her first novel as a teenager but never pursued what is now her greatest passion until becoming the lead witness in a federal case brought against the school district where she taught broadcasting and journalism. Writing Brylee's story as she waited two years to testify helped her through a terrifying time. She lives in Utah and has two children and two living grandchildren who help bring meaning and joy to her life.

A Note From Jan

Thank you so much for reading this novel. I'd love to stay in touch with you. Please consider joining my MAILING LIST so I can send you periodic newsletters about upcoming book releases, special offers and more. The link to sign up for my mailing list is: http://eepurl.com/dCPYVf . I promise that I will not spam you, will not sell your email information and will treat it with care.

One last favor: Your rating/review of this book helps me to keep writing. I would really appreciate it if you could leave a review. It shouldn't take more than a minute or two. You can reach the page directly at http://amzn.to/2BXNSdv

Thank you again,
JS Ririe

www.JanHillBooks.com
For contacting the author: JSRirie@JanHillBooks.com